Sophia

or The Beginning of All Tales

by Rafik Schami

translated by Monique Arav
and John Hannon

Interlink Books

An imprint of Interlink Publishing Group, Inc.
Northampton, Massachusetts

First published in 2018 by

Interlink Books
An imprint of Interlink Publishing Group, Inc.
46 Crosby Street, Northampton, MA 01060
www.interlinkbooks.com

Library of Congress Cataloging-in-Publication data:
Names: Schami, Rafik, 1946- author. | Arav, Monique, translator.
Title: Sophia, or the beginning of all tales / Rafik Schami ; translated
    by Monique Arav and John Hannon.
Other titles: Sophia, oder, Der Anfang aller Geschichten. English.
Description: Northampton, MA : Interlink Books, 2017.
Identifiers: LCCN 2017031326 | ISBN 9781566560313
Subjects: LCSH: Damascus (Syria)—Fiction. | LCGFT: Romance
    fiction
Classification: LCC PT2680.A448 S6513 2017 | DDC 833/.92--dc23
LC record available at https://lccn.loc.gov/2017031326

To request our complete 48-page full-color catalog, please call us toll
free at 1-800-238-LINK, visit our website at www.interlinkbooks.com,
or send us an e-mail: info@interlinkbooks.com

Printed in the United States of America

 The translation of this work was supported by a
grant from the Goethe-Institut in the framework
of the "Books First" program.

For Root and Emil, who always get a foretaste of my stories,
and for all those who take mirages for their Paradise lost.

I

1

Baptism by Fire

Damascus, summer 2006

Aida was still riding her bicycle unsteadily that day. Although she managed to keep her balance, her eyes stayed glued to the handlebar, as her front wheel drew snaking curves along the ground. Karim kept warning her, "Look straight ahead, forget about the handlebar." But her gaze remained fixed—as if hypnotized—on the gleaming bar between her hands.

Aida would call her ride down Jasmine Street that day her baptism by fire. On that afternoon she wore white sandals, blue trousers, and a red-and-white striped shirt. She had tied her long gray hair back in a ponytail. Time and again she would begin to wobble, and she would laugh out loud when she did, as if to drown out the sound of her heartbeat, while Karim kept a tight hold on the bike saddle.

It was a sturdy Dutch bicycle that he'd bought secondhand thirty years ago. He loved that bike and in all those years had never let anyone else ride it. He'd never imagined that anyone else would until, about a month earlier, Aida had asked him if there was anything he couldn't do that he had always wished he could. By then they had been together for over six months.

"Play a musical instrument," he answered immediately, and then hesitated. "Actually, conjure up my favorite tune on an oud," he added quietly and then almost swallowed the words, "like you can," because he was sure that

3

for him it was too late. His fingers were nimble enough, but he was already over seventy-five.

As a child, Karim had dreamt of playing music, but it was frowned upon at home. Although his well-to-do family owned a radio and his father would listen to an occasional song or instrumental piece, as well as the news, he forbade anyone to sing or play music. Karim's mother had a wonderful voice, but she only sang in secret, when his father was out. The day when his brother Ismail once dared to quietly play the flute he had bought, he got a beating. "That's gypsy stuff," his father scolded contemptuously.

Aida beamed at Karim. "I can teach you the oud in three months. If you practice hard every day, the melodies will find their way to your hands. All it takes is a bit of patience," she said, and then added while stroking his face, "and a sense of humor." He laughed self-consciously, trying to hide his shyness.

"Riding a bike is what I always dreamt of doing when I was a little girl," she went on. "I envied my brother, his friends, and all the boys in the neighborhood who could just float around on their bikes as light as feathers. But when I said I wanted to learn to ride, my mother nearly had a fit, just like she always did when she was frightened. She told me to put that idea right out of my head. Women stayed at home and didn't need bicycles. She said that riding a bike could have terrible consequences. And when I asked what they were she warned me that many young women had lost their virginity riding bikes. 'Try explaining to stupid men that you are still intact.'"

I couldn't believe it—it was like everything else that my mother said when she was frightened. She'd make such drama out of things that in no time you found yourself lost in a maze of superstition and fear: young girls grow beards

4

from drinking coffee, broken mirrors bring seven years' bad luck, playing cross-eyes can make your eyes stay that way, pregnant women should get all the different fruits they want or the baby could be born with a birthmark in the shape of the fruit they craved—the story was that Uncle Barakat rode all the way to Jaffa and back in four days just to pick up a basket of famous Jaffa oranges for Aunt Mary, who then delivered a healthy baby. As for me, riding a bike was just elegant—a balancing act like a circus artist walking a tightrope."

"You'll have it down in two or three weeks," Karim promised her, but then realized he was being rash. He would never break an arm or a leg playing the oud, but Aida very well could, riding a bike. Her dark eyes beamed at him, she jumped at him and kissed him full on the lips, banishing all his pangs of conscience like mist in the sun.

"Keep teaching me," she begged, and he could see tears of joy in her eyes.

It was amazing how long they both had lived with their secret wishes. Over the six months they'd been a couple, they had shared their pasts openly, yet suddenly they'd both discovered that they still had lots to learn about each other.

"Maybe I was afraid you'd laugh at me," said Aida, explaining her hesitancy. Karim concurred with a nod. "I haven't talked about my dreams since I was twenty. If anyone asked, I'd say I'd like to dance, and fly like a swallow. But I kept putting things off, and after my wife Amira died, I stopped dreaming."

"I could never relax when I was dancing," Aida confessed. "I always kept counting the time and watching my steps. So when I was ten or twelve, I gave it up. But I never stopped dreaming of riding a bike."

~

Aida was diminutive in height. When she was barefoot, her forehead came up to Karim's shoulder. She was slim and athletic, and if you didn't know that she was in her mid-fifties, you would have thought she was forty. When people paid her compliments, she'd say, "Love makes you young! Fall in love and you'll see," and then she'd laugh.

Aida had always been daring, as Karim soon found out. He worried about her and her high spirits.

Not far from the neighborhood where both she and Karim lived, there was a big parking lot that had belonged to a textile factory just outside the Eastern gate. It was almost always empty. They practiced bike riding there for a week until Karim thought it was time for her to learn how to ride on a busy street. He accompanied her to her street, which was a bit wider and ran parallel to Jasmine Street on the western side. Aida rode quite calmly, with Karim holding on to the saddle. Neighbors watched from their windows or from their doorways, shaking their heads in disapproval, but she wasn't bothered in the least. Soon Karim could let go of the bike without her noticing. He ran alongside her, and when she saw him she nearly fainted. "Hold me tight," she cried out, "have you gone crazy?" and she almost collided with the wall. Karim held on and she braked and came to a stop with a sigh of relief.

It took another five days before she was able to give Karim the okay to let go, after the first few meters. Off she went along the street, ringing her bell nonstop, turning around at the corner of Jew Street and riding back to him with a big wide grin. But she still was not so good at turning. Twice she skinned her knee against the wall after taking too wide a turn. Both her knees were bleeding and she had torn her brown trousers—but she hadn't fallen off her bike. After a week of solid riding, Karim suggested that she practice on Zeitoun Street, where cars were allowed to drive, but only slowly. Zeitoun Street was wide and rambling, passing the See of the Catholic Patriarch and the big Catholic Church.

Aida was not in favor. "It's swarming with priests and bishops over there, and just the sight of them makes me nervous." She smiled as she imagined herself kneeling in the confessional, something she hadn't done in fifty years, and saying, "Father, I have sinned."

"What have we done? How have we sinned—in thought, in deed?"

"Yes, in deed, with a bicycle," she answered. Her friend Sahra had told her that cycling made women come. "You know," Sahra said, "a saddle does a better job than most men." Without ever having ridden a bike herself, Sahra was convinced this was true.

"What about Jasmine Street?" said Karim, bringing Aida back to her lesson.

"That will do," she said. She wanted to show the neighbor women that she had become a full-fledged cyclist. "It would be best around three in the afternoon when they're all sitting in front of their doors," she said, laughing as she imagined the twin rows of open-mouthed faces. Karim rolled his eyes. It was his street. "If I can do that, I can ride through hell with no hands," she said. She had known that street for a long time, and since becoming Karim's lover she'd come to know the women there better, too.

~

Jasmine Street is located in the Christian Quarter of Damascus, near Straight Street, running parallel to Abbara Street and Zeitoun Street. You enter it under a stone arch, along a dark, narrow corridor not even a meter wide, and come out onto the street proper, which then widens out to four meters. This bottleneck saves the street from cars and motorbikes. Most tourists overlook the entrance to the street, which looks more like the door to a house. The view into the street from outside is blocked by the arch of two overhanging balconies that almost touch, completing the camouflage.

Until the 1950s, the entrance had been graced by a gate decorated with wrought ironwork and bronze, which mysteriously disappeared after the 1959 Gates of Damascus exhibition. Decades later, rumor still had it that an oil sheikh had paid the exhibition director a handsome sum for this beautiful piece, which he had then taken back with him to Kuwait.

However, even when curious tourists did go through the tunnel, they would only be disappointed—Jasmine Street had little to offer, except for an unusually well-kept flagstone surface, countless benches, climbing plants, and flowerpots, all of which made for a tacky impression. There were no strikingly elegant buildings, just the plain earthen façades of single-story houses lining the street, looking much the same on each side. Little did visitors know that these modest façades were actually a sophisticated disguise that had effectively protected residents for centuries, keeping both the envious and the tax collectors at bay. Inside, behind the doors, inner courtyards opened to the sky, bearing witness to the Damascenes' sensual way of life.

Five hundred meters farther on, Jasmine Street ended at Monastery Square, lined mostly with houses and with two shops selling groceries and household goods. Karim's large house stood on the corner; his door was the last on the left-hand side of the street. A second door in the long, high stone wall bordering the square led into his garden. Just next to it stood a weather-beaten, age-old bench that had been chiseled out of a single block of white stone and where Karim often came to enjoy his late-afternoon coffee in the summer. There he was always met by the unexpected sight of a little monastery, with sparse grass peeking out between the big stone blocks and the remains of the walls. Built in the tenth century and dedicated to Saint John, the monastery had been completely destroyed in 1157 by an earthquake, which had claimed eighty thousand dead in Damascus and the surrounding area alone. Two-thirds of the population were killed, but the Damascenes arose from the ruins, as so often before in their history, and built their city anew. They never rebuilt the monastery, though. Its stones found their way into the many houses of the Christian Quarter, as if both the monastery and its patron saint should live on in each of these dwellings.

Here the historic city wall in the background had been robbed of any vestige of beauty by the skimpy, rushed, and ugly repairs, which had made use of a variety of small stones from as many centuries, and which bore the unmistakable mark of the tragedies that had preceded them. Seen from the outside, the city walls reached over nine meters high above busy Ibn Assaker Street, but on the inside, on the edge of Monastery Square, they were barely three meters high. There the mass of rubble reached up to two-thirds of the height of the wall. This was because the Damascenes had not been allowed to carry the rubble left over from earthquakes and fires out of the city, so as not to destroy the surrounding fertile plain that fed its inhabitants.

In the midst of the ruins in front of the wall, two poplars reached proudly to the sky, lofty against the low background. Strangers scarcely noticed that every 23rd of June, at seven o'clock sharp, the sun would shine exactly between the trunks and light up the tip of the simple burial stele, a granite column two meters high that tapered toward the top. The modest grave beneath this monument was often covered in flowers. Most visitors know little about the lovers buried here, who were united in death when life had forbidden them to fulfill their love. But those who live in the Christian Quarter tell the story of Fadi and Fatima, whose different religions would not have them live together. They were buried where they lay entwined in a final embrace. Many a tale was told about their love and how the poplars had grown to whisper their story with every gust of wind. The funeral stone bore no marking, but all the children in the neighborhood knew the names of these martyrs to love. And every year, hundreds of women would come from the Christian Quarter and gather in a procession to the grave, where they would wait for the sun to shine through the poplars to sing a long lament over the injustice both lovers had suffered. The procession lasted two hours, and the women would return home red-eyed and tearful.

The well-kept street had fortunately been spared motorized traffic, and it looked like the inner courtyard of a housing estate. Except during the three months in the year that were cold and rainy, the women and the old men usually went out around three o'clock in the afternoon and sat down at the entrances to their houses. The children would be shooed away for two hours to play on Monastery Square or in the ruins with their balls, marbles, and scooters. This is when the street would be hosed down with water, not just to wash it clean but to make it cool and pleasant. Coffee and tea would be sipped, rumors collected and traded to much laughter. The session would end around five o'clock, and the children would reclaim the middle of the street with all their noise and their own raucous laughter.

There wasn't a peddler or a cyclist who dared to disturb the peace and tranquility of these two hours. The sharpness of the women's tongues was not feared only by residents of the Christian Quarter; many a street trader, postman, policeman, and beggar who ventured into the neighborhood had felt it, too. The saying went that the Damascenes had their legendary steel knives—and Jasmine Street had the tongues of its women. Karim knew about that. Aida, however, absolutely insisted on cycling past the women at that very time. She knew that many of them were envious of her love for Karim. As long as she had been a mere widow, the women had felt compassion for her, on her own street and on Karim's. But that a widow should fall in love, "ere the earth be dry on her late husband's grave," that was immoral. Yet love doesn't ask the heart for permission, much less does it worry about graves. The funniest thing about it was these were the very same women who mourned the death of the two lovers on the 23rd of June each year, although he had been a Muslim and she a Christian.

In the Christian Quarter, Aida wasn't despised only by the women for having fallen in love with the Muslim Karim, but by the men as well. "As if there weren't any Christian men," they would grumble when they spotted her. Although they took no small pride in their street being a peaceful home to the followers of many different religions, they regarded this love as overstepping the mark that they themselves had set. As if love checked IDs before conquering hearts.

And Karim? He gave his pat answer, whether at the greengrocer's or the barber's: "I'm not a Muslim, a Christian, a Druze, or a Jew. Love is my religion, do you understand?" But no one understood, whether they nodded politely, shook their heads, or smiled in embarrassment.

Aida had fallen passionately in love with Karim in the autumn of the previous year, and this made her look younger with every passing day. The women in the street had noticed that her clothing had become more colorful; not only that, but the way she walked, the way she laughed, the way she looked made her resemble a bold teenager going through life fearlessly and full of curiosity. But had they been honest and acknowledged this, it would have been an admission of defeat. That is why, on both streets, the inhabitants maintained that their dislike of Aida had to do with her loose morals and her disregard for her own Christian religion. It was quite beside the point that their knowledge of Christianity only ran as deep as the Hail Mary and Our Father, for most of them.

The women who'd invite any passerby in for tea or coffee now refused to show that hospitality to Aida. No, no one liked the widow anymore, that same widow who had landed this attractive, humorous widower before several of the women were able to weave their own plans for him. Aida knew about it all, and that is why she wanted this baptism by fire at all costs.

"I'll watch out for you," Karim promised, because he knew his own street very well and he could feel how unsure Aida had suddenly become. On that decisive day, he stood with her and the bicycle on historic Straight Street in front of the entrance to Jasmine Street. As so often, he wore a shirt and trousers of khaki cotton on that summer day. He gave her a long look. "Are you sure you want to do this?"

"Yes, definitely," she insisted.

"Then you can't turn around. You know the story about Lot's wife?"

"Yes, she was turned into a pillar of salt because she had no name, but my name's Aida and I shall turn into chocolate so that you can lick me up," said Aida, kissing him on the lips.

"Oh my God! We'll have to be quick, you already taste like chocolate," he said. Men never look back, Aida thought. They follow whoever can convince them and quickly lose touch with the past. Women will always turn around, moved by worry, longing, curiosity, or compassion. That's why they hesitate more often than men—it's always been that way.

"If you please, Madam Chocolate," Karim said, and off she went. Benjamin the tailor was just taking a little break at the door of his shop and drinking a mocha. He shook his head in clear judgment with a crooked smile.

Karim hurried after her. He could feel her insecurity in the narrow passage that the inhabitants referred to as "the corridor." He held the bicycle below the saddle without her noticing. The street was lined with women and old men. They looked up, and some whispered to each other. Scandalized looks enfolded every inch of her body. She could feel the sting of their looks and avoided eye contact, focusing on the handlebars and pedaling furiously.

An old woman sat at her window eating a slice of apple. She froze at the sight of Aida, shook her head, and shouted something back into the house. A plump young woman hurried to her side, pressing her hands to her mouth as if to stifle a scream.

Halfway along, almost at the cobbler's house, the confectioner's twenty-year-old daughter suddenly jumped up, ran across the street and sat on an empty chair next to her father's house, braying with laughter. Karim knew the young widow. The story went that her husband, a naval officer, had died at sea during an exercise and that she had gone insane with grief. She would often spend the night on her husband's grave in the Catholic cemetery, sometimes taking his favorite dishes with her.

Aida held her breath, swayed, and pulled the handlebars in the other direction, but with too much force. The front wheel grazed the knees of Afifa, the neighbor, and Tuma, the cobbler's wife, who both cried out and spilled some coffee on the ground. Aida quickly returned to the middle of the street and escaped at the last moment, instantly drenched in sweat.

"Look where you're going!" Afifa shouted indignantly.

"She needs glasses," said one woman, laughing.

"I'll buy them for her at the grocer's," a neighbor replied.

"She's gone mad!" shouted a portly woman whom Aida didn't know.

"She's having trouble with her hormones."

"Next thing you know, she'll be wearing red shorts."

"Karim's changed, too—and not for the better."

"He's losing his marbles."

"When old folk lose it just before the end, it's like a fart from the dearly departing," someone else shouted. "It upsets the mourners and drives away the angels who have come to fetch their soul, leaving only the devil! And that's…" Laughter drowned out the rest of the woman's words.

Aida couldn't place the voice, but a knot formed in her stomach. Could bicycle riding really spark such hatred? People laughed at her in other streets, but this was the first time she had heard such nasty remarks. This was hatred. Where did it come from? What did she take from them by loving Karim or riding a bike? Hadn't Karim lived lonely among them for decades? Had he wanted one of those women, he would have told her. Had envy led to hatred or had hatred been lurking in their souls for a long time before finally finding an outlet?

Karim felt goosebumps crawl down his back. He wanted to stop and rebuke the women. Harsh words prickled in his throat, wanting out but not being allowed. His throat hurt from the effort of restraining them. But he walked on silently, mechanically holding on to the saddle. When the laughter died away, he loosened his grip and ran alongside Aida to the end of the street. He stopped there while Aida circled Monastery Square. When she came back to him, she called out, "Stay there! I'll do one on my own and be right back." She rang her bell and rode back more confidently. She went straight along the street and turned where it narrowed to a bottleneck. Karim had a better view of her now because she rode standing up on the pedals. She rang her bell cheerfully and pedaled boldly, still balancing above the saddle and barely touching the handlebar with her fingertips. When the women suddenly jumped in front of her bike, she rang her bell, stuck her tongue out at Afifa, and rode away.

"This crazy woman knows no shame... If she did, it would have choked her," she heard Afifa call out. Finally she saw Karim with his arms stretched out wide, like Jesus on his cross, and she whispered, "I love you with every beat of my heart."

When she reached him, she braked slowly and dismounted with almost regal elegance. She leaned the bicycle against the wall of his house, next to the stone bench on Monastery Square, and held Karim tightly. "Thanks," she whispered into his chest. When she looked up at him, she noticed how he was covered in sweat. His forehead gleamed and pearls of sweat hung between his wrinkles like silver music notes. He stroked her head. "You were wonderful... and brave," he said, leaving the bike where Aida had leaned it against the wall and walking slowly with her to the square to enjoy the cool breeze in the shade. The stone bench almost glowed in the hot sun.

They sat on a stone block in the shade, and he started whistling a tune that Aida loved, but he had to stop and laugh as he remembered Afifa's expression. Aida ignored his laughter and took up whistling the tune, which sounded like a canary's song. When Karim whistled, it sounded like a squeaky old bicycle pump, or every now and again, like air escaping from a punctured balloon. Children were playing marbles nearby. They stopped, looked at the old couple, and had to laugh because they couldn't whistle while they laughed either, which made them laugh even more.

"It's no good," said Aida. "Laughing and whistling are arch-enemies. You have to pick one or the other."

~

Karim and Aida continued to sit on the stone for a long time. When shadows started to lengthen, they moved to the more comfortable bench outside the wall of Karim's garden. They talked, laughed, whistled, and kissed. A boy with red hair and a bright face full of freckles nudged his playmate who was aiming a marble. "Look, look, they're crazy," he said, but the other boy took no notice. His mother had long ago told him so, and he preferred to concentrate on his target, which was about three meters away. "They're as old as our grandparents and they're kissing like they do in the movies." The other kid hit the marble and jumped up shouting in excitement, startling his friend.

The shout also startled Karim out of his kiss. "Stay here, I'll be right back," he whispered to Aida and went into the house through the wooden garden door. He soon returned with a tray filled with two glasses, a bottle of *arak*, a glass carafe of water and ice cubes, and a bowl of salted peanuts.

The carafe was misted over and the ice cubes tinkled like distant bells with every step he took. Aida looked at him and fell in love once more with this generous, grateful lover of life.

They toasted the successful baptism by fire and put their glasses down on the tray.

"And now they're having a drink," said the red-haired boy. The other still didn't pay him any attention as he aimed at a marble—he didn't want to break his streak of good luck.

The last children ran home as the sun went down behind the houses, some skipping and jumping like foals. Aida and Karim watched in silence as dusk began to dim the colors of the houses and the green of the monastery ruins. Twilight drew its dark cloak over the world, meeting with no resistance save for a few tiny isolated lights in the dark body of the city. "I'm hungry," Aida said, looking at her beloved and adding, "and afterward let's play the oud for an hour or so."

Karim went first. Today he particularly wanted to spoil Aida and cook her favorite dish—baked kibbeh. He took the tray with the arak bottle, the empty carafe, and the glasses. Aida pushed her bike through the door into the courtyard where the bike shed stood.

Karim started whistling again, this time an old song that he had been hoping to coax out of the oud with Aida's help. In the kitchen he thought about how difficult he found it to pluck the oud strings precisely with the quill, while keeping the fingers of his left hand pressed firmly enough in the correct position on the strings.

Aida had given him an oud as a present. He had tried several instruments before finding just the right one. She showed him how to sit and hold the oud so that it would not slip away. Every day she trained his fingers and he learned how to hold down the strings and produce clear notes.

Karim marveled at Aida's knowledge. Not only did she seem to know everything about how an oud was made, she also knew all about its history.

"Prior to Islam the oud had three pairs of strings," she told him on the first day. "Then, in the seventh or eighth century, a fourth pair was added. At that time, each pair was associated with a humor and an element, and so the strings were colored accordingly. The uppermost string was yellow, for yellow bile and fire, the second one red, for blood and air, the next one white, for phlegm and water, and the last one black, for black bile and earth. Later on, in the ninth century, a fifth pair was added for the soul. Only the soul can unite the four humors in music."

"And what color is the soul?" Karim asked.

"That pair of strings was left transparent," Aida said, "for the soul is changeable and beyond our grasp."

"But I can grasp my soul," Karim replied, pulling Aida to him and kissing her, "and I can even kiss it," he added. She laughed.

"How am I supposed to teach such a lovesick student properly? Let's get back to our exercises." She tried hard to inject some severity into her voice but her laugh bubbled through again.

Every day Karim would practice patiently, but compared to Aida's playing, his simple exercises sounded painfully bad. He decided to take it in good humor, as it was worthwhile just to have Aida as a patient, caring, modest teacher. He still hoped to learn how to play the oud properly someday. He had to smile when a little inner devil suddenly held up a sign in front of his eyes that said: the hopeless feed on illusion.

But even devils can make mistakes.

2

At Memory's Gate

Damascus–Beirut–Heidelberg–Rome,
spring 1970–summer 2010

One summer day in 2010, Salman Baladi decided to return to Damascus. Forty years, two months, and seventeen days had passed since he had left Syria in 1970 on fake travel documents. It took him another six months to check out the situation thoroughly. He wanted to be sure that there was no warrant still out for his arrest. He'd read of cases where impatience, a desperate yearning to return to the land where you were born, or secret service tricks had led to the arrest of expatriates the moment they stepped off the plane, and to their confinement in a hell of torture and disgrace. Some did not survive. Other paid millions to escape. That's why Salman took his time double-checking everything, but it was difficult to do from Rome.

It wasn't until December, when he was certain that the secret service had nothing against him, that he boarded a flight out of Rome, his second home. His wife, Stella, and their fifteen-year-old son, Paolo, didn't want to come with him. Salman was fine with that. He wanted to return to the arms of his beloved city of Damascus in the same way he had left—alone and able to move about freely, without having to take care of any companions, explaining and translating everything for them.

Stella noticed how much the trip to Damascus preoccupied Salman. A general amnesty for all past political offenses had been proclaimed in January 2010. The government hoped to encourage new investment by enticing rich émigrés back to their homeland. The prime minister confirmed the amnesty in July, thwarting any rumors to the contrary that might prevent successful Syrians from returning. "Any official arresting one of our brothers at the airport," he declared emphatically from his podium, "or bothering them anywhere else shall be dismissed on the spot. The returning brothers are guests of His Excellency." The wily prime minister knew his fellow countrymen only too well—arrests outside the airport would have instantly set off a wave of scandal and contempt. Salman followed the prime minister's remarks live on satellite TV. The speech relieved—somewhat—his suspicions about claims made by the Syrian government.

During this time, Salman kept up his routine, going every day to his office on Via Principe Amedeo and working steadily as usual. But since June, he had begun to retreat each evening to his study, where he would listen to Arabic music and spend hours on the phone. To Stella's and Paolo's delight, he cooked more Damascene dishes than ever before, but apart from that he barely had time for them. He stopped accompanying Stella when she visited her parents in Trieste, attended birthday parties, or met friends at bars or restaurants. Their common friends in Rome increasingly asked about him. When they last met in October, Carlo, the goldsmith, had shouted to Stella, "Tell His Highness that we miss him a lot. With all respect to Damascus, he lives in Rome and we Romans also have a claim on him." Carlo wasn't pretending. With his charm and wit, Salman was the life and soul of the evening gatherings that took place at least once a week.

He was also missed at his favorite restaurants. The owner of New Station on Giuseppe Parini Street even asked anxiously if Salman had stopped dining there because he was mad at him for some reason. Stella reassured Giuseppe that Salman missed him—and his restaurant, too. But forty years had gone by since Salman had seen Syria. He wanted to visit his home country again, and the trip would not be easy. Stella felt a certain pride in Salman's being missed by so many people. His company, Oasi, had headquarters in Rome, with branches in Milan and Ancona. It had become Italy's largest importer of foods from Arab countries as well as an exporter of Italian specialties to the rich Gulf countries, where the company had two large branches in Kuwait and Dubai.

More and more Italians were curious about foods from the neighboring Middle East, while more and more wealthy Arabs were keen on imbibing in Italy's famous cuisine.

Despite an economic crisis in Italy that had generally decreased trade, Salman was satisfied with sales. He had been renting two stalls in Nuovo Mercato Esquilino since 2001, when the large indoor market first opened. Run by four diligent employees, the stalls turned over more profit than ever before. Salman's ambition was to create additional branches in Florence, Bologna, Naples, Turin, Palermo, and Trieste, as well as in other Arab capitals. He had entrusted the plans to a firm of investment consultants, but that spring he put them on ice. His trip to Damascus came first.

~

From that June until December when he left for Damascus, Salman spent more and more time thinking back on his childhood and youth in Syria. He listened to songs he re-membered on CDs or YouTube, but they were all over forty years old. He couldn't stand any of the current Arab music.

He got himself a large notebook and jotted down events and names of people who had been part of his previous life—friends, relatives, rivals he had lost track of, places and people he most wanted to see again. His memory started working at full tilt.

What was memory, really? As he wrote, he often crossed things out, and he realized that reducing his recollections to entries in an archive oversimplified them. After days of writing, he began to see memory as an invisible city, home to entertainment districts, secret lairs and repair shops of all kinds. Memory had a cemetery, a morgue, a crematorium, temples for the saints, a museum, dungeons for the hated, a boiler to bring heat and life back to old experiences, gardens to be watered and tended or neglected, and dark rooms better feared and avoided. It even had supermarkets for all the glittery rubbish, lies, and legends that he'd believed to be true when he was growing up at home, at school, and at church. He had stored them in this memory-mart and they had influenced his thinking without his conscious knowledge. It reminded him of a German proverb—*Lies have short legs*. Overhearing Paolo watch a football match on television in his room, he wrote in his notebook—*Lies have short legs, but they score goals!*

Despite all the scientific advances in Salman's lifetime, the workings of this strange memory-city were still as unfathomable as the ocean depths. One could forget a particular event for one year or even forty—*Time wipes away all traces*. But then, through the death of a loved one, an unexpected encounter with a person or place, or even just a fragrance, something happened and it all came flooding back. Salman suspected that his nose was his key to the gate of countless memories. The mere scent of a street in Rome was enough to summon a movie-like replay of an event that had taken place on his own street decades ago.

Salman had forgotten most of his eventful past in Syria, and he lived happily in Rome with his family. But he never forgot why he had left his country illegally: The shooting, the badly injured policeman with his eyes pleading for mercy... the flight and the threat of arrest that he had escaped at the last moment—they all haunted his nightmares, almost nightly during his first years in exile, but less and less as time passed.

In those early years away from Syria, his parents came to visit him every now and again, first in Heidelberg. But his father didn't feel comfortable in that old romantic city on the Neckar River, nor later in Rome. But his mother, Sophia, loved his friendly neighbors in both cities, and she was especially curious about their customs and cuisine. When Salman would suggest an Arab restaurant in Heidelberg or Rome, she'd reply, "I didn't come here to eat Arab food. I can do that in Damascus."

More inquisitive than an ethnologist, she observed the ways of life of the Germans and the Italians. She wanted to know in detail how they ate, laughed, had fun, married, and got divorced. Then one day Sophia showed up in the cemetery at the burial of one of his neighbors, dressed in black and weeping sorrowfully, although she had never met the deceased woman—not even once. When Salman asked his mother about it, she said, "I'm crying for my dead friends, for me since I've been separated from you, and for this suffering humanity that does not understand death."

His father, Yusuf, however, always remained in Salman's apartment, just sitting there with an expression like he'd recently eaten something that didn't agree with him. He was too frightened to go out anywhere alone, as if the Mafia were lying in wait for him on every street corner. Only when Stella invited him to join them did the old gentleman reluctantly do so, but he let it be known that it was only as a favor to *her*. He would mumble and grumble quietly in Arabic so that Stella couldn't hear how he missed his favorite café and his friends and his daily paper. Plus he found neither German nor Italian cooking to his liking.

Later on, Salman's father suffered a mild heart attack, which served him as a plausible excuse for refusing to travel anywhere. He was normally in good health. But as soon as his wife began talking about her son and about Rome, he went to bed and wouldn't get up for days. Once, his mother told Salman on the phone, laughing, that whenever she wanted to calm her husband down she would tell him she had just been inquiring about cheap last-minute flights to Rome. His father would immediately start running a measurable temperature, and she would be left in peace to visit her girlfriends in Damascus without her grumbling shadow.

Salman's connection to Damascus was weakened even more by his father's heart attack. It became limited to just one phone call a month, which always touched on the same things: what his mother was cooking, whom she had been to see, who was involved in a scandal, who had gotten married or divorced, or who had died. Salman often laughed until he cried during these phone calls with his mother. She was charming and funny, and had an inexhaustible supply of rumors and anecdotes on hand. Even so, the years that slept in his memory were not awakened by these phone calls.

Then, in January 2010, came the general amnesty for all politically motivated crimes. In March, the Syrian ambassador in Rome—Hassan Kadur, a very nice gentleman—once again inquired in Damascus whether any charges were still open against Salman. The answer came back in the negative. But despite the fact that the ambassador was extremely bright and worldly-wise, Salman was reluctant to meet with him in the Syrian embassy on the Piazza d'Aracoeli. Instead he invited him to the nearby upscale Gran Caffè Roma, which served delicious dishes and where they could talk in peace and quiet—without fear of being overheard.

Salman was taking no risks. He might have a German passport, but what good was that to him under a dictatorship? He recalled the story of the student and social worker Elisabeth Käsemann, who, before the eyes of the world in 1977, was arrested by the Argentinian secret services, tortured, and murdered. People were incensed by her death, but German politicians were unable to do anything for her. Salman knew of similar cases in Chile, Cuba, Brazil, Iraq, and Saudi Arabia. The moment people were arrested they were absolutely isolated, and the dictatorship that held them prisoner and tortured them ended up being dutifully courted by both East and West.

Fear sat deep in Salman's bones.

He asked his mother to contact his cousin on his father's side, Elias, and ask him to make inquiries in Damascus. After a week, Elias was able to assure them that in none of the fifteen departments of the secret service, and at none of the country's border posts, was there anything recorded against Salman. Elias would know—he was a senior officer in the secret service himself.

After Salman received this final reassurance, memories of his years in Damascus and his escape from Syria became so vivid that it seemed as if everything had happened only days ago.

3

Flight

Damascus, South Lebanon, Beirut
1960–1970

Images of events from decades ago flickered across Salman's mind like a well-preserved documentary. He remembered just how the moment of his escape from Syria tasted, how he breathed a sigh of relief as the shared taxi passed through the checkpoint on the Syrian-Lebanese border. The taxi driver assured the Syrian border policeman that everything was in order and handed over the passports of his four passengers. In the front, a corpulent lady sat wreathed in silence and a bad mood. She wore sunglasses and stared through the windshield, unmoving like a plaster statue, for the entire two-hour drive, without saying a word to either the taxi driver or her fellow passengers. Salman sat in the back by the right-hand window, next to a little old man who fell into a deep sleep as soon as people stopped talking to him. When the man woke up, he would curse the weakness of his advancing years and promptly fall asleep again. A dark-skinned, serious-looking Palestinian sat behind the driver.

Salman could hardly breathe. His heart raced. Although his passport was a skillful forgery, he was still afraid because he knew that—although there was no way of checking passports electronically at the time—border police had their own effective methods for identifying forged passports. But his worries proved unfounded. The policeman was friends with the taxi driver and took care of things himself without handing in the passports to the checkpoint in the building. In Syria, arbitrariness and a low sense of duty—even if they didn't often couple—could make all the difference when they did.

The policeman was dark-haired and stocky. Salman's heart pounded as he observed him—a Bedouin, he thought when he recognized the three blue dots on the man's chin, nose, and cheek. It was a primitive tattoo worn especially by all Bedouins. Bored, the man leafed through the passports, looking repeatedly inside the car and whispering the names to himself as he did so. Then he returned the passports to the driver and asked, "And what's for dessert?"

"Mandur—the best chocolate!" the driver replied slickly.

"Good, but God help you if you forget it!" the policeman said, waving the next car in the queue toward him. The taxi driver accelerated away, and when he was at a safe distance he commented, "Since he stopped smoking he's been addicted to chocolate. Before, a carton of American cigarettes used to cost me three dollars at the Beirut docks. Now a box of Mandur chocolates costs ten Lebanese lira— that's three dollars, too! That lousy Bedouin only likes Lebanese chocolates." Then he added, "Didn't I promise you folks you'd have a smooth ride with me? Sometimes passengers complain that I charge two lira more, but isn't that better than sweltering for an hour in the sun while they examine your passports inside?" With these words he waved at the Lebanese border police and drove on past them into Lebanon.

Salman looked back as the Syrian border guard slowly receded from view. He would have loved to shout out, "You're not gonna get me, you sons of bitches!" but he thought of the old man next to him who appeared to have fallen asleep again and didn't want to startle him. The woman hadn't spoken a word either during the whole passport control. The grim Palestinian now revealed himself to be a ladies' hairdresser. He told a long-winded tale about how he wanted to get a visa for Canada because ladies' hairdressers were much in demand there. He had paid two hundred dollars for this information, and the head of the hairdressers' guild had even given him a letter of recommendation.

Even the fool is thought wise as long as he keeps quiet, thought Salman as the taxi driver laughed and said with a sneer, "Sure, because it's so cold in Canada that all the ladies' hair stands on end." Salman forgot his own worries and had to laugh at the Palestinian's naiveté. "Boy oh boy," the taxi driver said to himself. "If you'd thrown two hundred one-dollar bills out the window, you might just have made a hundred kids happy." The young Palestinian fell prey once again to his gnawing doubts and put the mask of his bad mood back on. The taxi driver retreated into his own thoughts, smoked out the window, and gave Salman a searching glance every now and then in his rearview mirror. Salman closed his eyes and pretended to sleep, taking refuge in his memories.

~

Flight is like a fate, an omen, a constant companion in Arab culture. Jews begin their calendar with the creation of the world, according to rabbinical tradition in the year 3761 BC. Christians begin their calendar with the birth of Christ. But in Islam, the calendar is connected to the flight of the Prophet Muhammad from Mecca to Medina, which saved both his life and his mission. No attempt to reset the Muslim calendar to either the Prophet's birth or death has ever succeeded.

"Flight is beginning again. Flight is hope," Salman thought. "Flight is wisdom, and wisdom is often mistaken for cowardice." Now this same flight had helped him to cheat death.

So far, his life had been a chain of emigrations and separations. His mother had told him how he was born in 1945 on Baghdad Street, where she and his father, Yusuf, had been living. Three weeks later, his family had to flee Damascus because Musa Bandar, a gang boss, had threatened Salman's father that his goldsmith's shop would be raided and he would be killed if he didn't pay "protection" money.

So they fled to Aleppo where Yusuf was able to quickly open a new goldsmith's shop, with the help of his relatives. The well-to-do Baladis had been goldsmiths or merchants for centuries, and Yusuf worked there successfully for four years. They only returned to Damascus with their son after the criminal Musa Bandar was shot and killed by the police. For the next six years they lived in a little house in the modern al-Salihiya district. There Salman attended a Catholic school that he liked, and where his charm won over friends and hearts. But then his father bought the big patrician house on Misk Street in the Old City, near the exclusive Lazarist school, so that ten-year-old Salman had to start again as a complete stranger.

A theater lover in the wrong place

The French Order of Lazarists was founded in Paris in 1625 to help the poor, but in Damascus it was one of four exclusive schools for the sons of the wealthy.

Since the 1950s, the school had been run by Josef Ata—a Lebanese priest, a well-known theologian, and a strict but just man. From teachers and pupils alike he insisted on the same respect that he accorded them. Father Josef did not shrink from owning up to his errors and asking for forgiveness before his assembled pupils and teachers. In Arab culture it was considered tantamount to a miracle when anyone in power admitted to errors. As early as the 1960s, he had managed to attract to the school the best teachers in the country, and one of these was Father Michel Kosma. He taught ethics and rhetoric, and he had studied theater and philosophy in Paris in his youth. After falling hopelessly and catastrophically in love with a young actress, Kosma retreated forever into a theological shell. In 1956, he joined the Order of Lazarists in Paris and became a priest. Shortly afterward, he returned home to Damascus.

Father Michel was a gifted producer and director, and soon the senior students were putting on world-class plays that delighted audiences. Salman brought passion and enthusiasm to his acting. He learned to speak clearly and confidently, and to use facial expression and gesture. Father Michel treated him as he would his own brother. He called him *mon petit cousin*. At first Salman thought it was a nice joke, but later his father told him that their great-grandfathers had been brothers. Father Michel recruited senior students from the Sacré Coeur girls' school to play the female roles. He warned his pubescent students to treat the girls with consideration at all times. "Because they're being brave and also because they're your guests," he would repeat time and time again. But the boys' hormone-fueled brains saw only willing objects of their desires in the ripening young females, so that erotic romances kept blossoming, until the catastrophe of 1963.

One year prior to Salman's graduation, Father Michel suffered a bitter defeat. A pale female student from a powerful Christian family fell prey to the blind lust of a horny boy who would almost have raped her, had an attendant not come to her rescue at the very last minute. Maximus IV, then the patriarch of the Catholic Church, immediately banned theater at the Lazarist school, without granting the priest a hearing. Kosma was severely reprimanded and suspended from all his duties for a year. Salman often visited him in his room, a Spartan cell with a cot and a small shabby table. Father Michel cried like an abandoned child.

After his cousin's punishment and suffering, Salman lost any inclination to be at the Lazarist school, but another teacher came to his rescue. He was a young French priest named François Semeux, and he taught physics. He would visit Father Michel every day and was the only one who could make him laugh.

He started to look after Salman as if he had been ordered to do so by Father Michel himself. Unlike Salman's cousin, Father François was a left-wing radical. He supplied Salman with French books and discussed films and novels with him. Physics was his passion, but he was widely read and well versed in world literature.

Salman's friendship with the young Father François was sealed with a book of plays by Jean Genet. The two started meeting more often, went for long walks, and talked about everything under the sun. Just like Genet, Semeux was on the side of the weak. He confided to Salman that he had entered religious life so as not to have to carry a weapon. At the time, it was impossible to avoid military service in France, and any attempt to do so carried a prison sentence. Just like Genet, Semeux was also in favor of independence for the colonies, especially for Algeria.

Semeux lent Salman books on socialism and debated with him at length. They would read the writings of Saint-Simon, Camus, Sartre, and the great classics of the

Enlightenment. Salman lapped it all up and felt deeply indignant at the injustices in the world, but he could not yet imagine doing anything about it himself.

One night, on his way home, Salman saw a man sitting next to a trash bin outside a villa, eating food scraps that he had salvaged. Salman could not believe his eyes. He went up to the man and found out that in two days' begging he had received nothing and so he had been unable to eat. He was a farmer who had fled to the city to escape his debt. Salman gave him all the money that he had in his pocket and hurried away. That Sunday, his parents were entertaining business guests at home, with champagne, wine, and dishes of the finest delicacies. For the first time ever, Salman felt a deep aversion toward his father and his well-to-do family. He couldn't sleep that night.

~

In March 1963, after barely eighteen months of democracy, the Syrian army took power in a coup and declared a state of emergency. Among those involved were several factions fighting for the upper hand. Gradually, an unassuming air-force officer named Hafiz al-Assad emerged from the shadows to become the sinister new leader of the country. He could boast neither charm nor eloquence, but he was secretive, brutal, and a master conspirator.

In his heart of hearts, Salman became a socialist, but he wanted nothing to do with the Syrian Communist party. He believed it answered to Moscow, was corrupt, and just like the government, was led by a clan. The Communist party gradually became the Bakdash family's private enterprise. It was subject to both the Syrian regime and to Moscow at once. But along with his friends, Salman believed that selfless fighters were needed to topple the Syrian dictatorship by force.

At the university Salman studied mathematics and physics, but he also attended philosophy and history lectures. He studied in order to avoid the compulsory, brutal two-year national service. As long as he was in school, he was exempt. Also, he needed time to decide what he wanted to do with his life.

At the end of June 1967, shortly after the devastating defeat of the Arab states by Israel, Salman joined the armed underground movement with four friends and his cousin Elias, who had just turned seventeen. The purpose was to overthrow the Syrian regime. The overwhelming majority of Arabs believed that their defeat had been caused less by the strength of Israel than by the incompetence of the Arab governments, which had specialized in humiliating their own peoples. However, few members of the opposition were ready to sacrifice their lives to oust these regimes. Salman was one of the minority who was willing to be a martyr, if it came to that. From that moment on he was officially at arms and on the run.

Beirut—the Swiss mirage

The taxi driver honked his horn at a colleague driving past in the opposite direction. Salman opened his eyes and looked out of the window. His glance wandered over the green hills, where the apple trees were in full bloom. He breathed in their scent and thought that freedom smelled like apple blossoms. And for a moment he forgot all about exile and being on the run.

Lebanon was still at peace that spring. The civil war would not start for another five years, in 1975, and then rage for fifteen more. This little country on the Mediterranean was called "the Switzerland of the Middle East" for its banks and snow-capped mountains, its free

European lifestyle, and its neutrality in political conflicts. This description was popular, but inaccurate. It was a slogan, invented for helpless people groping for the first available signpost to safety. Lebanon was nothing like Switzerland in either its attractions or flaws. And Beirut, the great beating heart of that little country, bore no resemblance to any Swiss city. Compared to Beirut, Zurich was a neat little family hotel with a bank, a boutique, and a restaurant on the ground floor. Beirut was a planet with its own laws—or no laws at all. The city extended its generous hospitality to all: the innocent and the guilty, beggars and billionaires, pacifists and weapons dealers and drug barons alike. No other city in the Arab world printed as many books as Beirut. Most of them were meant for other Arab countries and made their way to their destinations legally or illegally, with the help of courageous tourists, dealers, taxi drivers, and passengers.

At that time, the opposition parties from every Arab country were active in Beirut. They agitated against the dictators in their respective countries and were more often than not financed by other dictators. Here people could live well under the radar, provided they studiously avoided treading on the toes of any of the more than twenty secret services operating in Beirut. The CIA, KGB, Mossad, and agents from Arab secret services were long-term guests in the city, which also played host to over ten armed Palestinian organizations.

Salman's own knowledge of Lebanon came from an illegal visit to a guerrilla training camp three years earlier. Germans and Japanese also trained there, alongside Palestinians and other Arabs.

At the time, Salman had gone to the Palestinians with a small group of Syrian men and women—for weapons training and to learn how to live and operate as an underground movement; in short, how to move "like a fish in water" among the "popular masses," as Mao had put it. Most of the fighters were former students who had read Mao, Ho Chi Minh, and Che Guevara, and wanted to imitate these revolutionaries.

At that time, Salman had lived quietly under an assumed name in a Palestinian camp in southern Lebanon. In the camp there was an atmosphere of cold mistrust among the various groups, and contact with strangers was strictly forbidden. The trainers were brutal, primitive sadists. The whole thing was more like a prison camp than a place where the idealistic project of a free future was being forged.

And now, several years later, here he was back in Lebanon, with false papers again—this time not to learn how use weapons and explosives, but simply to survive. This time he would be able to live at his Aunt Amalia's place. His mother, Sophia, had contacted him by roundabout means and informed him that if he got out of Syria alive, Aunt Amalia would gladly take him in. This surprised him because, while Aunt Amalia liked his mother, she was not at all on good terms with her brother, Salman's father.

Aunt Amalia and the three rebellions

The root cause for the hostilities lay more than thirty years in the past. Amalia had married the man she loved, not the man deemed suitable by her mother, her father, and her two brothers—Salman's father, Yusuf, and Uncle Anton, Elias' father. She had met Said Bustani at the university. Both had been studying literature and philosophy. He was Lebanese, highly gifted but from a poor family, and—as if that wasn't enough—an Evangelical. Salman's father never used this word. He used to say "Protestant" with his lips pressed together, as if to indicate that such people were poor ignorant Arab Christians who had been led astray by American and German missionaries. And although Amalia was a few years older than her brothers Yusuf and Anton, their opinions carried more weight than her own.

Sophia always used to say that Amalia embodied three revolutions. A woman who studied in the 1940s and who also smoked and drank was one revolution; then when she went and married the man that she—and not her family—wanted, that was the second revolution; and when this man was not even a Syrian Catholic but a Jew, a Muslim or, even worse, a Protestant, well, that was the third revolution.

Amalia's well-to-do Baladi family was ashamed of her. Honor killing never crossed their minds, but they treated their disloyal daughter as if she simply did not exist. This was even more humiliating than killing her, since her death as a martyr to love would have elevated her to a shining legend and caused much mourning in wealthy, enlightened Christian circles. But the Baladis would then have been regarded as heartless, primitive criminals. The clan was at pains to deny this triumph to their rebel. The family's ultimate disdain was, however, their refusal to even acknowledge their daughter's existence. One week after eloping with Said, Amalia was cast out from her family, dispossessed, and forgotten. Nobody was allowed to talk about her, or to name any daughter after her.

Amalia was unimpressed with all this. She loved her Said. He was a fine man. He became a professor at the American University in Beirut and wrote several books on philosophy, causing a sensation each time. Once he was even charged with blasphemy, but in liberal Lebanon he was acquitted. The accusation itself was the best possible advertising for the book, which ran to twenty editions over three years. When Salman read the book, he found the dedication very moving: *For Amalia, the woman from a worthy future.*

Aunt Amalia herself became an English teacher. Her only heartache was that she and her husband had had no children, although she loved them. The Baladi family in Damascus noted this with glee—superstitious as they were, they ascribed Amalia's childlessness to the curse that her mother had uttered while donating candles and incense to the Virgin Mary, so that she might cause her daughter's ovaries to wither and become unfruitful. Sophia laughed at that. "As if the Virgin hasn't anything better to do than cause ovaries to wither!" she cried.

When Aunt Amalia came to Damascus, she would stay with the family of friends. Salman's mother would invite her out to restaurants, but never to her home. That was forbidden. Amalia knew her brother, and she could understand her sister-in-law's attitude. However, when Salman and his mother came to Beirut, Amalia always wanted to welcome them into her home, but such visits were few and far between. It was only later that Salman learned both his mother and several other women in the family had tried in vain to convince Amalia's parents to reconcile with her. Even after George Baladi died in 1944, his irascible widow still refused to forgive her daughter. "No wonder," Aunt Amalia recalled, "that she suffocated on her own mucus during a fit of anger."

Later Amalia's husband came into money through an inheritance and bought the roomy apartment on Pasteur Street, in the middle of the beautiful Old City, the liveliest quarter of Beirut.

He died suddenly in January 1965, after a short illness. Amalia mourned the loss of her husband all her life, but she locked her grief away in her heart and lived alone as a widow in her spacious apartment. She had a generous widow's pension and resigned from her job. Free of all obligations, she was finally able to do what she had always dreamed of: reading, painting, and traveling. She always wore black. It kept away flies and lustful rats, she would explain ironically.

But Amalia had stipulated in her will that she was to be laid out in her coffin wearing a white wedding dress, as it was her wish to marry Said again in the hereafter.

Salman climbed out of the shared Syrian taxi in central Castle Square, took his suitcase, and waved down another cab. "Eleven Pasteur Street," he told the driver. He was curious to meet Aunt Amalia, whom he had not seen for years. He had no idea that his life would undergo a radical turnaround at his widowed aunt's home.

4

Aunt Amalia and the Great Crisis

Beirut, summer 1970

An oasis of tranquility

After the strains of surviving in the underground, evading arrest, and being pursued by the secret service and its informers, Salman's first few days in Beirut were a welcome relief. He had felt like a hunted animal, every captured friend, every betrayed bit of information shaking the ground beneath his feet and tightening a noose around his neck.

In the winter of 1969, his rebel group was crushed in a fierce battle south of Aleppo. Its leaders foolishly had thrown strategy and tactics overboard and provoked a direct confrontation with a giant army. The few surviving fighters fled in all directions. From then on, his cell of two women and three men wandered cross-country. But in an olive grove near Homs, they were drawn into an ambush and surrounded. Although wounded, Salman somehow got away. The two brave women died in a storm of gunfire, one partisan was captured and executed, another wounded and beaten to death in the vehicle on the way back to Damascus.

Salman wandered about aimlessly, lack of food tormenting him more than the wound in his right shoulder. Hunger clawed its way into his innards like a wild cat, scratching and screaming for bread. He dug for roots in the barren landscape, but whatever he found was inedible. He drank from streams to quiet the beast in his stomach and dragged himself on. One day he found a lone wild apple tree and, in great pain from his infected shoulder, picked and devoured a few apples. Then he sat down in the shade and thought about the disaster that had befallen his group. Why had they failed? He had no answers. He picked a few more apples and set off again, with a single thought—to shoot himself if he was threatened with capture. He started running until, exhausted and weakened from loss of blood, he collapsed.

When he came to, he was in a dark room, his shoulder heavily bandaged. A farmer had dug the bullet out and hidden him, risking the death penalty for saving a "terrorist's" life. Salman asked him why he had rescued him. The farmer answered that he had lost his wife because nobody was there to help her. While he was out working in the fields, his wife had fallen off a ladder while cleaning the windows and cut herself on a broken window pane. Alone, she had bled to death. "When I came home in the evening, she was gone," he said. He had found Salman lying on the dirt path, bleeding, just like his wife that time in the kitchen. Salman had been lucky; the bullet hadn't gone in deeply, and he had been able to dig it out easily.

Salman's stay at the farmer's passed quickly. His only memory was the strong fragrance of thyme all around. Once he recovered, Salman gave the farmer his Kalashnikov rifle, his pistol, and his expensive compass. Three weeks later, Samad, the farmer, took him via various back roads to his brother, who was a printer in Damascus. But unlike Samad, his brother was both bold and mercenary. In exchange for a gold chain and an expensive Swiss watch that Salman had been given by his parents for his graduation, the printer got him a forged passport and handed him two hundred dollars as pocket money, as well as a few hundred

Syrian lira for travel expenses. The watch alone was worth more than five thousand dollars, but Salman had no choice because he had to leave the country quickly. Being stingy or petty could cost him his life.

~

Staying at Aunt Amalia's allowed him to get his strength back. Embodying Arab hospitality, Amalia refrained from bothering her nephew with any questions for the first three days. But she spoiled him, and he made it easy for her with his gratitude and his charming, humorous, self-deprecating way of talking with her about his failures, catastrophes, and other painful experiences. Always outspoken, she pointed out that he owed his witty and brave personality to his mother. His father—her brother Yusuf—never demonstrated even the slightest inkling of humor as a child, teenager, or adult, and had snuck through life in the shadow of others. He was a tortured soul who could neither find, nor spread, peace. As his sister, she knew that firsthand.

Her apartment on the third floor was quiet and roomy, with a balcony from which Salman could look out at the harbor and the open sea. He never met the neighbors because he spent as little time as possible on the stairs, as a safety measure. Day after day, all he heard was Aunt Amalia's voice and her laughter. She laughed loud, long, and often, which was completely at odds with her widow's attire. He also found her accent strange because, although she had been born and raised in Damascus, she spoke with a Beiruti dialect. When Salman asked her why, she told him, "I want nothing to do with the Damascene dialect. It reminds me of my family, but the Beiruti dialect is connected with my love for Said and my escape from the clan."

Amalia looked like an Arab woman from North Africa. Unlike his father or his uncle Anton who had straight hair and light skin, a small nose, and thin lips, Amalia had a lion's mane of thick, grizzled, frizzy hair on her powerful head. Her large eyes, full lips, and dark skin gave her an alluring beauty. "I'm sure I'm the result of a secret love affair my mother had with an African," she was fond of saying, laughing aloud as if to proclaim her pride in her African relations.

Salman had hardly known his aunt, but her warm-hearted openness soon broke the ice. It didn't take long for him to trust her, and although he had not planned to, he began to confide in her. Eager for details, she praised his courage, his ideals and readiness to risk his life for them, and the fact that he had given up the security of an academic career to fight for freedom. But she also told him bluntly that his underground activities reminded her of children playing cowboys and Indians. Only this time lives were at stake, which made it all the more stupid. Forty years later, Salman still remembered how shocked he had been at her words.

A painful awakening

At around three in the afternoon, Aunt Amalia woke him gently out of his siesta. The smell of cardamom and mocha filled the air. They sat on the balcony and drank the strong coffee. Amalia wished to be candid with him. Looking out to the sea, she said that if she had a son, she would talk to him in exactly the same way, not holding anything back but also without any obligation for him to accept what she said. She lit a cigarette, exhaled, and watched the blue smoke disappear into the equally blue distance. "A completely different force is needed to overthrow the regime in Damascus." She grieved for all the young men and women who stood up so naïvely to face the cold-blooded killers of the Syrian special forces and secret services, and sacrificed their lives. Her best Lebanese friend had lost her only son in the fighting in the mountains. He had taken the name of Ali Che—in honor of Che Guevara—and, like his idol, had been captured and executed in cold blood.

Salman stroked her hand as a faint smile flitted across her face, followed by tears. "All these young people like you and Ali," she said sadly. "They all want a revolution so that we can live like human beings, in freedom and dignity. But they all die young, maybe as favorites of the gods, before a revolution led by a new gang of professional criminals can defeat the old, worn out ones. It was ever so—and so it shall remain." She looked into his eyes. "Listen carefully, son, nothing will ever change as long as rebellion is meant only to achieve social or political change. Your naïve fighters level mountains with tremendous self-sacrifice and pave wide roads with the tears of hope, only for criminals to drive up and enter the capital amid flags and fanfare, soon to be so intoxicated by the cheering, foolish crowds as to believe themselves to be gods.

"No change will ever come to Arab countries until the very structure of the clan that enslaves us, body and soul, has been destroyed. The clan is built on obedience and loyalty, and couldn't care less about democracy, freedom, or human dignity. It permeates and rots everything, like a fungus. Stick and carrot, a bit of security traded for a bit of dignity, and we suddenly find ourselves on a slippery slope looking merely for happiness and a way to satisfy our instincts. There is no dignity left at the bottom of the slide. We are just satisfied slaves of our clan leaders, priding ourselves on the fact that we haven't been arrested yet. But tell me what you think of all this…"

"How can I explain it?" Salman replied, searching for where to start. "I was shocked that we had given up on

the world long before the army even came on the scene...
There were just a few of us, close friends, and we felt like
we'd been going round in circles for years, only to come
back to where we started, like a mule moving a millstone.
Revolutionaries weren't rebels anymore. They'd become
just like the society they wanted to destroy... And all our
dead have died in vain," he said, and quietly began to cry.
Amalia kissed his eyes and hugged him. He took a deep
breath. She smelled of almond blossom.

"That's the nature of revolution," Amalia said. "Since
Nicholas Copernicus, the word *revolution* has meant the
unchanging orbit of a planet in a closed circle. It can never
mean a new beginning."

For two hours, she told him stories of intrigue and
revolution that might have come straight out of a detective novel, and Salman realized that none of his years with
the underground or his training could match the widow's
tales. Like a palace made of ice, his faith in revolution
melted away under Amalia's burning words.

Salman felt that, after this conversation, something
inside him had irretrievably broken into pieces. Afterward,
he couldn't sleep, so he snuck into the kitchen and returned
to his room with a glass of red wine. In the corridor, he
paused briefly and smiled when he heard Aunt Amalia
snoring in her bedroom.

Revolutionary hell and promises of Paradise

The next morning, Salman felt like he was paralyzed. He
didn't have the energy or slightest desire to get up or do
anything.

Why had he joined the armed resistance? Was he
reacting to the 1967 defeat of the Arab states by Israel, as
many of his friends claimed? Clearly not. Then what was

the reason? Slogans like "liberation of the fatherland" or "socialist justice" weren't enough. How many of these had he repeated without knowing what they meant? What did socialism even look like? The realities of socialism seemed dreadful. His rebel group rejected both Moscow and Beijing, and their client states, and although members praised the Cuban way, none of them had ever been to Cuba themselves.

And how did the cause of emancipating workers and poor peasants championed by his rebel faction relate in any way to his reality? A memory came back to him, strong and painful, the kind best buried once and for all. Because of his powers of persuasion, he had been sent for three months to Aleppo, the metropolis of the North. His assignment was to win over left-wing students to fight in the mountains and to build up an urban network of radical groups, as well as Kurdish fighters. Under a false identity and passing himself off as a student, he stayed at the house of a widow who was in her fifties. She had no children and worked in a textile factory. Every morning she got up at four, left the house at five, and returned at around seven in the evening, pale and exhausted after a twelve-hour day working and a one-hour return trip. The only light she ever saw was the artificial light inside the factory. Salman seldom crossed paths with her. She always seemed to be in a bad mood and unapproachable, and she never tried to get to know him. At the beginning of the month, without any comment, he would leave the rent on the kitchen table and spend his time debating the emancipation of the workers and peasants with others in his radical group.

"I'm moving out at the end of the month," he told her after about three months.

"Right," she said, and went to her room. Later he remembered that he had sometimes heard her crying, and he would have liked to comfort her, but his orders were to avoid all close personal contact.

It was only now, in Beirut, that he realized how detached from reality his life had been. The workers who lived in poverty alongside him could not be the reason for his fight. Only here, in Beirut, did he find the answer to why their group had failed. The rebels had suffered their bitter defeat without a single poor peasant standing by them. They looked on as if watching a savage war movie, frightened to death yet uninvolved. All the fighters, men and women, were heroic and self-sacrificing, but that was not enough. They knew a few of the writings of Marx, Bakunin, Lenin, Mao, and Guevara, but they didn't know the peasants and so remained out of place in the country.

But if not to defend the peasants, why had he fought? The answer alarmed him. It was because of a dangerous mixture of romantic notions about heroic liberation and Christian ideas about self-sacrifice, equality, and martyrdom, combined with the Christian minority's eternal longing to play a decisive part in a Muslim society. It was no accident that the Christians were always the first members—if not the founders—of the nationalist and socialist parties in Arab countries. Like the Jews in Europe, the Christians living in Arab countries did not want merely to establish their position—they wanted to show the majority that they, too, belonged. All these ingredients had combined into a lethal formula that had clouded Salman's brain and turned him into a useful idiot, ready to wage battle.

Salman now felt bitter and ashamed to have slandered the members of his group who had laid down their weapons and wanted nothing more to do with politics. They had been more honest and clear-headed than he had.

~

When he got up at around noon, Amalia was out. As always when she left the apartment, she had left him a note. He didn't want to eat, or to drink coffee, so he got dressed and went out and headed toward the sea. Fresh air for his lungs and wide vistas for his eyes—that was what he needed.

His thoughts raced. He felt cheated by the movement's leaders. The dream of a free and just society had made every sacrifice easy for him. Utopias were an effective drug on sensitive people, he thought on his way to the beach. Utopia is a blindfold, and he realized that he'd willingly put on that blindfold, searching for the way with outstretched arms. Now he had a bird's-eye view and could see how that leadership had laughed at and pushed him around. Up until now, all he had seen in his leaders was the fire of their pure hearts and their desire to fight and win an honorable life for all Syrians. But he had been too naïve to understand that revolutions also attract the dregs of society, like a magnet attracts iron filings. They came to settle personal scores and didn't give a damn about any values—stealing, killing, and raping.

Although Salman mocked and criticized clannishness in his own circle of friends within the ranks of his rebel group, he never risked an open confrontation. The people were intimidated by the regime, but so were followers by their revolutionary leaders, and they too held their tongues. The same fighters who bravely risked their lives for the revolution showed cowardice in concealing their uneasiness and their criticism of leaders.

It had never occurred to Salman and his fellow fighters that they had been given a single task—to put a new regime in place, with new big shots to rule over their subjects.

Amalia was right... it never had dawned on him so clearly.

Alia, the love-struck healer

On the beach in Beirut, he shook his head at himself. He had been a complete fool to fight as a guerrilla in the northern Syrian mountains with his Kalashnikov and his old Beretta, manufactured in 1955. In despair he shouted out at the sea, until a cool breeze slowly calmed him down. During the night he ran a fever and vomited several times. Amalia discovered him lying on the bathroom floor.

For three days, he had shivering fits and pains in his limbs. He kept vomiting, but only a yellow, slimy, bitter liquid came up from his empty stomach. He could hardly stand. Aunt Amalia looked after him around the clock. On the third day, his temperature hadn't come down, despite all kinds of herbal teas and cold poultices, so she called Alia, a young doctor who lived in the house next door. Salman experienced her visit through a daze but answered her questions and followed her instructions as best he could. Later, all he could remember of those days was the pale face of his aunt and the lemon-blossom fragrance that came with the doctor and remained in the room long after she had gone. Years later, his aunt wrote to him in Germany and told him that she had never been so worried about him in her whole life. She attributed his symptoms to the poisons of injustice and cruelty he had swallowed for so long. The same thing had happened to her after she decided to break with her family.

The doctor gave him an injection and several tablets, and he fell asleep. When he woke up, it was quiet in the apartment. He got up, washed his face with cold water, rubbed it with a rough towel, and peered into the mirror. He looked miserable and worn out.

Whenever he woke from his feverish dreams, the past washed over him like a lament. He was haunted, in particular, by the memory of a policeman he had seriously wounded.

The policeman had been a friendly, simple man. Together with his four colleagues, he had been unlucky to find himself assigned to a mountain police station, not far from Aleppo, at the wrong time. The secret service had captured five experienced opposition fighters in a massive surprise attack. One of them had been Salman's closest comrade in arms, Hani Khoury. Hani came from a Christian Damascene family. Although he lived not far from Salman's family home, they had only met in the mountains. Hani was a quiet, modest compatriot. He was the group's radio technician and explosives expert. Salman and he had vowed never to abandon each other.

On their way to the police station, the prisoners had been handcuffed and beaten like animals. Salman's heart nearly shattered at the sight of Hani. The leader of the secret service group called Aleppo, demanding reinforcements and a vehicle for the prisoners. Then he left the police station to hunt for the other freedom fighters in the nearby woods.

Neither the secret service nor the five policemen suspected that a rebel commando unit led by Salman had moved into position in the abandoned building opposite the police station. When the three white Land Rovers with the men from the secret service sped off in a cloud of dust, the commandos attacked the police station. The five policemen were poorly armed, elderly officers. Salman burst in first. Despite his experience, he was nervous because he expected at least one seasoned man from the secret service to have stayed behind. Scared to death, four of the policemen raised their hands to surrender, but the fifth moved his hand in a way that alarmed Salman. He fired at the man, hitting him in the stomach and gravely wounding him. The other four policemen shouted and begged for mercy. The wounded man looked up at Salman with pleading eyes, a look that would haunt him for years.

He had the four policemen handcuffed, called an ambulance, gave the name of the police station, and said that they should send a helicopter quickly, with an experienced doctor for a seriously wounded general. The injured policeman nodded gratefully and tried to smile. Salman then cut the telephone line to the police station and hurried out last behind his freed compatriots. Before the commando group left the village, a helicopter landed in the village square.

Salman never found out whether the policeman had survived his wound. He also lost touch with his friend Hani when the Syrian army sent a huge detachment to comb the mountains northwest of Aleppo, set fire to villages, and mercilessly hunt down the guerrillas. His rebel group disintegrated into small factions that scattered over the entire country and continued to fight. Salman and his companions became the target of an intensive manhunt.

Between bouts of fever, the details of those events came back to him, but he mentioned them to no one. Alia, the doctor, visited him every day, and slowly he recovered.

~

Salman was not the only one to notice that Alia was falling in love with him. So did Aunt Amalia. Alia was married and she had two children, both at boarding school since their parents had hardly any time for them. At the time, Salman had not gotten over his breakup with his last girlfriend, Lamia.

Lamia was a peaceful woman who would rather listen to music and look after the flowers in her parents' garden than talk about Vietnam, Cuba, or Palestine. She was in love with Salman and wanted a simple, happy life with him at her side. That was why she kept urging him not to associate with those "losers," as she called revolutionaries. When Salman went to the training camp in South Lebanon, Lamia turned her back on him for good. She wrote him a bitter farewell letter, cursing him for breaking her heart and calling him a brainless terrorist. She would soon marry, and he would lose sight of her forever. From that time on—three years prior to his escape to Beirut—he only related to women as political comrades or casual erotic partners. And that is how he became involved with Alia, without feeling anything for her.

Years later, the smell of lemon blossom would still conjure up the memory of the first time he had made love with Alia. She was sitting at his bedside on that day. She was witty. He lay in bed in his white summer pajamas, and she bent over him and kissed him on the lips. She stood up, drew the curtains, and undressed very slowly, almost as if in a dance. She looked different in the dimly lit room, with her sensual lips, large eyes, and seductive body. As if in slow motion, she took off her panties and went naked to him. Her scent bewitched his senses and he noticed that he was too aroused. He tried to put off the decisive moment by distracting himself and thinking of a complex chess gambit. Her breath felt scorching on his skin. He straightened up to distance himself from her but she pressed his shoulder down on the bed. She licked his mouth and when his lips parted, she sucked his tongue. Her mouth tasted sweet and smelled of licorice.

She undressed him, her lips slid over his throat and chest, and when she licked his navel he almost burst with arousal. He grabbed her shoulders and turned her on her back, she looked at him with a new expression in her eyes.

"Come," she whispered, pulling him over her. That had been the end of him. He felt ashamed, and she comforted him by making love with him again.

~

In Beirut he started to read again as a way to collect himself and understand what had happened. And in Beirut he could get books both in French and in Arabic. He read Manès Sperber's *Like a Tear in the Ocean*, and felt as if he was the brother of its hero, Dojno Faber. George Orwell's novels, *1984* and *Animal Farm*, confirmed everything that Amalia had told him. He was shattered. So many million people had died to help a troubled dictator come to power.

As for Amalia, she never again spoke with him about his past. She led a very active life, had many girlfriends, and whenever she was at home for a while, she would read English detective novels. Even after Salman's recovery, Alia continued visiting him every day. Whenever she turned up, Amalia seemed to have urgent business in town. Salman enjoyed his time with Alia... she was his first sexual mentor, and with her he explored the vast expanse of erotic fantasies. He learned that foreplay is an invention born of one's mind, not one's instincts. "A goat like my husband knows nothing about this," she said. "He mounts me as if I was a she-goat. The smell of his sweat is disgusting. He jumps off and soon he's snoring in his bedroom. But even though I take a shower, the stink of him lingers with me."

She was also the first woman who taught him how words are an important part of lovemaking. Usually he either remained silent or else parroted phrases like, "You're beautiful... I like you... you please me." Alia, however, adorned even the smallest stirring or softest touch with spontaneous, delicate poetry that was neither contrived nor vulgar. Salman had never experienced anything like that before.

At the time, Alia's husband was the director of the Beirut airport. That was all Salman knew about him, and he himself didn't breathe a word to Alia about his real identity or his past. She was curious and asked many questions, but it only made him all the more uncommunicative.

Alia talked openly about herself. Her greatest mistake, she said, had been to let herself be beguiled by outward appearances. As a medical student, she had been fascinated by her future husband's sports car and luxurious lifestyle. But now it felt as if she was living with her bags packed all the time. "If it wasn't for the children, I'd be long gone," she said.

~

The city throbbed with noises and smells, and early summer peeled away layers of winter clothing from people. Lively and colorful, they strolled along the streets, sat in cafés and bars, danced and laughed, sang and drank. Hippies were unknown in Arab countries, but the Lebanese took all that color and created elegance out of it. Hippies had nothing to teach them about a relaxed lifestyle, for they had been masters of it for centuries.

All that noisy life streamed past Salman like a long film. For the first time in his entire life, he had no inhibitions about questioning any of his past. Occasionally he would feel giddy when a rock of truth or a bottomless chasm of lies loomed up.

Each day he would spend long stretches sitting by the sea and talking to himself, silently or aloud, before returning home exhausted. It was during this time that he began to understand not life but himself better, and his first discovery was that he was no politician. Not that he was apolitical, but he simply was not cut out for political action. Every night before going to sleep, he wrote down what he had learned in a sort of diary.

It was only weeks later that he started to take part in the lively night life around him. It was on one of these nighttime strolls that he saw Alia with her husband. They were coming out of a bar in the nearby Gemmayzeh district. Alia's husband wasn't at all bad-looking. They were behaving like two lovers and they kissed in the middle of the street. Shortly afterward, they drove off in his Porsche.

When Alia visited him the following day and changed his dressing while badmouthing her husband, he felt a deep disdain for her, which he was able to conceal. He had never fallen for a woman so completely, so erotically, so fiercely as this time. He was quite unable to explain how it was that he felt such intense physical pleasure, while his emotions were stifled by disdain. Later on, it would be even more of a mystery to him how he would never again be able to remember Alia's face, try as he might.

He stayed in Beirut for three months, until his parents were able to secure a Syrian passport for him through bribery. Armed with this passport and his high-school diploma, he was able to apply for entry to a university in Europe. America was too far away, and too final. He wanted to be sure that he could return to Syria as soon as the dictatorship had been toppled. Salman was certain that the regime would not even last four years. Later on in Rome, he claimed that he had miscalculated by a zero.

He sent out countless applications, from Finland to Spain. His French was perfect, and so he hoped to be admitted to one of the many French universities in Paris, Lyon, Marseilles, Lille, Avignon, or Bordeaux. But the

French rejected him. Though the official at the French embassy in Beirut admired his French and his high-school grades, he eyed him suspiciously and asked, just before he left, almost as an afterthought, "Why don't you apply directly from Damascus? No problems there, I hope?" Salman understood perfectly the diplomatically concealed question—"What have you been up to there?" He came up with a labored, untrue answer, but the official was not convinced. He smiled faintly and gave Salman a weak, sweaty handshake goodbye.

But then Salman received two acceptances almost at once—one to study biology in Stockholm and one to study philosophy in Heidelberg. While he liked philosophy, the actual subject of study was of secondary importance to him. He opted for the romantic German city on the Neckar because it was more southerly and closer to France.

That year, July gave him a scorching taste of Hell. The sky burned and water fled, seeking shelter in the depths of the earth. At night, people filled pots and pans, bowls and buckets with water because the supply failed repeatedly during the day. If you opened the taps, all you heard was whistling, gurgling, and whispers from afar.

Farewells

On a sticky morning in mid-July, Salman got his German visa without a problem. He went straight down to the seaside from the German embassy and sat in a café for a while, enjoying this latest stage in his victory over death. Then he treated himself to some delicious fish in a nearby restaurant, accompanied by some cold white wine, and he tipped the polite waiter so generously that the waiter mistook him for a rich Saudi. It was only later that afternoon that he sauntered slightly unsteadily back to Aunt

Amalia's. There he found a note waiting for him. On impulse, Aunt Amalia had decided to ride the ferry to Cyprus with some girlfriends. She wanted to take a week's holiday and get to know the island. She had generously stuffed the fridge with all manner of treats, as if Salman was forever holding eating orgies.

Alia came over every day since her children were away on vacation at their grandparents' house in the mountains. They cooked together and would often spend all day in bed. Alia was his teacher in the kitchen as well. Not only was she an excellent cook, she was also a very good instructor.

There were tears when Salman told her that he would soon be leaving. She told him that he was her first true love. She had suffered a lot with her husband and had not known tenderness before she had met Salman. That was when he told her that he had been accepted to study medicine in Paris. There was a glint of joy in Alia's eyes. "In that case, I can visit you now and then because I'm in Paris at least once a year," she said, and he let her continue to believe that.

Years later, he still wondered just why he had lied to her so cold-bloodedly. He probably wanted to calm her down and still the flood of tears that would otherwise have spoiled their remaining time together. More likely, however, he wanted to make a clean break with the lie. The contempt that he felt for her whenever he thought of the lovebirds' scene between her and her husband flared up time and again.

~

Two weeks before his flight to Germany, he decided together with Aunt Amalia that his mother should not come to Beirut to see him off, although she would have loved to. Thanks to the newspapers, it was common knowledge that the Syrian secret service, which came in and out of Lebanon at will, dogged relatives' footsteps to lead them to where the fugitives were hiding. Amalia sent Salman's mother an envelope, with no return address, containing newspaper cuttings about three victims of the Syrian regime. Sophia understood and stayed in Damascus. Salman never learned that his father had read the same newspaper articles long ago and had advised his wife not to travel to Beirut. However, she would never have heeded his advice alone. His father arranged for Salman to receive eight hundred deutschmarks a month through a Lebanese bank—a lot of money at the beginning of the 1970s.

~

Salman liked the pubs by the harbor. They were simply decorated and their customers were dockers and fishermen. Tourists seldom wandered in. In one of these packed pubs, Salman spotted an empty chair at a little table. An old fisherman with worn, patched clothes was sitting there on his own, and when Salman asked him if the chair was free, the man laughed. "Empty yes, but the price for parking yourself is one arak," he said slyly. Salman sat down and ordered two araks, and another two, and then two more. When the old fisherman learned that Salman would be leaving the country in a week, he advised him that anyone emigrating needed a sharp pair of scissors to really cut through all the ties binding him to the old country. And then he said something that Salman would only understand forty years later. "When you go, don't come back, because you take your space with you. People won't like you because you come from their past, and many will see you as an uninvited witness for the prosecution." The old man was nothing but skin and bones, and the skin had been thoroughly tanned from a lifetime of sunshine, as if death had forgotten him.

~

The day before his flight was due to depart, Salman wanted to say goodbye to Beirut, but also to the life he had led up until then. So, that afternoon, he sat down on the ground with a bottle of red wine beside the sea where he had so recently screamed in desperation against the thundering of the waves. He drank slowly, savoring every drop. The sea played coquettishly with her blue gown while the waves caressed the soft sand.

Salman felt a sense of solemnity overcome his heart. He spoke softly to himself as if he was standing before an altar. Many of the couples that strolled past looked at him pityingly, as if they saw somebody who had been left by his wife, or who had just been fired from his job. "The man's drunk," a young blond girl said, pressing her mother's hand fearfully.

~

He found it hard to say goodbye to Aunt Amalia. She clung to him as if to her own son. He promised to write regularly and asked her not to reveal his address in Germany to anyone. Amalia smiled with tears in her eyes, "Above all I won't tell Alia. I'll say you've forgotten us. Yes, forgetfulness is the lot of the emigrant, but God forgive you if you forget me." She laughed and tugged him gently by the ear.

Salman raised his right hand and solemnly swore he would never forget his 'guardian angel Amalia,' and he kept his word. He wrote her very open and sometimes passionate letters right up until the time she died.

~

Amalia held back her tears at the airport until Salman began to cry. "You are my second mother," he said. "And what you told me in a half hour about revolution changed me more than books, parents, church, and school all put together. Aunt Amalia, I will always be grateful to you."

"You do that, but don't call me 'aunt' anymore. You know, in these three months with you, I learned for the first time that I can love children without them having to be mine, as Khalil Gibran advised. That was a great gift, and I do thank you. From now on I am your Amalia." She slipped a small package into his hand. "Wait until you're on the plane before you open that," she said, kissing him and stroking his face in farewell. She stayed where she was as Salman moved toward passport control at the entrance with the other Lufthansa passengers. He turned around again and waved. Aunt Amalia had gone.

Onboard the plane, he opened the little box and was shocked. It contained five thousand dollars and a note. "Reserve for use in case your father is stingy. Women love a generous man!" That was all it said, nothing more.

Salman's time in Lebanon had been the most intense and difficult of his life. Although it lasted only a few months, it spread out and took up more room in his memory than all his forty years in Europe. Later, another experience—a fatefully similar painful scenario—would also extend into an eternity and remain with him until his very last breath.

5

The Time before Sophia

Homs, 1927–1950

The power of memory… The first twenty or thirty years
in Karim's life were overshadowed for a long time
by his later experiences in Damascus. To him those early
years seemed bathed in a mist of innocence. It was only in
December 2010 that his childhood and adolescence returned
to him, banishing his later years to the remote recesses of
his mind. A certain visitor and a promise made now moved
him, to think back to these same beginnings, reflecting and
recounting. Not only was his dearest listener, Aida, surprised; he himself was amazed at all he had experienced.
And he recognized just how much a single event in all those
years had molded him into what he had become.

Karim was the oldest of seven children in the wealthy
Asmar family, itself a branch of a powerful Sunni Muslim
clan. His father, a rich timber merchant, owned estates on
the outskirts of the city of Homs that had been leased for a
time to tenants for market gardening. But when the sugar
plant opened its gates in 1948, his father took everything
back under his own management. His agent now oversaw
the planting of sugar beet year after year, and the sugar
plant bought up the harvest. Although the big farm was
located just outside the gates of the city, none of the children had ever seen it. It was simply a source of money for
Karim's father, who remained a city dweller through and
through. His father had studied philosophy and briefly
taught at a high school in Homs. But the timber trade,

which he had run as a sideline while he was a student, became ever more lucrative and ultimately his main profession. Still, he admired France and French philosophers and men of the Enlightenment. At the time, France was the occupying power in Syria, and Karim's father hoped that the French would make Syria into a liberal democratic republic. But Homs, his city, rebelled against the occupiers; many of his relatives took up arms against the French and regarded him as a traitor. After independence several of them were to become nationally known politicians.

Karim's father refused to be intimidated and sent his first three children—Karim, Saliha, and Ismail—to one of the elite Christian schools, until his daughter Saliha ran away with a Christian in 1950, a year after graduating. This came as a shock to their father, who was now jeered at by the rest of the more rural-conservative clan. It was all his fault for sending his children to the infidels for schooling, people said. Other relatives claimed it was a well-deserved divine punishment for being a traitor.

His father immediately took Karim's younger brother Ismail out of the Christian school and enrolled him in a Muslim school, together with the two younger brothers. Fatima, his second daughter, in her last year of elementary school, had to leave school since her father now maintained that the sheikh was right—school learning and books were the ruin of Muslim girls.

From that time on, all laughter deserted the house of Asmar. Karim would long remember his mother's tears and sadness, and how his father tormented her, reproaching her for the "soft" way she had brought up their children. Relatives showed an exaggerated concern for the clan's reputation. All this lay like a leaden weight upon the family, and so Karim took refuge wherever he could, in his school and afterward in cafés, returning home only when he was exhausted.

Since his daughter Saliha had fled, Karim's father had taken to hating Christians and prayed daily at the mosque. His mother and his younger sister now had to wear headscarves, and his father grew a beard. He still wore European suits—but no tie. Although this harmless accessory had originally come from Croatia, it was quite usual for conservative preachers to see it as symbolizing all things Western. Karim knew that his father's piety was all pretense and that the ugly brown prayer mark had simply been painted on his forehead instead of the prayer bump forming naturally as a result of repeatedly pressing it to the ground during prayers. Every morning, his father would touch up the stain. At the time, people would use the juice of green, unripe walnuts. Later they switched to European suntan lotions. This fashion was restricted to men. Karim's mother and sisters, aunts and female neighbors, although they actually prayed more often, never sported a cosmetic prayer bump.

But ritual displays, or even genuine expressions of piety, were not enough for the clan. So Karim's father announced one day, to his relatives' applause, that he would not rest until his honor had been washed clean with the blood of his daughter Saliha. After Friday prayers, he declared triumphantly that his firstborn son Karim be appointed avenger and executioner by the court of honor. This court had consisted of a single judge, Saliha's father.

Karim would never forget the meeting. The walls of the large drawing room seemed to have closed in on everyone present. The room was filled with relatives, friends, the imam of the Great Mosque, two senior army officers, and the Homs chief of police. More than ten people stood outside in the corridor. Tea and cakes were served.

Karim's father stood in the middle of a crowd of expectant faces. Karim felt wretched. A sad family affair had suddenly become a public spectacle.

When Karim's father gave his fiery speech and sentenced his daughter to death, the excitement of relatives and strangers alike peaked in a frightening climax. Shouts and applause resounded throughout the house. Saliha's brothers and sisters stiffened and turned pale at the exultation of the adults, who were then invited to share a celebratory meal.

This all happened in 1950, when Karim was already twenty-three. He had graduated from high school at eighteen, completed a two-year training course to become an elementary school teacher, and started work at a small school on the outskirts of Homs.

His sister's flight had been a major event in his life, but earlier on, something even more important had happened that changed his life forever.

Many years prior to his father's passing sentence, he had fallen head over heels in love with a young Christian girl named Sophia.

6

Stella and the Meekness of the Lioness

Heidelberg, Rome
summer 1970–summer 2010

The accordion of time

Whenever Salman thought back to his time in exile, he could hardly believe that so many years had gone by since he left Syria, or how much time he had spent in Heidelberg and in Rome. Happiness eases the passing of time, he thought, and leaves fewer traces in memory.

He could remember his first weeks in Heidelberg. Like a newborn reaching out for life, he had carefully made new contacts, savoring his first words in a new language.

Although he learned German quickly, it took him much longer to get to know the Germans. After catalyzing so many promising changes, the student movement had come to a standstill. Careerists emerged from its idealistic ruins, losing themselves in the labyrinth of a long march into institutions. Once they became ministers, directors, and industrialists, they stopped suffering for their revolutionary principles and started worrying more about their wallets and waistlines. What was most dangerous for Salman was the rise of German terrorists with contacts in Arab countries. A number of harmless Arab students among his acquaintances were arrested and deported because they were suspected of being intermediaries between German and Abu Nidal terrorists. So Salam kept his interactions with his fellow Arab students to an absolute minimum.

Instead, he threw himself into his new life, eagerly studying philosophy and history—and enjoying himself. His German friends saw him as an intelligent, articulate charmer. Many of the Arab students regarded him as an entitled, unapproachable upstart, who was more preoccupied with women's legs and gourmet meals than with Palestine.

This was probably overstating the case, but there was more than a grain of truth in it. Salman enjoyed cooking, which greatly improved his chances of scoring with German women since, in those days, most men wouldn't be caught dead near a pot or pan.

Still, most of his friends and girlfriends knew nothing of the torments that plagued him. They did sometimes wonder about his moods and his mistrust. Only his most intimate partners knew about his nightmares and how he would shout in his sleep. Although Salman had escaped physically, his spirit would long remain prisoner of the dictatorship that had expelled him.

~

He took pleasure in studying German philosophy in its original language, and his excellent recall made it easy for him. And for the first time in his life, it was a joy to study history. Unlike in Damascus, he no longer had to memorize dates, battles, and rulers by heart—now he could learn to understand historical backgrounds, without which the present remains a riddle. In his free time, he read widely about psychology and was particularly fascinated by C. G. Jung and Wilhelm Reich. He understood more clearly some of what he had experienced at home—his father's coldness toward him and the basic absence of feelings between his parents.

Freedom and the layers of the soul

Just as he had in Beirut, in Heidelberg he began to question things less fearfully. He read about the idea of freedom, but what he experienced every day was even more important for him than books—namely, being able to live in freedom, to be free from fear each day, to be able to speak openly without having to look over your shoulder, and be able to actually say what you meant. In Syria, he had never said what he thought, never believed anything he was told, and had always been careful to read between the lines.

Time and time again, he could see the crippling influence of the clan on his fellow Arab students. In Heidelberg, he knew Arab students who had been radicalized by the student movement, even going so far as to become anarchists, ardent Marxists or Leninists. But this was only until their parents or some uncle came to visit, when suddenly they became as meek as lambs, praying with their visitors, disowning their girlfriends, and betraying their political convictions.

He also became aware of his inability to form a relationship with just one woman. He couldn't fully understand this impulse, and thought less of himself for it. But inevitably, as soon as the first flame of love died down, he would start to notice his current girlfriend's shortcomings and become infatuated with someone else.

People envied him for being sociable, but this impression was deceptive. For all his adventures and erotic escapades, he was often lonely, especially when he most needed security, trust, or someone to comfort him. In those moments, Damascus drew him back. Wanting to return right then, he would steal a glance at his suitcase, which sat empty and dusty on top of his wardrobe.

Acknowledging this failing in himself did not seem to grant him the ability to overcome it. Salman had numerous affairs until he fell in love with Anna, and later it seemed that his love for her was really a form of self-love finding expression. At the time he needed a secure base, a haven to keep away the cold winds of loneliness.

And he was in a hurry—yet haste is never a wise counselor. Within three months they were married. As soon as the first bloom of passion gave way to the quiescence of everyday life, Salman had to resume fighting his budding attraction to other women. Although he didn't want to admit it, Anna's weaknesses stared him in the face. She was cold, didn't like guests, couldn't bear to see another woman around Salman, and disliked children. As if that wasn't enough, she wanted a dog, and Salman hated dogs. He couldn't even stand the smell of them.

Salman's mother, Sophia, wanted nothing more than a grandchild. Whenever they spoke, she would harp on it. "Grant me my second victory over death," she begged him once. "What do you mean, your second victory over death?" Salman asked, confused. He thought his mother was drunk. "Yes, my son, with you I have put one over on Death. I will continue to live through you, and when my genes are passed on to your child, it will be a second victory over the Grim Reaper. It would drive him mad."

Salman laughed. He loved children, but Anna wouldn't hear of it. She was independent, strong-willed, and tough. Salman was often drawn to tender, feminine women in need of protection. Three years into his marriage, he had an erotic affair. After that, he often let himself be seduced by attractive women, and Anna began to shut herself off from him.

Her relationship to Salman cooled even further after she had an abortion behind his back following an unwanted pregnancy. She accused him of tricking her, and the accusation was not totally unfounded. For Salman, the child had been one last desperate attempt to save his marriage. Little by little, they moved apart—geographically, physically, and spiritually. So when Anna told him one evening that she wanted to divorce him and that she would go and live in Amsterdam, he guessed that she had another man in her life. He asked her about it and she nodded. She told him that she had known about many, if not all, of his affairs. She had put up with them, but now she wanted to lead an honest life.

It seemed funny to him, in that moment, that he didn't care about the divorce, but later he realized he had already divorced her in his heart the day she aborted his child. He'd only stayed because he had been too much of a coward to take the first step himself.

That was the end of their story. Anna vanished from Heidelberg, and from his heart.

~

After graduation, he took odd jobs in Heidelberg to survive. His degree in philosophy was of as little help as his knowledge of history and psychology. He didn't want to stay in academia and do research that would only interest specialists. He dreamt of writing books that many people would read. For a while he worked as a publishing director, and later spent a year as another publishing company's representative. At the same time, he translated Arabic poetry and plays that had been rejected by publishers and theater producers. He wrote a love story whose heroes, an Arab and a Jew, finally decide to put an end to their lives. He imagined his novel acting as a warning against hatred and war. But the book was a total flop. A year later, when he inquired about the sales figures, the publisher retorted viciously that twenty-four copies had been sold and he could have the rest as a gift. Salman hung up and decided never to write again.

He sent out application after application, but it was difficult to find an opening. Heidelberg was a place for students and tourists, not for unemployed academics. Even his German passport was of little use.

How a Syrian with a German passport becomes a Roman

He finally received an offer for a one-year position as an editor with an Arabic-French publishing company in Paris. Shortly before going to the interview, he met Stella. On the main street in Heidelberg, she had asked him where the students' detention cell was. She spoke German, but with a strong Italian accent, and had said *shell* instead of *cell*. It was a tourist attraction, this detention cell where students of old had covered the walls with aphorisms and self-portraits during their incarcerations.

Salman gave her directions and even accompanied her partway, before inviting her to a restaurant in the Old Town. He liked this young woman, and her sense of humor piqued his interest. She was blond and blue-eyed, unusually fair skinned for an Italian. Her face was gentle, almost angelic.

Stella was from Trieste. Her maternal grandparents were Austrian, but her mother didn't like the German language. She spoke only in the Trieste dialect or, when she wanted to sound high class, Italian. Her father, Franco Leone, came from Rome, where he was the branch director of a large bank with its headquarters in the city. He had advised Stella to learn German because the Germans were Italy's major business partners. After all, Trieste had been a part of Austria until the end of the First World War.

Stella planned to start studying pharmacology in Rome in October. She was very serious about the subject. "Simply to know how a drug enters the body and takes effect, say in the ear or in the kidneys, is more exciting than any detective novel. Science fiction is child's play compared to all the adventures that go on inside the body," she said, and Salman was struck by her passionate curiosity.

Stella wanted to study in Rome. She would live in a small apartment that belonged to her father.

But for the moment she was "doing Europe." Her parents had given her the money as a graduation present. She had only planned to stay in Heidelberg for two days, but she liked Salman so much that she stayed at his place for a week.

Later she told him that she had already fallen in love with him on the first day they met, while they were walking through the streets of the Old Town and he had laughed so heartily at her jokes and banter that he was nearly out of breath. She had looked at him then and known that this was the man she wanted to live with.

His feelings fell into place two days later.

It was very early in the morning. Daylight peeked in shyly and furtively through a crack in the doorway before pouring all at once over Stella's naked body. Salman was just about to leave the room to buy fresh rolls and croissants for their breakfast, but he stopped and stood near the door for a moment. He was deeply moved by Stella's beauty, and at the same time he was afraid of losing her. It was then that he realized he had fallen in love.

One week after Stella's departure, Salman traveled to Paris to interview for the editorial position. The publisher was supposedly very interested in him.

The interview was scheduled for late in the afternoon. Salman had arrived several hours early, so he found a bed and breakfast near the Gare de l'Est train station. He paid the friendly landlady for a three-night stay, freshened up, left his suitcase in the room, and walked to the metro station.

At the top of the steps to the underground station, he was attacked. The young Algerian man who had smiled at him only moments before now demanded his wallet. Salman had learned how to fight viciously during his years in the opposition—he hit the man hard in the face and kicked him in the shins, knocking him to the ground. The young man started begging for mercy in Arabic, saying that his mother was sick in Algiers and in desperate need of money.

"You son of a bitch!" Salman shouted at him Arabic, and continued down the stairs to the metro. Not a single passerby lifted a finger, as if it had all been a show performed by two foreign street artists.

The interview went very badly. Salman stuttered, contradicted himself, got lost in irrelevant details, and muddled a simple translation of a paragraph from German into French. When the publishing director asked him if his German was really as good as he had indicated on his application, his response was belligerent. He would get the results of the interview two days later, and in the meantime he decided to see Paris.

As he'd expected, he didn't get the job. Salman returned to Heidelberg, cursing the Algerian who had ruined both his day and his interview. He also cursed the publisher, who had refused to give him a second chance. Last, but not least, he cursed himself for being so unlucky. He felt ridiculous, but cursing made him feel better.

Stella called him every day from Amsterdam, Kiel, Copenhagen, Stockholm, and Helsinki. Soon Salman began to sit near the telephone from seven o'clock in the evening on, waiting for her call. He longed for this woman and wanted only to be with her.

As soon as she was back in Rome, he reversed the game and called her daily. He had to take on more odd jobs in order to cover the expensive phone charges. He would translate advertisements, regulations, and instruction leaflets for medicines into Arabic and joke about it with Stella. "I'm paying for this conversation with a pamphlet for disinfectant, and if we want to keep talking, I'll translate another one for antibiotics and one for painkillers." At some point Stella managed to convince him that they could take turns calling, and he was impressed by her generosity.

Four weeks after her return, she invited him to her apartment. Autumn was beautiful in Rome, and she wanted to show him her city. "On one condition," she said firmly. "You're on my turf here and will pay nothing. You're my guest. Do you remember when we were on your turf in Heidelberg?" He laughed and recalled that, in fact, he had not let her pay for anything in Heidelberg.

On a lovely fall morning, he boarded the train for Rome. He didn't dare think yet about a lasting relationship, but focused on the promised delights of wandering through an unknown city, like in the movie *La Dolce Vita*. The trip took more than twelve hours and he had a lot of time to think. Doubts began to overwhelmed him. He was fifteen years older than Stella, and she was dead set on becoming a pharmacologist. This ambitious woman would definitely not start playing wife and mother for his sake.

Why was he drawn to such independent women? Never for a moment had he thought about marrying one of the many feminine, soft, home-loving girls he had taken to bed and who dreamt of having children. And now, after a few romantic days in Heidelberg and a few telephone conversations, he was already thinking of a steady relationship with Stella!

By the time he arrived in Bologna, he was almost in despair, and during the twenty-minute stopover, he thought three times about turning around and going home. But then his desire for Stella won out, and he told himself he just wanted to enjoy a few days with her, away from any thoughts about the future. Years later, he would think back to this time that brought about such a momentous change in his life.

Stella's apartment was located on the Via Giovanni Battista Morgagni, a ten-minute walk from the university. It was a nondescript building, but the apartments were very well furnished.

Stella loved the city, and she showed Salman its most delightful hidden corners. He was fascinated by Rome, and after only three days he thought it came closer to Damascus than any other city he had visited. He and Stella walked hand in hand, happy and in love, and Salman laughed at the fountain for dogs. It was the only one of its kind in the world. Pope Gregory XIII had taken pity on the dogs of the city that went thirsty on hot summer days, and had it built next to the church wall. Water trickled from the maw of a marble lion that bore witness to the ravages of time, yet still offered refreshment for the city's suffering dogs. A little farther on, Stella showed him a sign in the window of a wine shop and translated for him: "Those who drink only water have something to hide."

Stella seemed to have planned Salman's visit down to the last detail. Not only did she show him historical buildings and monuments like the Coliseum, the Castel Sant'Angelo, the Sistine Chapel, and other tourist sites, but she also introduced him to the city's lesser-known attractions, almost as if she wanted to make Rome seem particularly appealing to him. One such local institution was the Dolce Maniera bakery in the Via Barletta, which stayed open twenty-four hours, and another was the Castellino bar, a well-known refuge for night owls and insomniacs.

Salman had only intended to stay a week in Rome, but Stella didn't want to let him go. The fire of love moved her to show the courage of a lioness and risk everything in telling him her feelings. It somehow tickled Salman's vanity that Stella, the only daughter of a wealthy, respected family, should say to him, "I'm meant for you and you for me. That's why you failed with other women, and I with the few suitors that I've had. We've both lived through all that to gather experience and come together now."

She was sure that she only had to want something hard enough to achieve it, and that would remain her lifelong belief. As complicated as the formulas were for the medicines she worked with, her rules for success in life were simple. Not only as a student, but later as a highly regarded professor, Stella was absolutely trusting. She loved to laugh and had many friends who made her life beautiful and colorful. Guilelessness, she would say, was her key to good health.

Bowled over by her declaration of love, Salman first of all reminded her of their age difference of fifteen years. They were lying in bed, and Stella laughed and gave him a slap on his bare behind. "My mother is eighteen years younger than my father, and I have never seen two more passionate lovers. Your wild lovemaking with me makes you more manly and potent than a nineteen-year-old. And when you grow old and things start drooping down there, I'll find something in my laboratory to arouse them—to make a dragon out of the smallest worm, so to speak. So there, no need for you to start moaning!"

"And how about you? What will you do if you get pregnant?" Salman asked, now without a trace of vanity. The young woman's seriousness in its humorous guise was beginning to command his respect.

"I'll get pregnant when *I* choose. We, sir, are living in the twentieth century—haven't you heard about condoms, or birth control pills?"

"And what about your parents?" asked Salman doubtingly.

"You leave them to me, please. And now we should get some sleep," she said, and then kissed him and turned over. In a few minutes she was fast asleep. Salman stayed awake. He was ashamed of the cowardice that left him in the role of the cynical sceptic. Stella, on the other hand, was absolutely convinced that they were made for each other—and had the courage to come out and say it. Aunt Amalia had once claimed that women in love had the gift of prophecy.

"But their predictions are sometimes mistaken," he had replied in a know-it-all tone.

"That's all part of the risk of prophecy. Even Moses, Jesus, and Muhammad made mistakes—especially in choosing their disciples," she'd said, laughing so loud that the glass prisms in the chandelier above them tinkled.

~

With Stella sleeping peacefully beside him, Salman slowly allowed himself to become excited and even hopeful for the future. Deciding on Stella would require him to give up everything in Germany and start again from scratch in

Italy. But just maybe he could have the peaceful, fulfilling life and the family he had dreamed of, with this woman at his side.

He was sure he could be fluent in Italian within a year, but it wouldn't be enough for a position in philosophy or literature. How would he earn a living? As morning dawned, he remembered an acquaintance in Heidelberg who ran a stand with Syrian specialities, and who had asked him for linguistic help because he wanted to start an import-export firm. Salman had not taken him seriously at the time and had only helped him out of pity. But within a few years the man had opened branches in Frankfurt, Stuttgart, and Munich—and he was rich.

Why couldn't he try his hand at that himself? Salvation and death are both audacity's children. Yes, it was decided—he would import groceries from Arab countries and export Italian goods to the same countries.

He got up and dressed without having had a wink of sleep, bought two croissants from a nearby shop, and prepared the cappuccino for Stella's breakfast.

Stella awoke and noticed his excitement, but let him take his time in sharing it. Finally he said:

"Stella, I love you. So I want to change my life to be with you and start a family together someday. I've thought it over, and I'll give up everything in Germany and move here. But before that, I'll have to learn how the import-export business works. I'd like to start a company here, and…"

She jumped up from her chair and threw her arms around him. "I knew you were brave," she said with tears in her eyes. "And I give you my word I'll stand by you whatever happens." Her lips tasted of butter, sugar, and coffee when he kissed her.

7

Loving Means Rebelling against Death

Homs, 1927–1943

Karim's childhood was an innocent and happy one, spent in a house filled with hospitality for friends and guests alike. He would retrieve an old photo album from his bookshelf whenever he shared these memories with Aida. She was surprised that, in the thirties and forties, the family wore such modern European clothing. In one hand-colored photograph his father was pictured, dressed in a white summer suit, raising a glass of wine for the camera. His mother and sisters wore pretty, vibrant dresses and hats, and his brothers wore suits with ties.

However, Karim's experience at the Christian school was unsettling. For the first time in his life, he learned how it felt to be in a minority. He and two other boys from the richest Muslim families were the only non-Christian children in his class. Only Christian religious education was offered, and Karim was free to either attend the lesson or spend it in the library. He opted for the lesson, and he also went to church with the other pupils on Sundays. He was fascinated by the prayers, and the incense, and the activity of the priests in their colorful vestments at the altar—unlike his best friend Philip Derani, a pale boy with beautiful hands and a delicate, feminine face, who always seemed bored by the rituals.

But joining in was not to the same as being accepted. The Muslim children were teased by a gang of other students the moment the monitors looked the other way. Karim smiled

78

when he remembered all the stupid things the Christian children said about Muslims and Islam. Sometimes the taunts had really annoyed him, and he learned to hate the student gang. The eight strongest kids in the class terrorized the others, hitting them and grabbing their sandwiches at lunch time, and nobody dared to speak up or say anything.

One day they got him, too. Philip had to stay behind and repeat an arithmetic exercise during the lunch break. Five of the gang dragged Karim off to the toilet, and three others kept watch to warn the sadists if a teacher was coming. Karim was alone, and he struggled in vain. The little tyrants had worked it all out to a T.

Years later, Karim was able to look back and laugh at the boys' prejudice and stupidity. They had really believed that Muslims had their glans cut off at circumcision. Two of the boys were even convinced that the testicles were cut off, as well. It was not enough for Karim to insist that he had a penis and two testicles, just like them, and that only the foreskin had been cut away. Begging was no help either. Suddenly yesterday's friends became deaf and their eyes lost any gleam of humanity. They unbuttoned his trousers and pulled them down around his knees, along with his underpants. Disappointed, they left him standing there and scattered in silence. Filled with shame, Karim burst into tears.

When the teacher saw his injured knee and asked him what had happened, Karim lied, saying that he had fallen and scraped it. His injuries were painful, but the humiliation hurt even worse. From that day on, he never spoke to any of those boys again.

"Why did you lie?" Philip asked him.

"Because if the teacher punishes them here in school, they'll come after me on the way home."

"But we can't let them get away with this. Write down the names of these idiots for me," said Philip. He was a head shorter than Karim, but brave and a cool strategist. The two boys lived only a few streets away from each other.

"What are you going to do?"

"Just wait and see," Philip said, and a devilish smile flashed across his face. The next day, when the students came back in from break, none of the eight boys could find their exercise books for Arabic grammar. Mr. Safi was their Arabic teacher, and he had a very short temper. The pupils learned the difficult rules of grammar more from fear of his anger than anything. If somebody had not done his homework, Mr. Safi showed no mercy.

All eight of the bullies were punished. Philip just grinned when Karim asked him if he'd had had anything to do with it. A few weeks later, the newly bought exercise books disappeared again, and in their places were photographs of half-naked actresses. During break, there was a great tumult and tussle around these pictures until Mr. Safi came into the room. As quick as lightning, he threw his briefcase onto the teacher's desk and lunged toward the pupils in the back rows, his face clouded with accusation. The students froze, unable to hide the photos in time. The teacher confiscated all the pictures, snorted like a wounded steer, and shouted, "Hopefully this time you've all got your exercise books with you, as well as these porno pictures?"

He thrashed them all mercilessly with his bamboo cane. It was a totally one-sided fight. The cane whistled through the air and the boys howled like spanked puppies, but the teacher was deaf and blind with rage. One pupil ran to find the principal, who saved them from the worst of the teacher's wrath by dismissing class early.

The three eldest students were expelled from the school. The others were allowed to stay, but with a hefty punishment. They were regarded as spineless snitches, and from then on scared nobody else.

So that was Philip. He later became a famous pianist, emigrated to France with his wife, and died there, scarcely forty years old, of a heart attack after a concert in Lille.

As school friends, Karim and Philip often visited each other. One day, Karim met a new schoolmate and friend of Philip's sister Nora. Her name was Sophia. She was very pretty and almost too bold for a girl of her wealthy family background. But she also had a cold, calculating intelligence and a strong will, which only became clear to Karim later. Sophia fascinated him, and he was hypnotized in her presence. She seemed not to understand his hints and ignored his passes, somehow without creating the impression that she was uninterested in him—a tantalizing mixture.

It took almost a year for Sophia to respond to his advances, but she did so all the more passionately then. When she let him kiss her for the first time, she explained the reason for her earlier caution. "Any donkey with enough hormones can fall in love, but only a person with noble feelings can love." During a walk along the Orontes River, he broke it to her gently that he was only Muslim on paper and was really more of an agnostic. In class they had just studied the philosopher Ibn Arabi, who was buried in Damascus. His teacher admired the poet and philosopher, whose most important saying was: "Love is my faith, my belief." Karim even recited one of his poems for her.

Sophia told him she knew nothing about Ibn al-Arabi, and she couldn't care less about religion. What mattered to her was riches. She knew exactly what kind of man she wanted to marry, and she insisted—even during heavy petting sessions—that her virginity remain intact. "That's my marriage capital," she said. She scoffed at her sister Takla, who was just as attractive and bright as she was but didn't capitalize on it at all. "She's the commoner of the family, but I love her," she said.

Sophia, on the other hand, intended to find herself a wealthy Christian man, and made a razor-sharp distinction between love and marriage. Karim had hoped to win her over in both matters, but failed miserably. One sunny day in May, as she was getting dressed, she told him almost off-handedly that this would be the last time. That Sunday she was to be engaged to a goldsmith from the rich Baladi family. Karim shed bitter tears. Sophia comforted him, telling him she would always love him, but now she had to give her full attention to her fiancé and be a good wife. If they kept seeing each other, she would be torn between Karim and her future husband, and that would make her sick and crazy.

Instead it was Karim who fell ill—and seriously so. He spiked a high fever that left him too weak to leave his bed. His mother summed up his condition to a girlfriend of hers. "He's getting thinner and thinner, almost as if he's eating himself up." Soon he weighed a frail ninety-nine pounds. His friends visited loyally—Philip came every day and read adventure stories out loud. Only Sophia stayed away. One day he asked Philip's sister, Nora, to say hello to Sophia for him. He hoped that she would tell Sophia about his terrible state and that Sophia might feel sorry for him and come back. Sophia's reply was a healthy shock. She let him know that she had no use for wimps. If he had ever loved her, he should pull himself together, because love meant rebelling against death. He should fight and meet life bravely, or else she would be ashamed to have spent even an hour with him.

First he flew into a rage, but then he got up, studied, and worked. As his anger subsided, he realized that he loved her more than ever, but that it was a different kind of love, free from claims, plans for the future, or jealousy. Looking back, he was thankful for her reply, which had yanked him out of his destructive self-pity. Later, when he started teaching elementary school, he got a letter from her. She congratulated him and wrote that she was proud of him and would be happy to see him again. He was worthy of her love, her respect, and her support, and should he ever need help, she would be there for him.

He shook his head, convinced these were just empty words that Sophia had copied out of some cheap romance novel. But a time would come when just such an opportunity arose, a situation that would be the most disastrous of his life.

8

First Temptation

Rome, 1980–1995

The wibbly-wobbly man

Stella's parents were more accommodating than Salman could have imagined. Her mother thought him charming from the beginning, and he completely won her heart when he cooked for her. Salman was a sophisticated cook, unlike her husband, who could barely fry two eggs without the kitchen needing to be redecorated afterward.

Stella's father, an old banker, admired Salman's courage in leaving prosperous Germany to try his luck in Rome. The fact that Salman had a nose for business and a level-headed relationship with money impressed him. He was secretly proud of his clever daughter, who had managed to turn the head of such an interesting and worldly man.

Salman worked hard, and soon after the wedding founded his import-export firm, Oasi. Initially, he opened a shop in the Via Natal del Grande selling oriental spices and groceries, but competition was fierce and Arab cuisine in Italy was not well known then. The rent was also prohibitively high. Salman gave up the shop after two years, but Oasi earned money brokering the export of Italian products to Arab countries. This enabled him and Stella to live in modest comfort. He consistently refused help from his generous in-laws.

Life in Rome suited him. Here, he could finally give free rein to his native Damascene manners. Unlike in

84

Germany, people were seldom direct, but conversed in roundabout ways. They never said outright that they were not feeling well, for example. First everybody was fine; then, and only then, would there be intimations as to how one actually felt. People never criticized openly, but would politely hint at whatever did not appeal to them. Rome differed from Damascus in some respects, however. Romans seldom visited each other at home, often meeting at bars or restaurants instead. "The Romans have more style," Salman said one day on the phone to his mother. "They prefer to see each other beautifully dressed. At home, people used to turn up unwashed, unshaven, and in pajamas." His mother laughed. "*Used to* is right. These days nobody visits in their pajamas. They dress like they're off to a fashion show."

Salman was able to export more and more Italian products through his contacts in the Gulf states. These states had once been looked down on as "the Emirates," but they had developed into a considerable economic power. He successfully expanded and built three branches in Qatar, Dubai, and Kuwait—but then, at the end of 1984, came a setback like a bolt out of the blue. His partner, a prince of the ruling clan, swindled and ruined all three branches. Salman lost all the capital he had invested there, but managed to remain debt-free. When Stella was appointed to a post at the Faculty for Pharmacology, they at least had some measure of financial security.

Then, as if heaven-sent, a large legacy from Aunt Amalia saved them.

Salman only learned of her death belatedly. His mother was in the hospital for a hip operation, so his father, his Uncle Anton, and all the other relatives traveled to Beirut for the funeral. Not that they wished to make their peace with her memory, nor did they go to honor her in death as she had fought them in life—they went to see if they had been left anything in her will. Three days later they returned to Damascus empty-handed, each nursing their own grudges.

A week after Amalia's funeral, her lawyer called Salman in Rome. The lawyer informed him in as few words as possible that his aunt had split her estate between him and a Lebanese association for the defense of women's rights. Salman flew to Beirut, went to Amalia's grave, and laid a red rose on the modest marble slab. He was deeply grateful that Amalia had rescued him yet again. The legacy would prevent his firm in Rome from going bankrupt, and would put him back on his feet again. A few years later he opened a large grocery store, this time in the Via Giovanni Giolliti, opposite the train station.

In 1995, his son Paolo was born. That same year, his import-export company Oasi opened two more branches, in Milan and Ancona, whose sales soon surpassed that of the flagship branch in Rome. He opened another market, Nuovo Mercato Esquilina, six years later. Salman leased two stalls and saw steady earnings from them. He set up an office around the corner, from which he ran Oasi as it continued to flourish.

"Our son-in-law is a real *misirizzi*—a wibby-wobbly man who always bounces back from adversity no matter how many punches he takes," Stella's father said to his wife at the opening for the market. "If we had a thousand guys like him in Italy, there wouldn't be a crisis."

Stella had become a professor of toxicology at the *Dipartimento di Fisiologia e Farmacologia*, named after the brilliant pharmacologist Vittorio Erspamer. To teach at the same university where she had studied filled her with pride. By now she had published dozens of articles and established an international reputation in her field.

In the summer of 2002, Salman bought a large apartment in Trastevere. This popular district of old Rome had once been a home to the poor, to foreigners, to the marginalized. Many Jews had lived there, establishing more than ten synagogues. Even Rome's first Christians had settled there. Centuries later, Trastevere became Rome's thriving international district, also known as "the village in the city." During the Roman revolt against the papacy in 1848, it had been the rebels' stronghold. Salman liked to stroll over the bridges, stop, and look out across the Tiber, thinking of the Barada River in his native Damascus. He soon discovered little Belli Square at the beginning of the district's large main street, which was also called Trastevere. There in the small square was a monument to the poet Giuseppe Gioacchino Belli. *Dedicated by the people to their poet* was inscribed on the marble slab. Belli had been a great dialect poet who had described life in Rome at the start of the nineteenth century in several thousand, mostly satirical, sonnets. But he also worked as a censor for the Vatican and fought against the publication of Shakespeare, Verdi, and Rossini. Not far from the monument was a marble plaque commemorating the birthplace of Guillaume Apollinaire, the French poet. Salman laughed bitterly, thinking that there should be monuments on every street corner in Damascus to poets who had been arrested. The city's walls would be covered with enormous plaques listing the names of all the poets, intellectuals, journalists, painters, and musicians who had been locked up in its prisons.

Salman and Stella's apartment was on the wide Viale di Trastevere, not far from the Ippolito Nievo stop. It was a handsome corner building with four large wings, a yellowish-orange façade, and a view overlooking Ugo

Bassi Street. Their apartment was on the sixth floor, with a large balcony offering a wide view of the gardens, the picturesque houses, and the Tiber. A rickety elevator from the 1940s took them up and down each day. There was a bus stop just across the street that had a quick route to the metro station. After that it was just a ten-minute walk to Salman's office, even less by streetcar.

Car traffic had become one of Rome's biggest problems, a veritable inferno, so Salman preferred to take public transportation whenever possible.

When they'd first moved in, he'd tried to paint their new neighborhood in glowing colors to Stella—but what interested her first and foremost were the primary and secondary schools and the routes to and from them. Paolo was due to start school that autumn. She finally settled on the Scuola Francesco Cesana, which was on the Via Napoleone Parboni, not even two hundred meters from their apartment. Paolo ended up being very happy there—he never wanted his parents to come with him, and insisted on walking himself to school each morning.

The Liceo John F. Kennedy High School was also within walking distance for Paolo when the time came. He had to walk along Ugo Bassi Street, at the end of which was a set of handsome stone stairs leading up the hill. Paolo never complained about the steep walk, but Salman was soon out of breath when he accompanied his son one day. He counted eighty-four steps on the first set, and then there was a steep path through a mini-wilderness, followed by another long set of stairs.

"And you walk this every day?" Salman asked, almost shocked. Paolo laughed. "Sure," he replied, seeming a bit surprised.

Metamorphoses of a marriage

When Paolo was born, much changed. Until then Stella and Salman had lived like two singles in love. Although they had been married for more than ten years, they would sometimes feel such a burning desire for each other that they would find any excuse to meet, whether to eat, sleep together, or just share a glass of wine. They would laugh like two conspirators, like schoolchildren playing hooky from a boring lesson.

But when their beautiful boy was born, Stella changed completely in Salman's eyes. She started behaving very coolly toward him and seemed only to have room in her heart for her little son. Sometimes she didn't even notice when Salman came home. He would quietly watch her kissing and cuddling with Paolo, and feel jealousy rise up in his heart, and silently go out again. Salman often felt very lonely. But when he tried to talk to Stella about it she didn't seem to take him seriously, and would admonish him with distracted affection. "Be reasonable. He just needs me, that's all."

"And what about me?" Salman would ask. He found it ridiculous to compete with a baby for his wife's attention—and lose all the time. "Don't be silly," she would say. Often he would have to decamp to the living room sofa because Paolo had woken up happy as a sandboy and wanted to play with his mother, while Salman needed to sleep.

Immediately after the birth, Stella seemed to lose any desire for Salman. His urges and appetites were met with yawns, and when that did not suffice, she would put Paolo in a portable cushioned bassinet between herself and Salman, like a sort of chastity barrier.

Salman wondered if it was possible to love a child without it being at the expense of your partner. He grew restless. Jealous was not the word for it, because he loved Paolo and knew that it was not the child's fault. But he noticed the distance between himself and Stella increasing.

Suddenly and unexpectedly, Salman yearned for Damascus. Rome had become a wasteland for him, and he missed his home.

~

And then he met Tina. It was a cold Sunday in February., and Salman was in a bad way. Just like every other Sunday, he and Stella had gone to bed after lunch for a nap. Stella was lying next to him in see-through silk pajamas, while Paolo slept in his little cot a meter away. Salman woke up suddenly after an intense erotic dream. He was choking with desire for Stella, whom he had not been allowed to touch for over two months. With his hand—just like he had always done—he first stroked the pajama top and then the naked skin of her bewitching belly. But instead of this putting a smile on her beautiful mouth, she sat up with a start, wide-eyed, looking at him as if he had done something evil, and pushed his hand away forcefully.

"You can't do that," she spat at him, "I don't feel well…" she hesitated slightly and glanced at their sleeping son. "And Paolo," she added as if this tiny baby was an obstacle.

"And Paolo?" repeated Salman in bewilderment. She didn't reply, but only got up quickly, went into the bathroom, and came back fully dressed. He cursed himself and felt ashamed, put his clothes on and left the apartment.

He needed to talk to someone. What was the matter with him? He found his own reactions so primitive. How did other new fathers manage?

"The Germans are best at this sort of thing," he thought to himself on the Garibaldi Bridge. Yes, the Germans are world champs when it comes to analyzing *twosomes*, as they call love relationships. The Arabs and the Italians are not as well-versed in this art. Germans talk about their infidelities, sometimes even with their partners. Arabs and Italians are different. They cheat on their partners, but they don't talk about it. "*Si fa ma non si dice*—you do it but you don't talk about it," says the Italian, as if he were putting the Arab's most secret thoughts into words. "That's dishonest," says the German. "It makes life easier," say the Arab and the Italian. While Germans may not be thought of as romantics, they are born analysts. Salman headed toward the Via dei Condotti, and Caffè Greco. This favorite café of Salman's attracted not only tourists but also German journalists and staff from German companies and media firms. As old as the hills, the café had been opened in 1760 by a Greek, Nicola della Maddalena. Salman liked the many ancient portraits, paintings, and figurines decorating the rooms. He'd heard that Goethe had stayed there, as had Schopenhauer, Ludwig I of Bavaria, and Franz Liszt. There was also said to be a poet who suggested replacing the word "Greco" with "Tedesco"—German.

Salman knew the young waiter, Giuliano, who had worked there for more than five years. Since Salman was always charming and generous to him, Giuliano always found him an especially good table.

A woman came in soon after he was seated. He felt a warm breeze accompanied by a light, pleasant scent. Then she came into view and he saw she had thick blond hair that fell in generous waves to her shoulders. She sat down at a nearby table and shrugged off her wine-red jacket. She was wearing a black blouse, a red vest, and black trousers. She took an Italian women's magazine out of her large leather bag and started to read. Her lips were also dark red and her legs were slim and well-proportioned, ending in a captivating pair of red shoes.

Salman took in every movement that she made. Soon she put the Italian magazine back in her bag and took out a German fashion magazine. "She's German," whispered Giuliano, who had read Salman's glances. "She works nearby at the fashion firm Lancetti. I think she was at Giorgio Armani's before that."

"Your secret service is very well informed," Salman replied softly and laughed. The lady briefly raised her head, looked at him, and smiled.

"But she's gay," Giuliano whispered, and hurried away to help an elderly couple, hard of hearing, who were having difficulty finding the table they'd reserved.

Was that possible? The woman put down her magazine and moved toward the restroom, chased by Salman's gaze. He wanted her in his arms. When she came back, she seemed surrounded by an invisible wall. She read, ate, and drank as if she were completely alone. After a while she waved Giuliano over. "*Il conto*," she said quietly. The waiter nodded and disappeared. Soon he was back with the bill. The woman paid, drank her last sip of red wine, slipped into her jacket, and left the café.

Salman finished the dregs of his Campari, paid his own bill, and went off in the direction of number sixty-one, the address of the fashion house Lancetti. He slowed his pace, his heart pounding frantically. There she was, on the telephone, standing at the shop counter. In her hand was a sheet of paper like an order or a purchase instruction. From his vantage point in the street, Salman had an even better view of her than he'd had in the café. She was exquisite. When the woman looked in his direction, he glanced away and acted as if he was just strolling by.

He was not in love with this woman—how could he be?—but his body and mind were possessed by her. And he would be happy, he was sure, if he could hold her just once, just for a moment. What should he do? For the moment, at least, he could do nothing. He went back home in high spirits and noticed that he was more considerate toward Stella, that his resentment toward her had mysteriously subsided.

The next day he learned from Giuliano that the lady's name was Christina—her friends called her Tina. Since Giuliano also knew Stella, Salman played down his attraction and asked about the names of other customers as a cover. Giuliano saw through his game and played along. But Tina didn't show up at the café that afternoon, although she had been lunching there on a *tramezzino* sandwich and a glass of red wine every day for over a year. She was not to be found behind the counter at Lancetti, either. Salman checked four times before going to his office, and he could hardly concentrate on his work that day.

A week went by that felt like an eternity, and then she showed up again. He nodded to her as she entered the café. "You've been away a long time," he said in German.

She seemed surprised. "You speak German!" she said, as if she didn't catch his hint.

"I studied in Heidelberg."

"Ah, Heidelberg! Such a romantic city. I spent a week there once for a fashion show," she said. She tried to speak High German, but couldn't hide her Saxon dialect, which sang happily between her words.

"Have you just been to a fashion show?" he asked.

"No, unfortunately not. We had some problems with our suppliers in Milan."

"I understand. That's our stock-in-trade in the import-export business."

She took her magazine out of her handbag, slowly and discreetly, but Salman took it as a clear sign. He pretended to be engrossed in the newspaper he'd bought that morning at the kiosk near his apartment.

When Tina said goodbye and walked past him, he felt strangely aroused. Her fragrance stayed with him after she left the café.

He gave himself a month to move closer to her. Hearing her voice had strengthened his desire. But the shock came on the day when he cautiously invited her to dinner. She gave him a long look. "May I be frank with you?" she asked. Salman nodded silently, suspecting the worst. "It's not possible. My partner is the most peaceful woman in the world, but she's jealous. She will never understand. It's bad enough that I neglect her because of my work."

If Salman had been made of glass, he would have broken into a thousand pieces, but he was supple flesh and so he remained stuck to his chair. He didn't know where to look, and he was lost for words. He felt himself turn pale.

"I wanted to be honest with you," she said. "You seem charming and interesting. If my frankness hurt you, I apologize."

"No problem," Salman replied, trying to act nonchalant. When she left, he cursed, the way Arabs do, the mother who had brought this creature into the world. He was relieved that Giuliano was not there to hear him.

A month later, he saw Tina in the company of a dark-skinned woman. It was at the nursery Fleur Garden, which was on the same street as his apartment. He wanted to buy some flowers as a birthday gift for his colleague, Chiara, on his way to the office. Tina wore jeans and sports shoes, as if she had the day off. She greeted him from a proper distance in the spacious shop, but the woman who was with her still surveyed him suspiciously. Tina stroked her hand reassuringly. Outside, while he was waiting for the bus, he saw the two of them walking to the streetcar stop. And he noticed that, as attractive as she was, Tina no longer aroused or interested him.

He stayed at the office until late that afternoon. When he got home, he did not go directly to the elevator. He greeted Tomaso, the caretaker, in his lodge. With his round, ruddy, forever smiling face, Tomaso seemed almost simple-minded, but he had a knack for all things technical and was a gifted observer—and he knew how to keep a secret. Tomaso knew exactly who was in mourning in his building, who was lonely, who had just broken up from a relationship, who had met their lovers in secret, which children had their birthday. He always had a friendly greeting or bon mot ready, as precise and polished as chiseled marble. He was one of those rare, gracious beings who are in danger of extinction. A few years ago the real estate company in charge of the apartment complex had wanted to let him go to cut costs. Salman had reacted quickly, mobilizing the ten owners and all the tenants in the building, convincing them that Tomaso's dismissal would make a severe dent in the quality of their lives. And he succeeded; the company withdrew its proposal. From that day on, Salman had a faithful friend who rejoiced at his little gifts—above all, Tomaso loved white wine and tinned tuna fish.

Salman went into the tiny inner courtyard of the complex. There a loquat tree grew out in the open, together with a large oleander bush and a small but sturdy palm tree, just like thousands in the East. Salman paused in front of the palm tree. Even as a child he knew that these are sociable and sensitive plants… according to an Arab fable, God made them out of the clay left over from Adam's creation.

"O sister, we are both prisoners. When will our wings grow?" he heard himself whisper in Arabic to the palm tree.

9

The Fire of Love and the Water of Reason

Damascus, 1950–1970

Whenever Aida was sad, she would think of her childhood and let the water of her memories quench her thirst. She was the second child of a well-to-do Christian family. Her parents loved each other passionately. She was seven or eight years old when she slowly realized that—unlike her and her brother Sami—her parents did not immediately go to sleep when they said, "We're off to bed." Her bedroom was in between Sami's and their parents'. Sami was fifteen and as strong as an ox. He was already a student but still lived at home as was common at the time.

Aida was never afraid at night. She knew that her parents would protect her, and so would big, strong Sami. If she was afraid, all she had to do was to knock on his door and he would show them all, even if they only wanted to touch a hair of Princess Aida's head. "Even if it's a lion, I'll tear it in two. And if it tries to get rough, I'll rip it in four. All you have to do is knock three times, or shout 'help!' and I'll be there for you," he'd say to her time after time. Once she wanted to try it out, so she called out quietly, "Help!" Sami immediately tore open the door and jumped into the middle of her room. He brandished a sword, an heirloom from their great-great-grandfather, who was supposed to have been a great hero way back when. Sami looked very funny in his underpants, carrying the sword. Aida laughed until she cried. "Where's the lion? Where are you, you cowardly lion?" he shouted, and then he kissed her on the forehead and went back to his room to sleep.

No lion ever turned up, but Aida knew she could rely on Sami, so she was never scared of the dark.

Their parents tried hard to be quiet in their love play, but passion was stronger than restraint. Their laughing, gasping, sighing, giggling, slurping, and whispering could be heard through the wall and would wake up Aida time and time again. She would lie awake, enjoying herself, until she was rocked back to sleep by the laughter from the next room. She tried to imagine what it was that her mother and her father might be doing just then, but she couldn't. Once she thought that the two of them were putting on circus acts with her mother balancing on her father's head while he turned her round in a circle, and she would call out eagerly, "Yes, more... more!"

Another time, she imagined her father disguised as a mouse. He would hide under the bed and her mother would play the cat. "Slowly, you'll eat me up! Not so fast!" the mouse would call out in a shaky voice, and the cat would laugh and say, "Come, little one! Let yourself finish!" Aida would have to laugh. Later her burgeoning imagination would cause her even greater amusement when she learned from her school friend Amal how simple it actually was, what man and wife did when lovemaking.

Her parents did love each other—the whole world could see. They kissed in front of relatives and neighbors and didn't care who knew it. That sort of thing was frowned upon in Damascus at the time. The fact that they were still in love after so many years of marriage led to a certain amount of teasing from their relatives, who called them "turtledoves."

After Sami, Aida was the first child to survive. Four children died before her. This meant she was pampered around the clock by her mother, father, and Sami too. She did not even need to ask for anything. Sami was her hero, friend, protector, and clown. He was a born inventor and made many toys for her out of wire, wood, and cloth, all of which she kept, even fifty years later, as priceless treasures. She was seven years old when he gave her a kite made of colored paper for sailing in the sky, with her name written on it in big letters. She was so excited that she cried with joy. The next time that happened was fifty-three years later, in the arms of her beloved Karim.

Sami left the country as an engineer when he was only twenty-five. First he went to Saudi Arabia, because salaries were better there. From there the American firm he worked for sent him to New York, convinced of his talent. In New York he made a career for himself and was soon in charge of the research department at a factory for machinery.

And then, one spring day, the terrible news arrived. It was March 21, 1965, a Sunday. She would never forget the date. She was just fifteen. It was already as warm as summer, and her parents were drinking coffee in the courtyard of their little house in Abbara Street when the telephone rang. Her father answered. It was Sami's wife, Nathalie. Aida's father spoke good English, as the head of a newly founded cigarette factory. He stiffened and shouted into the telephone, in English and Arabic, "What? What? Why, where did it happen? How? For God's sake! Where did it happen?"

Her mother dropped the cup from her hand. She shouted, "Sami, oh God, Sami!" He had drowned in the sea on a sailing trip with his friends, in a sudden storm. Aida's mother idolized her son, and she lost faith in God after his death. "Why did you take my son from me?" she screamed up at the sky. "You're not a god of mercy—you also abandoned your own son Jesus. Heartless traitor!" She cried for days, weeks, months. Aida could not remember how long it took until her mother had cried herself out of her senses. Meanwhile her father swallowed his grief and tried to console his wife, but in vain. She no longer recognized anyone—not her husband, not Aida.

"Why don't you take her to the hospital, or put her in a nursing home where she can be looked after?" Aida protested as her father continued his devoted but futile care. "She doesn't know you anymore."

"But I know her, my child," he said and kissed her mother on the forehead. Her mother stared into a faraway world, not even aware of him.

Out of fear that his wife might injure herself, he brought in an elderly aunt to help Aida watch over her until he came home from work in the evening. He no longer wanted to visit friends of colleagues, or be visited by them. He read to his wife, fed her like a baby, and stroked her hand. She would not eat, she hit herself and hit him, and he endured it all with the patience of a saint. Finally, when she fell asleep, he would cry like a child as he washed the dishes in the kitchen.

However, his great heart was not strong enough to endure his grief. He died on his way to work, a year after his son had died. It came suddenly, without warning—or rather, in spite of the many little warnings that nobody except Aida had noticed.

Her father's death pierced Aida to the core. For years she was unable to understand why her brother's death had engulfed the whole family in misery. Why had her father not recognized that he was ruining himself by caring for her delirious mother? She had fought the demons of her madness in faraway worlds, and neither her husband nor daughter had been able to help her. Why had her father not understood this? He was usually so clever. Had love robbed him of reason? Had he been infected by his wife's madness and become mad in his own way? Was love still love if it had the power to engulf such a caring person in misery? Had it chained her mother and father together so that the one could not exist without the other?

It was only years later that Aida realized these questions had helped her recover from her father's death. They put a distance between herself and her parents' madness that was her saving grace. But this bitter experience was also a warning—she would never let herself be chained to anyone by love.

A week after her father's funeral, her mother committed suicide during an unguarded moment while Aida was at school. Her aunt was diligent in looking after her mother, but when the postman rang the bell and she went downstairs to open it, her mother threw herself headfirst out of the second-story window. Aida's aunt, who was still signing the receipt for a registered letter, saw her mother jump. She hit the ground just steps from the postman, and she died at the scene.

Strangely enough, Aida hardly felt any grief for her mother. And if her shame had not held her back, she would have said to neighbors and relatives, "Stop pretending. It's good that she's finally at peace."

~

Aida liked to read, but only if a book interested her, which was why she did not like school. She stoically endured the boredom for love of her father, who had ambitions that she should become a pediatrician. She loved music, but the

101

only possibility at school was singing in a girls' choir, since musical instruments were reserved for men. Soon after her mother's death, she stopped going to school and started an apprenticeship as a ladies' hairdresser.

She was almost twenty and coming to the end of her apprenticeship when she fell helplessly in love with a pale young man. He was a poor window cleaner who, for a few piasters a week, came to clean the display windows of the high-end shops downtown.

One morning Aida was arranging the new hair-care products on the shelf. As she looked up, the young man had just finished wiping away a stripe of foam on the window pane and could see into the shop. When he looked Aida in the eyes, he stiffened and a pained smile flitted across his face. He reminded Aida of a painting of Jesus Christ before Pontius Pilate, surrounded by his tormentors. It was the first of fourteen pictures hanging in the church, which depicted the Stations of the Cross, from Christ's condemnation to his burial. Made by an Italian painter, they never failed to fascinate and unsettle Aida, so much that she was able to picture all fourteen images down to the last detail.

The young man looked at her with his head tilted slightly to one side. He appeared to have completely forgotten what he was doing, and the bubbles of foam on the window pane began to burst and run down the glass in little rivulets. Her older colleague Farida took notice. "Looks like someone's fallen in love with our Aida!"

Aida was frightened. She put down the shampoo bottles and disappeared, blushing, into the stockroom at the back of the salon. After work, she hurried to the church and looked at the first picture of the Stations of the Cross. There was no mistake. It was the face of the young man. That night she couldn't sleep and could only think of him.

The next morning, Salma, a jaundiced assistant, laughed at Aida when the window cleaner returned and smiled at her again. "He's put on his best clothes just for you. Now he looks even more wretched," she called out. She had a tongue as sharp as a cheese grater and a voice that could drown out any radio.

"If I were you," Salma said when the young man had finished his work and left, "I'd run off with him, clean windows, and enjoy the fresh air all day." She blew a large bubble with her chewing gum, popped it, and laughed. Aida felt so angry she could have throttled the woman. Farida just shook her head, patted Aida on the shoulder, and gave Salma a look that, had it been made of copper or lead, could have pierced the tough hide of a wild boar.

At home, consumed with longing, Aida was unable to do anything but think of the young man. When she went to work early each morning, she always hoped to see him somewhere along the way, but she was never so lucky. Later he would appear in front of the salon window, smiling silently, and work deliberately and slowly to clean the large glass pane. Aida had to hide. She'd find reasons to go to the back of the shop, where he couldn't see her, and stay there, later despising herself for her cowardice. Almost two months went by like that, and every morning when he would smile she could almost hear her heart pounding.

One day he stopped coming. Suddenly, without warning, without saying goodbye. A week later, an older man took over the window cleaning on the street.

Aida drifted around the shop listlessly, her heart yearning for the young man whom she loved without even knowing his name. To annoy her, Salma sang songs about unrequited love, where at the end the lovers either went mad or committed suicide. Aida's boss noticed her misery and understood. He ordered Salma to spare him from having to listen to her dreadful voice, or else go outside and torment customers in front of his competitor's shop with her whip of a tongue. Salma shut up.

Around noon, Aida started feeling very weak. She tried to put on a brave face and show enthusiasm for her work, but her boss took pity on her. "Go home, child. You look so pale, and there's not much going on in the shop today, anyway," he said in a fatherly tone.

That night she ran a fever. When she started vomiting, her old aunt, who had been living with her since the death of her parents, called the doctor. He prescribed some pills and bed rest.

It was two weeks before she was back on her feet. And she was no longer the same. The time off had allowed her to think, and she realized that she was acting like her parents, doing the same thing that had killed them both. What did she know about the young man anyway? Nothing! And yet she was obsessed with him. She didn't even know his name! The whole affair had been like a silent movie that ran every morning for five minutes. The windowpane was the screen, and she had fallen desperately in love with a picture, an actor. Who knew how many other women he had smiled at every day?

Aida took herself severely to task. When she went back to work, she was completely different. Salma was the first to notice it. "Lovesick," she mocked, but Aida laid into her.

"With no waistline and such an ugly face, you wouldn't dare fall in love because you know you wouldn't have a hope in hell of seducing a toad!"

"Congratulations, child, things will be quieter around here, finally," her boss said at lunch.

~

Thanks to her father's generous life insurance policy, Aida was able to open her own chic salon in the New City. She quickly made a reputation for herself in the wealthy neighborhood, so much that she was able to employ three hairdressers. But her real passion was music, and so she began to play the oud—late in life, but with all the more enthusiasm. Her idol was the famous singer Jamila Nassour, who, after a short conversation with Aida, decided to take her on as a pupil, free of charge. Aida returned the favor by adorning the singer with the most beautiful, fashionable hairstyles she could create.

For nearly forty years, Aida did not allow herself to fall in love again. The memory of her parents and the pale young man held her back. She thought that romantic love was an illness, somewhere between a migraine and diarrhea. Rational thought must prevail.

And so it did until many years later, when the cool waters of reason finally yielded to passion's fires.

10

The Rift

A party with consequences

For years, summer parties were a speciality of Alfredo Angelini, successful architect and genial host. Every year in August, one hundred guests would gather to help him celebrate his birthday. The Italian elite were invited to Milan. Each year featured a glittering party with a carefully planned program of dancing, music, comedians, and magicians, followed by long, quiet moments for conversation. The evening's program remained the host's jealously guarded secret until the very last minute. Attendance was always high because Alfredo never failed to surprise his guests, and because the networking was so good.

Stella and Salman were invited every year, not only because she was Alfredo's cousin, but also because he thought so highly of her. As a pharmacologist, she was his trusted consultant for all the medicines that he, a notorious hypochondriac, consumed in vast quantities. Salman worked as a consultant for Alfredo whenever he had a contract for a project in an Arab country.

That year, Stella didn't want to go to Alfredo's party. She used Paolo as the reason, since he wasn't yet eight months old. Looking back, she said that she'd had a premonition of catastrophe. But Alfredo and Salman both insisted that she attend. And since Alfredo provided lodging for all his guests at the best hotel in Milan, so that they could enjoy a farewell breakfast with him the following morning, Stella had no choice but to find a babysitter for Paolo. She asked her parents to come from Trieste, and also found an experienced nanny to help them. Salman laughed about it. "All that's missing are two bodyguards at the entrance to the building and a helicopter circling overhead." Stella slapped him on the backside. Even her mother had to laugh.

"That's Stella. Always two hundred percent," her father said, almost apologetically. Paolo cooed happily in his cot and seemed to enjoy his grandmother's cuddles.

"She never kissed me that much in my whole life," Stella said quietly to Salman as they were leaving the house.

"Grandparents celebrate their second victory over death at the birth of a grandchild. That's why they love them so much," he responded.

"And they can afford to love their grandchild to pieces and totally ignore the big picture of upbringing, education, and morals," Stella added.

Even in Milan, Stella was still worried. Salman was not the only one to notice. Alfredo whispered to her, "Have a glass of champagne—you'll feel better. You can be sure that Paolo is fine. The chaos of grandparents suits children." His voice was fatherly, and Stella was embarrassed to burden her cousin with her excessive worry. She had a few glasses of champagne and forgot all about Paolo.

It was past midnight when Stella and Salman left the party. A few night owls kept on celebrating, but most guests began to leave shortly after the midnight singing of "Happy Birthday."

Stella was cheerful and slightly tipsy, and she slipped her arms around Salman. "I've been watching a few women today. If their eyes had had teeth, there wouldn't have been much left of you. I'm in love with you, you lovely man," she said.

"And what about me? I had eyes for no one else. You still have a hold on me."

When they got into bed, Stella forgot about everything else. She was not lying in an elegant king-size bed in a luxury hotel... she was racing through space with Salman, and she felt breathtakingly happy.

Two visions of life

It took a few weeks for doubt to raise its ugly head, followed by the paralyzing fear that she might be pregnant. Salman soothed and comforted her, but then she took a pregnancy test, and it was positive. Salman's attitude toward Stella changed immediately. At breakfast one morning, he said that it might be a gift from heaven if Paolo were to have a little brother or sister. They could play together and never feel lonely.

But Stella wanted no more children. She wanted to get back to the university as soon as possible. She cried and shouted that she'd rather die than become a housewife. She scolded Salman for wanting to push her further into the role of being a mother, which—along with the idea of the perfect family—had become just a myth, a pretense, in Italy. She had not forgotten her own mother, "a piano virtuoso at sixteen... she shrank into the role of a simple housewife who was glad to bring me into the world after four miscarriages, to finally make my father happy." She knew that her mother had only been so cold toward her because she was unhappy.

"That's just you being high and mighty about housewives," Salman replied angrily. "Without them, there would be no life or culture on earth."

"You're right," she said calmly, but it sounded more like a threat. "Then you'll just have to become a stay-at-home husband. I'm working and my salary is enough for the family," she added. They went on arguing, and Stella taunted him that he, who had once fought for freedom in the mountains and risked his life for his country, had transformed into an ordinary businessman.

Salman would later realize that he had made two stupid mistakes at the time. Arguing for a second child, he kept insisting that the standard of living they had achieved was enough for Stella to give up her job at the university. But his selfish insistence blinded him to the fact that she was not doing research for the money, but because she was truly passionate about her work.

His second mistake had more serious consequences. Stella told him in confidence about an abortion pill that was illegal in Italy, but allowed in France and in Germany. She would take a week's leave and book herself into a clinic in France, where an experienced doctor could perform the abortion.

Salman panicked. He alerted her parents, who came immediately. He had called them because he felt helpless, but to Stella it was a betrayal. Her mother shed floods of tears and her father reminded her that abortion was a mortal sin. Stella felt lonely and weak. She was on the verge of running away, but she decided to stand her ground. Politely but decisively, she asked her parents to leave her house. Salman was at the office. He felt guilty about having abandoned Stella to her parents. He was beginning to find her father ridiculous with his "mortal sin," and her mother seemed able to burst into tears at will. Stella was growing nervous because the abortion became riskier with every passing day.

He drove home to find Stella packing her suitcase. He pleaded with her not to go to France, but to have the abortion done in Rome by a gynecologist. He'd gotten an address from friends and had already spoken with the doctor. He agreed to the abortion, he said, crying and begging her for forgiveness. As if on cue, Paolo started crying piteously. Stella put her suitcase down, went to sit in the kitchen, and thought for a long time. In the end, she decided to have the abortion in Rome, illegally.

The procedure went badly. The embryo and the amniotic sac were not ejected completely and had to be removed surgically. An infection set in, and Stella had to stay in the hospital for two weeks.

During that time, Salman took devoted care of Paolo, refusing any help from his in-laws or a babysitter. He learned to feed, wash, and change Paolo. Meanwhile his assistant, Chiara, ran the import-export business. She called him, asked for advice, kept him informed about how things were going, and reassured him. Every day Salman would take the baby and visit Stella for an hour.

"Paolo is blossoming in your care," Stella said, praising him during one visit. "Maybe I should stay in hospital longer, until he finishes high school," she joked, and kissed Salman on the forehead as he bent to pick up Paolo. The baby beamed and stretched out his arms to Salman.

"No, Rome is a desert without you, and both of us are lost," Salman replied, close to tears. Stella looked pale and thin. He didn't tell her he had already made a plan so this would never happen again.

11

Sophia, a Savior in an Hour of Need

Damascus, 1950–2005

Karim drove to Damascus in the autumn of 1950. Years later, Aida would tease him, saying that he had come to make sure that his future beloved would be born. He shook with laughter at this because his first visit in the city had been cursed with misfortune. At the time, he was twenty-two and already brokenhearted because Sophia, whom he had loved so much, had married the rich Damascene goldsmith. Karim lived in Homs, where he had become a primary-school teacher. As a newcomer, he was assigned a position in a school on the outskirts of the city, where poverty was rampant. The children needed to learn to read and write and, if at all possible, count a little—such was his ultimate goal as a headmaster.

The children were hungry for bread and knowledge. They saw Karim as a magician who could disclose the secrets of letters and explain natural phenomena to them. But young as they were, they had already learned the grammar of survival and knew more than he did about some things. Every one of those schoolchildren was a bold fighter and gifted actor, since that was the only way they could survive. Young as they were, they knew that school could be their salvation, and they learned passionately.

Karim loved his pupils, but he was not able to stay on in Homs. After his sister Saliha had fled with her Christian lover, the family had chosen him to kill her. He loved his sister, but the family council had decided. "We are putting

111

the family honor into your hands," his father said as he was leaving, "and you can be sure that you'll spend your two years in prison like a prince. I'll make sure of it and you'll come out a hero." He fought back tears as he said these words and handed Karim a pistol and a small box of ammunition. Everyone applauded.

Karim left Homs in a daze. Money didn't matter. He had been given enough cash and, if necessary, was allowed to borrow as much as he needed from a Damascene business partner of his father's. Karim didn't even know just where his sister lived in Damascus. But he could at least hope to meet Sophia there, his former girlfriend who had since become the mother of a five-year-old boy. Had I married her, he suddenly thought, her family would have killed her. He found his sister's house surprisingly fast. Her husband, Anton Tarasi, was a well-known doctor. Karim signed in to a room in a hotel opposite the house. The following morning, he waited until his brother-in-law left the house, got into a black Citroën, and drove to his surgery.

In his whole life, Karim would never forget the moment when, with a pounding heart, he rang the bell of his sister's house. Saliha opened the door and was so surprised that she nearly fainted. They embraced and kissed, cried and laughed like children. His sister knew that he was there to kill her on behalf of the clan. She told him he should just do it, and she wouldn't cry out because she loved him. She wouldn't hate him either, because she knew it was his duty.

Karim kissed her and cried. "Never," he said, "I would never kill you. I've come to warn you. Run away with your husband. As long as I stay here, you'll have enough time. I'll stall our father and tell him that I'm still looking for you. Hurry, before it's too late and someone gets suspicious."

His sister agreed. But his brother-in-law didn't want to hear about it. He wouldn't leave Damascus. He had studied medicine in France and believed that every human being had the right to love and marry whomever they chose. Karim was amazed at such naiveté, but he swallowed his disappointment and tried to convince his brother-in-law of the danger. He explained how the rule that prevailed in this country was different than in France, and that Anton needed to disappear with Saliha for a few years. Still he refused. Anton Tarasi was a kind but stubborn man who worshipped his wife with the innocence of a child. He was the first man that Karim ever saw cook and wash dishes.

"You must go back to Homs and tell your father that you're not willing to kill a human being and that I love your sister very much," he said. "This is how we can move society forward, not through escaping time and again."

"That won't help us," Karim replied. "They'll despise me and send someone else instead." But Anton did not want to believe him. To prove it, Karim offered to call his father and have Anton listen to his father's reaction. He would tell him that he did not want to kill his sister. So Karim called his father and told him that he loved his sister and that he could not think of killing her. She would never find a better husband than Anton, who treated her like a princess. His father threw a fit. He cursed Karim, saying he was a dishonorable, unprincipled, and ungrateful scoundrel. If he would not save the honor of the family, he would disinherit him and send another man—with more courage and backbone.

Karim was amazed that his brother-in-law still refused to take his father's words seriously. He suggested that the two of them live in Beirut, Amman, or Cairo and hide their identities for a time. His brother-in-law was a good doctor who could have worked anywhere, but he did not want to leave Damascus. The brother of Colonel George Tarasi, the police chief, Anton was convinced that no one would dare harm a hair on his wife's head. He refused to see that the clan acknowledged neither state nor any law besides its own. And Saliha would not move an inch from her husband's side.

~

Karim had started looking for Sophia on the very next day after his arrival, but with no luck. He eventually came across a former schoolmate who told him that, for his wedding, he had bought gold jewelry from Yusuf Baladi, Sophia's husband. He didn't know where Sophia lived, but he showed Karim the magnificent goldsmith's shop, which was located close to the Umayyad Mosque. Karim waited until Sophia's husband closed up the shop to go home and then followed him all the way to his doorstep. The next day, he knocked on Sophia's door. She was pleased to see him again. Karim told her about his trouble.

From that day on they met regularly, and the old flame was rekindled. Sophia rented Karim a room in a bed and breakfast in the modern district of Salihiya, far from the Christian Quarter where his sister lived. That way they could meet every day, except Sundays when the goldsmith's shop was closed.

Karim was haunted by nightmares in which he would hear his sister's cries without being able to help her. Sometimes he was wandering in a dark forest, sometimes he was stuck in clinging mud up to his knees. One Saturday, he wanted to visit his sister and again implore his brother-in-law to take his advice. But it was too late. An ambulance and a police car were parked in front of the house.

The killer had shot Saliha and her husband, and left a

fake letter by Karim claiming responsibility for the crime. The letter said that he had restored the family honor—a ridiculous piece of evidence, full of contradictions and mistakes. Why would anyone be so stupid as to implicate himself in a murder and then disappear? But the police chief was blind with rage and he wanted to avenge his brother. Truth and vengeance have always been enemies. Two days after the murder of his sister and her husband, an official manhunt for Karim began.

The murders were a shock to Karim and to Sophia. She came to see him, pale with fear, and brought him the latest issue of the local paper.

Karim would never know another woman who recovered from fear as quickly as Sophia did. "Your picture will soon be everywhere," she said. "You must go into hiding, and I'll make sure that they search for the murderer and hopefully arrest him."

Just how Sophia would accomplish this, she did not know herself. And Karim was a complete stranger in Damascus. "But where will I disappear to until then?" Karim replied helplessly. "The owners will recognize me here, and inform on me to the police…"

"I'll find a place for you, darling, that's for sure," she said and kissed him.

Sophia had a very old aunt, named Munira. She had no children. After her husband died, she lived alone in a small house in the elegant neighborhood of Salihiya, not far from the parliament building and Karim's bed and breakfast. The old lady hardly ever left her house. She tended her little garden, and Sophia visited her once a day. Her aunt would not have any servants or a nurse.

By the following day, Sophia had already told her aunt about everything—the murders, the manhunt, and her love for Karim. The aunt, who couldn't stand Sophia's husband, was delighted that her niece had a lover. "Did he do it?" was her only question. And Sophia swore by the Holy Virgin that she had been with Karim at the time of the murder, and that he was incapable of it, because he loved his sister Saliha so much.

"Let him come, then," Aunt Munira said. "Finally! I'll have a bit of entertainment." Karim was still afraid, but Sophia swore by her love for him that her aunt would not betray him.

And she was right. Aunt Munira was a witty, generous, and brave hostess. Karim would never forget his time with her. Even thirty years after she'd died, he would visit her grave every month and lay a handful of jasmine blossoms, her favorite, on the marble slab.

But in Karim and Sophia's renewed love, there was a catch. He was no longer allowed to touch Sophia. That was her condition. Aunt Munira joked about these two strange lovers. "It's like love between a nun and a priest," she said. But Sophia was insistent. She didn't want to abuse the right of hospitality that she had claimed for Karim's protection. His desire for her seemed to leave her cold. Pleas or attempts were of no use. She wouldn't bring her son Salman with her, either, although Aunt Munira often asked her to do so. She was crazy about the beautiful boy. "No, he's bright beyond his years and he might somehow betray Karim."

Karim respected her strong will, but he wondered whether she loved him as much as he loved her. When he asked her if she desired him, the way he longed for her, she smiled. "If the fire in me could catch you, you would have turned to ashes by now. Your life matters more to me than my desires."

~

So Karim lived in hiding at Aunt Munira's house as if in a monastery. Munira was small, but not weak or helpless. She enjoyed letting herself be waited on hand and foot. Karim looked after her garden, helped her in the kitchen, and played cards with her and Sophia. He even forgot he was a wanted man. But then he heard that the police chief had given orders for him to be shot on sight, because he was afraid that Karim would get off with just three years in prison. Then as now, honor killers were treated like heroes and given only mild sentences.

Damascenes saw Karim's face on wanted notices and leaflets. Sophia brought one for him to see. Aunt Munira laughed. "Even Sophia and I wouldn't recognize you from that. Don't worry." It was in fact a badly enlarged photo of Karim taken for his ID card five years ago. In it, his head was almost shaved and he looked stiff and tense. His father had given the photo to the police. Even so, Karim didn't dare leave the house.

Then one morning, Sophia came to Karim with an idea. She would persuade a member of his clan to come to Damascus and tell the police the name of the murderer. She would make sure that the witness remained anonymous and escaped safely to live in Baghdad. Sophia's favorite brother Farid was a rich carpet merchant there and could help her.

She asked Karim who in his family could do this. "If anyone would dare, it would be my brother Ismail," he replied.

Ismail was two years younger than Karim. He had loved Saliha very much, and she had been very fond of him. Both Saliha and Ismail resembled their mother, while Karim was the spitting image of their father. So off Sophia went to Homs. She told her husband that she missed Homs and her parents. She wanted to spend a week in the city where she was born, on the banks of the Orontes River. She also wanted to see Takla, her favorite sister, who was in the hospital with pneumonia. When Sophia arrived, Takla had already been discharged. She was at home, still in bed but happy. Her fiancé, a poor Damascene carpenter, sat next to her, looking paler than she did from care and worry.

The following day, Sophia got in touch with Karim's brother Ismail. He was in mourning for his sister but wouldn't reveal the murderer's name. Sophia assured him that nobody besides herself and Karim would know about his flight to Baghdad. She was even prepared to pay for his ticket. Her brother could use an assistant from his native city of Homs.

But Ismail was too afraid, and Sophia returned to Damascus disappointed. Karim would need to be patient. She would find another way out, she said.

Karim was bitter about his brother's lack of courage but deeply grateful to Sophia for everything she was doing for him. "How can I ever repay you? I would do anything for you, even die," he said, deeply moved.

Sophia laughed. "Start by staying alive. I haven't finished—you're only halfway safe. You're not rescued yet." She stroked his head. "I'm sure I'll think of a way for you to pay me back. Don't worry!" She laughed gently. It sounded like fresh water trickling down a stream.

12

Double Lives

Advice from a reptile

Looking after his son while Stella was in the hospital was not as tiring as Salman had expected. There were still quiet times. Paolo was a baby with a sunny disposition. Salman could take him everywhere, and he would lie quietly in his stroller. When necessary, he would take Paolo with him to the office. Chiara liked the boy and could watch him while Salman dealt with business. Apart from that, Salman dedicated himself to the child. He also read many books during that time.

Once Paolo had been washed and fed in the morning, he would sleep for two hours solid. Salman would put the baby monitor near his crib and go to the Caffè Arabo, less than a block away. There he would read the paper and indulge in some people watching, but after an hour at most, he would hurry back to Paolo.

One day, an old man he had known for years asked Salman why he was so sad. He found it strange that the question should come from this man, whom he didn't like. He was nearly eighty, and small, with a perpetual frown. Three scars on his face complemented his cold, protruding reptilian eyes. It was rumored that he had been a Mafioso, but his miserable demeanor was not in keeping with the legend. He did his best to appear elegant: white shoes, white hat—a cheap imitation Fedora, blue jacket, white shirt, and a red tie. And he always clenched an unlit cigar in the corner of his mouth. He would read the newspaper, comment on the news, greet all the customers, and never drink more than a single espresso.

In all those years, Salman contented himself with a polite nod and avoided addressing the man. If he was in an especially good mood, he might add a "*Buon giorno.*"

But that morning, Salman began to chat with him. "My wife is in the hospital," he said, wondering about his openness. As if on cue, the man came immediately to Salman's table.

"Oh, nothing serious, I hope, is it?"

"No, no. It's…" Salman hesitated.

The man leaned toward him over the small bistro table. "An abortion?" Salman nodded silently.

"Oh, that can be dangerous. I lost my first wife, Emma, after an abortion… in 1960. We went to one of these criminal 'angel makers.' The woman's work wasn't clean, and Emma died three weeks later. I had myself sterilized afterward."

"Isn't sterilization dangerous?" Salman asked, hypocritically, since the only danger he cared about was loss of potency. But the reptilian eyes smiled in reassurance.

"Don't worry, young man. I may not be Fellini's Dottore Cazzone, who recorded ten thousand lovers on tape, but I've had my thirty lovers—ten before the operation and twenty after. I never fucked better in my life than after the operation, because you can then fuck without any fear or guilt. I could never be content with one woman, but I kept worrying about producing children left and right. Ilse, my second wife, lacked for nothing, and she let me service the other women. She had a big heart."

He lifted his hat, massaged his thick but cheaply dyed

hair, pressed the hat down to his forehead, and grinned.

Only then did Salman notice that the old man had just greeted an old lady wearing too much makeup, who walked past and gave the man a prolonged smile.

"Her too?" Salman asked mischievously.

"Don't be deceived by the wrinkly exterior. Gabriela loved nothing better than to suck me up to the neck."

Salman realized that the lady's erotic play with the old man had once been wild. His eyes followed the old woman as she put on an elegant gait, but he stuck to his role as hypocrite.

"Maybe I should be celibate. It would be best for everybody."

"What are you talking about?" the old man shouted indignantly. "Bacteria and viruses can be celibate—not human beings. Even a worm wants to fuck, and if it can't find another, it will fuck itself… When I kick the bucket," he said, laughing so much that his eyes became alive for a short moment, "I will tell the Lord of the Worlds that if He wants to save humankind, He must immediately start producing hermaphrodites."

~

Stella was touched when Salman told her, one week after she had been back from the hospital, that he had made an appointment at the urologist. And because he described the operation in dramatic terms, she seemed impressed by his courage. Salman seized the opportunity and asked her to invite her parents to a reconciliation dinner. He felt guilty about her fighting with them. Stella did not object. Her parents came on the same day, and they were grateful to Salman for all his help with Paolo. They spent the weekend in Rome and returned to Trieste feeling relieved.

The operation was actually simpler than Salman had imagined. It required only a local anesthetic, and Salman was able to go back home after one night at the hospital. But then he was haunted by terrible nightmares: men with giant knives or shears castrated him and left him lying there.

Stella seemed to have become indifferent to sexuality. She would kiss him on the cheek in almost sisterly fashion. Whenever he wanted to make love, she would pretend to be tired to hide her listlessness or find some other excuse.

"I'm not in the mood," she would always say when he kissed her passionately. Instead she was hungry enough for a whole company. She had never eaten so much before. She was soon back to her old freshness and energy. Then one day she passed one hundred and forty-three pounds and started to become fat. All around her rejoiced. Salman, however, thought that she had lost her charm and erotic charisma. In less than a year, Stella put on over twenty-six pounds. She was becoming, more and more, a real Italian *mama*, her mother exclaimed delightedly. Salman's Arab acquaintances in Rome also found Stella more beautiful, and more feminine. He laughed at that. "The hunger of your Bedouin ancestors is still deep in your bones, and when you see a woman you want to eat her up. And the rounder she is, the heartier the feast."

A year passed by and Salman realized, bitterly, that he had only had sex with Stella once in all of those twelve months. He felt like a stranger in Rome again and no longer really at home with Stella, and he dreamed increasingly often of returning to Damascus. It wasn't until much later that he would learn that the Damascus he dreamt of in his loneliness existed only in his imagination.

~

So one January day in 1996, he decided to visit a prostitute. He didn't want to love anybody else because he loved only Stella, but the need to make love to a woman was nearly making him ill. So he looked for a love that was strictly commercial, so that he could fulfill his desire in a way that was completely detached from any pleading or begging.

In doing so, Salman didn't even realize that he had now become like those Italians who differentiate strictly between sex and love. You loved your wife from afar and you let off steam with prostitutes. He consoled himself with the fact that he had been faithful for more than fifteen years. And in all those years, he hadn't even noticed once when someone had been interested in him. His entire focus had been on Stella.

Violetta

It was pure chance that in January he had an appointment with Claudio, his tax advisor. After they had finished their work, Salman invited the old, witty widower for a drink in a bar near the train station. Claudio, however, was in a hurry. He just wanted to have a quick red wine and then catch the train for Bologna. He gulped the wine down hastily, thanked Salman, and left him standing at the bar. A young woman was talking to the Indian bartender. As she turned and faced Salman, he smiled. She smiled back. He found her very attractive and liked her deep voice. When she left, Salman paid and followed her.

It was raining and she stood there under the awning in front of the entrance, waiting. "There's room for you under my umbrella if you'd like," Salman said. The woman laughed, "How could I refuse such a kind offer?" she replied.

He opened his umbrella. She stepped out with him and took his arm under the umbrella.

"Where do you want to go?"

"Home. I live just nearby, three streets farther on," the woman replied. Outside, her beauty was more clearly visible than in the bar's subdued lighting. She had a dark, well-proportioned face and long black hair, with the fragrance of exotic fruits about her. When Salman, somewhat embarrassed, asked her what she did, she said, "Companion," and laughed. It transpired that she didn't actually live just nearby, but quite far away, in the Via Giovanni Battista de Rossi. They walked through the streets for almost half an hour, and Salman kept the umbrella up, although by then the rain had eased off. With his face hidden by the umbrella, he accompanied Violetta and they almost seemed like a couple in love.

"Your little lie reminds me of a saying of the Bedouins in the desert. When asked how far it is to such-and-such a place, they're fond of replying 'a stone's throw away.' Do you know how far the sons of the desert can sling a stone?"

Violetta laughed. "I had to get a feel for you first. You never know who's out looking for a woman in Rome."

"And? Did I pass the test?" he asked.

"Sure. Otherwise we wouldn't be here," Violetta answered seriously.

They had stopped in front of a three-story house with a pretty front, but modest compared to the others. "I live here," she said. Salman followed her with his heart pounding. He had never visited a prostitute before. He despised pimps and had always regarded prostitutes as exploited women, martyrs of a sort. Violetta's small apartment was tastefully furnished and more pleasant than he had expected. She said she had been living in Rome for a year and had taken up prostitution of her own free will, not as a result of a hard childhood or abuse.

Violetta poured Salman a glass of wine and answered his curious questions. With total pedagogical detachment, she talked about prostitution in Italy and about how happy she was to have her own apartment. Poorer prostitutes rented more modest apartments or just a room in a rundown hotel. The poorest prostitutes, particularly the foreign ones, worked on the exit roads. They were called *lucciole*, or 'glow-worms,' because of the little flashlights that they carried in order to be seen in the dark.

Salman was ashamed that he had lived so long in Rome without the slightest notion about any of this. His shame didn't last long, however. Violetta was so gentle with him that he quite forgot that she was a professional. She exuded calm and affection, as if he was the only one in the world for her. He paid generously. She asked him if he wanted to come again. He nodded. She gave him her telephone number. He lied to her, saying his name was Roberto, but his friends called him Robbie. After years of working as a university professor, he now enjoyed a reputation as an intellectual and had been a widower for two years. He was back living with his old but very rich mother.

She didn't ask any further.

He returned home, satisfied and mellow in spirit. To his surprise, he only felt pangs of conscience just before falling asleep. The following morning, they were gone completely.

When Stella asked him at breakfast why he was so relaxed, he lied to her, saying, "Business is booming." This first lie plagued him for days. Like the first murder in wartime, it was the most difficult, but after that it was much easier to put off Stella with excuses.

From then on, it no longer bothered him that Stella only had eyes for their pretty little baby. Actually, Salman felt relieved about it, to a certain extent. He never pestered her again, but would wait until she came to him, something that seldom happened, but was all the more passionate when it did. Sardonically, Salman referred to it as *seasonal sex*, which made Stella laugh.

Violetta, on the other hand, seemed to wait for him. She behaved like a lover, albeit for money, but things were clear—no tears, no infatuation, and no threat to his marriage. That gave him a sense of security. Here his needs were satisfied; there he had love and family. He loved Stella, but the thrill of each secret meeting with Violetta, the possibility of slipping into another personality gave him tremendous joy. One evening at Violetta's, he was reminded of two pictures by Caravaggio. They hung next to each other in the small room of the Galleria Doria Pamphilj on the Piazza del Collegio Romano. One picture showed Mary Magdalene, the other showed Our Lady resting on the flight to Egypt. Caravaggio had chosen the same model for both Marys.

In summer, the gardens of the villas on Violetta's street blossomed into a delight for the eye. Her apartment was on the third floor, with an unrestricted view of the beautiful surroundings. Diagonally across from them, in the garden of a white, supervised villa was a splendid bougainvillea that had been artistically trimmed by the gardener into an enormous lilac bouquet. Sometimes, Salman would gaze out over the flowers and trees, and imagine he was an angel hovering and caressing his beloved.

~

For ten years, it was Tuesdays and Fridays at Violetta's, always for exactly two hours. Each time they met, she was as happy as she had been that first day, spoiled him thoroughly and totaled up for him the price she charged her luxury clients, as she called them. He would joke with her, "Don't you do a bulk discount? No loyalty points?"

She'd laugh. "Yes, when you get one hundred points there's a frying pan. You get that over the head if you ask any more stupid questions."

Violetta wasn't curious. Salman didn't ask about her work, or her feelings, either. She knew nothing about his marriage, because he never wanted a woman to be able to compare herself to his wife. In his eyes, that was the absolute difference between an affair and paying for sex. A lover who knows about a wife, feels superior to her. She might envy her being able to live with her lover, but as long as the wife doesn't know about the lover, she remains the inferior.

Once, when he couldn't get it up in bed, he ordered some Gigante XXL virility tablets over the Internet. Violetta didn't notice anything or, if she did, she hid it well. Stella, also, didn't seem aware of Salman's secrets—or if she was, she hid it well.

When Salman first met Violetta, she was in her late twenties, and she was in her late thirties when she gave him his marching orders in the summer of 2005. One evening she said off-handedly, "I've no time next Tuesday."

"What about Friday?"

"I'll already be in Montreal with my husband."

"What? You got married?"

"Not yet. On Wednesday. We're flying off on Thursday," she said. She then told him a little about her new life partner and about how tired she was and gave him a little peck on the cheek. "You're a generous, good-hearted man. You're going to have to strangle your mother soon, otherwise you'll be stuck with her forever," she said with a smile.

"But who's going to comfort me?" he asked, sadly.

"Here's the address and telephone number of Lola. She's Polish but she speaks good Italian. She knows the score and is looking forward to seeing you—and your money."

He stuck the slip of paper into his trouser pocket and left. Years later, he still remembered how lonely and abandoned he'd felt that night.

Removing the dust of forgetfulness

Salman often thought about the past and wrote down in Arabic whatever thoughts came to him. He was obsessed with Damascus. He spent every waking minute thinking about how he would manage his triumphant homecoming. That would be the only way to heal his wounds. Day after day, he thought of how happily he would live on his return, but talked about it to nobody. How could Stella, a child of freedom, understand how the wounds of exile felt?

He found himself noting down one phrase again and again: "My soul is in Damascus, wandering the streets of my childhood." He described the Damascene streets in the gleaming colors called for by his yearning, while he still sought, from the safety of Rome, to uncover just what risk such a journey might entail.

He also wrote about his life with Stella. The simple fact of writing it down seemed to blow away the dust from everything he had experienced. He thought about his first days with Stella in Rome, and how Rome had changed in the last thirty years. Mass tourism, traffic chaos, and cheap shops had all conspired to deface the city. It was heart-breaking to stand by and witness to what extent reality had surpassed the horrific visions and fears of a Pasolini or a Flaiano. The gentry had moved into what had once been colorful and lively districts. The outskirts of the city were becoming rundown and dangerous.

Evening after evening, Salman committed his thoughts to paper under cover of Arabic script. Neither Stella nor Paolo could read Arabic. While they each had their many failings, they respected each other's privacy and secrets. That was what allowed him to write so openly about his wife and son. Paolo had brought him a lot of happiness, but his arrival had robbed him of his beloved. His son seldom caused him any concern, and the quiet little boy always did well at school. Paolo's sunny disposition attracted lots of friends and he was never seriously ill. It was only through his son that Salman had really come to understand everything that his own parents had done for him. When he thought of just how much he had neglected them, he felt ashamed—but never for long.

Three or four times a year, he and Stella would invite friends to their home. On Christmas Eve, their acquaintances could visit anytime between eight o'clock in the evening and three o'clock in the morning. Arab cuisine was the order of the day. There was no obligation on anybody, but all their friends could come and celebrate their "open day," as Stella called Christmas Eve, with them.

Stella was not fond of cooking. When she did cook, it was either spaghetti or minestrone. She preferred to eat out. Salman, on the other hand, enjoyed cooking. He'd had lovely dinners with his German friends, but it was more difficult to cook for Italians. The Germans would try anything, even pizza with pineapple. For centuries, German traditional cooking had offered very little in the way of exotic dishes. In Italy, however, blessed as they were by the Mediterranean cuisine and an ideal climate for growing vegetables, wine grapes, and olives, people were normally mistrustful and rather superior when faced with any new food. And if a guest ran out of arguments, he could always fall back on an old standby: "It tastes different at my mama's."

13

Thirty Years Sailing on Quiet Water

Damascus, 1972–2005

Aida was twenty-three when she married the lawyer Nadim Intabi. He was a widower and twenty years her senior. Nadim had fallen in love with Aida when he defended her rights against the rich property owner who wanted to evict her from her hairdressing salon. The location was much sought after, and a car dealership had offered the owner a much more substantial rent.

The year before, a rich young hairdresser had already fallen in love with Aida and was courting her passionately. He begged her to marry him. He overdid the passion, such that she was more frightened than charmed. She even found him ludicrous at times, once writing to her that he would be willing to die the moment she allowed him to live with her for just one day. It sounded like something out of those cheap Arab romantic films that she hated. And no, she wasn't interested in any maze with no safe way out. What she wanted was a boat ride on a wide, calm lake.

That's why she chose the fatherly lawyer who allowed her to work and indulge her passion for music. He asked her to move into his villa with him, since there was more room there than in her parents' small house on Abbara Street. She was glad to leave the house, which was still alive with memories of her parents' recent deaths. The only thing she took with her was the toy that her brother Sami had made for her. She sold all the furniture and appliances to a junk dealer. Then she rented the house and moved into her husband's villa.

Aida had a good life with him. Nadim was a smart, reasonable man and living with him might have been a little boring, but it was very much like a faithful friendship. She was content and convinced that she could forever do without any other kind of love. Ten years later, she gave up working as a hairdresser but went on playing the oud daily.

There were no children but the marriage lasted over thirty years. Passion may have been lacking, but it was full of mutual respect. Nadim was a reliable and caring partner. Aida cherished him with all her heart, and she never betrayed him, not even for one second. He died of cancer in June 2004. She would sit with him every day in the hospital, sometimes as long as ten hours at a time. A few days before he died, she asked him, "Is there anything you'd like?" It was a hot summer's day and she was hoping that he'd ask for a pistachio ice, so that he might leave this earth with its sweet taste on his tongue. He smiled at her. "Pistachio ice, but only if you promise me that you will not mourn me more than thirty days, one day for every year together, and that you will look around for a good man. I'd be very happy if you go back into life with your music and your big heart. If there is a hereafter, you can be sure that I'll be blessing your happiness from above, and if there is none, I'll just be phosphate fertilizing the earth—and that's no reason to remain sad and lonely for a lifetime."

She cried and hated herself for being weak. He stroked her head and calmed her. "Now where's my ice?" Nadim was a noble soul in all things, including dying.

Aida did as he wished and donated his wealth and his villa to a child welfare association. Nadim had arranged with an insurance company for her to be paid a lifelong pension. This is how, on one day in May 2005, Aida returned to the little house in Abbara Street with a suitcase full of clothes, the box with her childhood toy, her oud, and her memories of Nadim. When the tenants had moved out, she had the house renovated and completely redecorated.

She had just turned fifty-five and she planned on leading a quiet life. She was pleasantly surprised to see that, despite all the grief surrounding Nadim, she was still getting friendly signals from the world around her. A whole army of children and youngsters wanted to run her errands for her, while neighbors invited her for meals and coffee almost daily. Occasionally, Aida had to resort to white lies for some peace and quiet. The neighbors loved it when she played the oud, and when she did, there would be absolute quiet in the nearby houses and apartments. Radios and televisions were switched off, and a whole troop of youngsters would make sure that nobody sounded their horn on busy Abbara Street and that no street vendor hawked his wares too loudly.

Autumn had entered Aida's heart and she contemplated the arrival of winter with equanimity.

14

Munira's Suggestion and Karim's Risk

Damascus, 1951

One evening after Karim had finished eating dinner with Aunt Munira, she had him bring up a bottle of red wine from her vaulted cellar. When he came back, she had set out two bowls with pistachio nuts and pumpkin seeds on the table. They clinked glasses, and he noticed that Munira had something to say.

"You must go out! You'll always have a place here, but apart from me and Sophia and a neighbor sometimes, there's nobody here to draw you out of your grief. Out there are women who dream of meeting a charming man like you."

"But the police are looking for me. There are wanted posters everywhere and…" Karim protested.

"The posters have all been covered over and the wind has blown all the leaflets and flyers out of the city."

"But I'm not looking for anyone," he said, unwilling to mention his fear.

"You're not supposed to look for anyone. You're supposed to open your heart. Take a rocking chair in your heart, go around the city and pretty soon you'll find a woman sitting in it. Sophia has conquered every last corner of your heart and it will always stay that way. But you can't wait for her all your life."

"It's my fate and I accept it. You have to look at things reasonably. She's married and can't do as she pleases. I…"

"Reason, reason—a fig for your reason! You can comfort yourself with reason, you can use virtue to explain your cowardice, but neither will quiet your passion. Only love can heal love's wounds."

Karim remained silent for a long time. Munira kept refreshing his glass. Finally, he looked up. "And Sophia? What will she say?"

"Leave that to me," said Munira.

All that night he lay awake and only managed to fall into a light, fitful sleep at around dawn.

Sophia came just after lunch. Karim was in a bad mood and didn't say a word. Munira made coffee, and they sat in her big kitchen. Finally, Munira took a big gulp of coffee and said, "Sophia, forgive me if I tell you that you cannot save Karim this way. The police may not have caught him, but your care is holding him prisoner."

"That's not true," Sophia said and looked to Karim for help, but he avoided her gaze. "You'd rather preserve him in olive oil and lock up the jar," the old woman continued. "But Karim needs air. He has to get to know Damascus and seek his salvation there."

"But that's dangerous," Sophia protested. Yet, Munira would not be dissuaded. "No, no. He's always welcome here." She turned to Karim. "You're the perfect guest. No host could hope for more. You're helpful, charming, funny, but that's not the point. Here you are, living with an old lady and a lover who has a five-year-old son and a decent husband. I don't like Yusuf, but we have to be fair. You can bet your life that Sophia would rather die than leave the two of them. Haven't you already had a taste of her iron will?" she asked.

Karim cracked his fingers uneasily. Munira didn't wait for an answer.

"This woman here is so full of life, and she's managed to turn herself convincingly into a nun," she said and turned back to Sophia. "I respect your decision, but that doesn't give you the right to keep Karim a prisoner. He must leave the nest and spread his wings. Only then will he really be free. Only then can he love you without waiting for you."

Sophia was distraught and in a complete turmoil. Her Aunt Munira stroked her head, which she had laid on Karim's shoulder.

"You're right," she whispered in a scarcely audible voice.

That evening, Karim again lay awake for a long time. Just before he fell asleep, he decided he would go out the next morning and get to know the city. Until then, Damascus hadn't meant very much to him. Homs was his first love, the city of his birth on the banks of the Orontes River.

The next morning, wearing ordinary clothes and a red-and-white *keffiyeh* head scarf, he went out into the street, looking like the hundreds of farmers who streamed into Damascus each day. With every step he took, he became surer of himself. Who's going to recognize me, he thought in relief. Munira was right. None of the wanted posters put up by the police, offering a reward of three thousand lira for information leading to his arrest, were visible anymore. They had been pasted over with layers of advertisements, film posters, and notices for plays, sports events, and festivals.

He was certain that his walk would end as harmlessly as it had begun.

15

A Swallow in Exile

Rome, spring 2005

Enter a doppelganger

Salman's desire to return to Damascus had come and gone in waves, taking on clear contours before disappearing back into a sea of forgetfulness. One day in the spring of 2005, Hussein, a Lebanese employee of Oasi, called from the stall at the New Market. A man named Francesco Mascolo was insisting on meeting the boss of the import-export firm. This wasn't unusual, but Hussein's voice seemed overly excited.

Along with its two stalls in the New Market, Oasi's branches in Ancona and Milan sold Arab groceries and spices directly to the public. Together with his assistant, Chiara, Salman oversaw the wholesale operation from his office on Via Principe Amadeo, a short walk from the market. Oasi's list of long-term customers included over a hundred firms, restaurants, and specialty shops in Italy and the Emirates. Salman was now worth a small fortune.

"You won't believe your eyes, boss," said Hussein in Arabic, which the Italian stranger, listening along to the conversation, didn't understand. "He's the spitting image of you. You only find something like this in fairy tales. You've got to come and see."

"Tell him to wait for me in the Indian restaurant Mahavir. I'll be there in about fifteen minutes. I need to finish up something here."

The "something here" was a tricky situation demanding attention. A Chinese firm was offering Salman's Gulf customers Italian products at half price. That could only happen with the help of the Italian Mafia moving falsely labeled goods through customs. What was needed was a way to beat his competitor at his own game: corruption.

Salman had excellent connections in the region. He would bring in the brother of the ruler of Dubai through paid middlemen. They would start an embargo on all Chinese firms supplying Italian pasta. Salman would invest half a million dollars each year in this system—half his Gulf profits—to defeat the attack.

~

Meanwhile, Hussein was giving the stranger directions to get to the Indian restaurant where Salman often had lunch, and trying to calm the man down. "He'll be there in a minute. You can talk quietly at the restaurant." He turned to an old lady holding a small bag of lentils. "Want to pay for that, Signora?" He took the little bag from her hand and rang it up on the cash register. "Anything else with that?" he asked without looking at her.

The six employees running Oasi's two stands had their hands full at this hour. The Italian stranger left and disappeared into the surging crowd on the busy street. Hussein and the others running the stall laughed and shook their heads in disbelief. Except for their voices, Salman and Francesco were as alike as could be. The only difference was that the Italian's voice was high-pitched, like a eunuch's.

A crazy idea

Twenty minutes later, Salman arrived at the restaurant. Francesco stood up. Salman looked at him in shock. Both whispered *"Buon giorno"* and shook hands, slightly dazed.

Francesco divulged that he was an actor, then gazed down in embarrassment. He had some Lebanese friends who often shopped for Arab groceries at the market. They had told him that the stall owner, a Syrian named Salman, looked exactly like him, and while he wasn't quite speechless, he was genuinely surprised at how closely Salman actually resembled him. "Did your father ever travel in Italy?" he asked. "I don't think mine ever went to Syria."

Slowly recovering from his shock, Salman laughed at the thought. "No. My mother has been to Rome several times, but only since she turned sixty!"

They both laughed, and Salman invited the man for an espresso, and then to have lunch. The doppelganger, Francesco Mascolo, was quite poor. He lived in Trastevere, in a tiny apartment in a rundown development of six-story buildings with dark and dismal stairwells. Francesco never used his balcony because the tenants in the building opposite only used their rusty, rundown balconies as rubbish bins for their broken furniture and household appliances. The building was surrounded by a vandalized garden with sun-bleached grass and dead trees.

Like most Romans at the time, Salman and Francesco were soon talking about the changes that Berlusconi's government had visited upon Italians.

"Eighty percent of the rich in Italy live in dream villas in Rome," Francesco complained. "But just around the corner, it looks like slums in the poorest countries."

Salman agreed that in Rome, luxury and misery rub up against each other all the time and leave their marks. He saw the same gulf between rich and poor on his business trips through Asia. His best business partner, Vikram, lived in Kolkata. The owner of a large wholesale company for tea and spices, he lived in a villa with bodyguards and surveillance cameras. Misery lurked around the corner. The villa stuck out like a white island of wealth in a dark ocean. Salman noticed that in Rome, too, the super-rich were now increasingly ensconced behind walls, cameras, and gates.

Salman was well-off, but he wanted neither to live in a villa nor to leave his district. There was nowhere else in the world that resembled his Damascene home as much as the neighborhood where he lived. His roomy apartment was no more than several hundred steps from Francesco's miserable dwelling. Francesco told him about an old lady, his neighbor, who would knock at his door over and over, asking him to help her do something about the cockroaches, so intense was the disgust and fear that they provoked in her.

Salman made a quick call to the office and took the rest of the afternoon off. Then he ordered a bottle of red wine and kept chatting with Francesco, who hadn't landed an acting role in six months. His high voice sounded squashed, rough, almost incomprehensible at times. He often cleared his throat.

"Something happened to my voice three years ago. They call it hyperfunction. When I speak, I get a lump in my throat. The doctors can't do anything for me. And actors make their living with their voices," he confided regretfully.

They talked for hours, and Salman ended up inviting him for dinner at his favorite restaurant, the New Station, not far from where they both lived. The restaurant resembled a small train station, with signs hanging from the ceiling: Platform 1: Rome-Paris, Platform 2: Rome-Vienna, Platform 3: Rome-Madrid. That evening, the place was quiet and Francesco talked a lot about himself. It gradually emerged that they had friends and acquaintances in common.

Suddenly, Salman looked thoughtfully at his doppelganger. Perhaps the wine had made him bold and sentimental, perhaps missing his home city had suddenly become too much for him. He took another long sip. Then he told Francesco the daring idea that he had just had. What if Salman flew to Damascus using Francesco's Italian passport and a tourist visa, and secretly visited his parents and all his childhood haunts? Of course, Francesco would be generously rewarded.

The suggestion took Francesco by surprise. But he agreed almost at once. Salman hugged him and invited him to dinner at his house the following evening. "Then we can talk about details for a bit and get to know each other better. I'll have to play the part of you," Salman said, laughing. What he really wanted to know was whether the striking resemblance would convince his skeptical wife.

That day, Stella was to be back home a bit later. Paolo would be at a schoolmate's birthday party and would also be spending the night there. It couldn't be better. Salman slid the eggplant stuffed with onions, meat, tomatoes, and spices into the oven, set the table with the care of an experienced head waiter, enjoyed another glass of red wine with his guest, and waited for Stella to arrive.

Salman made sure that Francesco combed his hair the same way he did, and that he wore clothes similar to the ones he was wearing—a white shirt over jeans with a wine-red vest. Salman had five similar vests. He loved them because they had some elegance and left his arms free.

When she came into the dining room, the two men grinned at Stella from behind the table. Stella was startled, but quickly regained her composure. She laughed out loud. "Salman, am I drunk or do you have a twin?" Test passed.

~

Francesco was only a moderately successful actor but a good-natured and sensitive human being. After thinking about it more, the idea of Salman flying to Damascus under a false identity began to seem extremely risky, not only to him but to Stella. But he was determined to travel to his native city, no matter what. Stella warned him against this dangerous idea. "Your desire to go is making you underestimate the Syrian secret service," she said sternly. "It could cost you your life. It would be easy for the government to accuse you of spying for the Israelis."

It took days for Salman to change his mind, reluctantly, and with a heavy heart. But he gave Francesco a generous present for his goodwill, taking over the rent on his apartment for a year. Even Francesco seemed relieved that his double had given up his reckless scheme. And Salman soon forgot about it, but not his desire to return.

An insistent nightmare

Sometimes dreamers get lucky. Their dream tells them something about people they've met, desires they've felt, stories they've gotten caught up in. It may happen only rarely, but Salman had such a dream.

In it, he met Francesco at the Caffè Arabo. His look-alike had brought his passport with him. Salman was touched. On parting, Francesco hugged him. "Look after yourself," he whispered—in Arabic, surprisingly enough.

Salman then traveled with his doppelganger's passport and a tourist visa to Syria. Stella and Paolo came with him. It was during the two most beautiful months in Damascus, September and October, when you can sit out in garden cafés until midnight and sleep in milder temperatures than in August, which Damascenes refer to as the "taste of Hell." They decided to travel by sea via an Italian Grimaldi Lines ship departing from Civitavecchia, some seventy kilometers north of Rome, to the Syrian port of

Latakia. The captain was Greek. Amused, Stella observed how the captain flirted with her. Paolo was bored. He was the only young person among the other passengers, all of whom—except for his mom and dad—wore Hawaiian shirts and oversized sunglasses.

"Why didn't we fly?" Paolo whined. "We could have been done with this whole thing in three hours."

"I'm a creature of earth and water," Salman replied. But Paolo had already disappeared. Suddenly, there he was, waving to his parents from the bridge of the ship. He had befriended the captain, who was patiently explaining to him everything about ships and sailing, in a futile attempt to get into the good graces of the kid's beautiful mother. Salman and Stella saw through this stratagem and smiled at each other. The captain had shown up at just the right time to drive away Paolo's boredom.

After a lovely journey of several days, they arrived in the Syrian port. Strangely enough, when the ship entered the port, owls flew around it, not seagulls. A customs official looked directly at Salman and asked him if he had any thoughts or goods to declare. Salman said that he didn't, without really understanding the question.

A policeman consulted his computer and shook his head. "If your name's Francesco Mascolo, how come your Arabic's so good?" he inquired confidently, as if he'd finally stumbled on something suspicious.

"Because my grandparents and parents were Syrian. I'm third-generation and I went to an Arab school."

"Oh?" said the official, somewhat surprised. "An Arab school in Rome?"

"Yes, it's financed by the Saudis. That's why my son won't go there. He hates the Saudis," Salman added, playing up the bad relations between the Alawite regime in Damascus and the conservative Sunni regime in Saudi Arabia.

"Good boy," said the official. He was, Salman could see, a successful mixture of ignorance, arrogance, and self-confidence. He handed Salman the three passports, without checking Stella's or Paolo's.

They left the harbor building, and Salman looked around to see if they were being followed. But Stella never turned around. She only ever pressed forward. To his surprise, there weren't the usual taxis at the harbor entrance, but instead two horses. A friendly man handed the reins to Salman, gratefully accepted his tip, and disappeared, smiling shyly. Stella was unsure of herself and asked Paolo to mount behind his father. And so they rode south, side by side, with Paolo hanging on tightly to his father and whooping for joy.

Finally, they reached Damascus. They stood there, at the front door to his house on Misk Street. Salman rang the bell. His mother opened the door and called out happily, "Your suitcases arrived three days ago! Where have you been all this time?" She kissed him and Paolo, and ignored Stella. "Come, light of my heart," she said to Paolo, guiding him into the house with her. The boy looked back at his mother, in embarrassment. She was left standing alone in the street, in front of the house. Salman motioned to her to come in and could hear her whisper, "Old witch."

Salman ran joyfully through the old Christian Quarter, still without Stella, sometimes with Paolo, or on his own. Finally, he was able to keep his promise to Paolo and play marbles with him in the street. They hadn't been there ten minutes before a group of local children were playing with them. Salman slipped away quietly.

Paolo was able to make himself understood by the children on his own, using Italian, English, and "handish," as he called the language of gestures he had invented. The children could follow him and even taught him a few bits of Arabic. Salman leaned against a wall. And when he heard a Syrian boy call out, *"Tocca a me*—it's my turn," he knew that Paolo had been accepted.

In the evening, they were sitting around the dinner table. Suddenly, Salman heard sirens, and Stella ran out of the house with Paolo, her face pale. "I have to get to safety with Paolo. Your mother wants to have me arrested," she called out to Salman.

It was true. Salman heard his mother yelling in the house, "Arrest the Italian woman. She wants to kidnap our grandson and make him an Italian!"

He ran out of the house. There was no trace of Stella or Paolo. He stayed out in the street in the dark. The sirens faded away. Morning finally came and he was sitting on the doorstep murmuring, "Stella, don't leave me alone." An old man appeared. He was pasting posters on the wall. Salman stood up and approached him. "What are you pasting up?" he asked.

"No idea. It's mostly ads for shirts or aftershave. But I can't read. They pay me a lira per poster. Two hundred posters earn me enough for one meal a day." Salman looked up. A photo of himself was staring out at him from the poster. Beautiful photo, he thought. He looked like Marcello Mastroianni in it. And under his picture, in big letters, was the word WANTED. Somehow, Salman wasn't surprised.

He walked slowly down the street to the nearby Eastern Gate to catch a taxi to the airport. But at the gate he encountered a cruel surprise. It had been covered over with bricks. A smooth, solid wall also sealed off the Old City at Thomas Gate—Bab Tuma.

"You need to be able to recite by heart the names of all the gates of Damascus before the city will let you go," his mother called, standing on the doorstep of her house, drying her hands on her apron. Just as in life, Salman could only name four. He woke up with a start, bathed in sweat. Stella was still asleep next to him. He needed a moment before he knew where he was.

~

In the morning, when Salman told Stella about his dream over their morning espresso together, she could see her fears confirmed. "Forget the trip. Just stay here," she begged him. "Dreams are messages. In this one all I can hear are warnings."

He did not reply.

Lately, they'd been arguing almost every day about this trip. She accused him of toying with her happiness and breaking his promise never to leave her on her own. He was hurt and replied that *she* was the one leaving him in the lurch. Instead of coming with him and bringing Paolo, she was letting him crawl back alone, like a beaten dog, to the country of his childhood, after so many years of being away. He'd have to explain to everybody why his wife and son hadn't come with him. People would think his wife was too much of a snob to visit his parents. How often had he helped *her* parents and tried to satisfy all *their* wishes? And all that for one reason—because he loved her, he loved his Stella… How often had he entertained her professors, friends, and colleagues like royalty, just to please her. Now she begrudged him her support and couldn't even bring herself to encourage him.

He kept on ranting and raving for a long time. Stella left him to it and went into the kitchen. Then suddenly he was quiet. When she came back he was in the bedroom, sitting on the edge of the bed, crying bitterly. Stella sat down next to him and started crying, too. This wasn't a married couple or a pair of lovers. It was two children, weeping over their wretched fate—Salman because he felt abandoned, and Stella because she was afraid of being abandoned.

Finally, she stood up and kissed his eyes. "Stay here," she pleaded.

But he was determined to go.

Out of pride, Stella couldn't admit to Salman that she feared for his life. She had a premonition that he'd be killed on this trip. And she didn't have the courage to tell him.

~

Salman washed his face. Then he switched on his laptop in his study and looked up the names of the seven gates of Damascus.

16

Longing for Childhood Hideouts

Stella didn't want to go on a vacation that summer. Instead, she wanted to stay in Rome with Salman, because she was afraid he would do something rash. Also, Paolo had gone to a summer camp in Grado with his school class. She noticed how Rome's summers were changing. There were more poor people, as well as the usual tourists. Many domestic workers—mostly Filipinos—came out for brief strolls, while their high and mighty masters were away, either in the mountains or at the beach.

One day Stella invited her friend Luca Azzari to the Caffè Greco to chat. She had known Luca and his wife, Gina, since elementary school in Trieste. They both had lived a few houses away from Stella on Via Commerciale. By fifth grade, Luca and Gina had already fallen in love with an intensity that was at first laughed at by staff and pupils alike, and then viewed with concern. Even their own parents tried to break them up. It was all in vain. Now, forty years later, their love was still going strong. Gina was a well-known painter, Luca a counselor.

At one point, Luca and Gina had left Rome for New York. Luca found a good job at a hospital, working with children in the trauma unit. The work was satisfying, and he and Gina lived in a beautiful little love nest of an apartment. But Luca couldn't stop feeling a burning desire for their home city of Trieste.

Stella joked with him over the phone. "I really need

your advice and I'll pay in food and drink—all you can eat," she said laughing. "I wouldn't do that if I were you," Luca replied. "I haven't eaten for days."

Like Salman, Stella, too, liked the elegant Caffè Greco. Giuliano, the lively old head waiter, thought highly of them both, because they had always been so generous and respectful toward him for so many years. He reserved a small table in a quiet corner for Stella and Luca. Giuliano led them to their table. Luca just ordered a red wine. As Stella confided to him her worries about Salman's travel plans, he listened quietly.

Luca felt that Stella needed to try to understand Salman. "Yearning for the places of our childhood is so deeply rooted in us, as if we were a salmon or a swallow," he said. "It can be so powerful that someone living in beautiful circumstances might wish to be back in the squalor of their childhood. You can't change it by criticism or preaching. The only thing that helps is actually visiting those places. But when we do, what do we find? Our imagination can create illusions. The only cure is the shock of reality. Otherwise, we could end up searching for, mourning, our childhood forever."

"But how could Salman suddenly feel this way after so many years?" Stella wondered. "In all this time in Rome—and before that, in Germany—he never talked much about missing Damascus, where a death sentence is probably waiting for him."

"Maybe he didn't tell you because he would rather avoid a conflict. That's how I know him. He loves you and wants to live with you in peace. He's kept this part of himself to himself. That's legitimate. People who've been forced to leave their country learn to protect themselves from dangerous questions that are too critical. They avoid them and live like animal tamers who keep their wild beasts at bay to keep from getting eaten by them. Those who don't could end up committing suicide.

"Your Salman's love of Damascus causes him a lot of heartache. A year ago, he happened to tell me that he'd had a dream, time and again, that Damascus was destroyed in a war. But Damascus is the most peaceful place in the Middle East. And as we get older, our longing for our childhood keeps getting stronger and stronger. Life is a circle, and in old age we come back to our beginnings."

"But why does this make me feel so angry with him?"

"Does it make you feel that your love is not fulfilling him, may not be enough for him? Yearning for childhood places has nothing to do with loving another human being. We can be attached to places and not able to stand the people who live there. Attachment can overcome us, Stella. It could happen to anyone."

"Yes, but honestly, I don't miss Trieste at all."

"Maybe not now, because you call your parents every week and visit them every month. But someday, when you haven't been in Trieste for a long time, you may look back and feel differently."

Stella sat still. Softly she said, "Sometimes words force their way out of me from deep inside. As soon as I open my mouth, they burst out like a storm and destroy everything in their way. I end up feeling ashamed, because I've added to Salman's burden instead of sharing it."

"Stella, just hold out a loving hand. Let him go look for his childhood paradise," Luca insisted. "He'll be surprised and wonder if he went to the wrong address."

~

Stella returned home relieved and was tender toward

149

Salman that night. She felt a love and empathy for him that seemed boundless, as if for someone who was sick—homesick with longing.

But Luca had nearly foretold the future that evening.

Paolo and his father's childhood

That September, Salman's nightmare recurred three more times. Each time, he was unable to recall the names of all the city gates of Damascus, although he kept trying to memorize them. Why was his memory rejecting these names? The beginning of his dream kept changing, but the ending—imprisonment in Damascus—stayed the same. The third time he dreamt it, Salman was already on his way to the next gate, Bab Tuma, knowing that a wall was waiting for him and that he would then hear his mother's voice and wake up.

He had experienced a dream like this when he was around twelve. The same dream, over and over, for years. In it, he'd been paralyzed in an accident. A young nun was pushing his wheelchair through an unfamiliar ground-floor apartment. Suddenly the nun laughed. "Nobody can see us," she called out and then she bent toward him and gave him a long kiss on the lips. Then she straightened up and pushed the wheelchair down a long corridor, faster and faster. Salman's heart was beating in his throat. The wheelchair shot along the corridor so fast that the pictures on the walls turned into a brightly colored blur. Abruptly the sound of the nun's footfalls stopped, and a stairwell opened up at the end of the corridor. When he turned around, the nun was gone, and he was falling, falling in the dark. He woke up.

In the months that followed, he came to know what would happen in his dream after the nun kissed him, but he couldn't do anything to prevent it.

Salman wondered if Paolo's presence in his dream was bringing out what he had always tried to keep private. Out of consideration for Stella and for Paolo—who now had his own friends and life—he didn't want to keep telling them about his desire to someday walk through the streets of Damascus with his son and show him the school he'd attended, his parents' beautiful home, the *hammam*, all the places Paolo couldn't get enough of whenever his father would tell him stories.

In fact, Paolo had never once expressed the least interest in seeing the places of his father's childhood. When asked, he would shrug his shoulders, or say defiantly, "I think Rome's better, and I'd rather to go to the beach in summer."

Salman's mother, Sophia, yearned to see her grandson in Damascus. But neither Stella nor Salman would send him there. Also, Paolo didn't want to fly to Damascus by himself. And while Salman could fly anywhere in the world on his German passport, as a Syrian citizen he would be arrested immediately in Damascus, and Stella never wanted to travel to a country that persecuted her husband.

Still, there was one decisive reason why Salman wanted to return there, even if just once, and which he told no one. It was the humiliation he'd suffered at being driven out of Damascus. That wound would not heal, no matter what success he might achieve elsewhere. Whenever he met guests or friends coming from or traveling to Damascus, the scab would break open and the wound would begin to bleed again.

Salman wanted to stand up to those who had expelled him and say, "You can never take Damascus from me." The casualties of expulsion are wounded souls, and thoughts of home only reopen and burn into them, like salt. Over his years of exile, he had never given up hoping to overcome his violent uprooting.

Salman realized he would never trade Rome for any other city. He had lived in Rome longer than in Damascus. It was Rome that offered him everything. All the same, he'd decided now to fly back to Damascus, despite all the warnings. His need to stand again in the city of his birth, with his head up, drove him. He had transferred powers of attorney to Stella so she could withdraw money for ransom, if necessary. In Syria, every prisoner had his price.

At his final meeting with the Syrian ambassador in preparing to leave, Salman surprised himself by confiding in him that Stella was afraid for his safety. The ambassador laughed curtly. "Women are emotional. My wife is always afraid for me. You're rational. That's what I like about you."

Salman would curse his rationality, and even his desire to heal the wounds of his exile, for endless days to come.

17

A Rocking Chair in the Heart

Damascus, 1951–1952

Karim wandered the streets and alleys of the city, one district after another. When he stopped, he found himself in the Christian Quarter of Bab Tuma, far from his hideout at Munira's. Not a single wanted poster with his picture could be seen.

He went into a small café near the historical gate, sat down, ordered a mocha and watched the passersby. People strolled along the street, shopping. Old men at neighboring tables argued and cracked jokes about the different governments that had followed each other in Damascus in recent years. Karim envied them. He yearned for inner peace, felt harried and alone. Finally, he paid and stood up to explore this district he'd heard so much about. He went wherever his curiosity led him, and by midday, he felt hungry. A queue had formed in front of a falafel stand. Nearby there were two other places also offering falafel, hummus, and other fast food, but they had hardly any customers.

Some ten men and two women, the older one in a headscarf and the younger one in European clothing, were waiting patiently, which was not a virtue of your average Damascene. Karim glanced at the stallholder. He was small, hard-featured, and in a bad mood.

"And he's mean, too," said the last man in the queue. "But his falafel is the world's best. With the first bite I forget how long I had to wait, with the second I forget his bad mood, and with the third I forget my mother-in-law." The man had red hair and a light, handsome face that made him look like a brash schoolboy when he laughed. The young woman turned around and laughed in agreement. She was standing self-confidently in the men's queue. When Karim finally got his falafel sandwich, he looked around. Several people were standing in small groups on the square in front of the stall, enjoying their falafel and the fine weather. The woman was standing alone. She smiled at him. Karim went up to her and said hello. They chatted about the food, what a good idea snack stalls were, and the city. And they introduced themselves to each other. Her name was Amira.

"From the way you talk, you're no farmer," she said suddenly and looked at him in amusement. Her smile melted into the bright sky above her.

"No, I'm not," he sighed, feeling as though he'd been found out. "It's hard to hide the way you talk."

"Why hide? But no, I shouldn't have asked."

"Not at all, but the answer is a long story." And one that Karim didn't wish to talk about just then. "Perhaps I'll tell you one day. Do you live around here?" he asked, feeling that the young woman with her bright eyes had just opened the door to his heart a tiny crack. He was right in the middle of the Christian Quarter and was wary of falling hopelessly in love with yet another Christian woman.

"No, no, I've just been to visit my grandmother to help out. She insists on holding my little brother Hamid's circumcision party this evening. I've set and decorated the banquet table and set up about a thousand bouquets," she laughed. Karim suspected that her laughter was washing away a sharper comment.

He loosened the red-and-white *keffiyeh* headdress he had wrapped around his head and put it loosely over his shoulders like a scarf.

"You look much better like that, almost like someone from the city," Amira said. It was Karim's turn to laugh. Amira looked at her watch, "I have to get to the hospital."

"You're not sick, I hope?" Karim asked.

"No, no, I'm doing an internship there, every day except Fridays and Sundays. It starts at two o'clock. The French hospital has a good reputation."

"Are you a doctor?"

"Not yet. I'm a medical student, but I've only got another year to go. Then I'll work on the children's ward for three years, and afterward, maybe I can to go to Paris for an internship."

"Interesting," said Karim. "And may I accompany such a talented medical student to the hospital?"

"Yes, if I may learn what it is you do, apart from disguising yourself so badly as a farmer."

"I'm a teacher," Karim replied. "Elementary school."

Karim accompanied Amira to the hospital, and when they reached the entrance, she extended her hand to him. "Today is going to be tiring. When I've finished here, I'll take a carriage straight home, change, and head back to Jasmine Street to my grandmother's where we'll be celebrating until midnight."

"And what will you be doing tomorrow?" asked Karim, not letting go of her hand as if it were a float meant to rescue him from the ocean of his loneliness.

"Tomorrow I have no more lectures from ten o'clock on. I only have to be back here at two."

"Shall I pick you up from school?" he asked, not having the slightest idea where the university was.

"No, better not. It's a long story. Let's meet up at eleven at the falafel stall and look for a café from there. You can tell me your long story, and I'll tell you mine. Then we'll see which one is more boring." Karim pressed her hand one last time. She went through the entrance and, before she opened the inner glass doors, she turned around one last time and waved to him. Then she disappeared into the interior of the building.

For a while Karim stood there, rooted to the spot. A total stranger, yet he already felt such closeness and unbridled joy that she had allowed him to accompany her. He turned and went off walking, for hours. Late that afternoon, when he arrived at Aunt Munira's house, Sophia had already gone home after dropping in briefly. Her husband had invited the bishop for the evening. She and three assistants had to prepare the feast.

Karim was so excited he could hardly eat anything. Munira glanced at him and smiled. The next morning he was up at six. He drank a coffee and waited impatiently for Munira to wake up. She took her own sweet time with everything.

"In a bit of a hurry today?" she asked.

"Yes... I mean no. I'm meeting someone in the Old City."

"Fine, take your time and finish your coffee with me, and I'll give you money for a horse-drawn carriage. Then you'll be there in a quarter of an hour."

Karim smiled in embarrassment. He had more than enough money from Sophia, but he loved the walk through the city and the fresh air. By the time Amira arrived at five to eleven at the bus stop opposite the falafel stand and waved to him, he had been there for fifteen minutes. He'd already heard the life story of the stallholder, Abu Yassin, and learned why he was always in such a bad mood. Nevertheless Abu Yassin now managed a tired smile for Karim and Amira. They enjoyed their falafel, then went for a stroll in a nearby park. Amira spent the whole day with Karim until evening. When they parted, he kissed her. He walked her as far as the bus stop. She wanted to go home alone, although her parents also lived in Salihiya, only three streets away from Munira's house.

Night closed in over the city, scattering darkness in every corner, but hope began to grow in Karim's heart.

Amira came from a rich Muslim family. Her father was a respected industrialist who had sent his three sons and two daughters to the university. Amira's sister, Hala, was studying pharmacy. Amira was the same age as Karim, but despite a very liberal upbringing, she had never had a relationship with a man. Her father rejected veils and headscarves alike. His wife and daughters dressed fashionably.

Although Amira was petite and her face had a softness to it, there was something quite manly in the way she behaved. Later, when Karim got to know her sister Hala, he thought that their father had brought his daughters up the way he had so that they could survive in a conservative male society. Although she was attractive, intelligent, and well-to-do, Hala was to stay single all her life and run the largest pharmacy in the city successfully on her own.

Amira was also very pretty. One of her teachers, a famous surgeon, wanted to marry her. He spoke to her father, but was told that Amira was an adult and should decide for herself. Amira found the professor boring, and besides he smelled strange. When she politely turned him down, he was very angry. From that time on, he became jealous. Up until then, Amira had always happily joked with her colleagues, but now she tried not to provoke him. That was also why she didn't want Karim to meet her at the university. She still had one examination to pass. "And afterward he can be as angry as he likes," she confided to Karim. She was strong, almost too strong for a woman in an Arab society. Damascus, however, was buzzing with optimism, so colorful personalities like hers could lead relatively undisturbed lives. Later, Amira often joked with Karim that his love had successfully melted through her protective layer of ice—now she not only dared to appear feminine but even enjoyed it. "It was only through your eyes that I came to see the beauty in me," she said. Karim told her all about himself, including about Sophia, despite the fact that he was worried that Amira might be jealous. She wasn't, but she did ask him to promise never to cheat on her, and Karim agreed. That, for him, was the natural thing to do.

Sophia was happy for him, and Munira even more so, when he told them both a few days later that he'd met and fallen in love with Amira.

Shortly afterward, Karim's brother Ismail arrived in Damascus and looked up Sophia. She had given him her address herself and took him to Munira's.

Ismail described how he had at first refused to appear as a witness because he didn't want to end up in Iraq. In the meantime, a friend had secured him a visa for the United States and passage on a ship. So he was now prepared to testify and provide proof that Karim was innocent. He would need police protection. Once the murderer had been sentenced, he would emigrate.

Karim felt ashamed he'd suspected that out of cowardice, his brother hadn't wanted to testify. He asked Ismail for forgiveness and wept with him when he heard just how much his brother had suffered at their sister's murder.

Sophia also accompanied Ismail to police headquarters. The evidence was overwhelming. Ismail named the murderer, a cousin, and showed handwriting samples that were compared with the incriminating letter that Karim was supposed to have left at the scene of the crime. When a police patrol car picked the man up, he called out to neighbors that he was glad to go to prison because he had saved the family's honor. During the interrogation, he boasted of what he had done and recounted details that convinced both the police and the judge that he had indeed committed the crime.

Karim was now completely free of any suspicion. During the long months in hiding, he had almost completely severed all ties with his clan, who had given him up for dead. Karim had totally seen through the clan system. The whole thing was based on members blindly following their chief—in this case his father—oblivious to the fact that he was leading them to ruin with a pack of lies. Everyone had known that Karim wasn't the murderer. In spite of this, they had allowed their innocent brother and son to be hounded and hunted, not because they hated him, but because his refusal had jeopardized the clan system.

"No, I don't want to see them. Relatives like them don't deserve the time of day," he told Amira, when she tried to put in a good word for Karim's mother. "The only person to stand by me, Ismail, now has to leave his home and live abroad, otherwise he would pay for his honesty with his life." Karim's brother Ismail emigrated to America and became a successful baker.

The courts still handed down very mild sentences for honor killings and the murderer was sentenced to three years in prison. But the police chief was contemptuous of both the court and sentence. The prison governor reported directly to him, and the police chief gave him strict instructions to put two thugs in the same cell as the murderer. Day after day, the two would beat and humiliate him.

Compared to what he suffered, death would have been a merciful gift. The thugs were not to kill him. They even stopped him from committing suicide on two occasions. "He is to suffer—right up to the last day of his sentence," the police chief had reportedly ordered. That was his personal revenge. A day before his release, the prisoner was shot by a warder. Apparently, he had tried to get hold of his weapon.

~

Karim and Amira soon got engaged. Amira's parents accepted the fact that Karim did not invite his own family to either his engagement or to his wedding. In his speech to the guests, Amira's father said, "Our country needs such courageous men as Karim who renounce primitive revenge. Bedouin vengeance belongs in the past. Long live the free citizen! It is my honor to welcome Karim into our family as a son, not just as a son-in-law."

Amira graduated and started work on the children's ward in the French hospital near Bab Tuma. Karim found a job as an elementary school teacher in a Christian school. He continued to study Arabic literature and history so that after four years he could become a high-school teacher.

In a small apartment near the hospital, Amira and Karim lived together in harmony, enjoying both their love and their work.

Once a week Amira would visit her grandmother, and cook and eat with her. On these days Karim would visit Munira. Sometimes Sophia was there, as well. She seemed relaxed and wished him a happy life, but she didn't want to meet his wife. Once when Amira came with Karim to visit Munira, Sophia refused to come, to everybody's disappointment.

One day Karim was preparing a fish recipe for Munira.

He had turned on the radio and was singing along a song by his favorite singer Abdulwahab. Suddenly Munira and Sophia were standing behind him. They laughed at his surprise. They sat down happily together at the table and enjoyed the meal. When Munira briefly went into the bedroom to fetch her tablets, Sophia told him that her husband was away for three days, that she desired him and they could spend an enjoyable hour together at her place. Karim froze. "I can't," he said quietly, just as Munira came back into the room. Sophia didn't reply, but when he stood up to say goodbye to Munira, she quickly followed him outside.

"Why not?" she asked, clinging to his arm. He saw the disappointment in her eyes. Wishing to avoid a scene on the busy street, he turned around and went into a quiet alley.

"Because I love Amira," he said softly.

"What about me? Don't you love me anymore?"

"Of course. But it's different. You're my dearest friend. I'll never forget our beautiful time together and will always be grateful to you. You saved my life. But I want to stay faithful to Amira."

"What harm will it do her if you make love to me? She'll never know. I need you. I'm dying with desire and I can't stand this cold husband of mine any longer. You're talking to me about being faithful? Did you suddenly become a saint?"

"No, I have my faults. We can talk for as long as you like, even about your life with your husband, but I'm not going to touch you. It would be an injury, not just to Amira, but to my self-respect. I promised her…"

"You won't touch me? I'm a leper now?" Sophia retorted furiously.

"Please, calm down. You're just as beautiful as ever,

but I can't, and not just because of Amira…"

"Amira, Amira," she broke in, "And me? What about me? Don't my feelings for you count anymore?" she shouted and started to cry. Karim was ashamed to see this proud woman crying. "If I have to kiss your hand, that's what I'll do," she said, finally, and before he could do anything, she grabbed his hand, kissed it and bathed it with her tears.

Karim recoiled and pulled his hand from her grasp more roughly than he had intended. Sophia stumbled. She managed to regain her balance and gave him a hard slap.

"That's for your cowardice… for your ingratitude…" she shouted and ran away.

He stood there in turmoil. He didn't understand what had happened, but he felt that he had lost Sophia forever.

Amira's grandmother died five months after the wedding. In her will, she left her house on Jasmine Street to Amira and Karim. Amira mourned her beloved grandmother for a long time. They moved into the large house with its inner courtyard where lemon trees, jasmine, and roses flourished. This made Karim indescribably happy, and his happiness was crowned with the birth of his daughter, Maha. She came into the world exactly one year after his first meeting with Amira at the falafel stand.

18

A Hurdler's Fears

Rome and Damascus, December 2010

Elias the chameleon

Salman hadn't anticipated that preparations would take so long. He wanted to fly to Damascus in autumn, the most beautiful time of the year in Syria. But a warning delayed his departure. The Syrian ambassador in Rome, with whom he was now on friendly terms, had assured him that there were no charges against him in Damascus. But then a strange call came from Salman's mother, asking him to wait a little while longer until a good friend had checked everything, because there was still a problem. Since she was afraid that her telephone was being tapped, she mentioned to Salman a visit to her girlfriend Asmahan in Beirut. He understood. His mother made the tiring hundred-kilometer journey just to explain the whole thing to him clearly, without fear.

Salman remained on cordial terms with the ambassador, although he'd been as naïve as a twelve-year-old to give credence to the man's bureaucratic boasting, and was tempted to tell him so. As a diplomat, the ambassador was used to pretending that he had more power than he did. When Salman told his mother of the ambassador's assurance, she came right out and said the man was full of hot air.

"If they bother you at the airport in any way, just give me a call and I'll deal with them," had been the ambassador's spirited instructions. He was completely serious, and actually believed it. Salman could just imagine telling one of the gorillas arresting him at the airport, "Stop. Just a minute! I want to call the Syrian ambassador in Rome— he'll deal with you!" They would have laughed themselves sick.

Two days later his mother, now in Beirut, called again. She told him about a visit from his cousin Elias, who had become a high-ranking officer in the secret service. Elias had discovered that two of the fifteen secret service agencies—all in competition with each other—still had Salman on their wanted list. It was urgent that this be cleared up before his trip.

"Salman, my heart, I don't want you to be arrested," his mother said. "That would be the death of me. Let's wait until Elias has fixed everything. Your father has asked him personally to do this, and he knows he has to hurry since you are already sitting on your suitcase."

~

As a teenager, Salman had liked his cousin very much. He was three years older than Elias and had always been a head taller. Elias was small and athletic. He had an open, light, and inconspicuous face. He had been daring and overconfident as a child, provoking older and stronger children or even teenagers, and getting into fights. The girls didn't like him because he used to laugh at their little blemishes. To make things worse, he was stingy and didn't buy them things to win their affection. Salman became his cousin's guardian angel and was on his side whenever he was in trouble. Together they joined a revolutionary rebel group, trained in South Lebanon, and fought in northern Syria, west of Aleppo.

Elias seemed to have finally found his true calling. He was intelligent, cold-blooded and keen, and immune to any luxury-induced softening. His comrades feared and respected him, but he wasn't liked. Hani, then a close friend, said they regarded him as dishonest, never saying what he meant or meaning what he said. He was also particularly aggressive toward female fighters. He couldn't stand women with weapons and would make fun of them, making even more enemies. One of them, Samia, once said, "Elias is the only Christian Islamist!"

But Elias was dead set on revolution, and he distinguished himself through reckless bravery that brought him some recognition. Still, reservations about him persisted, although Salman put the others' mistrust down to misunderstanding and envy and continued to defend his cousin.

"Our judgment is often influenced by our first impressions. Che Guevara would never have become so famous if he had been bald, with a bulbous nose and big ears," Salman argued to rebel leaders one stormy night. He was furious at them for suspecting Elias of maintaining secret contacts with shady characters—informers—in the region. Meanwhile, Elias was lying sick in the hospital tent. He was running a high temperature, and Salman suspected that he had malaria. "You should take care of him so that he regains his strength. I'll check out his contacts."

After two weeks, Elias was able to leave the hospital, but he had gotten wind of the suspicions. He cursed the leaders and he wouldn't even speak openly with Salman. He reacted angrily when Salman asked him privately about three men from a nearby city with whom he was in contact. The first one was a pimp, the other two well-known thugs and informers in the city. From that time on, Elias avoided Salman.

Two weeks after Elias recovered, his group was lured into an ambush. Three of its best fighters were shot. Elias disappeared. Leaders were now certain that Elias had steered them into the ambush, where a special squad from the secret service was waiting for them. His disappearance seemed to confirm those suspicions. At the same time, other rumors and legends grew. Elias was not a traitor but had fought bravely, been wounded, arrested, and died under torture, or he had been invited to Havana. Salman wasn't sure what to make of all this, but he no longer completely trusted his cousin.

In a call to Salman in Heidelberg, Aunt Amalia related what she had read in a left-wing Syrian newspaper in Beirut. Elias had been a traitor from the start. He had infiltrated the resistance to spy on its leadership and, if possible, turn them over to the secret service. Believing the story to be true, Amalia cursed the coward.

Shortly after his escape, Elias joined the police academy. Three years later, he was sent with a small group of young police officers, first to Moscow and then to Prague, to complete a basic course in secret service methods and techniques. When he returned to Damascus, relatives and friends knew that he was working for the secret service, but no one knew exactly what he did.

Whenever Sophia visited her son in Heidelberg or Rome, she always told him news about all their relatives, and Salman enjoyed their morning gossip over coffee. That was how he found out about his cousin's advancement through the secret service ranks, for which Salman despised him. But he enjoyed his mother's stories about Elias' wife, Isabella. She was a head taller and fifteen years younger than Elias, and very feminine. Salman's mother enjoyed exaggerating Isabella's curves as she mimicked them with her hands.

Salman had initially thought that Elias would support

him and erase his record at the secret service because of their shared past. Then his mother had told him, "Your father has promised him ten thousand dollars, and for that amount Elias would even convert to Islam!"

The delay drove Salman crazy. September and October, his favorite months, inched by and he was plagued by new nightmares. Stella was puzzled to see his previously speedy travel preparations grind to a halt. Whenever she asked him, Salman's answer fell into a monotonous, nearly irritated tone: "As soon as everything is one hundred percent sure, I'll get a signal, and the next day I'll be on a flight."

Salman suspected that Elias was taking his time on purpose. It seemed as though he wanted to show his uncle, Salman's father, what a big job it was, perhaps to get even more money. Salman had heard that one of the president's cousins had extorted two hundred thousand dollars from a rich family for releasing their only son, a talented musician. There were price lists for buying the freedom of those who were wanted or held prisoner. Poor people were obviously not on those lists, and they had to go on suffering in the cellars and camps of the secret service.

Then came the scandal reported first by the Italian press, then by media worldwide. The Syrian ambassador in Rome was dismissed at the beginning of November. He had refused to take the blame in a case of money laundering, for which the president's corrupt cousin was responsible. After saying goodbye to his few friends, including Salman, he disappeared in fear for his life. Salman was astonished. Could it be that a diplomat of the regime, who had been checked a hundred times by the secret service, who'd had to bow and scrape to them for so many years, had finally shown some backbone and put up resistance against the constant money laundering and corruption?

Throughout November, Salman felt paralyzed. As agreed, he would ask his mother once a month about Asmahan's health. As long as there remained a problem, Asmahan stayed sick. If they received a positive report from Elias, her health would immediately improve, and as soon as all problems had been resolved, all would rejoice at Asmahan's happy recovery. From then on, his mother would be able to speak openly with him.

Finally, on November 25, his mother told him that Asmahan was feeling miraculously better. The following day, Salman booked an Alitalia flight to Damascus for the beginning of December. He went to visit his in-laws in Trieste to say goodbye to them. On the way, he prepared himself mentally for a difficult discussion. He expected criticism from his father-in-law and tears from his mother-in-law.

Stella's parents had moved and now lived in a splendid house on the Strada del Friuli. It was actually a villa, but his father-in-law didn't like to call it that. He was an old-school banker, gifted with much common sense and even greater discretion.

To his great surprise, Salman's decision met with the approval of his in-laws. Not only did they understand the reason for his journey to the places of his childhood, they also gave him fine, expensive gifts to bring his parents. Salman was speechless.

The flight to childhood places

Stella hugged him as they stood outside the airport. "There are hundreds of thousands of Italian men. Why did I have to fall in love with a Syrian?" she said, laughing through her tears. Salman took her face tenderly in his hands and kissed her tearful eyes.

"Because you know that no Italian would ever love you as much as I do."

"That's true, and that's why I also…"—she gulped down the words "fear for you." She shook her head. "How silly of me. Instead of sending you off with a laugh, here's me in tears."

Salman kissed her on the lips once more. "It's only a visit, and next summer we'll all fly to Damascus so I can play marbles with Paolo in my street, just as I promised him." He turned to his son. "And you, look after Mama until I'm back, okay?" he said, brushing him lightly on the cheek.

"Yes, boss, will do. Already got the shotgun under the bed," Paolo said, laughing and high-fiving his dad. They embraced and Salman took in the scent of his son. He tore himself away and started to walk off. Then he turned around again briefly, and waved.

December definitely lived up to its reputation, with the temperature two degrees above zero and a raw, blustery wind. The sky was full of heavy clouds, but it was still dry. Stella walked slowly back to the parking lot, her head still in a whirl. Paolo, however, led her straight to the car. She hugged him. "Am I happy that you're here with me," she said.

As they were leaving the airport parking lot, it started to rain.

Salman went into the departure lounge. He was much too early, but he hated goodbyes and didn't want to make his separation from his family more difficult by prolonging it.

Check-in went quickly. Salman felt relieved to see his big suitcase roll onto the conveyor belt. He took his boarding pass and his baggage receipt from the attendant at the

Alitalia counter, who wished him a pleasant flight.

International airports are all alike, he thought. If the departures board hadn't said *Partenze*, Salman could have believed he was in Frankfurt or London.

He still had an hour to wait. The departure lounge was slowly filling up. An old man nearby was laughing at his wife's worrying. "If we crash, it'll all be over fast. We'll be dead before you know it." A scrawny man called out to his corpulent friend who was sitting a few rows farther away, "I think passengers should pay by weight, don't you? Then we'll see how many people travel by plane!"

Salman laughed. He thought of going on a diet, and then smiled at the absurd notion of traveling to Damascus with this resolution in mind. As soon as he set foot on Syrian soil, he would forget any resolutions and begin to feast.

Finally they called his flight.

The fears of the fathers

The three hours passed quickly. Salman read, chatted with the stewardess now and then, closed his eyes, and relaxed. Two seats ahead, an Egyptian poet, a heavyset man with an ugly face, was telling a passenger next to him that he was going to Damascus to recite a story at a literary festival. His astonished neighbor, a Syrian—in his late seventies, slim and sprightly—asked in a deep, warm voice, "What? You're a *hakawati*? When I was a kid, I only ever knew of three coffeehouse storytellers, and now they're coming from all over the world to meet in Syria?"

"No, no," the author replied, almost insulted. "I'm not a *hakawati*. I'm an author, you understand? An author!"

"But you just said you were going to tell a story at a festival," said the man.

"Yes, but it's a literary festival. It's not just about

entertainment. The Syrian Ministry of Culture invested about seven million dollars for the three hundred Arab poets who are invited."

The old man whistled through his teeth. "Seven million! If our *hakawati* had heard that, he wouldn't have died. Seven million dollars. That comes to three hundred and fifty million Syrian lira. All that just to tell stories?"

The Egyptian didn't reply. Salman smiled, and it occurred to him that he was actually sitting in a plane that was taking him to Damascus. There was no turning back now. It was as if he had burned all his bridges. He had a strange, uneasy feeling, and for some reason he thought of a parachute.

Suddenly his father popped up in his thoughts. Why was he—unlike his sister Amalia—always so reserved and fearful toward Muslims? Perhaps he had suffered under the fear of Salman's traumatized grandfather. Uncle Anton, Elias's father, had been deeply mistrustful of Muslims, as well. Aunt Amalia had laughed at both of them. "Just like us, they're made of skin, bone, flesh, and fears," she had told her brothers.

Salman's father had told him the story of why they had the surname Baladi. Originally his family name had been Kosma, and they had come from Aleppo. As the result of a love affair, one of the sons of the family had moved to Damascus. He was a goldsmith and who had five children, all born between 1845 and 1855.

One week before the great massacre of 1860, his eldest son George had traveled to his aunt's home in Aleppo. That visit saved his life. In a barbaric pogrom lasting six days, the Ottoman governor of Damascus allowed more than ten thousand Christians to be slaughtered. The once prosperous Christian Quarter was reduced to rubble.

George's ten-year-old brother Yusuf was the only one to survive, when a Muslim family hid him in their house. His parents and his three sisters were murdered. Their home was plundered and burned to the ground by an enraged mob.

The strange thing was that, at the time, there were no attacks on Christians in other cities, such as Homs or Aleppo. To this day, the exact circumstances of the massacre remained unclear. Both the governor and the killers who participated in the mob were summarily executed without trial.

George never wished to return to Damascus. His aunt adopted him. He married later, in Aleppo, and his great-grandson was the famous priest Michel Kosma. After the bloodbath, Salman's great-grandfather Yusuf suffered from a strange fever for months. The shock almost drove him mad. Day and night, he would repeat the same phrase until he finally fell asleep, exhausted: "*hada baladi*, that is my home." He would wander through the streets and sit on the ruins of his parents' home and weep, crying out, "*hada baladi*." People thought he had gone mad, and many called him by this phrase that he used, Hada Baladi. Soon they shortened this to Baladi for convenience.

The family that had taken him in treated him with patience and generosity for three years, until he recovered from the shock. He didn't want to return to his relatives in Aleppo, but remained in Damascus and was devoted to the Muslim family for the rest of his life. His parents had owned commercial land and large irrigated farms south of Damascus. With this legacy, it was possible for him to have the house rebuilt and to open a goldsmith shop, and when he married in 1876 he had himself recorded in the new Ottoman register as Yusuf Baladi. He named his only son George, after his brother. Like his father before him, Salman's grandfather George Baladi became a goldsmith and married the daughter of a rich textile manufacturer. His wife chose the name of their first child, Amalia. George didn't like his dark-skinned daughter right from the start. The next child was a boy. He named him Yusuf, in memory of his father, and because he looked a lot like him. The third child was named Anton because he was born on June 13, the feast of St. Anthony of Padua.

In the spring of 1944, George became the victim of a drunken soldier of the French occupation forces. The soldier shot his weapon wildly in all directions, injuring many passersby severely and killing George. His children, Amalia, Yusuf, and Anton, were already married at the time.

Amalia was studying at university, and Yusuf, Salman's father, had also become a goldsmith. Anton took after his mother and was interested in textiles. His grandfather on his mother's side supported him. Anton, who was later to become Elias's father, showed little talent for business and went bankrupt. However, his share of the legacy of the wealthy George Baladi allowed him to live a life of idle ease until he died.

Yet it wasn't the occupying French Army that was remembered and blamed by the family, but a Muslim mercenary who had gone on a crazy shooting spree. As a result, both Yusuf and Anton were always mistrustful and reserved toward Muslims. And, as absurd as it sounded, the soldier from the French occupying forces became, in Yusuf's version, a Moroccan Muslim sent by the Angel of Death to Damascus to kill his father. Legend lives longer than truth.

George Baladi had lived very modestly. He had,

however—known only to his wife and three children—always kept a packed suitcase in the cellar with two thousand English gold coins in it. Each one of the coins had the image of St. George slaying the dragon on one side.

Yusuf, Salman's father, had inherited these coins and locked them in a safe. Anton, and even more his wife, would tell all and sundry that Yusuf had received more gold and money than he had. Soon the brothers only visited each other at Christmas and Easter. They did so more out of a sense of duty, and such visits were prickly affairs. There was only one thing the brothers managed to agree on, and that was their dislike of Amalia. Salman's father liked to live splendidly, without being wasteful. He bought a large house on Misk Street for a lot of money and had it renovated according to the original plans.

These stories and images from his childhood filtered slowly through Salman's imagination. The house where he had grown up was in the Eastern patrician style, with several living rooms, bedrooms, servants' rooms, and pantries. It didn't have a garden, but it had a courtyard that was open to the sky, with the floor covered in geometric patterns of dark and light marble. All around were citrus trees, jasmine, and roses. A large fountain was the centerpiece of the courtyard and of life there.

Two servants and a cook worked all day looking after the house, the fountain, the trees, the potted plants in the courtyard, and cooking according to his mother's instructions. Salman remembered that hardly a week went by without a festive meal. His parents loved to feast in the courtyard with friends and relatives. The exclusive Lazarist school that Salman attended was not even thirty steps away from his house.

~

Within ten years after Salman's escape from Syria, his father had lost nearly all his wealth through bad investments. He sold the house for a lot of money, paid off his debts, and bought a big, fine, modern apartment on quiet al-Akhtal Street, which ran parallel to busy Aleppo Street, not far from the Christian Quarter. From then on, his parents stopped having servants. There was only a cleaning lady who came twice a week. His mother had written to him at the time, humorously as always, that she finally enjoyed her food.

Salman smiled and opened his eyes. It seemed strange to be so disturbed. He remembered an anecdote about a white American driving a car, with an Indian passenger. The American was driving too fast. Suddenly the Indian man shouted, "Stop!" The frightened driver braked, and the Indian leisurely got out and sat down on the curb. "What are you doing?" the American asked. The Indian man replied, "I'm waiting for my soul. It can't move that fast."

For Salman, it seemed to be the other way around. He was sitting in an airplane moving at incredible speed, yet his soul was traveling even faster through time and space. It had reached the Damascus of his childhood long ago.

When the stewardess came again with drinks, cakes, and coffee, he declined absentmindedly in Arabic. The young Italian stewardess replied in Arabic. Salman got talking with her and found out that she had been involved with a Syrian man. Pressured by his family and his clan, he had ended up marrying his cousin in Damascus, and he had been arrested three months ago.

"Why? No reason?" Salman asked, feeling like a fool.

"No idea. I often speak to his sister on the phone,

and even she doesn't know why. He's not even allowed a lawyer," the stewardess replied, smiling bitterly.

19

Sudden Departures and Slow Failures

Damascus, 1952–2005

Amira was driving with Aunt Hanan, a young woman full of life, to the wedding of a cousin in Qabun, a village north of Damascus—nowadays a suburb of the capital. Karim didn't like this cousin. He preferred to stay home with the baby and was happy that little Maha was content, full, and already tired enough to fall asleep so early in the evening. He opened a bottle of wine, filled a bowl with pistachio nuts and roasted pumpkin seeds, and got out a book about the Qaramitian Republic in the tenth century that he had been wanting to read for a long time. Strangely enough, the reference work had been written in 1886, not by an Arab but by a Dutch-Friesian scholar by the name of Michael Jan de Goeje.

Karim was delighted when he read the chapter on equality between men and women in Qaramitian society. As backward as they may have been in some ways, the Qaramitians had been in the process of creating a society where women were neither exploited nor oppressed. And this society had lasted for more than a hundred and fifty years. Official history books paid little attention to this long period and disapproved of the unbelieving Qaramites, but devoted hundreds of reverent pages each time a caliph passed gas.

Karim smiled, allowing his attention to wander. Doesn't such a society come close to Paradise? he thought.

177

Around eight that evening the phone rang. Karim stood up slowly and picked up the receiver. Amira was on the line. She laughed and told him that the feast was better than she had feared and that she would be home by midnight. Karim told her about Maha and about the good wine. "And by the way," he added, "I now know why I not only love you but also treat you with respect. I come from the tribe of the Qaramites, but then I was catapulted here by history and landed in my clan by mistake." Karim laughed.

"Qaramites? Never heard of them. Who are they?"

"I'll tell you tomorrow while we're having tea."

He knew that Amira had the day off.

"The reason I'm calling," said Amira, "I'm ashamed, because it occurred to me that I haven't kept my promise."

"Which one's that? You've made me a lot of promises," Karim joked.

"To teach you the tango. It came to me at the party when two couples were dancing to the fantastic music by Carlos Di Sarli. My cousin had gotten the records from Beirut, and the guests were really surprised. They only wanted to do Arab dances at first, but soon it was like they were enchanted, and everybody wanted to learn the tango. Didn't I promise to teach you the tango in a week?"

"Yes, yes, you did. And I'm sure you'll keep your promise," he replied.

As a little girl, Amira had loved to dance. Her mother used to send her to a girlfriend of hers who had lived for a long time in Argentina, and the friend had taught her several dances. Amira particularly liked the tango Argentino and was soon dancing it better than her teacher. She collected records by Carlos Di Sarli, Anibal Troilo, and Osvaldo Pugliese. When Karim heard this music and saw Amira dancing with one of her cousins, he wished he could be in that dancer's place and whirl her around just as passionately. In his home, dancing had always been something that just the women did. Here, however, he could see the drama of two lovers expressed in their movements.

"Right, no more delay. I swear to you by my love for you—we start tomorrow."

And then she told him about her plan to build a playhouse for Maha in the garden, and how she longed for the sea. He laughed and reminded her that Maha was still a little baby, but he did promise her that they would spend two weeks by the sea during the summer holidays. He hung up happily. At the other end of the line, Amira stood still for a moment, closing her eyes and savoring the prospect of a holiday by the sea.

~

The shrill ringing of the telephone jerked Karim awake. He had dozed off on the sofa while reading. He glanced at the wall clock. It was twenty minutes after midnight.

It was a relative of Amira's on the phone. His words were stumbling and confused, so much so that Karim could barely make sense of them. There had been a terrible accident near the cousin's house where the wedding had been celebrated. Amira's aunt had been drunk and had driven her Ford straight into a truck while passing a bus. Amira and she had died on the spot.

~

Amira's death shook Karim like nothing before or after in his life. The world seemed like an overwhelming, featureless enemy, and he felt small and helpless. He wept in despair. All night he looked at the baby, time and again, sleeping peacefully. All night he cried the grief out of his body. His tears that night were his saving grace, otherwise he would have died of grief.

Faith in God's goodness deserted him. He never went to the mosque again after his wife's funeral. The sheikh would try repeatedly to get him to come at least to Friday prayers, but Karim refused. When he had finally had enough, he told the sheikh to his face that he had lost his faith. The sheikh, a patient old man, regarded Karim in his youth and anger. "My son, your suffering will be all the harder and longer without the comfort of religion."

"Better than pretending and going to the mosque and staring at your backside!"

The sheikh left the house as if the Devil himself was on his heels. He never came back.

Amira's parents and the whole family loved Karim and took pity on him in their own mourning. They were generous and helped him wherever they could. For six years, Nihad, Amira's widowed aunt, would come every day at seven o'clock in the morning, drink coffee with him, and look after Maha until Karim came home from school.

Karim had locked up Amira in his heart and thrown the key into the sea of his grief. He wanted only to be with her. It was not that he lacked for offers of female company—with or without ulterior motives—but he declined them all politely. Soon he was regarded as an odd character and, behind his back, the whispers ran that his grief had driven him mad. The reality, however, was that he was a prisoner of his memories of Amira. It wasn't until many decades later that his love for Aida knocked down the walls of this prison, and his memory began to put what he had experienced into some sort of rational order.

Raising his daughter, studying literature and history, taking his examinations, and learning to teach high-school students all helped keep him busy. And when he found any spare time, he would occupy himself as his own handyman in his large house. He did all the jobs himself. He laid tiles and installed water pipes so there was access to water everywhere in the garden and in the house. He restored the old wall and floor mosaics, and in addition to the quince, apricot, and citrus trees, he planted a vegetable garden. Now he was able to feed himself and his little girl from his own garden. And in all that he did, he asked Amira in his heart if it was pleasing to her.

His pain left him solitary and unsociable, but he had a few friends who understood him and respected his reclusiveness. They afforded him the distance he needed and always made sure that he knew that they felt for him.

Maha quickly grew into an independent little girl. She loved her Aunt Nihad who had looked after her so lovingly during her first six years. But once she turned seven, Maha would accept almost no more help. "She's a miniature version of Amira," her aunt would say, laughing, "and just as stubborn." And Maha did, in fact, look like a smaller version of her mother.

Karim and his daughter were a good team. People often saw them playing together in their yard, or out in the street. In those days, men seldom played with their daughters in public, which was why the neighbors would smile at the widower. But this didn't bother Karim. He would concentrate on his marbles, so as not to lose against his deft little daughter. But loneliness would overcome him at night. He missed Amira. The grief for a lost loved one is like a faithful dog; no matter how often you chase it away, it keeps coming back.

Later he would say that there had been little to recount about the time between Amira's death and meeting Aida, except that he thought of Amira every day, and was proud of his gifted daughter, and hardly had any free time between school, the garden, and cooking for himself and Maha; as for pleasure, he took an hour for reading every day, if that.

Maha graduated from high school with honors. She'd already wanted to be a lawyer by the age of ten, so she studied law and earned money tutoring pupils from rich families.

One day stood out in his memories. In June 1972, shortly before summer vacation, he got into an argument with his school's new principal, a fervent supporter of the new coup leader Hafiz al-Assad. Karim already knew the principal from when he had been a teacher. At the end of the fifties, he had been an ardent supporter of Nasser, and then, after a pilgrimage to Mecca, he became all in favor of Saudi Arabia. When the Saudis paid him no attention, he fervently supported the left-wing government under Atassi, which was defeated by Assad and his clan in 1970.

"Of all the beings full of fervor, the only ones I like are glowworms," Karim remarked sardonically after the principal delivered one of his fiery speeches in front of eight hundred pupils and forty teachers and staff. An informer reported him, and he was dismissed on the spot, not just from the school but from the whole education system. At first Karim thought of emigrating. At the time, the Gulf States were frantically looking for teachers, but this would have taken him too far away from Maha, whom he saw almost every day, and from Amira's grave, on which he laid flowers every week. So he took a job at the reception desk of a big hotel and ended up as their chief accountant. On the side, he taught at private institutes that were just becoming fashionable at the end of the seventies, since state schools were getting worse and worse, teaching more ideology than knowledge.

With his jobs, Karim earned more than he had as a teacher; he lived as frugally as a cactus and was proud of Maha, who excelled at her studies and became a successful lawyer. He retired in the mid-nineties and was finally able to read all the books that he had collected but barely had time to open.

One day in autumn 2002, three years before he met Aida, his friend Gibran, a well-read carpenter, made him a present of a slim volume with the intriguing title *The Fortress of Love*. Gibran was shy and quiet in everything he did. He always visited Karim on Saturday evenings, drank only one glass of wine, chatted with him for an hour, and went away as quietly as he had come.

The book lay unnoticed on his bedside table for weeks. Karim thought it was a love story. One night he was sleeping fitfully, plagued by nightmares. At some point he picked up the little book. It was the collected wisdom and advice of a man that the editors called al-Hakim, the wise. Gibran and other Hakim followers called themselves the Selfless. The book had been published anonymously, printed on cheap paper, and badly typeset. But the more Karim read, the more he understood why both editors and publisher had wished to remain anonymous. Every line, every word, was a call to resist dictatorship and its loss of freedom and dignity. Gibran had shown Karim great trust in giving him this book. The editors left the readers in no doubt that the secret service would have anyone who possessed the book killed quietly and in secret, without any trial. Even al-Hakim had been murdered, as the editors stated at the end of the book.

The modest appearance of the little book was misleading. Its title was honest, but also an effective camouflage. The text was so condensed that it demanded careful reading and long reflection. Karim was so moved that he stayed up reading and pondering until six o'clock in the morning.

He always got up at that time when he was a teacher, and still did so now that he was a pensioner, using quiet of the early morning to plan his appointments and ready himself for the day before the din of life took over. He did not feel the least tired on that October morning. He kept thinking of his daughter because, despite her intelligence, her behavior was the exact opposite of the wisdom contained in the slim volume. She had turned fifty, was living alone after a divorce, and had become an unhappy rich woman. She seemed to have forgotten everything that she had learned from him. Perhaps that was why she had succeeded—and was now unhappy.

To top it all off, she had joined a conservative Islamist women's group a year ago. She had given up drinking and smoking, although she still drove her sports car. Now she wore a headscarf that turned her beautiful head into an ugly egg, and coats in the summer, and long-sleeved, ankle-length clothes. She would argue with her father about every glass of wine he drank. She seemed to have forgotten all about joy and pleasure, and longed only for the Paradise of the afterlife.

Where had her life gone so wrong? Karim wondered helplessly in the autumn dawn, and took a sip of coffee.

II

20

Mosaic of an Arrival

Damascus, December 2010

Return to an ancient city

There was already a long queue for passport control. Salman smiled. Queuing is totally foreign to the Arab mentality, but after so many years of dictatorship, these Syrian queues, at least at the airport, seemed as orderly as their faded forbears from the Eastern Bloc countries. Everywhere the image of the All-Father Assad and the Son Bashar looked down; everywhere armed soldiers stood with stony faces. After ten minutes waiting, Salman counted eighteen men and women in front of him and twenty-seven behind. Disgruntled murmurs rippled through the ranks of those waiting. Everyone was disappointed that immigration was not going as smoothly as they had been told it would.

Someone from the Ministry of Culture took the Egyptian poet out of the queue and past passport control. The old man who had sat next to him on the plane called out to him, slightly envious, "Oh, Allah, I should have been a hakawati, instead of mucking around with glue, wood, and knotholes." He then explained to those around him that he was a carpenter and had been to visit his son in America.

The young official, who was in a bad mood, was on duty in a booth under a portrait of the severe-looking president with the long neck. He took Salman's passport from him and gave him a long, hard look. "You're an Arab with a German passport? Why?"

"*Kismet*," replied Salman, grinning at the officer, who leafed briefly through the passport and put it on the scanner. Salman knew full well that his reply was of no importance. All that mattered was what the computer at headquarters decided.

Visibly disappointed, the official pushed the passport aside, a sign that nothing had been found. The thought shot through Salman's head that Syrians regarded the state as their enemy, yet acted as though they respected its representatives; whereas officials despised the people and even hated them, but acted as though they were doing as the people wished.

A telephone rang and the official took the call on his cell phone. He turned his back on Salman and the others still waiting. From what Salman could gather, something had gone wrong the previous day. The official was protesting that he had done everything in his power. Finally he put the cell phone away in a furious temper and stormed out of the booth. Salman heard those waiting behind him quietly cursing the official's clan back into the mists of time—to his great-great-grandparents at least.

When the official returned five minutes later, he seemed to have forgotten both Salman and the queue of people waiting. His eyes flickered as if he was drugged. He looked at Salman and asked him in a slightly slurred voice if there was anything missing. "My passport," replied Salman, forcing himself to smile.

Damascus, the city that he loved, was showing him after only a few minutes that it was one of the oldest cities in the world. Such cities do not change quickly, and the Syrian official, the modernity of the airport notwithstanding, was treating people as if they were all still living in the nineteenth century.

Salman stuck his passport in his pocket and followed the other passengers to customs. Two officials were standing behind a big table. The older and smaller of the two asked in a sleepy voice if Salman had anything to declare. Salman said no and made as if to open his suitcase, but the small man behind the table waved him on. Just moments before he had rummaged through the suitcase of the passenger in front of Salman, a gray-haired man who wore horn-rimmed glasses, even taking out the man's clothing and underwear and shaking them. Well, that had always been the way in Damascus—chaos and caprice wherever you looked. The other official, slightly corpulent and mistrustful-looking, wanted to take a closer look at Salman's bag, but after a brief glance at the contents, he waved him on with a bored expression. "Dear God, they're worse than Italian customs officers. What if I had contraband in my suitcase?" Salman railed quietly as he reached the large table where passengers repacked their suitcases and bags. The man with the horn-rimmed glasses laughed and said, "Smugglers use another exit. There they serve them refreshments."

He was busy trying to stow his underwear, which somehow didn't want to fit, back into his suitcase. Salman helped him, forcing everything back in, and it took the two of them to finally close the wheeled suitcase.

"Thanks," said the man, out of breath. "Every year I visit Damascus, and every time they search me, I swear never to set foot in this city again. But then after a few months I'm sick with longing and I have to come back."

Outside the airport was dark and icy cold—December could be very unfriendly in Damascus. Despite the damp, the air smelled of dust mixed with diesel, a strange scent that Salman had missed for years. The taxi drivers were loud and pushy, just like they had always been. They fought for every fare and before Salman could stop him, one of them carried his suitcase to his taxi.

"But we haven't agreed on a price yet," Salman protested.

"That doesn't matter. Pay what you like. You're a generous gentleman. We're not going to fight."

No, that was the old trick taxi drivers played on tourists and emigrants returning home. To most taxi drivers, both sorts were rich idiots to be fooled easily. First you drove them, then you demanded an outrageous fare, and when the passenger refused to pay, the driver made such a scene that the passenger finally felt ashamed and paid up.

"I swear you all have learned nothing in forty years. I'm a Damascene—not an oil sheikh, and you want to try and trick me in my own city? How much to al-Akhtal Street?" Salman had dropped the polite Arabic and now spoke in the broad Damascene dialect.

"Say two thousand five hundred lira, right to the doorstep in al-Akhtal Street. After all, it's at the back of beyond, isn't it?"

Al-Akhtal Street was in the new district that had been built in the 1960s and, at the time, was at the northernmost edge of the Christian Quarter. Salman had often Googled the route in anticipation. It was about twenty-five kilometers, and the taxi driver was asking for the equivalent of fifty euros. It was over twenty-five kilometers from Fiumicino Airport to the Viale di Trastevere, and that trip came to forty euros. Besides, prices in Damascus were much lower than in Rome.

"A thousand lira. The street isn't in Honolulu, it's just parallel to Aleppo Street. And if you're going to try the one about your twelve hungry children, I'm taking another taxi." Salman's tone became more aggressive because he could see that it wasn't just the Syrian official who despised him. This scam artist clearly did too, and Salman had taken a dislike to him.

"No, no, sir. Don't get excited. I don't have any children. Okay, one thousand two hundred. After all, I carried your suitcase for you."

"I didn't ask you to, but all right then, twelve hundred," agreed Salman. Then he quickly took out his cell phone and called his mother.

"Hello, Baladi," he heard her say.

"Got a small cup of mocha for a nomad?" he asked.

"Salman, heart of mine! Where are you?"

"On my way to you. I'll be there in half an hour."

"May the Blessed Virgin Mary protect you. Why didn't you tell us when you were arriving?"

"I didn't want you both to wait. I thought they'd question me for hours. But they were very nice to me and only made me wait two hours." He laughed and enjoyed the curse that his mother laid on the bureaucrat, wishing him yellow fever.

"But I'll be there soon," he went on and looked at his watch. "Twenty-five past eight. Is there going to be coffee or not?"

"Oh, there'll be coffee for the whole world!" his mother exclaimed and Salman knew that she was weeping for joy and relief. He climbed into the taxi and off they went. On the way from the airport into the city, Salman thought of his old friends and schoolmates; of Lamia, his great platonic love; and also of Rita, an adventurous young woman with whom he'd had the most intense erotic encounters without the slightest hint of feeling. In his mind, they had all stayed young.

There were military vehicles parked at every cross-road. "What's going on?" he asked the taxi driver, pointing to the soldiers.

"Nothing. What about it?" the man replied as if the soldiers were invisible to him. Perhaps people were all blind in one eye. Perhaps they didn't notice the giant posters of the president and the monuments to the president's father everywhere, either. Both father and son looked stiff, misshapen, and off-putting. Salman refrained from any comment that might provoke the taxi driver. The latter was eagerly inquiring where Salman came from, why he lived abroad, and how long he was planning to stay in Damascus. Salman remained silent, watching people hurry along the dark streets. The taxi driver gabbed on as if he had swallowed a radio. Salman just let it all wash over him; all the whining about the economic crisis that had forced him—a former teacher—to become a taxi driver, his unmistakable hints at "certain eminent persons" who were now billionaires, and his coarse jokes, with which he tried to make his taciturn and gloomy-looking passenger laugh. He hated Kurds, Christians, Druzes, Jews, women, homosexuals, and his parents-in-law who sucked his blood like vampires.

"Do you hate Alawites, too?" Salman finally snapped. He knew that the taxi driver had deliberately and spinelessly excluded this minority because Assad and his clan were Alawites. One wrong word about them and a person could look forward to a year in prison.

"No, for God's sake, I don't hate anybody!" he replied quickly, glancing at Salman anxiously in the rearview mirror. From then on, there wasn't a peep from him. When they finally arrived, he thanked Salman obsequiously and drove quickly away.

Salman took in the fine three-story building where his parents lived. Although there was an elevator, he walked up to the second floor and rang the doorbell.

He was deeply moved to see how his mother had aged. She seemed to have become smaller and frailer, but her bright, kind face had hardly changed. She greeted him and hugged him fiercely, weeping with joy and pain. "God should punish these bastards who have separated us. God should punish all who separate mothers from sons. At last you're here, my heart, light of my life!"

Salman didn't feel at all like crying. Instead, he felt like a victor. They had neither managed to stick him in jail nor to punish him. He had returned, rich and with his head high.

"I told you I'd be back," Salman said and smiled.

His mother looked at him, enraptured. "You've not forgotten that promise, *either*?" This last word, lightly emphasized, showed her character. She was sparing with her words and affection. 'Softly, softly' was her way, in life as in love. She was frugal with her sympathy, too, whether for a person or a thing. You had to be an excellent listener to keep up with the subtlety of her jokes. Decades ago, in his last call from Beirut, he'd shouted into the telephone, "Just you wait and see, Mother. I'll be back. They won't break me." There had been pride and defiance in his voice. How often had his mother taken this promise to bed with her? How often had she started her day with it? Only mothers know the answers to questions like these.

Behind his mother floated the scent of mocha with cardamom, and it was only then that Salman caught sight of his father in a wheelchair. He looked tired and ill, though he had managed to celebrate his eighty-ninth birthday that May. Salman was startled, but he covered his shock with a loud laugh of joy at seeing his father again.

"Leave something of our son for me, Sophia," his father called out. And when he noticed the worry in his son's eyes, he said quietly, "I managed again to escape Death's clutches, but very clumsily this time. My legs have given up carrying me." Both he and his wife had concealed from Salman the stroke Yusuf had suffered the previous year, as they had also done with his cancer diagnosis, for fear of worrying their son. Salman bent down, put his arms around him and kissed him, and then it was his father's turn to weep.

"Why don't we stop crying and be happy at Salman's return, and drink coffee with him?" his mother said.

"Shrewd, this young woman. First she cries enough tears to make the desert bloom and then she tells me I should stop."

His mother brought in just a few light snacks from the pantry and the fridge, but Salman found them all delicious. While they were eating, his mother came up with reasons to get up time and again, walk behind him, and hug him. His father sat on his right, stroking Salman's hand shyly and smiling in embarrassment. He ate very little, since he and Sophia had already had their evening meal.

There was no end to their questions. Before Salman could finish answering the first, the next one would come, or sometimes even two—one from each direction. But Salman was amused by it. And when his father quietly inquired about his financial situation, he replied proudly, "Five million euro!"

Yusuf Baladi beamed. "Well done, young man! I'm proud of you. But here in Damascus we prefer to keep that sort of information buried deep, otherwise you'll be like a drop of honey attracting too many bothersome insects."

It was a splendid evening, and the only thing that got on Salman's nerves was the television constantly running in the background. Back in Italy, however, Salman had decided that he was going to enjoy his first visit in so many years with quiet gratitude, and to criticize as little as possible.

Shortly after supper his parents retired to bed. Salman telephoned Stella, glossing over the arrival at the airport and praising the joyful reception his parents had given him.

Salman's mother had put him up in the beautiful room looking out onto the street. The furniture came from his old bedroom—the fine wardrobe, the big bed, the oriental-style sofa that was old but still good, his walnut writing desk, and his favorite chair that still looked almost new.

Even slips of paper on the cork notice board were still there, a little yellowed and brittle. They were still legible, though. "Help A.L.," "Call B.M." Unfortunately, he couldn't remember who A.L and B.M. were. He found a slip of paper with a telephone number in a drawer, under which it read, "Call Hala a.s.a.p.!" Strangely enough, he still remembered this young comrade. He also remembered that the number on the slip was her parents' telephone number. He smiled, imagining how it would be if he rang up and said, "Hello, this is Salman. I was supposed to call Hala forty years ago!"

He felt something akin to happiness, looking at all these objects from his past, but he also recognized how absurd it was to think he could preserve anything of that time. His initial joy faded away. Suddenly, he felt indifferent, not just to the slips of paper but to all the other pieces of the puzzle making up his past.

Salman couldn't fall asleep for a long time. Damascus was noisy and loud, and it wasn't until dawn that the city seemed to tire—but not for long. The muezzins' calls to prayer could soon be heard. These days, they were played from CDs or cassettes, and reached every household via loudspeaker.

The strangeness of places

It was already after nine when he woke up the next morning. His parents smiled indulgently. He hastily ate breakfast, wanting to leave as quickly as possible and visit the Old City district where he had grown up.

"Lunch is your favorite, *kofteh* with potatoes straight from the oven," said Sophia. Salman knew exactly what that meant: no snacks on the way and be back here ready to eat at twelve sharp. For as long as Salman could remember, his father had always eaten lunch at twelve, even when he had his goldsmith's shop.

"And we have guests this evening," his father told him. "Three or four of your cousins will help your mother. That was the compromise. I wanted to order everything from my favorite restaurant. Their cooking is excellent, and they send the dishes you order with staff to serve them. But Sophia didn't want that. She thought that would be inhospitable. But I didn't want her serving twenty people."

"Twenty people?" replied Salman in surprise.

"Of course, what do you think? They've been waiting for months to say hello to you. We can't just offer them coffee and cakes," his mother explained. "And Yusuf's right. I can't manage all that on my own now. You'll get to know your cousins this way. Some of them were either babies or not even born when you left."

"I can't wait," Salman lied. He had never liked these big family get-togethers. They were loud eating orgies where it was impossible to carry on a conversation. He found them boring—but there was no getting out of it. He anticipated that the cousins would arrive in the early afternoon to do the cooking and prepare the big drawing room for the guests.

Monday was cold but sunny. Salman dressed warmly and set off for the Old City. First he went to the Glass Palace, a café and restaurant in the Christian Quarter that was almost a hundred years old. He still knew the old owner, Christo Dahduh. The place's heyday had been in the forties and fifties. It had been the favorite meeting place for poets, politicians, actors, and singers. Renovated and smaller now because the street was going to be widened, it had lost much of its charm.

Although he knew these streets, they seemed strange to him. While people were dressed in more modern fashions than he remembered, the women wore headscarves and the men beards. Most were busy with one or even two smartphones. Arabs have to exaggerate in everything, he thought, smiling to himself. He eavesdropped on people's conversations in the café and on the street. They may have been speaking Arabic, but he often didn't understand what they were talking about. There was one phrase he kept hearing: "*Ma dachalna!*—that's none of our business."

An hour later, he reached the house where he had spent his childhood. It was now a plush restaurant. The door to the inner courtyard stood open. Salman went in. A young man in an elegant black suit came up to him. "Welcome—come in. The weather is much too cold to sit outdoors. It's much more comfortable inside."

"Please excuse me, I just wanted to have a quick look at the house. I grew up here. My name is Salman Baladi. I lived here until I left for Europe."

"Oh, really?" said the man in surprise. "My name is Nasser Darwish. I'm the tenant. Mr. Musawi, the owner, lives in Aleppo."

"Yes, that's it. My father sold the house to a Mr. Musawi—an architect, I think."

"May I invite you in? Some tea in this weather is bound to do you good," the landlord said in a friendly voice. Salman followed him inside. He didn't recognize anything in the large dining room. The owner had torn out the dividing walls and made one room out of three. The room was decorated with three beautiful arches. The light streaming through the colored glass windows gave it a church-like air. But the decor was close to kitsch, and the bar at one end didn't really fit in. It was cold, gleaming steel.

"Where in Europe do you live?" the tenant asked.

"In Rome."

"A beautiful city. I visited it once. And what do you do there?" he asked after a waiter had served them tea.

"Food import-export," Salman replied.

"Oh, good," the man said, but then he was called away to the telephone by one of his staff. The call was urgent, apparently. Salman slowly finished his tea and looked around discreetly once more. There really was nothing in this place to remind him of his childhood, or his youth. He stood up and went back through the door into the inner courtyard. The only things that remained were the octagonal fountain and the marble ornaments on the ground and walls. Salman looked closely at the precise design of the ornaments and felt how the play of line and colors composed a visual music, like good calligraphy.

The fruit trees had been cut down to make room for as many tables as possible. Circular stone benches with a round marble table in the middle now stood where a garden shed had been. It was where his mother used to meet her lover.

Salman had once been a witness to this, quite by chance. A couple had come to visit. They had sat with Salman's parents in the living room. Bored because the couple had no children, he had gone up to his room. From there he was able to sneak into the garden without anyone noticing him. He decided he would conceal himself, as he often did, in his hideout—a little Indian tepee just across from the garden shed. There he kept a secret store of nuts and chocolate in jars that were sealed so the mice couldn't eat any. That was where he saw his mother hurrying out to the garden shed with his father's friend, kiss him, and close the door. It was absolutely quiet in the garden and so he could hear his mother moaning. The man didn't make a sound. After a quarter of an hour she came out again, smoothed down her dress, and went into the house. The man came out somewhat later, lit a cigarette, and also went back inside.

This friend of his father came to visit almost every week. While his wife would make polite, if awkward, conversation with Salman's father in the living room, Sophia and her lover would carry out a hurried rendezvous in the shed. This went on until one day Salman's parents had an almighty argument, and from that day on the friend never came to visit anymore.

"Do you like it?" The tenant's voice yanked him back into the present.

"Yes, sure, but everything's changed so much," said Salman. Then he thanked his host for the tea and left. He felt lost outside on the street, and a bit dizzy. He kept walking to the next street, past his former school. The schoolyard was full of noisy pupils on their afternoon break. After nationalization, the Lazarists' School was renamed after the caliph al-Mansur.

Father Kosma, Salman's favorite teacher and his cousin three times removed, no longer taught there. He now worked at the See of the Patriarch.

Out of politeness, Salman wanted to invite the priest to a meal. When he rang him up, the secretary explained that Father Kosma was away with the patriarch on a short trip to Lebanon. Salman left word that he said hello and that he would love to see Kosma on his return, because he would only be in Damascus for two weeks before returning to Rome.

They had even renamed his family's street. It was no longer Misk—meaning musk—Street, but was named after a Lebanese poet. Dictatorships are never that inventive, he thought, and continued along until he reached the main street, Bab Tuma. From there he strolled slowly through the Christian Quarter. The houses had hardly changed, but everything was louder and more colorful, and there was much more cheap plastic for sale in the shops.

When he arrived back home for lunch, his mother reported that even more friends and relatives had said they would be at his welcome-home feast that evening. He enjoyed his favorite kofteh dish that his mother had prepared, and the fine red wine. After the meal he called Paolo, who told him that he missed him very much. Stella was out delivering a lecture at a symposium of toxicologists in Rome.

His conversation with Paolo touched Salman greatly. At that moment he wanted to fly straight back to Rome. He felt a void spreading inside him until his eyes closed.

The strangeness of relatives

At about three in the afternoon, his mother knocked softly
on his door and asked him if he wanted coffee. He could
hear laughter and loud voices, so he quickly got dressed
and came out to meet people. He immediately recognized
his Aunt Takla, his mother's younger sister by five years.
She looked very much like Sophia. After a moment's hesitation, he also recognized Mona, his aunt's daughter-in-
law and the wife of his favorite cousin, Tarek. Next to her
stood a young woman who turned out to be her daughter,
Samira. "It can't be!" Salman cried out in surprise, giving
her an affectionate kiss on both cheeks, "I carried you
around everywhere in Rome. Do you remember?"

"How could I ever forget it, Uncle?" she replied,
hugging him tightly and weeping with joy. Her mother
immediately joined in. Samira and her parents were very
grateful to Salman, since he had paid all the hospital costs
for her treatment twenty years ago. Samira was seven
when she had broken a leg, an arm, and both collarbones
in a bus accident. She had received thoroughly inadequate
treatment at the city hospital in Damascus, which had left
her with a limp and lingering pain. Salman's mother had
asked him to have the daughter treated in Italy. Samira's
parents didn't have the money, so Salman's father paid
for the flight and Salman paid for the little girl's surgeries
and rehabilitation. Soon afterward she was skipping again,
happy and healthy.

"Let's not cry now," Sophia said.

"Where's your father? Is he alright?" Salman asked.
She nodded and wiped her tears away. "He's coming this
evening."

"And your brother, Amir, is he coming too?"

"No, unfortunately—he's been working in Kuwait for

a year," said Samira. "But he wants to call this evening to wish you welcome." Sophia stopped herself from reminding her son that she had already told him several times about Amir's job in Kuwait.

Salman noticed that all this time a dark-haired woman in her early forties had been admiring him. "And who might you be?" he inquired with great interest.

"I'm your cousin Maria," she said shyly, her voice brittle but warm.

"Don't tell me you've never heard of my youngest daughter?" joked his aunt.

"Yes, of course, but she was born the same year I left the country. Just a minute, you were born in the summer, right? I got the news in Beirut at the time."

"Yes, that's right. In July," Maria said and laughed.

"And you've been married to Subhi for about ten years, and he works as a chemist in Saudi Arabia. Right?"

She beamed at him, full of pride. He kissed her on the cheek and she hugged him tightly. She smelled of lemon blossom.

What surprised Salman most was that even now, in the middle of the party, his parents kept the television on. If somebody switched it off, like a sleepwalker, his mother would walk over and turn it back on.

His father had withdrawn from all the commotion. He sat in their bedroom in his wheelchair by the window, solving a crossword puzzle.

"You don't want any coffee?" Salman asked him.

"I seldom drink it, and never at these ladies' get-togethers," he replied.

Salman decided to call Stella. He looked at his watch. She normally worked until three on Mondays, but maybe the symposium had already finished. He got up and left his parents' room. In the corridor he ran into Maria, who was carrying a big bowl of parsley.

"What's this for? Are you going to feed a lamb?"

"It's for the tabouleh," she said, laughing. She reminded him of a young Claudia Cardinale.

When he got through to Stella, she excitedly bombarded him with news about her appearance at the symposium, and a new research contract she'd made. Only then did she ask about him and how things were going in Damascus. "Eating, eating, and more eating," Salman replied.

"You could just as easily have done that here, *amore*."

~

The guests continued to stream in. Salman stopped counting at thirty-eight. As if by a miracle, everyone found a seat and was served. Salman was greeted, pressed, kissed, pinched, and stroked. Many of the relatives he didn't recognize at first. Some of his political friends were there, as well. Two of them, Josef Samuel and Ahmad Hariri, had been with him in the mountains, but had quickly laid down their arms. Mahmoud Bardoni and Jirgi Sairafi had been taken prisoner and released only after years of torture. All had reached retirement age and were now more or less wealthy.

The one comrade he worried about was Hani. Salman was shocked at the sad sight he made. He seemed very downcast and somehow absent. People whispered that torture had driven him mad. In the kitchen, Sophia confirmed that Hani had been in for psychiatric treatment several times, and she wondered why his wife hadn't come with him. "An intelligent, capable woman. Without her, the café they both run would have gone bankrupt a long time ago."

Salman and Hani had met when they were under-ground fighters in the mountains. They became close friends. But when the fighters scattered after a large-scale attack by the army, and Salman's and Hani's faces were plastered on wanted posters all over the city, Salman had lost touch with him.

It was only later in Italy that Salman learned from his mother that Hani had visited her and asked for him. He had left his address and telephone number. When Salman called him, he told him that he had been released after ten years in prison, had given up politics for good, and was running a little café with his wife in the New City, near the al-Kindi Cinema. Salman and Hani telephoned and wrote each other letters, first on a regular basis, then less and less until it was only a letter or a postcard at Christmas—still, Salman considered him a dear friend. But now Hani just sat there, without a trace of his old sense of humor. He didn't say a word to his former comrades, either. He soon left.

Only his Aunt Takla's family was a breath of fresh air that evening. They all pitched in so that his mother didn't have to lift a finger and could sit proudly by Salman's side. Amir called from Kuwait and was pleased to have reached Salman in Damascus.

Salman's father came to supper to be polite, but he remained steadfastly silent, picked at his food, and made his excuses around nine o'clock, saying he had to take his medicines and go to bed. He was more uninterested in the guests than unwelcoming. His father's indifference an-noyed Salman. For forty years, his father had nagged and badgered him to come to Damascus. And now the joy of seeing each other again seemed to be over and done with after twenty-four hours. Sophia tried to comfort Salman.

His father had become very run-down in recent months. But he loved his son, she said, and admired how he had been able to work his way up from humble beginnings in a foreign country. Meanwhile, the guests shrugged off the departure of the head of the household and continued their merry celebration. Again and again, someone would raise their glass of wine or arak and toast him: "To Salman and his arrival!"

When the meal finally ended, the women cleared the table. Some relatives made their excuses and left because they had a long trip home, while others stayed until after midnight. Sophia laughed at Salman's worry that their guests might be disturbing the neighbors. "This is Damascus. The whole street knows what's going on and is celebrating with us," she said, as if it was the most natural thing in the world.

The following day, and the day after, visitors streamed in and out. Mostly they would come after seven in the evening, with the last guest not leaving until after midnight. Salman was often bored on these evenings, but his years in Europe had not erased his good manners. Despite the fact that he himself was only a visitor, he was cast in the role of host, and in Syria a guest was revered almost as a saint. "If a guest feels at ease in your house," his mother had taught him when he was very young, "he will bless your house in his heart." In Europe he had learned to yawn with his mouth closed, and he hid his boredom so well that only his mother could notice it.

Each evening, before he fell asleep, he thought that if he came here again with Stella and Paolo, he'd only spend the first night at his parents' home. After that he'd travel around with his two dear ones and stay in hotels. He'd show Stella and Paolo his beautiful country and take them out to eat in fine restaurants—but only ones off the beaten track, where there were no tourists. Stella was bound to like the quirky proprietors of such places. "Yes, you owe me that, at the very least," she had said on the telephone, laughing, when he had promised her that he'd someday play tour guide for her and Paolo in Damascus.

Salman wondered at the fact that many guests seemed so surprised and disappointed that Stella and Paolo hadn't come with him, although his mother had told them months ago that he'd be traveling alone. They called the boy "Bulos," the name of the church founder in Arabic, as if they didn't want to acknowledge that Paolo, first and foremost, was an Italian boy.

Friends and relatives asked Salman about all sorts of things, studiously avoiding the matter of why he had stayed away from home for so long. He had several variations on a noncommittal answer ready, to avoid any problems should there be an informer among the guests. But nobody asked him, at any of the evenings. The Syrian propensity for self-censorship was more thorough than he had anticipated. Any question about his exile could have been construed as criticism of the conditions in Syria that had led to his flight.

When the last visitor had left the apartment and Salman had gone to bed, it was a long time before he could fall asleep. He was dead tired, but the guests still managed to irritate him. He felt like a stranger here. They were polite, friendly, helpful—and exhausting for exactly those reasons. He noticed how he had been spoiled by European freedom. For all their happiness, the people here were not free. They spoke a lot to conceal what could not be said. Even during the day, it was impossible for him to find any peace and quiet in Damascus because nobody ever left him alone. The prevailing opinion was that anyone who remained alone was either ill, had problems, or was an outsider. Salman became acutely aware of the extent to which he had changed. Everything that interested his guests, he found shallow and dull. What was important to him, they found ridiculous, reckless, or even childish. Each side tolerated the other with superficial charm, but, deep down, each found the other unbearable.

His old friends who came every day, with the exception of Hani, he also found intelligent but boring, since the main use they made of their intelligence was to conceal their discontent. Hani seldom came, was often silent, and when he did speak it was with the bitterest sarcasm. He was mainly concerned with how to lay his hands on enough money to get his revenge—how and on whom, Salman never learned. "Perhaps a bank robbery," Salman's father said jokingly. "But only with a water pistol, please," added Josef Samuel, a former comrade in arms of both Salman and Hani. Everybody laughed. Hani's irate glance at Josef silenced him. Salman found the very idea of Hani as some jittery bank robber absurd.

But the aim of coming by a lot of money quickly, if possible without work, was common to everyone. The members of the ruling clan were their secret role models: yesterday dirt-poor farmers, today billionaires; and the poorer the visitor, the crazier his ideas about Europe. Poverty, thought Salman, is truly the best fertilizer for the imagination. There were occasions, however, when he could hardly contain himself—when a cousin his age, or someone he had been to school with, out of pure jealousy made fun of everything Salman had achieved. The politeness incumbent on a host forced him to hold himself in check. But it deeply annoyed him when someone who had never set foot outside his street suddenly claimed to know Rome and Italy better than Salman did.

His mother could often recognize his disdain for these blowhards by the crooked smile he would give her, and she was pleased with her discerning son who, after two or three days, had once again mastered so completely the rules of that complicated game of how to be charming to idiots. There was hardly anyone who understood him better than she did, and before each visit, she would ask him to remain polite and not get excited over any stupid remarks, since he'd be able to return to Rome soon. But if he let slip the mask of the perfect host, his bad reputation would remain for her and Salman's father to deal with.

Just as Damascene values and life in Damascus had changed, so had their language. The word "security"— once completely harmless in meaning—had become synonymous with the terrible secret service, with fear and state terror. "'He writes,'" his mother said, "used to mean someone was an author. 'He has beautiful handwriting' used to mean someone was a calligrapher, but today, both phrases mean such and such a person is an informer."

Salman liked Damascus by day. Sometimes he would simply get on a bus and ride around the city. He would listen in on conversations, trying to get a glimpse under the invisible cloak that his fellow passengers cast over what they said. But the evenings were a torment for him, because the conversations were so repetitive. One evening, Sophia was even brave enough to politely, but firmly, snub a cousin, twice removed, who maintained "just between us" that European women were all whores, at the same time asking pardon for being so direct. In the sudden silence, Sophia replied that she knew that he had problems with Syrian women and suggested he seek help, "then we can talk about European women together." The guests laughed at him, and he didn't dare talk back to the older woman. He got up and left. Salman nodded his thanks to his mother. He was slowly coming to understand that his father did not withdraw from such evenings out of coldness, but because he couldn't stand the guests. He could hide behind his illness. When Salman mentioned this to him, he smiled mischievously and nodded.

"Yusuf, you're a clever old fox," Salman said, kissing his father tenderly on the forehead. His father hugged him tightly. "I'm not clever," he said. "But I've put up with enough boredom in my life to last a hundred years, so I reckon I can take the next fifteen years off." His eyes twinkled merrily.

How distance unburdens

"What has happened in this country?" Salman wondered the night after this little incident. The visitors appeared to be friendly and polite, but at the same time they were indifferent toward the guest who had insulted Salman. And something similar somehow happened almost every evening. A neighbor, a friend, a relative would start to run down Syrians who had left their homeland in the lurch, got rich abroad, lived with immoral women… Nobody got excited about this. But if any guests overstepped a certain limit, Sophia could be relied on to teach them a very public lesson. She was protected by her sharp tongue and her age. No one was allowed to insult an elder.

There are customs and traditions that have grown up over millennia, thought Salman. A guest was treated with generosity and should feel at ease, but he also remained a prisoner to politeness toward his host. Such customs had once governed life like an unwritten law. Many of these traditions had long since died out, but Syrians had not buried them to serve as fertilizer for a new way of living. They had let them rot and mistook the stench for a new tradition. These guests in his parents' house seemed to have lost any vestige of politeness. They received telephone calls all the time, stood up and walked up and down while they talked on the phone as if the other guests were wax figures, as if his parents' living room was an airport concourse.

One guest acted as if Salman had been born in America until Salman politely asked him to keep in mind that he had been born in Syria and only left his homeland at the age of twenty-five. The man seemed unimpressed and continued to repeat reproachfully, "You can't understand that because you didn't grow up here."

And the others? They were either not even listening or busy texting. It was an insult to deny his childhood in Syria. But why would anyone want to insult him? Had the fact that he had escaped and lived in freedom filled these acquaintances with hatred or jealousy because they had suffered under the dictatorship, but were never allowed to admit it in public?

He could find no answer.

Early on the morning of the fourth day, while he was sitting at the window watching the sun come up, he wondered, does a person who is imprisoned in a fortress under siege, or finds himself on a sinking ship, have the right to hate or envy those who have managed to reach safety? And he realized that was it, exactly. He should remain neutral and not take their anger or frustration to heart, and remind himself that he would be leaving soon. Suddenly he felt calm. He went back to bed and slept more deeply than he had for a long time.

The following evening his mother was surprised at how relaxed Salman seemed. He cracked jokes with everyone and was unruffled by the sharp remarks and pointed questions. That evening, Sophia also noticed for the first time how her beautiful niece Maria hung on Salman's every word with an expression of adoration. She came every day and helped diligently with looking after the guests—how else was she supposed to pass the time in a big apartment without her husband?

Maria's husband was mean and bad-tempered. He only came to Damascus twice a year, staying a week each time. He sent her very little money, although he worked as chemist at an oil refinery in Saudi Arabia and earned an excellent salary. Maria had tried to live there with him, but she hated the strict, misogynistic laws in that country and returned alone. Since then relations between the two of them had been strained.

~

When Salman got up after his siesta one afternoon, it was unusually quiet. His parents were sitting in front of the television watching a soap. "Where are the others?" he inquired and immediately felt absurd for asking, as if the relatives were part of the furniture.

"We're having *safiha* this evening, you remember?" Salman loved the little flatbreads stuffed with meat, spices, and pine nuts. "Takla insists on serving them to you and the guests, so she, Maria, and Mona are getting everything ready at home. The flatbreads will be baked at a nearby baker's, and he'll deliver the food fresh from the oven at seven o'clock. They'll also be bringing all the starters, salads, and your favorite dessert with them."

"Crème caramel?" asked Salman. Sophia nodded.

"Dear God, you've gone to way too much trouble for

me," said Salman, deeply touched.

"Your mother tried everything to talk her sister out of it, but you know your Aunt Takla. She has a mind of her own—made of granite," his father interjected, laughing.

Sophia nudged him gently in the ribs. "You always accuse me of that," she complained, but her voice sounded more amused.

"Yes, different color, same hardness. Must run in the family," Yusuf replied.

"Look, here comes your favorite comedian," Sophia said suddenly to her husband, pointing to the television. An anchorwoman was announcing the popular program. "You ask and our learned Sheikh Hussein Dakelbab answers."

A corpulent sheikh sat centered at a table. He filled up about eighty percent of the screen. The subject was the decline of morals in Arab countries. Unsurprisingly for Salman, the man started off on a tirade against women running around unveiled, and demonized men and women even touching each other before marriage. Yusuf laughed himself to tears over the sheikh, who got more hysterical by the minute, to the point where saliva was flying from his lips. When a viewer asked him if it was a sin to marry a beautiful, very feminine singer who would be able to finance his life, he flew into a rage, pelting the man with harsh words like stones cast at a sinner.

One caller asked why smoking during Ramadan was a sin, since the smoke entered the body via the lungs, not the stomach. The sheikh waxed abundantly and at length, but without answering the question. Another asked if it was a sin to masturbate on a space shuttle. Embarrassed, the sheikh had to hedge his answer since there wasn't a single sentence in any of his books about sins committed beyond the Earth's orbit. Yet another asked whether prayers said on a Chinese rug were valid if it had a compass attached showing the direction of Mecca. "Naturally," the sheikh replied rashly. "Naturally, nothing," the viewer shot back coldly. "I've heard these cheap rugs are so manipulated by these Chinese infidels that the compass always points in the direction of Beijing. That's why I recommend Turkish rugs."

Almost delirious, the sheikh now railed, not against the Chinese, but against the lifestyle of Europeans, which would surely lead them directly to Hell without the need for any compass.

Salman's father laughed until he cried.

"This is supposed to be funny?" asked Salman, disconcertedly.

"Yes," his father replied. "He's a hypocrite. A year ago a journalist discovered that this sheikh owned a palace in London, where his four wives are looked after by an army of servants. His three sons are studying in the United States. The Americans are declared enemies of Islam at least once a week."

"And the government allows someone like this?"

"Yes," his father answered, "because for thirty years he has been saying regularly that our dictator was sent to us by the Grace of God."

"The Israelis send their satellites into space and Arab television stations send their sheikhs into Arab homes by television airwaves," Sophia added.

He wasn't surprised at his mother's incisive comments, but he wondered about his father's radical views. Both his astonishment, and the admiration accompanying it were short-lived, however, when his phone rang. It was Stella. Salman passed on her greetings to his parents, as usual, and went up to his room. When he came out an hour later, he was pleased to see his cousin Maria who had just arrived with the salads. He had long since forgotten the conversation with his father.

Concerning strangers — near and far

Salman rejected all suggestions to host or visit during his remaining afternoons, declining invitations from Aunt Takla, lovely Maria, and his former friends and girlfriends. The period of time between the mandatory early morning coffee with his parents and the evening meal belonged to him. He no longer wanted to return home for lunch.

He wandered through the city, combed its streets, its old and new districts and quarters, in search of everything Damascus had once meant to him. It was only the Old City that retained part of its fascination for him. The rest of the city was nothing more than a juggernaut of more than five million inhabitants and commuters.

Salman was shocked to find that everything—streets, houses, doors and windows, even his acquaintances and relatives—was smaller, narrower, and darker than he re-membered, and he wondered if it was memory that made everything seem bigger, lighter, and more idyllic.

For the first few days, he was under the impression that he could go wherever he liked and talk to anyone. Perhaps the secret service was having him watched, but they must have been very clever "tails" because Salman, for all his experience with the underground, was unable to identify a single one.

He usually returned home late in the afternoon, lay down for an hour, drank a strong mocha with his parents, spoke on the phone with Stella and Paolo for a long time, and leafed through the tabloids that his father seemed to buy by weight. Afterward he sometimes met up with old schoolmates and friends in cafés and bars. They all kept what was happening in the country at arm's length, and their attitude was almost one of indifference. But he couldn't help noticing that they went about with two faces. When they were with friends or relatives, they would only talk about topics that would not endanger their safety, and that was little enough. In private conversations with Salman, they were candid and more critical. He had the feeling that, while they weren't suspicious of him, they had somehow become resigned. This left him disappointed and turned his former comrades into strangers.

The most pleasant surprise was Aunt Takla's family. He described to Stella his glowing impressions of this friendly, lively family that had stayed loyal to him—not just Tarek, his wife Mona, and their bright daughter Samira, but also Aunt Takla herself, who had previously seemed tame to him but was now a funny and courageous old lady. And his cousin Maria, who was there almost every evening although she lived far away, was in his eyes the rose of the family.

Aunt Takla was there every evening. Under her coat, she wore a colorful, simple housecoat like his mother—like thousands of Italian and Arab mothers. She helped in the kitchen and served the guests as if she was on staff at a restaurant. "For years I've missed you. For years you've been away; now I'd like to see you every day," she said. Salman was very moved at this. He kissed her. "And you were always like a second mother to me," he said. Aunt Takla wiped away a few tears and hugged him warmly.

"We get a day for every year you've been away," Maria chimed in.

"For God's sake, how many years do I have to stay here for? My company will go broke and my wife will divorce me," Salman replied, kissing his aunt on the forehead and laughing.

"No woman leaves a man like you," Maria objected, "unless she's lost her mind."

"I'm flattered that such a young flower among women should find me so likeable. But I have to be back home for Christmas—Stella always has her relatives over to celebrate. Italians make a big thing of Christmas. And at New Year's, all our friends come to our place and want to enjoy our Arab specialities." He kept to himself the fact that he would have preferred to fly back to Rome that very evening.

21

Love's Price

Damascus, autumn 2005

Amal, an old school friend of Aida's, was a remarkable woman. Although her marriage was a miserable failure and she had lived alone for decades, she never gave up hope. "Despair is a luxury I can't afford," she often would say cheerfully.

One day in September, she invited Aida to a social get-together. It was a group of men and women who met once a month and called themselves the Selfless. Amal told her that she had only been with the group for two months. They were peaceful idealists who met to sing, eat, and hold discussions. Amal invited Aida to one of their talks, and she asked Aida to bring her oud. This time the meeting was to take place in a house near the Bab Tuma steps.

Aida welcomed the invitation. She wanted to get to know people outside her street. Her neighbors were nice and obliging, but she didn't feel any bright sparks of connection, and she sometimes felt very lonely.

Amal was a bubbly little woman with beautiful green eyes and red hair. She and Aida had been friends since childhood and confided in each other things they wouldn't share with anyone else. While Amal was the same age as Aida, she was always a little bit more advanced than her, including in matters of love. When she was eight years old, she told Aida that she was scared of dogs, rats, and the word "love." She had been severely punished for her love.

Amal's first love was her father who was a tall, handsome, high-ranking officer in the police. At the age of seven, she fell hopelessly in love with him. She yearned for an embrace from him, but he never touched or kissed her. She would dance around him when he came home in the hope that he would pick her up in his arms. When he wasn't paying attention, she would jump into his lap, just to be close to him. Each time, her father's reaction was one of horror. He would raise both hands in disgust, as if she was covered in dirt. He didn't say anything, but his eyes spoke volumes. What's all this? What do you want from me? It was a long time before he really noticed what was driving his daughter. One day she took his hand and laid it on her chest to show him how hard her heart was beating. That was the last straw. He thrashed her mercilessly until her mother begged him to show their daughter mercy. The following day, Amal told Aida, "I'll never love anyone again. Once is enough. Every bone in my body hurts." She had bruises everywhere.

It wasn't until two years later that Amal's mother explained to her that love had not been created to hurt but to spread joy, and that her father didn't even touch her, his own wife. "He's probably been this way since his childhood," Amal's mother said. "He loves order, and love is the opposite of order."

~

Amal was waiting for Aida at the steps that led to Bab Tuma Square and took her arm when she arrived. She explained to Aida on the short way to the meeting that the Selfless followed the teachings of the Master. According to Amal's description of him, he was a modern version of St. Francis. He didn't go barefoot, he didn't talk to animals, and he didn't forsake all pleasures, but he did regard possessions as inventions of the Devil. "He who possesses nothing is possessed by nothing," said Amal, summing up the essence of his teaching. What was the Master's name and where did he live, Aida wanted to know. Amal replied that he had no name, as he wished to avoid any cult of personality. As a result, he had quickly become popular, which was why he had withdrawn from public life, and soon afterward disappeared completely. Some said he had emigrated to India, others maintained he had been assassinated. But the teachings of the Master lived on in his followers.

And suddenly they had arrived. Amal rang the bell. A young woman opened the door and greeted them. Her warm, dark eyes gave Aida a friendly glance. She had already heard so much about Aida and her music from Amal, she said. "Amal always exaggerates," Aida replied, earning herself a dig in the ribs from her friend.

To Aida's surprise, there were about forty people gathered in the courtyard on this mild autumn day. Everyone was wearing light, bright summer clothes, as if they refused to accept that it was already fall. Aida had to smile at the picture she'd had of the Selfless. These men and women didn't look that selfless. They positively exuded elegance and riches. A gray-haired woman, witty and self-deprecating, told about her visit to a '"mountain saint" in the north. People had claimed that he was the Master, but he had been a swindler. She laughed at her naiveté in thinking that she could come across the Master and then bring back to the group the glad tidings that he espoused. "The mountain rogue," she called out, and some laughed, "is a cunning charlatan. It was a very good performance." When one of them asked her what she meant, she told them that, like a magician, he had conjured up three devils out of her nose and then eaten the little wriggling black figures. Something must have been put in the drink that the visitors were given before they were allowed to see the saint—and after paying a tidy sum. "He put on a real show, hovered in the air, dripped olive oil from his hands..."

"Did you try it? Was it good?" somebody shouted. Many laughed, including the woman who was speaking.

"I was so confused I would have taken gasoline for olive oil. I could hardly walk afterward. After the audience, I was taken into a room where dozens of people were recovering from the effects of the drug. The helpers claimed that meeting with the mountain saint had shocked us and left us all in a daze. My head was still buzzing two days later. Dear brothers and sisters, I shall never again seek out a saint, be he from a mountain or from a valley." The audience applauded, and Aida smiled. A sick society will always look for a savior, she thought.

Three or four men and women took turns telling about incidents in their lives, and the listeners gathered around them in small groups. Some wandered from one group to another. People spoke without any fear; some expressed criticism of the political situation. The experience was unusual for Aida, and she felt as if she was on the set of a movie instead of in an ordinary Damascene house.

The atmosphere reminded her of the debates on Speaker's Corner in Hyde Park in London. She had been there once with her husband. He knew London well and had taken her to see these passionate speakers. He had explained that they could talk unannounced about everything but the Queen and the Royal family. This circle was similar. People would criticize the situation in the country, but not one word was said about the president and his family.

They all ate together afterward, and then the hostess requested silence for the music. Aida played her oud and felt that she had never played so well before. She concentrated on several difficult pieces by Riyad al-Sunbati, her favorite musician and composer. The joyful music swept the audience away. She looked up and her eyes caught the smile of a gray-haired man. He was looking at her dreamily. The moment she had finished her piece, he was already standing near her. He was very handsome, suntanned and athletic in simple but elegant clothes—an old white shirt, white trousers, and plain leather sandals.

"You play really wonderfully—Amal didn't exaggerate," he said and held out his hand to her. She pressed the strong warm, hand and felt embarrassed. Her heart was pounding. "I'm Karim Asmar," he said. She repeated his name softly. He moved his chair closer to her and she breathed in the pleasant smell of him. He didn't smell of deodorant or perfume, like many men in Damascus did to hide the smell of sweat. He smelled of fresh earth. She looked at him.

"I'm thirsty," she said, and he immediately jumped up and came back with two glasses; one with water for her and the other with red wine for himself. "Just water?" she protested and laughed. Later Karim told her that he had fallen in love with her laugh. Prior to that he had only admired her.

"Then you take both glasses, and I'll get myself another glass of wine," he said, handing her the glasses and disappearing again. They quickly struck up a conversation, and Aida enjoyed the closeness of this man. She kept looking up to the clear sky. Is this alright by you? I'm about to do something silly, she said in her heart of hearts to her deceased husband Nadim.

That night they sat together for a long time, and Aida discovered that Karim lived on Jasmine Street, not twenty steps from her street. He offered to walk her home, and she nodded and packed up her oud. They walked through the night, the darkness covering them like a cloak. The dusty old lanterns were so weak that they hardly lit anything.

She felt a new feeling starting to bloom inside. There was something about this man that made her heart race. Was it his deep voice that always sounded as though he was thirsty, or the way he lightly touched her hand when he stopped to explain something to her? Was it his eyes that seemed to laugh and cry at the same time, his sense of humor, his love of music, or his deep respect for her? It was all of that and more.

Normally it would have taken them fifteen minutes to walk from the Bab Tuma steps to her house on Abbara Street. That night they took an hour. By the time they were at her house, he had just started telling her a story. She stopped him. "It's unfair to stop just when it's getting exciting. Come in and tell me how it ends," she said.

He laughed cunningly, as if he had counted on it. Later she would tease him that he had deliberately started his story of a daring drive down a winding road just as they turned into her street, and deliberately got to the exciting part just as they arrived at her door. He vehemently denied any such intention. "Superstitious people would say it was fate, but I think it was pure chance," was his mischievous defense.

So he went inside with her, and they told each other the story of their lives. As morning dawned and Damascus began to wake up, Aida made strong coffee. "I'm hungry," she said when the last tiny cup of mocha had been drunk. Karim knew a restaurant on historic Straight Street, not far from the al-Bizuriyya spice market. The owner opened as early as five o'clock in the morning so that shift workers could have their breakfast there. Karim and Aida strolled to the restaurant, and when Aida tripped in the street, he grabbed her hand. She didn't let go, including on the way back through their street. Neighbors and passersby looked at them in surprise. Aida stopped in front of the doorway to her house, hugged Karim, and kissed him on the lips.

"When you've had a good rest, come to my place, I'm cooking for you today," Karim said and went home with a spring in his step.

Aida woke up around twelve. She was even more tired than before, but she was excited at the same time and wanted to go to Karim's as quickly as possible. First, however, she still had to buy a few things at the grocer's. She was standing before the canned vegetable shelf, looking for corn, artichokes, and peeled tomatoes when her neighbor Walide came up to her. "Look, it's not really any business of mine, but I'm worried about your good name," she said.

"Why? What have I done that's so bad?" Aida replied jokingly, because Walide could also be very ironic.

"Stop this nonsense. I'm serious. You're getting involved with that godless Karim. The neighbors saw it all."

Aida was shocked. Walide, of all people, who claimed she was her friend, had just shown herself to be a gossip and a tattletale. Aida had expected Walide to share her happiness.

"Well, that's quite an achievement. I was with him for four hours and you've already got a sermon ready. But there's no need to worry about my reputation. I can do that myself."

"But you kissed him at the front door!"

Aida was furious at Walide's insincerity. "I'm a grown woman in my mid-fifties, and even if I was seventy or eighty, I'd kiss him at my front door or even in bed. He tastes great, if you must know."

Walide was so angry that she turned and walked away, but others had overheard the conversation. Aida saw the women eyeing her and pointing. She busied herself with her shopping list, gathered the items she needed, and went to the checkout. "Yes, it's true—she's getting involved with an old Muslim, as if there were no Christian men," one woman standing in the queue told her friend, just loud enough for Aida to understand every word. Aida packed her shopping in the basket, flashed the two women a poisonous glance, and walked back home with her head held high.

Was Karim a Muslim? She hadn't known about that. He had said that he had banned all organized religions to the museum of his recollections, where they could be admired. But love was the true religion, and that particular one knew neither war nor racism nor the Inquisition. He had adopted the thoughts of the Andalusian Sufi philosopher Ibn Arabi, who was buried in Damascus. Aida had disagreed, and couldn't imagine how it was supposed to work. She worried that just another corrupt institution of power might emerge from the most beautiful of all human emotions if it were to become an official religion—just like politicians and the church had later turned Jesus Christ's words of brotherly love into crusades, murder, and manslaughter. Yet it was brave to claim that your only faith was in love.

She had thought that Karim was a Christian. He had drunk wine during the party and he lived on Jasmine Street, where only Christians lived, just like in Abbara Street. But that wasn't completely true... on her street there were also three Muslim and two Druze families. Maybe

Muslims also lived on Jasmine Street, and Karim was one of them. His name meant "the Generous" in Arabic—and it could equally have been given to a Jew, a Christian, a Druze, a Yezidi, or a Muslim.

Fine, she thought, he only believes in love, but everybody else sees him as a Muslim. "So what?" an inner voice said, frightening her. Who was talking now—her heart in love or her reason? Or were they joining in unison? What is it about a Muslim that should stop me from loving him? Indeed, even if Karim was a believing Jew, Druze, or Buddhist, who or what prohibited her from loving him? Aida thought of her friends and acquaintances. All religions were represented there... friendship was obviously allowed between people of different faiths. Why was love forbidden?

22

Encounters and Deceptions

Damascus, December 2010

The healer

Several days after his arrival, a healer visited Salman's father. She came at around ten in the morning and, that day, Salman stayed at home because he wanted to see her.

His father waited for her with anticipation. Salman's mother told him that the healer only paid house calls for three patients—his father and two rich, elderly ladies. Everyone else had to go to her and ask for an appointment. His father's privileged position was due to the fact that Salman's cousin, Father Michel Kosma, was her mentor and patron. To Salman's surprise, Marina was a pretty young woman. When she came into the living room, she quietly held out a hand to him and seemed to see right through him.

His father was waiting for her in his room, and Salman heard how she loudly ordered him around. "In the Name of the Holy Virgin! In the Name of the Holy Virgin, get up," she kept repeating. Soon they both came into the sitting room. His father was walking alone, without his stick and standing straight. "You see, it's your faith, not me, it's your faith that has helped you."

She knelt in the middle of the sitting room and prayed while Salman's father stood next to her, folding his hands to pray too, seemingly lost in a distant world. The television was on as usual, a report on a literary festival. The report was accidentally funny because several poets from Syria and other Arab countries seemed to be outdoing one another in singing the president's praises. For each poet, only two or three verses were broadcast, all mentioning the president. The Egyptian whom Salman had met on the plane came last. His distressed face now filled the screen. "Pray, great leader, forgive my frankness. Syria is too small. You should lead the whole world!" he shouted into the room. "Forgive me for being so in love, but how can my heart resist? Your beauty has bewitched me."

The audience in the hall went wild.

"The poor president. This elephant wants to go to bed with him," Sophia whispered smugly from behind Salman. Barely able to contain himself, Salman ran into the kitchen and burst out laughing there. He thought of the simple carpenter who had sat near the poet in the plane and kept calling him *hakawati*. Salman didn't know whether Marina could hear him laughing in the kitchen.

After she finished praying, she left. Salman's father held on to her hand. "My nephew, Father Kosma, is coming here tonight. Would you like to join us? We'll be eating together." He hesitated for a moment. "I mean, you can also bring your husband." Then he added, "Salman would be happy." Salman nodded. He was standing behind Marina, and his thoughts were not as pure as his father's.

"Unfortunately, that won't be possible," she said. "And Father Kosma knows about it, too. Some seventy pupils are coming with their teachers to pray at my place today." Marina nodded an abrupt goodbye and left.

Salman called Stella. He was still fascinated that he'd seen his father walk again. Stella laughed and told him not to lose his mind just because he'd been back in Damascus for a few days. She had a friend who was married to an

Egyptian. He was very modern when he was in Rome, and left-wing. But no sooner did he land in Cairo than he changed completely. He prayed every day, grew a beard, stopped drinking and smoking, and forced his Italian wife to wear a headscarf. Salman felt hurt that Stella would compare him to such a conformist.

Stella didn't seem to understand his anger. She repeated that she didn't believe in this nonsense of healing through prayer. She suspected that Marina wielded power over weak souls, such as his father's, by taking advantage of his gullibility—just like the placebo effect for drugs. The conversation faltered and then petered out to routine pleasantries. This was the first phone conversation that Salman had felt something like alienation from Stella.

The phone rang soon after. His mother picked it up, and her eyes revealed her astonishment. "Just a moment, please," she said, calling Salman over. "Lamia," she whispered.

"Yes, hello. What a surprise!" Salman said, drawing a deep breath. Lamia, whom he had worshipped, lived in Homs and had learned of his arrival. "My goodness, you found out so quickly?" he asked her. Lamia laughed. One of her girlfriends had been among the guests who had visited him in the last few days. Lamia told him about her happy life as a housewife and a mother of seven children and about her nice husband. Salman thought she had married a slave master who had turned a bright woman into a dull housewife, but he kept that to himself.

He was bored by Lamia's report. He courteously brought the conversation to an end, hung up, and felt shocked at his indifference.

The evening meal with his cousin, Father Kosma, was disappointing. There was no trace of the once critical spirit of a brilliant artist. Kosma seemed totally convinced by the healer and he cursed the Vatican for refusing to recognize her. His eyes shone when he spoke of her. Salman felt embarrassed and he let out a sigh of relief when the priest left the apartment with his driver.

A few days later, Salman's father sat in his wheelchair again, unable to get up. He was not pretending, he really couldn't. "Miracles don't seem to last long these days," Salman told his mother.

"That's blasphemy," she replied quietly, and crossed herself.

~

When Salman woke up the next Sunday, he realized that he had already been in Damascus for a week. He wanted to buy presents for Stella and Paolo, so he set off for the souk al-Hamidiya, the large covered market.

Even after searching for a long time, he couldn't find anything suitable in the market. So he continued on foot to the New City, and the sight of the congested streets and ugly high-rise buildings distressed him. First the Mongols had destroyed Damascus between 1259 and 1300, and now the Damascenes had done it themselves.

Back home that evening, an unexpected visitor turned up—Rita, his former lover. She scolded him for not coming to visit her yet, like he had promised, although she had been to see him every other day. "It reeks of family, morality, and hypocrisy here. You'd be free at my place," she breathed in his ear when she arrived. Salman attempted not to hear her.

"Yes, sure," he said almost absentmindedly.

On her first visit Rita had surprised him. He had hardly recognized her. She was now blond and had lost twenty years with the help of a Parisian cosmetic surgeon.

Salman was three years older than Rita; he had met her at a party given by a rich fellow student. She was nineteen, with coal black hair and a sensual aura. She always was surrounded by men and wasn't interested in him at first because he had been hopelessly in love with Lamia. At that time, Salman was quite a Romantic—aside from Marxist writings, he read mostly poems about unrequited love, which made up most of traditional Arab poetry.

Lamia loved him, but premarital sex was a mortal sin for her as a practicing Catholic. He promised her that he'd believe in God, Jesus, Moses, and even Muhammad if only she'd kiss him, but she refused. Salman protested. "The early Christians allowed themselves to be devoured by wild animals to convert others to Christianity. And you won't give me even one kiss to drive the darkness from my heart!"

It wasn't just premarital sex that divided Lamia and Salman. She also disapproved of his political commitment. But the more she distanced herself from him, the more he loved her.

Rita told him later that his indifference toward her then had drawn her into his spell. It was his very aloofness that challenged her. She was a born huntress.

Just like the other students, Salman had no idea that the young woman who danced at student parties had married at the young age of seventeen. Her husband was twenty years her senior, a wealthy consultant and horse breeder. Soon after her wedding, she'd found out that her husband didn't have much time for women. He loved pure-blooded horses and young outdoorsmen—she was just meant as window dressing. Half the city knew about his inclinations, and she found her position ridiculous. One piece of advice from a friend was to enjoy the riches and give her heart free rein. "The world is chock-full of young men dying to lie at your feet!"

And so Rita became an erotic adventuress. And since she believed in discretion, she became a comfortably kept woman. Her husband was generous, and she spent money hand over fist. She had lovers from all social classes—that is, until Salman came into her life. She quickly fell for him, but he kept her at arm's length. At first he didn't react either to her presents or her letters. From then on, she was mainly seen in student circles, where the people she met were fundamentally different from her husband's acquaintances.

When Lamia got married, Salman had to come to terms with the fact that his love for her had finally reached an impasse. So he let himself be comforted by Rita, and he liked it. Although he noticed that Rita was in love with him, deep down he remained frosty toward her, which kindled her love even more. She had never known a man who had been able to resist her charms for so long and who cared so little about her money. Without noticing, she had become the victim of her own thrill of the chase.

At the time, Salman was already leading a double life—one public and one in the underground, well concealed. Rita proposed that they run away together to America. She had money enough for both of them. Salman refused. He found her too unreliable. And he didn't want to flee, he wanted to be a part of the Syrian revolution. He could feel the conflict between his political convictions and his association with this wealthy woman whose arrogant words against the world's poor filled him with indignation. Sometimes he would humiliate her in retribution for the downtrodden, but his cruelty seemed only to make her become even more enamored with him.

When he joined the armed resistance, he broke off his

relationship with Rita for good and disappeared without saying goodbye. For her part, she vowed never to get involved so deeply with another man, and she once more became the huntress she had been before—only with a scar on her soul.

~

After an hour of social chat, she left early that evening. As Salman accompanied her to the door, she turned to him and gave him a lingering kiss. "Will you come and visit me? I have good espresso," she said, handing him an elegant visiting card from a golden case. Salman laughed, refraining from reminding her that she had already given him an identical card on her first visit, a few days earlier. "Only espresso?" he said jokingly, caressing her back. He somehow felt sorry for her that her life was so filled with disappointment.

"I swear I'll keep my hands off you," she said as she left the apartment.

"That old woman has her eye on you. Did you know each other?" his cousin Maria whispered to him when he returned to the other guests. That evening she was seated to his right. Salman was startled and lied, "Only slightly."

In that moment he heard his mother calling in the corridor: "At long last! Where have you been all this time?" Salman looked up. His cousin Elias had arrived, accompanied by a woman wearing a lot of makeup.

"Oh no! Time to go now," Maria whispered again, pressing Salman's hand and disappearing quietly.

~

Elias had grown older, but he had hardly changed. "Our prodigal son has finally returned," he called out. He did not embrace Salman, but gave his hand a squeeze. Salman wondered why his former comrades had shown such

231

deference to Elias, who seemed to grow several inches taller whenever they shook his hand. Had he humiliated them, possibly had them interrogated and tortured? Elias seemed to inspire respect from the other guests, too—a fear mingled with hypocrisy. Some of them called him "Colonel Elias."

"So this is Salman," his wife Isabella said. "Finally, a real male in this wishy-washy family," she called out, uttering a vulgar sound somewhere between a gurgle and a snort. She was probably fifteen years younger than Elias, and Salman took an immediate dislike to her.

Salman's father treated Elias like someone deserving special courtesy. He paid his respects to him and stayed up until shortly before midnight, in high spirits, mixing with the guests in the drawing room. When Salman went to the kitchen to get some wine and told Sophia how amazed he was at his father, she cursed softly. "He wants to show him how grateful he is," she said, "as if the ten thousand dollars weren't enough." Salman felt a helpless rage. "Elias doesn't even caress his wife for free. That's why she needs so many lovers," Sophia added contemptuously.

Everyone accepted Isabella as a necessary evil. She was a loud, pretentious name-dropper who would only refer to people by their first name in order to emphasize her close connection with high-ranking officers—General Ali, Colonel Maher, General Assif. The circle of her acquaintances did not include anyone below the rank of colonel. Salman sat in the armchair next to his comrade Josef Samuel. He had been the best blasphemer among the fighters, and although he was now running a furniture factory with over five hundred employees, he had lost none of his vicious tongue. Giving up his seat so that Isabella could sit next to her husband, he whispered to Salman, "She's the sweetest revenge on Elias-the-monster. The whole city knows about her whoring."

The evening babbled along. People talked about everything except politics or the economy. That was Sophia's express wish. "The Syrian survival principle" as she called it. "Let them rule in peace and they'll let you live." Salman followed her advice and kept his cool at Elias's snide remarks, which he filed under the heading "envious attacks." He consoled himself with the fact that those who envy are the only ones who suffer more than their victims from their deeds.

By some morbid coincidence, six members of his rebel group found themselves sitting together in the same room after more than forty years. Elias had become a high-ranking officer in the secret service, Salman was a rich merchant living in Rome, Josef Samuel ran a large factory, Ahmad Hariri owned two car dealerships, Mahmoud Bardoni was a wholesaler in agricultural products, and Jirgi Sairafi owned a chain of hotels. How would the six of them have reacted at the time if this had been foretold for them?

Conversations buzzed over the background noise of some television program, punctuated by smartphone ringtone melodies. His friends left shortly before midnight, offering the remaining guests their well wishes. Salman saw them to the door. They promised to return the following day. "Let's hope the traitor doesn't come, too," Josef Samuel confided in his ear, and Salman nodded.

"We're lucky Hani wasn't here tonight. Who knows? He might have strangled Elias," Sophia said later, as Salman drank one last glass of water in the kitchen. Little did she suspect that Hani's absence would turn out to be lucky for her son.

23

Deliberate Provocation and a Wager

Damascus, December 2010

Why aren't there any good
Arab detective novels?

The church bell chimed ten o'clock as Salman returned to the large drawing room. "Funny friends you've got there, cousin. Half of them have done time and the others are gay," Elias mocked with a laugh. Only his wife laughed with him. Salman ignored the remark. Later he kept saying that Elias had come over that evening just to provoke him. And when that failed, he proposed a bet, which he had planned long beforehand.

Elias had made cutting remarks all evening, and Salman had deliberately ignored them. Even Salman's father had tried to moderate his arrogance, saying, "Let's all be happy that Salman has returned safe and sound." Looking back, Salman appreciated his father's sensitive antenna for Elias's provocation and the danger it concealed. Yusuf's attempts to maintain harmony were not in the least naïve, as they might have seemed at first, but were an astute and friendly gesture toward Elias. They were meant to make clear that people had seen through his provocation, and to feed his vanity. He did all this to peaceably nip aggression in the bud, hoping that Elias would drop his animosity toward Salman. "You're cousins," Salman's father said, appealing to the last vestiges of clan solidarity in Elias's lost soul. "And what is a cousin, if not like a brother?" But Elias had gone deaf to any appeals to conscience.

Salman's father had stayed up until before midnight not to honor his nephew, but because he feared an argument. Struggling against the fatigue caused by the painkillers he took, he finally gave in and fell asleep in his wheelchair. Then Sophia pushed him slowly into the bedroom.

Hardly had she left the drawing room when Elias opened up. He didn't wish to offend anyone, but nobody should abandon the Fatherland. "Let's assume a man is educated. He has studied or learned a profession here and then he goes as a doctor or a grocery merchant to Germany or Italy, and offers his work or his knowledge, for which neither the Germans nor the Italians have paid a single lira. His sin against the Fatherland is twofold. He leaves it in the lurch in the struggle against Israel and wastes its patrimony, making a present of it to a former colonial power. Do you see what I mean?"

Some nodded. Others understood what he was driving at but found his objection inappropriate. Salman came within a hair of answering him that the greatest waste of Syria's wealth could be laid at the door of the dictator's clan. Billions squirreled away abroad and fifteen secret services had bled the country dry. But he bit his tongue as his mother stroked his back unobtrusively. She was also afraid of Elias. "It's treason," Elias went on, "and someone like that belongs in jail until he's paid off the cost of his education in Syria. That would come to a tidy sum for the Fatherland."

Some laughed. Salman's cousin Tarek spoke up. "That's ridiculous. We'd be better off sending the Germans the bill—a hundred thousand dollars for every doctor. I heard there's at least two thousand Syrian doctors there.

That comes to two hundred million dollars. That's what Germany owes a little country like Syria. They should send Elias the money, otherwise there'll be war," he said, showing that he'd understood Elias's hint and wanted to help Salman.

·"And what'll we do if we win the war?" his neighbor Abdullah asked. "Then we'd have to rebuild Germany, just like the Americans did. That costs billions. No, better not!" He laughed out loud. Elias's expression darkened.

Sophia whispered, "The gentleman from the secret services is making a fool of himself."

Salman was visibly enjoying the situation. He somehow felt above all these ridiculous accusations and snide remarks. Probably in an effort to steer the conversation in another direction, Isabella suddenly started waxing poetic about a Swedish detective story that she'd seen on television. She was surprised that the Swedes could write and tell such spine-chilling stories.

Salman loved detective stories, not just Scandinavian, but also those by the witty Sicilian Andrea Camilleri, with his Commissario Montalbano.

Sana, the daughter of his parents' neighbors, asked why there were no really good Arab detective stories—at least, she hadn't come across any yet. She was in film studies at the university. Sana's brave, Salman thought, asking an interesting but dangerous question. The young woman's complexion was pale and delicate, "as if light was her only nourishment," as Sophia used to say, and she wore her hair boyishly short.

The guests, including Salman and even Elias, confirmed the young student's comment. "But why are there no good detective stories? A little country like Sweden, with a population no more than half the size of Syria, conquers the world with its detective stories. Every single author has written more quality detective stories than all three hundred million Arabs put together. Something seems to get in the way of Arab detective stories," Sana argued. Many Syrians knew the exciting Swedish detective stories, which were also shown on Syrian television or in the cinema.

"I think it's because we're too hot-headed," said a small man with a moustache, the husband of one of Salman's cousins. "We prefer to find a culprit quickly and haven't the patient, cool thinking of the Swedes and English." Some guests laughed. "A month ago," he went on, "a young man killed his sister, a woman with a bewitching voice. And why did he kill her? All the neighbors knew why—because she was a Muslim woman in love with a Christian man. She was eighteen years old. The police closed the case in five minutes. The brother gave himself up. He'd killed his sister because she'd dragged the family's honor through the dirt. He's sixteen and bound to be sentenced to a maximum of two years. He'll do eighteen months of that and will be treated like a hero when he's released, as if he'd liberated Palestine. But, as I said to my wife, the case is more complicated than that.

"A good inspector would have found out that the parents of the young man had egged him on against his sister. An inspector would also have found out that one of his uncles on his father's side also belonged in prison, since he pumped the boy full of arak and gave him a pistol. And he would have asked why the idiot killed his own sister and not the lover. The boy wouldn't have been able to answer, because his parents forbade him to shoot the man without giving a reason. The lover comes from a powerful clan, and the family of the murdered girl would have been afraid for their lives. That would have been a great detective story.

But as it is, it's stuck being just another one of these stupid honor killings."

Sana's mother joined in. "Yes, a good detective—man or woman—would have figured out that all of Arab society belonged on trial. That would have led to a decent debate about the mess we're in. Arabs have been wounded and humiliated in the name of honor and dignity for centuries, and what do we do? Instead of rebelling and standing up to our tormentors, we hide our honor between a woman's legs," she said. "Suddenly I'm no longer a woman but a treasure chest for men's honor. That's just plain cowardice, isn't it?"

"Men should stick their honor between their own balls. It'll be safer there than with us," Sophia added, and both women burst out laughing.

"You've forgotten something else," said Isabella, getting drawn in. "I just saw a French film that had a woman inspector successfully solving the case. Just imagine, a woman inspector in Saudi Arabia." She laughed. "Maybe in a bikini?" she added, laughing even louder, joined by many of the guests.

"But Sana's question is justified and unanswered," Salman reminded them. "Why are there no decent Arab detective novels?"

Elias replied, "Well, obviously in northern countries it's different than here—always dark and cold. The London fog drives people to commit murders that are difficult to solve, and in ice-cold, thinly populated Sweden, it's child's play to make a corpse disappear. That means that living conditions demand a capable inspector."

"Fog and cold may be important factors in a detective story," Salman objected. "But Spain, Greece, and Italy are no colder than our country and they've produced very good detective stories." Sana nodded vehemently. She was an enthusiastic reader of the French versions of detective novels by Manuel Vásquez Montalbán, Andrea Camilleri, and Petros Markaris.

"It's also surprising," said Burhan, the neighbor from the second floor and a professor emeritus, "that our writers have imitated all the masters of world literature, from Tolstoy to García Márquez, Kafka and even Hemingway, without ever emulating Edgar Allan Poe, Agatha Christie, Arthur Conan Doyle, or Georges Simenon. Why is that?"

"You're right, the only famous murder mysteries that take place in Arab countries have been written by Agatha Christie—*Murder in Mesopotamia* or *Death on the Nile*," Isabella confirmed. "And they're actually her poorest ones," she added. Salman nodded. She was right, Agatha Christie did not know the Arabs very well.

"That is truly amazing. Why the hell is that?" Professor Burhan asked.

"I believe…" Salman started, after deciding to talk about Arabs in general instead of Syrians, so as not to provoke Elias. "I believe that no Arab can imagine an inspector being allowed to ask the questions that will explain a murder, no matter how honorable, smart, or conscientious he may be. That's why no Arab can believe that an inspector can successfully investigate, if the people he wants to interrogate are, say, members of the ruling family."

"And why not?" Elias asked irritably.

"Because in life as in novels, investigations require a freedom that can't be found in any Arab country. Imagine a murder taking place in the palace of the Saudi king. What inspector would dare question even a cousin three times removed?" Salman deliberately chose the example of Saudi Arabia to keep Elias satisfied, because the regime in

Damascus hated the Saudis. "I don't mean to be political, but in order to solve a murder, purely on a technical level, the inspector must be allowed to ask *everyone* about *every* detail. The freedom to ask questions is the life and death of an investigation. Even in Lebanon you're not allowed to ask just any question of just anyone." He felt like a complete hypocrite for again not mentioning Syria.

"I don't believe that. In our country, everyone is allowed to ask whatever they want of anyone, don't you think?" Elias asked coolly.

Salman felt his mother's hand on his back, warning him to measure his words. "I really don't know. After all, I've been away for forty years," he replied evasively.

But Sana laughed out loud. "Not at all, Colonel. I love our president, and I'd be the last to talk down our country. But Salman is talking about the whole clan structure in Arab society, and it's no different here than in Yemen or Egypt."

"You're right," Salman agreed. "But it's not only that. In Europe, detectives enjoy high status, but here they're on the lowest rung of the ladder."

"That's the way it is all over the world," Tarek interrupted. "Berlusconi is basically a criminal, and I've always wondered how the Italians could elect such a con man time and again instead of sending him to jail. There's corruption in France, Spain, Germany, Great Britain, even Scandinavia."

"Thank you, dear Tarek," Elias said. "But my famous cousin here forgives the Italians for everything. He lives among them courteously and avoids any criticism. It's only when he's here, in our country, that he would like to tear apart all rulers and drive them naked through the streets. That's not decent," he concluded, his voice shaking with emotion. Sophia unobtrusively pressed her son's arm. Salman took the hint and said nothing.

"Let's stop talking politics," Sophia broke in. "I know a good inspector nearby, and I've heard him talk to the grocer. His salary is barely enough for three, yet he has five children, a wife, and sick parents who live with him. This man cannot concentrate on solving a murder when he's constantly worrying about how his family will survive until the end of the month. So it's not a question of politics. The problem is the lousy civil service pay. It's the same with teachers—many of them need a second job just to make ends meet."

Elias calmed down. He nodded, because the problem of lousy civil service pay also applied to the secret service.

The wager

"So what do detectives need so that they can work effectively and we can finally have an exciting detective novel?" Sana asked. Everyone started talking at once, throwing suggestions all around. Once they had all calmed down a bit, Sana said, "I think detectives should have a free hand, and this has to come from the top—from the president— who must give them absolute freedom to question anyone. But, that should not lead to any defamation of the persons being questioned, who should remain innocent until proven guilty... and detectives need better pay."

Elias laughed gleefully. "I've got a better method for convicting a criminal, and it's already been used to expose public enemies. Sure, they were political criminals, but their aim was to destroy our Fatherland and that is much worse than murder."

All present hastened to agree with him. Salman was completely unmoved by this patriotic prattle from a member of the secret service.

"What sort of method?" he asked.

"It's a bit complicated," Elias replied quietly, "but I can explain it using an example. Just imagine a sheep living in a meadow surrounded by a wire fence to protect it against predators. Night is falling and the sheep can hear the wolves howling nearby. When they reach the fence, the sheep becomes terribly afraid. The wolves discover a post which has been loosened and they hurl themselves wildly against it. The fence starts to shake, and the sheep can already smell and feel the wolves breathing down its neck. It runs around in circles and notices that its pen has become a prison. And while the wolves are busy with the fence post, the sheep discovers a hole in the fence on the opposite side. What do you think the poor animal will do? It will be surprised and will hesitate for a bit. But when it hears the wolves growling again, it will forget its doubts and leap out through the hole, not suspecting that death is lurking on the other side of the opening."

"Yes, and then we can soon put it on the grill," the man with the moustache said in amusement. Isabella laughed hysterically until she was quite out of breath. "Yes, we'll grill it," she repeated through her tears.

"There's nothing new about that method. It's a sinister one used in the Eastern Bloc," Salman said, ignoring his mother's hand. "But it didn't help them. Where are the wolves of the past? They beg among yesterday's sheep. You could have learned a bit more during the Prague Spring in Czechoslovakia than what you had to cram at the police academy," he said.

"Unfortunately it's too late now for me to tell you everything I learned in Czechoslovakia, but I'll bet you ten thousand dollars that my method will convict any criminal, while a respectable citizen will not only have nothing to fear—he won't even notice the whole hunt." Elias's tone had hardened, and the guests held their breath.

There we go, ten thousand dollars again, Salman thought and almost said aloud, remembering the money Elias had taken from his father. But Sophia now pressed on his back so hard that it hurt. He swallowed his caustic reply because he didn't want to argue with this dangerous opportunist. His mother was right. Elias was spineless, powerful, and threatening.

So he replied, "Fine—I don't believe you, but I never bet. Do you hear, dear cousin, I never bet, because I always lose my wagers. I once wagered that a young man had character—and I lost."

A leaden silence descended, but did not last long.

"What a pity," said Isabella with a sigh. "Elias always wins his bets, and it's about time we had a Jacuzzi in the bath." She brayed with laughter again. Elias smiled crookedly.

"That's cowardly, coming out with all that fancy talk and then dodging the consequences... That's our lefties for you, especially when they've become millionaires among the Romans."

Deep down, Salman knew that he'd defeated Elias without any provocation. None of the guests were aware that Salman had vouched for Elias in the mountains when their comrades had suspected him of working for the secret service.

Elias stood up to leave. Salman played the courteous host, inviting him to stay longer. When Elias excused himself, saying that he had to get up early the next day to fly to Moscow with a delegation, Salman jumped up and accompanied him and his wife to the door. Sophia followed slowly and stood in the middle of the corridor, a little away

243

from the couple. Salman helped Isabella into her fur coat, and she gave him a goodbye peck on the cheek. "You must come and visit us. A successful man who has seen the world is always an asset," she said.

"Why won't you bet, you coward?" Elias joked, punching Salman lightly in the chest.

"I'm a born loser. The wager was a joke, wasn't it?" Salman said innocently to cover up his dislike.

"A pity I have to go to Moscow tomorrow. Otherwise I'd have enjoyed tempting you into another wager," Elias replied, laughing cheerfully before disappearing down the stairs.

~

That night Salman stayed awake for a long time. Why did Elias dislike him so much? Could it be because Salman was the only one in the family who knew about his betrayal? Or because Salman had escaped and now returned with his head held high? And he, the high-ranking officer, had to live with this betrayal in his heart, and go on being dependent on bribes in order to be able to pay for his wife's expenses and the megalomania of his cripplingly expensive villa.

Elias's provocations and his absurd story of the sheep and the wolves made Salman fear that his cousin was plotting something against him. He calmed himself with the thought that Elias was bound to have more important matters to deal with in Moscow than tormenting his cousin. But he would soon find out that his suspicion was more than justified.

24

Hope Reborn

It was two in the afternoon when Aida stood in front of Karim's door with a basket. She was bringing two bottles of red wine, a jar of quince jelly, and a jar of salted pistachio nuts. Three times she had filled the basket with treats, and three times she had emptied it. She didn't wish to come empty-handed, neither did she want to bring anything that Karim didn't like. From the previous evening's feast when they had met at the Selfless, she knew that he was fond of red wine and pistachio nuts. And she had a passion for quince jelly, of which she cooked twelve jars every year, one for each month.

Karim opened the door, smiling as he pulled her inside, locking the door behind her and kissing her with all his heart. He wore an old pair of jeans and a white shirt. Later she had no idea how the basket had landed on the floor safely from her hand.

For the first time ever, Aida felt a special warmth rise up within her, as if she had just taken a sip of strong hot coffee. It was almost unpleasant. She felt the ground become increasingly soft beneath her feet as she clung to Karim. When she pulled herself back into the moment, she looked deep into Karim's eyes and found him even more attractive than the day before.

Was that the meaning of the famous kiss turning a frog into a prince? She could feel her heart beating as if it wanted to jump out of her chest.

"I thought you wanted to have a meal together—but something edible, not me!"

"I've prepared everything, but I'd like to eat you up first, I'm so hungry," he said, kissing her eyes.

"Me too, for you," she said softly, hugging him tightly.

He walked beside her, holding the basket in his left hand, and Aida had a strange feeling as if she had always known his house. From the gate of the property, a beautiful mosaic-paved path led to three wide steps on the left of the house, and onto a slightly raised terrace. The right-hand side opened into a large, luxuriant garden, which was magnificent now in the autumn. There were vegetables, roses, citrus, apple, and plum trees.

A bistro table and three chairs stood on the terrace near a decorative wrought-iron railing that separated the house from the garden. Across the terrace, a path led under three arches to a small inner courtyard. An octagonal fountain in colored marble splashed and bubbled in the courtyard's center.

"Take a seat," he said, and only let go of her hand once Aida had sat down at the bistro table. The soft noise of the water calmed her.

"Would you like a coffee?"

"Yes, gladly," she said, although she would have preferred to nuzzle up to him in bed right away. He smelled as delicious as fresh bread. His mouth tasted of cardamom. Obviously he had already had a mocha.

He went into the kitchen. From where she was sitting, she could see how he almost danced while preparing the coffee. She looked around her; all the rooms had doors and windows opening onto the courtyard. A railing lined the narrow corridor that ran around the upstairs perimeter. She saw a large room with a wide terrace leading to the garden. A large vine was growing there. It bore light green grapes and gave shade to the terrace in summer like a sun umbrella.

She heard Karim whistling a melody. He whistled with devotion, but out of tune. He brought out the coffee, and she savored it along with the "nightingale's nest," a Damascene pastry with pistachios and thin noodles.

"Shall I show you the house?" he asked.

"No, I'll look at it later," she replied, and helped herself to another nightingale's nest.

~

An hour later, she was lying covered in sweat under the thin bed sheets, watching him as he held up an earthenware jug so that the water flowed in a high arc out of its spout and into his mouth. She had never been able to do that. As a child she had always envied her brother who had never spilled a drop, just like Karim was doing now, when he would empty half the jug like this. "It's child's play," he said, "just breathe through your nose and swallow without closing your mouth." She never managed it. She would choke every time.

Karim stood there, slim and almost athletic. If she hadn't known that he was over seventy-five, she would have taken him for a prematurely gray fifty-year-old. Aida smiled. Love is guided neither by date of birth nor religion. It takes people as God made them, with no religion and no money, all equal in our nakedness.

He came to her in the bed, which stood opposite two windows looking out over the garden. The room was spacious, and Aida saw an orange and a lemon tree in front of the high garden wall, and the blue sky beyond. Karim kissed her. It had been a long time since she had felt so soft and relaxed.

"It's a beautiful place you have here," Aida said, letting her glance stray to the bookshelves that stood against the walls on both sides of the bed.

"Yes, but it's a lot of work. I'd be really lost without Farida."

"Aha," she teased him and gave him a gentle nudge in the ribs. "Did you also bewitch her with your charm?"

He laughed. "You'll soon meet her. Farida can't be bribed with charm. She makes her living as a housekeeper to widows and widowers. She washes, irons, and cleans the house twice a week. And each time she needs two pots of coffee just to keep her in a good mood."

He handed her a pair of fresh white silk pajamas. She laughed and tied the slightly generous trousers at the waist with a small cord, then rolled up the sleeves of the shirt and the trouser legs. "You look enchanting," he said, "like a little girl who has slipped into her father's pajamas."

They went to the kitchen and he quickly chopped up the lettuce that had already been washed. She wasn't allowed to touch a thing, just to watch. "Let me at least set the table," she said. She had never once in her life been spoiled by a man. He kissed her. "Princesses let others serve them. Remember that." The table in the living room next to the kitchen was already laid. The *kibbeh* in the oven smelled of allspice and roasted pine nuts. On the table stood a carafe of red wine and two glasses.

~

After their meal, he wandered through the big house with her. He not only showed her the rooms, but also photos from his time with his late wife, Amira, and his daughter, Maha. At the end, he also showed her his workshop, the two guest rooms, and the childhood room of his now grown-up daughter. And while they were standing together on the first-floor terrace enjoying fresh grapes straight from the vine, Karim waved to two women who were trying to observe Karim and Aida as discreetly as possible from the house next door.

"Now they've got a juicy bit of scandal to drive away their boredom," Aida said and laughed.

"Don't be so heartless. If our love is useful to them, even if it's just to drive away boredom, then it's a worthy thing," he said, and she didn't know if he was joking or not.

And before the rooster from the neighboring house had crowed the next morning, every last woman on Jasmine Street knew that Karim and Aida were lovers and that Aida had stayed the night. The first part of the rumor was true, the second part wasn't.

It was after midnight when Aida sat up in bed. She had never made love to a man three times in a day. Karim "the insatiable"—as he called himself—slept next to her, as peaceful as a baby. The temperature in the room was pleasant. Outside, the full moon bathed the garden in its cool light. She slipped naked to the window and marveled at the beauty of the night as if she were seeing it for the first time. No wonder, she thought, that Arabs have always sung of the night so passionately.

When she turned around, Karim was awake. "What are you doing at the window?" he asked.

"Getting some fresh air and swimming in the moon-light," she said.

"Come to me, I can't swim so well without you," he said, stretching out his arms.

"I've got to go home," she replied. That disconcerted him, and he wouldn't understand it later on, either. But Aida insisted. Even if they spent most of their time with each other, whether at his place or hers, they were not to spend the night together. "That way, each time we meet will be a precious, exciting adventure," she said, kissed him, and left.

III

25

The Hunt Begins

Damascus, December 13–14, 2010

Strangely enough, Isabella came by to visit the next day, Monday, but this time alone. She rang the bell just as Salman was about to leave the house that morning. Isabella was dressed elegantly and enveloped in a cloud of perfume. She wanted to see Salman again before he vanished for years again, she joked. She had been fascinated by the previous evening's conversation about detective novels. When Salman's father asked about Elias, she told him he had left for Russia early that morning. He would be there for ten days to two weeks. She shouldn't really be telling them that he was away on a secret mission, but everyone was family here. Elias sent his best to Salman, she said.

Salman asked Isabella if there was anything he could send her from Rome when he returned home in a few days. As if she had been waiting for just this offer, Isabella took a slip of paper out of her handbag on which she had written the names of two skin creams and an expensive perfume. Stella used the same perfume. Salman told her he would send everything and refused the money she offered. "Either as a gift or not at all," he said.

"Do come and visit me, and let me spoil you. I'm bored all day," Isabella whispered as he finally helped her into her coat. Salman was speechless. She hugged him just a little too firmly and he felt her soft, warm body; if his mother hadn't been standing behind him he would have really kissed her. He wanted this woman. Isabella looked at him conspiratorially, as if she had understood, smiled, and left in a hurry.

"That's why she came," Sophia murmured, pointing to the slip of paper when Salman was back in the living room. Her husband chided her gently that Isabella had come with the best intentions, but Sophia always found a reason not to like Elias and his wife.

"A silly goose. She's a huntress and as soon as the prey is in her claws, she lets it wriggle," Sophia said on her way back to the kitchen.

Salman found Isabella sexually attractive and desired her. But he didn't contradict his mother; he hadn't done so since his tenth birthday.

His reason served to cool down his lust. In the few days remaining, he had to avoid a provocation at all costs. Knowing Elias, he would be sure to have his wife watched, perhaps even with cameras. A cold shiver ran down Salman's back, washing away the last of his lust for Isabella.

~

Salman went to the big souk al-Hamidiya again. He found a golden brooch and a necklace for Stella, both of the finest craftsmanship, perfect examples of the goldsmith's art. For Paolo there was a large box made of precious wood, with fine marquetry, and a music box that played *Eine kleine Nachtmusik* by Mozart, a piece Paolo loved. As a young child, he couldn't hear it often enough. Salman spent the rest of the day in Tarek's workshop. He was moved to hear how his cousin had always admired him, seemingly without a trace of envy.

That evening, he was invited to dinner with the patriarch of the Catholic Church. The previous day, his cousin, Father Michael Kosma, had called him to say that the head of the Catholic Church would be pleased to welcome such a successful son of the Catholic community to his home. Father Kosma had joked, "Dear rich cousin, just make out your check beforehand. Our patriarch is bound to mention the orphanage."

"Isn't it enough that I recognize the patriarch even though I'm a former communist?" Salman replied. Kosma's laugh sounded forced. "The patriarch knows nothing of your past. Let's keep that to ourselves."

The evening with the patriarch was mostly formal, but all three men were on their best diplomatic behavior. To Salman's joy the patriarch proved able to hold his liquor, even the excellent Lebanese wine. Salman said goodbye toward midnight and wanted to call a taxi, but the patriarch insisted on having him taken home in his chauffeur-driven black limousine. Salman handed the head of the Catholic Church an envelope containing two thousand euros. "For the orphanage," he said quietly, although the patriarch had not even mentioned it once. Father Kosma grinned.

"Christ's representatives travel so comfortably," Salman commented from the back of the splendid car, and he leaned back luxuriously.

"Our patriarch represents several million Catholics in the Holy Land. He can't just go around in a 2 CV," the insulted chauffeur replied, sparing Salman from any further conversation.

~

"There were so many people here... I'm very proud of my popular son," his mother confided to him when he arrived home. "But I consoled them. After all, you're here until the twenty-third," she laughed. "My sister Takla cursed the patriarch for depriving her of an evening with you—yes, her very words."

The following day, Salman's mother wanted him to visit an aunt who was over a hundred years old. She was in intensive care with pneumonia at the French hospital, which was officially known as the St. Louis Hospital. Salman would only be there for a few more days and should say goodbye to his aunt who had loved him so much when he was a child, his mother said.

The aunt didn't recognize him. She smiled, yet her smile didn't seem to be meant for Salman, but for some invisible companion. She spoke in disjointed phrases that were perhaps part of a secret conversation with her ghosts. He stroked her pale bony hand where the blue veins protruded under the thin skin. She didn't react. At that moment, Salman felt such sadness that tears welled up in his eyes. This aunt had been the liveliest woman imaginable, and now she was just a breathing husk. How lonely the dying are, he thought, even when they await death comforted and cared for, and not in a miserable hovel. Salman left the room.

~

He needed an espresso. He glanced at his watch and was surprised to see that he had only spent a half hour with his aunt. He sat in a small café nearby and drank an Italian espresso. Suddenly, as he was swallowing the last sip, his glance fell on the front page of the government daily paper *Tishrin* that a man sitting across from him was reading, and he saw his own picture. It wasn't a large photo, but the headline was clear. The police were looking for this man, the alleged murderer of Fatima Haddad. He couldn't make out anything more. He paid quickly and left.

It was like a slap in the face. His first thought was that he had to buy a pair of sunglasses. There was a supermarket nearby, but he didn't dare go in. Just before Burj al-Rus Square he found an exclusive optician's shop.

There he chose an elegant pair of sunglasses, put them on, and breathed a sigh of relief. Perhaps he was just imagining things and the murderer only looked like him. He felt protected by the sunglasses and hoped the whole thing would turn out to be a mistake.

He bought a copy of the paper at the next kiosk, sat down in a small café, and read the short report, his heart pounding. There was no mistake. It was a ten-year-old photo of him that had been taken in his Rome apartment and which he had sent to his parents. Underneath was the name Ali al-Ahmar, his cover name in the resistance all those years ago.

He didn't know the murdered woman. The story about her said that Fatima Haddad had been the wife of the minister of culture, who had once been the head of the secret service. She had been shot in their home at the beginning of November, which meant four weeks prior to Salman's arrival. The police suspected that the murder attempt had been planned by Islamists and was actually aimed at the minister. Surprisingly, he hadn't come home that evening but had attended a celebration at a newly opened steakhouse with friends.

Fatima herself had been a member of an Islamist splinter group in the mid-eighties, whose members had been tortured by the man who was to become her husband. She had also been his prisoner, but he had treated her so kindly that she had fallen in love with him and renounced armed struggle. When Fatima got married, her former friends distributed leaflets saying that she was a secret service informer. People ridiculed her because she had been transferred from a large cell into solitary confinement with her monster of a husband. In Rome, in the eighties, Salman had heard about the merciless waves of arrests and about the Islamist revenge killings. The idea that Salman could have killed this woman, before even setting foot in Syria, seemed like a cruel joke.

But the report didn't stop at the woman's murder. He was also accused of having seriously injured a policeman in the north, a few years ago. He was regarded as violent and to be approached with caution. The police were asking for information leading to… Salman stopped reading. He could hardly breathe. He was the wanted man. The heinous murder of Fatima Haddad was more than a month old and involved Islamists and their enemies, which didn't implicate him at all as a Christian. But what good was that? The second part of the report was enough to land him in jail for life. And that part of the report was substantially accurate, although the incident took place so many years ago in the past. But nobody cared about that. If he was caught, he'd be forced to admit to everything they wanted to hear under torture—even to the murder of someone who hadn't been murdered at all. He smiled in despair.

Salman turned back to the front page and read the murderer's name again—Ali al-Ahmar. At the time, he had decided on this name because the typically Muslim first name Ali hid his Christian origins. The "al-Ahmar" part, in Arabic "the red," alluded to his sympathies, while at the same time referring to a large clan that was spread not only all over Syria but throughout the Arab countries. Now he understood why his real name, Salman Baladi, was not mentioned. The Baladis were a well-known Christian family. How could someone with this name be an Islamist murderer? Ali al-Ahmar, on the other hand, clearly sounded Muslim. A masterstroke play!

Next to the photo of the murdered woman, they had printed another photo of Salman. This one showed him in a Palestinian training camp in southern Lebanon, together with two comrades from the radical group that he belonged to at the time. Each of them was holding up a Kalashnikov in their right hand. He and his friend Fuad Abrash were giving the clenched-fist salute with their left hands. The man on the left in the picture, Hisham, was holding out a book by Che Guevara.

The caption said, "Ali al-Ahmar, with two other Islamist terrorists near the city of Kandahar, Afghanistan. They are holding the Qur'an." There wasn't much for the reader to identify. The photo was far too old and blurred, but Salman remembered it well. Now he was certain that Elias had organized the dragnet for him, carefully and cold-bloodedly. Elias himself had taken that picture back then in southern Lebanon—Elias, the former guerrilla and now colonel in the secret service. The cover name and information about his past could only have come from Elias.

Salman's first impulse was to go to the police. He would explain that he couldn't have been the murderer, because he was in Rome at the time the crime was committed, and because, as a Christian, he had nothing to do with Islamists. "But that's the hole in the fence," Salman thought to himself, remembering the story that Elias had told. The criminal investigation department might listen to his story, but they would defer to the secret service. He would be arrested and handed over to them. A cold hand clutched his heart. Suddenly he was sure that Elias had not flown to Moscow at all, but lied to his wife for her to spread this news around. "He's sitting at secret service headquarters directing the operation," Salman surmised.

He dialed his parents' number. The line was dead. He walked slowly along al-Akhtal Street, past the St. Louis Hospital. When he rounded the bend and reached the

Caffè di Roma, he saw several police cars and white secret-service Land Rovers parked in front of the building where his parents lived. There were two white minibuses parked on the other side of the street in front of the Ajami grocery. He asked a man coming from that direction what was going on. The man either didn't know or didn't want to talk about it. A woman came hurrying toward them. "What happened?" he asked her.

"A murderer is holed up in the building. That's where his parents live. He's killed several people. How terrible for the poor parents!" she said breathlessly and hurried on her way.

He called Stella on his cell phone and told her how much he loved her and Paolo. She laughed and replied that she missed him so much, especially his hands and lips, but it would only be a few more days. She also said that she regretted not having come with him. He suppressed his tears and assured her that it had been thoughtful of her to remain in Rome with Paolo. She shouldn't worry, but it might be that he could no longer call every day. He hung up before she could ask for details.

Helping hands

Now he was caught in a trap and he cursed both his trip and himself. How could he have been so naïve as to trust these people? Where should he go now? Tarek first came to mind, not least because his faithful cousin had repeatedly offered to be of help. Tarek felt a deep gratitude toward his Aunt Sophia, her husband, and his cousin Salman because they had all helped his daughter Samira regain a happy life. Tarek was five years younger than Salman, and they had been friends since childhood. He'd actually wanted to become a lawyer, but had given up his studies after two years and an argument with a professor. Since he loved woodworking, he went to work in his father's large carpentry workshop. After his father's death twenty years ago, he'd taken over and modernized the workshop. He lived with his mother—Aunt Takla—and his wife Mona on Masbak Street, near Bab Tuma Square. His daughter Samira lived not far away with her husband. His son Amir lived in Kuwait.

Now was the time when Salman needed a helping hand, a compass in the midst of a jungle of anxieties and abandonment, to guide him onto a safe path. Tarek was just the one to help. Salman called him and asked if he could speak with him about a big favor. "You're always welcome. Just come over to my place. I'll be taking a break in a couple of minutes anyway. We can eat together."

Salman was surprised, then he looked at his watch. It was already twenty past twelve. He suddenly felt hungry, because he'd only had a croissant and an espresso all morning. He took a taxi, and half an hour later he was sitting at the table with Tarek, Aunt Takla, and Mona.

~

He looked so wretched that when she saw him Aunt Takla whispered, "Holy Virgin watch over him." Mona quickly brought the mocha pot. Salman took a sip and told his story. His relatives knew nothing, since they hadn't seen the newspaper yet. Salman told them he suspected that Elias was behind the all-points bulletin. He told them about the decisive photo, which only Elias had, and about the police and secret service vehicles in front of his house.

"But Elias is in Moscow! Your mother told us yesterday that Isabella was at your place and…" Mona broke in.

"Nonsense," Tarek interrupted her. "Isabella did exactly what Elias intended, without realizing it, while he's sitting at secret service headquarters. It's fitted out like a hotel for officers working on a case for days or even weeks. He says to his wife, 'I'm flying to Moscow,' stressing that it's a secret. His wife is a dyed-in-the-wool Damascene. If you want a piece of news spread quickly, tell a Damascene it's a secret. Isabella knows nothing, because he doesn't trust her. She's his companion and tool."

"You really think he's here?" his mother asked.

"I'm sure. He'd never launch a case like that unless he could direct and control it. Salman's right. Who else in this country would have an interest in pinning a murder on an old emigrant that happened four weeks before he arrived?"

Salman told them openly about his past in the rebel underground, the armed struggle, and the shots fired at the policeman.

"Stop it," Aunt Takla said. "You don't need to tell us that you're innocent. I'm convinced Elias is behind the whole thing. We know this son of a bitch all too well. He's got a heart full of poison and he enjoys tormenting innocent people. The whole city knows it. But why is he hunting you?"

"I don't know," Salman replied, barely audible.

The meal smelled delicious, but Salman had no appetite. He picked at his food. Everyone was lost in silence, searching for an answer to Takla's question. After finishing, when Mona brought the mocha, Aunt Takla suggested they move into the drawing room, but Tarek advised that they stay at the table, because people might be watching the drawing room from the street or from the houses nearby. After a while, he went alone into the next room, switched on the radio, and turned the volume all the way up. He then returned and closed the door behind him. "Now we can talk without being disturbed," he said and sat down again.

"I don't think revenge is enough of a motive," Tarek said. "I'm sure Elias is after a lot of money. The ten thousand dollars that Aunt Sophia told us about isn't enough for him. He knows you're rich. Let's be honest, in Syrian terms, you're super-rich. From what I've heard, Elias has overreached, with his big villa and extravagant lifestyle. He's up to his eyes in debt. So he sees you as a gold mine, it's as simple as that. A year ago, they suspected the jeweler Henri Halabi of being a CIA agent, and he was arrested. Can you imagine? The CIA is so foolish that it doesn't target the whole smart set around the dictator who do have secret information, and who wouldn't hesitate to sell out for a few dollars! Oh no, they employ an eighty-year-old jeweler as an agent! But the family forked out two million to the president's brother-in-law and suddenly our jeweler walked free, and all the accusations vanished into thin air."

"But what will he do if Yusuf and Sophia can't pay? They really can't. What will he do then?" Takla asked.

"Elias knows which way the wind blows. Don't underestimate him. I used to think he was stupid because of his poor, peculiar way of speaking and his surly look. But that's just a mask. He knows how attached your sister is to Salman, so he's assuming that she'll mobilize the whole family to raise, say, a million dollars. And he knows for certain that once Salman is back in Rome, he'll pay his family back every cent. So at the end of the day, he's only taking revenge on Salman. He's killing two birds with one stone—he has his revenge and he can pay off his debts."

"Tarek is right," Mona said. "And we would be the first to mortgage our house to raise a hundred thousand dollars from a bank or a loan shark."

"I know, and Sophia and I have cousins in Homs and Aleppo who are rich—very rich—and Elias knows that," Takla said.

"Exactly," Salman said. "Two of them are my business partners. Every year they export several tons of Syrian sweets and spices to Italy. They would definitely be willing to advance me the equivalent value. I'm just wondering why they didn't raid us and have me arrested, like they usually do."

"That would be too simple for Elias, too obvious. It wouldn't satisfy his sadistic streak. Because he enjoys frightening you and your relatives, luring you into a trap and playing the puppet master," Mona said.

"It sounds too much like a movie plot. I don't know..." Salman said.

"I wouldn't put it past him," Takla replied.

"I think Mona put her finger on it," said Tarek. "We often act like we're in a film we've seen, rather than go by tradition, or listen to reason. Look at weddings here in Damascus. They're bad copies of tacky movie weddings, right down to the horse-drawn carriages, throwing rice, and black tailcoats with bow ties in the heat of July! What people eat, what we name children, how we talk, laugh, dance, how we dress and have tattoos, it's all like in the movies. Why wouldn't a monster like Elias take his cruelty right out of a thriller?

"But he's taking a risk letting me run around free. What if I manage to escape?"

"The way I see it," Mona said, "he'll have had your house under surveillance since yesterday and people dogging your every footstep. You can't move a step without him observing you. This is a professional hunt. Elias is no amateur."

Takla looked up in alarm. "Does that mean they're right outside the door?"

"No, the old secret service would have done that—taking up positions that were stupidly obvious. But I'm sure they're nearby," Mona replied.

Salman suddenly felt in his pocket and pulled out his cell phone. "The secret service can locate me just by tracing my phone," he exclaimed in panic. "A friend of mine in Italy showed me on my smartphone that I was at his place, and where I'd been before that… one location after the other. He's a private detective, and he was able to follow a woman from her house to the hotel room where she met her lover. It's against the law, but every secret service can do it."

Takla was speechless. "They know where you're going? Mother of God!" Tarek was also afraid that Salman's phone could give him away. With the hammer Tarek gave him, Salman knelt on the floor and hit the phone until it was flat.

"I'll get rid of the scrap metal on the way," Tarek promised and packed the bits into a shopping bag.

Just to be safe, Salman wrote Stella's and Paolo's numbers on a slip of paper and gave it to Tarek. "In case something happens to me."

"Hopefully we'll never need it," said Mona, while Tarek hid the slip of paper between the pages of a cookbook on the shelf.

"Of course we'll need it—to set your wife's mind at ease," said Takla. "We'll have to call her regularly, otherwise she'll go crazy."

"Where will you be able to call from safely? And who's going to call?" Salman asked. "How would Stella know for sure that the call was coming from us and not the secret service?"

"Mona's cousin Sahar lives in Beirut," said Tarek after a moment's thought. "She speaks several languages and is reliable. I also have an old school friend who is loyal and discreet. He drives a bus between Beirut and Damascus. He could carry messages to Beirut and hand them off to Sahar, and she could then call your wife."

"Each letter should be just a few words, like a short love message. That and a piece of information that only you two know. I could send one every three or four days."

Salman agreed. Tarek stood up and retrieved a small exercise book. "Write down three short personal details for me that will tell Stella the messages are real," he said and handed Salman the book. Salman wrote while Tarek went from room to room, listening.

When he came back, Salman handed him the exercise book. "Here are four memories that only Stella and I know." But Tarek was distracted.

"They're at the door," he said, his face pale. "Listen," Tarek said firmly, "I'll get you from our house to Bab Tuma Square over the roofs of our neighbors' houses. From there, take a taxi to Maria's. We'll do everything we can to get you out of the country and we'll tell your parents. If we've been under surveillance, they know we visit Aunt Sophia once or twice a week—since way before you arrived. So we'll continue to visit and keep her informed. And if something happens, you can slip out through the passageway in my workshop. Remember?"

"Yes, the door is on Deir Street, right?"

Salman was familiar with his cousin's large carpentry workshop. They'd both played and tinkered there as children. Although he was the younger, Tarek had always been more skilled than Salman. The workshop was nearby and had a large gate that led into a small front yard where

Tarek parked his truck and a Ford Transporter, and also kept his wood. From there, the way led through a second big wooden gate into Tarek's sizeable workshop.

At the back of the hall were two doors, one of which led into a small kitchen with enough space for four people around a rickety table. Tarek would sit there to drink tea and negotiate with his customers. Tarek loved to joke about how tailors ran around half naked, shoemakers always wore the worst shoes, and carpenters ate off rickety tables.

The second door led into a large bathroom with a toilet and a shower. This bathroom provided a second way out that led through a narrow corridor, almost like a tunnel, under the neighboring houses and ended at a door after about fifteen meters. The door opened onto Deir Street, not far from the Maronite church. Tarek kept the key to this door because the corridor belonged to the workshop, and had for centuries. Many stories had been told about this curiosity, but they were long forgotten—much like the corridor itself. The door on Deir Street looked like a house door, but there was no number or family name on it. All that was written on it was the word 'entrance.'

"You can have our second key for it right now, so you can get in," said Tarek. "Then, wait in the corridor and call me from there. Let it ring three times and then hang up. If it's safe, I'll open the door to the corridor. If I don't come, either I've got a customer or my two workers are still there. The workshop closes at five, and the gate into Masbak Street is shut."

"But how do I call you from the corridor without a cell phone?" Salman asked.

"There's an old phone on the wall that my father had installed. In case a fire blocked off the telephone in the workshop, we could call the police or the fire brigade. I test it once a month. That telephone has never failed in thirty years. Thank God we've never had to use it. Just dial one, that's my office."

Takla and Mona listened with sad faces. Salman was touched when he looked at his aunt. "Can't he stay the night at least, just for today?" she pleaded.

"No. I think they're outside because they suspect he's here."

"Take care of yourself, my heart. May God punish those who torment us. I will hurry to my poor sister Sophia. What we mothers have to put up with!"

"Wait for me, both of you," Tarek said. "We'll go to Aunt Sophia's together."

Then he set off with Salman. From the dining room, they were able to get onto the first-floor terrace. Tarek leaned a ladder against the wall of the neighboring house, and before he climbed up he turned to Salman. "Wait here, I'll be right back," he said, then clambered up onto the roof and disappeared. Salman felt like it was an eternity, but when he looked at his watch, only fourteen minutes had passed when Tarek reappeared at the top of the ladder. "Come quickly."

Salman climbed up the ladder and followed Tarek. They made their way to the next roof, where Tarek politely greeted one of his mother's old friends. She looked up briefly and then turned away from the window to continue watching television. There wasn't a soul in the yard of the second house. In the third, a woman who Tarek quickly introduced as a distant cousin was trying to light a paraffin cooker. Thankfully, she also did not seem very curious about their presence. Tarek led Salman down a narrow set of wooden stairs, across a terrace, and down a second, wider set of steps. "From here you can get directly to Bab

Tuma Square," said Tarek when they reached the house door. "You've got Maria's address, right?"

"Yes," Salman said, his heart pounding. Once again he checked his wallet for the small slip of paper with the address and telephone number that Maria had given him. Then he put his hand on Tarek's shoulder, "What you're doing for me puts you in danger," he said, deeply moved.

"If someone like you is called a criminal and we keep silent, then we are criminals," Tarek said almost shyly, as if asking permission to stand up to the secret service.

Salman patted his cousin's shoulder. "Now hurry!" Tarek said and made his way back over the rooftops to his house.

26

Maha and the Impossibility of Educating Parents

The more money Maha made, the more she wanted and the more hard-hearted she became toward everything around her. She gravitated toward rich and cynical clients and, like them, ascribed all the world's ills to the laziness of the poor. Karim noticed how, unobtrusively but inexorably, a wall of coldness was rising between himself and his daughter. He tried, unsuccessfully, to point this out to her.

Maha was married to Hassan, a friendly lawyer from a modest background who had preferred a secure, but poorly paid, job as a civil servant in the Ministry of Justice to the risky existence of a law practice. He loved Maha and was more faithful to her than her shadow. But she humiliated him whenever possible, mocked his fears and anxieties, and boasted about her own success. Karim urged her to tone things down, but she refused to listen. One day, Hassan called Karim to say goodbye—he and Maha were separating. The only thing she'd had to say about his decision was, "I'll be able to breathe more freely without your petty-minded civil service mentality."

A year later, she fell in love with a professional basketball player, a glamor boy and well-known womanizer. She married him, but before the year was out she had divorced again. "I'm married to my profession—that marriage is the durable one," she said, laughing defiantly. But there was loneliness in her words.

She soon felt so isolated that she seldom laughed. Karim visited her often. He cooked for her and tried to cheer her up. But he also told her that although she was smart and had all the ins-and-outs and loopholes in the law at her fingertips, she was still as clumsy as a kitten when it came to life and love. "Why do I always have such bad luck with men?" she asked him. Karim replied that, given the way she lived, she wouldn't attract an honest man, and if one did come her way, he wouldn't last long. She behaved like a magnet for exactly the type of man that Karim could only warn her about. He reminded her that she had recently complained that she didn't have one real girlfriend. Gently, Karim encouraged her to see that friendship and love are the highest things that anyone could aspire to. He tried to explain to her how senseless it was to pursue money alone, but she wouldn't listen.

She never spoke to her father about her loneliness again. When she hosted a showy celebration in a five-star hotel for her fiftieth birthday, Karim felt so lost that he didn't even attend. Friends tried to console him, saying that Maha was an adult and responsible for what she did with her life, despite the upbringing Karim had given her. But in his heart, he felt guilty. He knew it had been his vanity that had led him to believe in the brilliance of his little girl. Maha had been hardworking, but practicing law didn't call for genius; just stamina, a good memory, and some eloquence—all qualities Maha possessed. But he had built her up into a combative, eager little bantam of a pupil. If he was relentlessly hard on himself, it had been he who had fostered her ambition, ignoring the fact that she hadn't shown the slightest interest in other children at school. The fact that there had been no girlfriends—and certainly no boyfriends—who could have spoiled his little

Maha had suited him far better. She had lived the life of a
nun in the house of a hermit.

~

And then came 2006, the year he lost Maha for good,
something he could never have imagined in his worst
nightmare.

Maha had met Aida the previous autumn. At first, she
was curious about his girlfriend and admired her strong
personality. She gladly accepted Aida's invitations and let
her cut and color her hair. She had enough experience to
recognize that this relationship between Karim and Aida
was not just some old man's passing erotic adventure but
a deeply felt love.

Maha herself had been quite happy since the beginning of 2006. She had fallen in love with a man named
Murad, a university professor. Karim was glad for her. He
was eager to meet this well-known mathematics professor
and asked Maha to pass on an invitation for a meal. But
Murad declined the invitation, and for months thereafter,
Maha refused to visit her father, without any explanation.

In April, however, she finally showed up, alone and
completely changed. As usual in Damascus, it already felt
like summer. Still, Maha insisted on wearing an ankle-
length gray coat over a long green dress with sleeves down
to her wrists, and a headscarf tied so tightly around her
head that her face was almost squeezed out of shape.
Murad had guided her onto the right path, and she had
become a believer, or so she said. She had given up wine
and had come to see cigarettes as a sin. She was preparing
herself for her wedding and was purifying herself, both
spiritually and physically.

For a moment, Karim thought she was playing a joke on
him. But she was serious. "And why the gloves?" he asked.

271

"So that unbelievers cannot touch my hands," she said.

Karim swallowed hard. "Have you been taking drugs?" he asked, as he couldn't conceive of any logical explanation for these grotesque changes.

"No, I've finally found the shining path to God and I'm very happy about it."

What was a father to say to his lonely daughter, who had found a man who, instead of spoiling her, had set her on such a path? But Karim didn't want to react hastily. "I wish the best for you," he said when she left. But he felt wretched, particularly as he realized that for the first time he felt relieved she was gone. He had always enjoyed drawing out their time together. But now she was preaching that he should stop drinking wine, attend the mosque, and repent his sins. She even started to threaten him. "Think on this—one day you'll stand before the Great Judge and he will recount all your sins to you."

"Well then, on that day I'll hire you as my lawyer," Karim said, trying to inject some humor into the situation.

"Nobody can help you, father," she said and wept with religious fervor. He came close to losing his temper.

~

Aida hadn't been there that day, but she was more understanding of Maha than Karim had expected. "Leave her alone, she's finding her way," she said after he shared his concern. "Did the Master not recommend accepting and loving all men, even if they walk false paths? Didn't you tell me once that this attitude reminded you of Jesus Christ? Or is tolerance only reserved for strangers, but things have to dance to our own tune at home?" Karim felt ashamed and decided to accept Maha regardless of how she was behaving and how she might turn out. His decision, fed as it was on love, pity, and courage, was to break into a thousand pieces on the hardness of reality.

A few weeks later, at the end of May, Maha brought her friend to visit. She had told her father that Murad had studied mathematics in London and taught in America before he had realized that living there was not right for him. He returned to Damascus and became strictly religious.

Karim's stomach turned at the sight of him. Murad was a large man, and his unattractive face was framed by an enormous beard. His high forehead had the famous brown spot called a "prayer bump," which reminded Karim of his own father's hypocrisy.

The professor wasn't a believer, he was a zealot. He ignored Aida the whole evening and questioned Karim about how often he prayed. Karim replied, "I pray about three hundred times a day. When I get up, I marvel at life, at the fact that I'm still here and that the sun still comes up, that bees still make honey, and Aida still loves me."

Aida was delighted. Unable to contain herself, she stood up and kissed Karim. "God protect these lips," she said. The professor rolled his eyes. Maha, normally glib and quick-witted, was dumbstruck, and when she did say something, she merely echoed Murad's opinions. Both of them refused to eat, so everyone drank tea. Maha didn't touch the biscuits, since Karim wouldn't give a clear answer about whether they contained alcohol or pork fat.

"As far as I know, butter comes from a cow, but who knows what dirty tricks it's got up to with a hog," he said, biting off a piece with relish.

That was the professor's first and last visit. Karim and Aida let out a sigh of relief when Maha and her friend left the house. Karim opened the windows and uncorked a bottle of red wine that they drank for the rest of the evening.

~

He had no desire to join in the celebrations for his daughter's engagement in June or her marriage in August because Aida hadn't been invited. Aida cautioned him not to be so sharp in his answers to these invitations, to plead other engagements, trips perhaps, as reasons why he couldn't attend. But this was only putting off the inevitable confrontation. Maha's initial fondness for Aida now turned to hateful aversion. During her visits, she made countless sarcastic remarks about infidel Christians and pointed out that what they both said was love, was in fact sin. Sometimes Karim would laugh, in an effort to bring the evening to a peaceful close. But Maha gradually became more impolite toward Aida, who was unable to match a lawyer's cutting remarks.

When Aida wasn't there during Maha's visits, Karim would patiently try to make clear to her how happy he was with Aida. And he begged her, even implored her, to stop hurting Aida with her barbed comments. He didn't want to lose his daughter, but she should stop trying to play the part of his caretaker. He had to live with her rejection of Aida, but he wished that Maha would accept that he loved Aida, just as he wished Maha a happy life with her professor, whom he couldn't stand. They should both show a minimum of friendliness. Maha nodded, but deep inside, the most she consented to was a ceasefire, never peace.

One week later, in mid-October, Maha came to visit again. Karim was enjoying the late-afternoon warmth with Aida and drinking a cool white wine with her out on the terrace. The smell of earth and roses was all around. Maha looked in disgust at the two of them and immediately began a sermon excoriating Aida. She threatened to break off all contact with her father if he didn't stop drinking alcohol and living with this sinner. Karim stood up, softly but firmly took hold of Maha, and led her to the front door. "Nobody threatens me," he said quietly and shut the door behind her, leaving Maha to curse Aida as a "black widow." Returning to the terrace, he talked with Aida for a long time about what had happened.

Aida had never loved so passionately and intensely before in her life, and that night, Karim seemed to let sixty years slip from his shoulders. It was dawn when Aida went home, drunk with happiness.

When Karim woke up the next morning, he quickly drank a coffee before calling Maha at her office. He apologized and invited her to lunch at her favorite restaurant. She refused. Either me or Aida, was her reply. He hung up. It would be more than four years before he heard from her again.

27

The First Dead-End Street

Damascus, December 14–15, 2010

The taxi ride took twenty minutes, but to Salman it felt like another eternity. He sat in the back, depressed, looking out at the street, and thinking about the bitter comedy of the situation and how everything could be brought crashing down by a single piece of bad luck. Fires, wars, floods, invasions, or persecutions robbed you of all security, even down to your self-confidence. Back in Rome, he had naïvely thought this visit to his native country would finally enable him to bring the long chapter of escape in his life to a close. But now it had reopened, more fiercely than ever. Here he was, on the run again in a city he no longer knew, without any contacts to professional helpers or to the underground.

Given their total lack of experience with situations like these, how long would his family be able to hide him? How much danger was he putting Aunt Takla and her family in? How would he ever manage to leave this country again? Someone had told him that, thanks to the Russians, all borders were watched so closely, electronically and via satellite, that it had become impossible to flee, by land or sea. Surveillance at airports was so strict that nothing escaped the secret service.

"Caught!" he thought to himself, paralyzed with fear. The taxi driver was the silent type, a pleasant exception to the rule. He drove slowly, stoically, putting up with the traffic jam and weaving his way through the chaos of weary pedestrians, overloaded carts, aggressive sports-car drivers, trucks, and buses.

They finally reached the Mazzeh district. Because of the tangle of one-way streets, the driver had to make several right turns before turning onto Marrakech Boulevard. Salman had him stop in front of the building of the World Food Program, tipped him generously, and got out. The second building from the World Food Program was four stories high. It had been built in the eighties and was one of those architectural sins that seemed ripe for demolition the moment it was finished.

"Hello, Uncle Salman," a teenage girl called out from the entrance to the building. She was just leaving with a few friends, all dressed as if they were on their way to a party. Salman flinched. He didn't know the youngsters. His relative, a pale girl with an indefinable hairstyle and an expensive pink smartphone in her hand, came up to him and smiled at him innocently. "Mom and I came to see you and say hello with Aunt Maria. My dad and Aunt Maria's husband are brothers. But they work in Saudi Arabia."

Salman pressed her outstretched hand and quickly ran inside, the girls' giggles echoing after him. He knew that his cousin Maria lived on the second floor. He already suspected that he would soon have to leave Maria's apartment again.

~

Maria was astonished when she opened the door and found Salman standing there. She smiled at him. "What a joy," she said, hugging him and inviting him in. Salman felt unnerved, still thinking about his encounter with the girl.

"I'm really out of luck," he began. "I wanted to hide at your place, they're looking for me…"

"They're looking for you?" Maria asked, frightened. She had no idea what had happened because she never read the newspapers. She reached for his hands.

"I'm supposed to have killed someone called Fatima Haddad. The whole thing happened a month before I arrived here. It's all over the front page of the newspaper. There's even a photograph of me. I think Elias is behind it. Aunt Takla, Tarek, and Mona sent me to you."

"Why would damned Elias do such a thing?" Maria asked, without expecting an answer. She looked at Salman and hugged him again. "You're safe here."

"That's what I thought too, but a young girl recognized me downstairs at the entrance. She said she'd come to see me and say hello with you and your mother."

"Oh my God, that's true! On your second evening in Damascus, my sister-in-law Nadia wanted to meet you because I'd told her so much about you, and she brought her daughter Lamis along. They live on the ground floor. Don't move, I'll be right back. Nadia's reliable," she said, hurrying out. Salman wanted to ask her not to tell her sister-in-law anything about his flight, but then that struck him as absurd. Maria would have to find some kind of explanation why her sister-in-law should keep quiet. He entered the bright kitchen and leaned against the wall.

Fifteen minutes later, Maria came back. "Nadia has promised to keep her mouth shut. Her brother had to go into hiding for eight years—then he was betrayed and shot during the arrest. Lamis is out with her friends, and she's turned off her phone. But sit down, let's have a coffee and not worry about that now," she said, smiling at him. Her smile restored his confidence a little.

~

Just as Maria was greeting Salman, Sophia was opening the door to her apartment. She looked wretched. Her sister Takla hugged her tightly and Sophia started to cry. "I don't know, I just don't know," she kept repeating. Takla, Tarek, and Mona came in. Salman's father sat in his wheelchair, his face toward the street. He returned their greeting without turning around. Takla and Mona sat down next to him. Mona patted his hand.

Takla really liked Yusuf and had often felt sorry for him. She had been very close to Sophia since childhood, and they knew all the intimate details of each other's lives. Yusuf had helped her and her husband a lot. Takla had married a young carpenter, Amin, after a stormy love affair. He had worked in a shop not far from his parents' house in Homs. He was twenty and she seventeen. Her parents had haughtily rejected the poor man, but Takla was already pregnant. She eloped with him to Damascus, where Tarek was born.

Yusuf had paid the rent for the young couple's apartment and had gotten Amin work in a large carpentry workshop. Later Takla's parents made up with their son-in-law and helped him financially because they were ashamed of their daughter's poverty. Yusuf and Amin remained firm friends until Amin's death, and Yusuf never wanted repayment for the money that he had advanced them, not even when Amin had his own workshop and made good money.

How awful, Takla now thought, looking at her brother-in-law. As if all his life's failures weren't enough, this rotten nephew Elias now had to destroy the old man's few friends too? Takla had quarreled with Sophia a few days earlier because Sophia had claimed that Yusuf took no interest in Salman. "You must be crazy," Takla scolded her. "Have you forgotten how much he suffered when Salman lived underground, and later when he fled to Europe? You said that Yusuf was cold and didn't care about what happened to Salman. But I knew that Yusuf was often at Amin's and cried because he was afraid for Salman."

"But why doesn't he show me that?" Sophia had asked angrily.

"He can't. Why should everyone be able to do everything? Amin couldn't even boil an egg without destroying the kitchen. He was as brave as a lion but he fainted whenever he went to the dentist—once he even fainted on the doorstep."

Yusuf now sat in front of them, looking miserable. "May God punish those who torment my Salman," he said. Sophia felt guilty about badgering Salman for all those years to come back to Damascus. Tarek took her by the hand and led her into the kitchen. He put his index finger to his lips and took a piece of paper. He sat at the table and wrote that Salman was safe and that they were not to talk about it at home, because the apartment was bound to be bugged. He would pass on all news to Salman. Sophia breathed a sigh of relief. She didn't need much in the way of explanation. Men from the secret service had come that afternoon, traipsing around the apartment and asking questions.

But swear to me that you will keep me truthfully informed and not treat me like a silly old woman! Sophia wrote on a new piece of paper in firm, vigorous handwriting that surprised Tarek.

"Dear Aunt Sophia, I'll always tell you the truth, even if it's bad news, so that we can find a solution. I swear I'll keep my word." He then wrote warning her to be careful when she spoke with her husband on their daily walks because their conversation could be picked up by directional microphones, even from far away. *Talk about Salman as much as you like and with whomever you like,* he wrote, *but not about his hiding place. From now on, Takla will no longer be told everything. It will be safer for her.*

And where is he today? Can't I call him, just to hear his voice?

He's at Maria's, Tarek wrote back. *Salman has destroyed his phone because the secret service could locate him that way.*

Sophia nodded in relief. She tenderly pinched Tarek's cheek. He stood up, tore up the paper, put the scraps into a frying pan, and lit them. When the scraps had been reduced to ashes, he opened the kitchen window to let out the smoke and washed out the pan under the faucet.

~

It was already evening when the telephone rang at Maria's. "I'm calling so that you don't worry, my child," Takla said after greeting her. "We've been accosted by a crowd of secret service men. We're fine, but they turned the whole house upside down looking for Salman. He'd come and paid us a short visit before driving away. Of course, they didn't find anything. The officer was very polite and apologized for the misunderstanding. Our own neighbors had informed on us, can you believe it? And now we're calling everyone to reassure them. You know how it is here—before we'd even had time to clean up the mess, the telephone was ringing and some cousin of Mona's three times removed asked if it was true that they'd found hashish at our place. No, we said, only chocolate and pistachios."

"Should I come over and help you tidy up?" Maria asked, playing innocent.

"No, there's no need for that, but you could go and visit your Aunt Sophia every now and then, and comfort her. She's very fond of you," her mother said, and then hung up.

Maria went into the kitchen. Shortly afterward, she

came into the sitting room with a bottle of wine, bread, and small bowls of cheese, olives, peanuts, and pistachios. The wine was delicious and Salman marveled at his ability to relax while he ate and even laughed at the secret service. Old man, he admonished himself, they're on your heels. You're just a few steps ahead of them. But even the idea seemed almost absurd to him at that moment because he felt so secure at Maria's.

Maria ate little but drank a lot of wine. The later it got, the more talkative she became. She talked about her troubles with her husband and begged Salman not to breathe a word to a soul. Nobody in the family knew about them, she said. They'd all been against her marrying Subhi because they thought he was cold and tightfisted, and unfortunately they'd been right. After they were married, she discovered that Subhi was even more indifferent and miserly than her family had suspected, and he resisted any attempts by Maria to influence or change him. That was why he didn't want her to live with him in Saudi Arabia. He made a pile of money there working as a chemist, but sent home so little that she was forced to accept help from her mother and sister-in-law.

Salman could feel Maria's bitter disappointment. It seemed to him as if she were sitting there with her bags all packed, just waiting for someone to pick her up.

Worn out from the chaos of the day, Salman went to bed shortly after midnight. He quickly fell asleep after all the red wine he'd drunk. When he woke up it was still dark. He felt Maria lying behind him in the narrow bed, holding him tightly as if they were both sitting on a motorcycle. He lifted her arm, turned on his back and, after a short hesitation, put her arm on his chest. She stirred and smiled.

He stroked her head. "How did you get here?"

"I walked," she said, turning over. Soon he could hear her steady breathing again. She was still lying there when he woke up early in the morning. He kissed her on the forehead, then got up and tiptoed into the kitchen. Soon after, he returned with a small pot of mocha.

Maria looked at him. In her men's pajamas, she looked like a character straight out of a sixties Italian film. "Did I keep you from sleeping?" she asked, savoring her mocha.

"No, but tonight we'd better stay in our own beds."

"Oh," Maria replied a little sadly.

~

They had breakfast together, and afterward prepared the windowless storage closet in the hall as a hiding place for Salman. "Nobody will find you here. And my husband's not back until June," Maria said, laughing at the possibility of Salman living with her for such a long time.

To take his mind off things, Maria asked him to cook real Italian pasta Bolognese for her. Salman wrote out a long shopping list, and Maria was surprised. "All that for spaghetti?"

"Do you have a delicatessen?"

"Yes, they also have Spanish and Italian groceries," she said. Before she left, she insisted again that he wasn't to answer the phone or open the door for anyone but her.

Salman turned on the television. The report about him had made the news. His picture faded in while the newscaster described his alleged crimes. The photo was different from the one in the newspaper. People would be able to recognize him from this one.

After a while, Maria returned, weighed down by two shopping bags. They cooked together and laughed, drank wine, and giggled like two children. With dexterity, Salman kept this playful woman who liked him so much at a distance. As they were having another coffee after the meal, Maria suddenly became thoughtful. "Why does Elias hate you so much? I mean, after all, he took ten grand from your father." She seemed preoccupied by this question.

"He wants to get rid of me, or to kill me because I'm the only one in the family who witnessed his betrayal. Now I'm sure that he was sent by the secret service to infiltrate our underground group right from the start. Your brother thinks that Elias doesn't want to kill me, just blackmail me for a great deal of money, since he's up to his eyes in debt. He knows I'm worth several million euros and would like to get his hands on at least a million. He also knows that my parents will give in and pay up."

"I wouldn't put it past him to do both—collect the ransom and then have you killed," said Maria.

~

After the meal, he went to his closet to lie down and sleep. He was woken with a start by the loud ringing of the doorbell, and it took him a moment to find his bearings and remember where he was. As he listened, Maria opened the door. It was her sister-in-law, who started talking breathlessly. She said that yesterday her naïve daughter had called her grandparents on her phone and told them how she had met Salman at the building's entrance. Maria's in-laws were faithful supporters of the president, and they were already on their way over to find out if this was true. The sister-in-law said that she was so sorry, and then left.

Maria came into the closet. "What business is it of those stupid in-laws, who I see and who I don't?" she said angrily.

"Don't get upset. Of course their daughter-in-law's security is their business. They'll betray me to the police, not because they have anything against me or you, but because they fear for your reputation. It was just a silly co-incidence—five minutes earlier or later, the girl wouldn't have seen me."

"It's my fault. Why did I have to take that silly brat to your place?"

"Don't talk like that, and don't blame yourself or the girl… she's innocent. Please listen to me. I'll be grateful to you for this day as long as I live. Your hospitality has wiped away my fear, and this is a first small victory against Elias."

Salman could think of only two people he could go to—Adel, his former schoolmate who still lived alone, and Rita, his long-ago lover. Adel had come to visit him twice but had gotten bored quickly and left. Since then, Salman had spoken to him on the phone nearly every day. He valued Adel's sense of humor, and his sarcastic comments about Arab society made him laugh.

But Salman decided to contact Rita. He longed to be close to another woman who would make him forget his plight for a while, as Maria had done. He called her from Maria's telephone and told her that he'd like to take her up on her invitation to visit. Rita was delighted.

He wondered if he should tell Maria about his new hiding place. But the fewer people who knew his where-abouts, the safer everyone would be. In the meantime, he had to assume that Tarek's phone was being tapped too.

"I'm going," he told Maria. "Just tell your father-in-law that I only had a coffee with you yesterday before going to my relatives in Aleppo. If he turns on me, they'll have nothing to go on. If I get out of this alive, you have to visit us in Rome. Will you promise? I know lots of interesting Italian men who would throw themselves at your feet."

"I'll start learning Italian tomorrow," she said through

tears. "And I'm sure you'll defeat them all and return safely home." He kissed her and she clung to him tightly for a moment. Salman cursed himself and cursed Elias for bringing such worry upon her. Then he tore himself away, went out into the busy street, and disappeared into the crowd.

28

Words Unsaid

Damascus, 2005–2010

Life and death

Karim was returning from the funeral of a young neighbor who had worked for an insurance company. He didn't know him all that well, but he often crossed paths with his wife while shopping and she was always friendly, even after his unpopular love for Aida became known. He felt for the young widow, who now had to live on a small pension with her two young daughters and her old, sick mother-in-law. Aida had stayed at home and was working in the garden. She didn't like funerals.

Karim badly needed a coffee. He brewed a pot and looked around his kitchen at the familiar cupboard, the colorful cups and plates on the shelves, a pair of his spectacles on the countertop. He took a tray with two cups of coffee out to the terrace, where Aida already was seated at the table.

"Look at these things," he said, thinking aloud, gesturing to the dishes on the tray. "They have no mind, they don't worry about life, and they'll be around long after we're gone."

"Yes, but they don't know about love. That's why eternity for them is just a string of dead hours," Aida replied.

Quarrel and reconciliation

It was as if an invisible hand had pushed the thin volume, *On Harmony*, off the bookshelf. Karim had actually wanted

287

to pull out a collection of detective stories, to take his mind off things. But this title was fitting. He hadn't yet gotten over an argument he'd had with Aida. She had come over to his place in a bad mood that day and hadn't felt like giving him an oud lesson. She had been angry at a neighbor, who had snapped at her on the street that this wasn't America and women didn't stroll around holding hands with men, or kissing them. And while you respected members of other religions, that didn't mean getting involved with them.

Aida had responded that she lived neither in Damascus nor America, but in her very own world, and she didn't go around kissing just any old man, she only kissed Karim, so the man shouldn't get his hopes up. This neighbor called himself a Christian but obviously understood nothing about Jesus. Had Jesus not said, love your enemies? And here this man was, forbidding her from even loving her own neighbor?

"She's gone mad," a woman shouted down from her balcony, while the man had been left dumbstruck.

"What a shame that you're too stupid and ugly to either love or be loved," Aida had yelled back up. The woman had burst into tears. She looked like a muezzin begging for listeners' pity.

Karim thought Aida should have controlled herself and refrained from hurling that last hurtful remark at the woman. That was when Aida exploded. "Haven't I told you that she was the first one who tried to humiliate me, a few hours after we kissed for the first time at the shops? And she's involved in all the tongue-wagging behind my back, when they whisper so loud that I can hear every word."

"It's only a front. She's lonely and envious," Karim replied. Then they started arguing. In the end, Aida got up and went home. It all happened so fast. And he felt like a fool, like a fat preacher counseling the hungry to go on a diet.

So he dove into the little book *On Harmony* to take his mind off things. It contained the last short talks and answers given by the Master to his pupils before disappearing. Contrary to popular belief, the wise man said that harmony never arose from sameness. When things were made the same by force, supposedly for the sake of harmony, this was one side's dominance over the other. It led to monotony, desolation, boredom. Only a vivid combination of different—even opposing—colors and tones, only a lively coming together of people of different temperaments and opinions, could give rise to a living harmony. It was a balance of opposites that could only occur among people through respect and love, but above all through reason. Once achieved, such a balance outlasted by far any coercive control.

"Aida will like that," Karim thought, putting the booklet into his pocket and setting off for her place. She had been gone two hours, but to him the time already felt like forever.

Getting old

One afternoon, soon after they made up from their silly fight, Karim stood in front of the large mirror in his bedroom, examining himself. He lamented his deteriorating eyesight because he enjoyed observing everything closely, and he read a lot.

"You should be happy, young man," Aida called from the bed. "Glasses are a good help and they suit you." She thought of how tender he had been before the afternoon nap and pulled the thin blanket between her legs. Sure, she would suffer a lot if her hearing were to lose its acuity. It had been good so far, but her friend Amal had recently needed to start wearing a hearing aid. She didn't like it at all and would pretend to have forgotten it on her bedside table. "I hide it from myself when I get up in the morning," she'd said, laughing.

It was strange. Since Aida had fallen in love with Karim, she felt as if age had increased her capacity for pleasure. Her body was like a castle whose mysterious chambers even she did not know. And she wondered how Karim had found the key and made her body into an oud from which he teased out the most beautiful songs. It sang her pleasure louder than ever, not only while they made love in a way she had never known, but in every single moment. Indeed, she had always known that death doesn't make appointments and strikes blindly, but now age was teaching her that everything might be happening for the last time. Holidays in beautiful resorts, meeting old friends, listening to music or playing her oud, laughing in the garden with Karim, picking fruit. Rejoicing to meet him in the morning. Death is a reason to savor the present moment to the full, she thought.

"Don't look in the mirror," she said as he started looking for warts on his body. Karim was afraid of warts. "It'll only show you how afraid you are of getting old. Look at me and you'll feel younger."

Karim came to her. He knelt near the bed and looked deep into her eyes. She was right. Her eyes were so full of love that he felt like a seventeen-year-old and blood rushed to his cheeks. There was so much he wanted to tell her, but he kept silent. He felt as if the words were rising from his throat to rest on the soft cushion of his tongue, but were then content to stay there to avoid the cold outside. And so it was that many words allowed themselves to be persuaded to join the things unsaid.

29

Faded Love
or the Second Dead-End Street

Damascus, December 15–16, 2010

The taxi pharmacy

Salman tightened his scarf around his neck and hurried to a taxi, whose driver was leaning against the car, smoking a cigarette. "Are you free?" Salman asked. The young man with glistening hair and cowboy boots nodded, took a couple more drags on his cigarette, and threw it on the road.

"Souk al-Hamidiya," Salman said. He still had some money, but nothing else. He needed to buy underwear, pajamas, shaving supplies, toothpaste, and a toothbrush. Salman checked his watch. It was three o'clock in the afternoon. How long could he hide at Rita's? He couldn't trust her for long. The most important thing was not to jeopardize Maria or himself, and to win time. But as he thought about Rita, he also realized that he had left the Gigante XXL potency tablets in his suitcase.

The taxi headed toward Umayyad Square to reach the souk via Shukri al-Quwatli Street and Marjeh Square. Salman suddenly remembered an old cinema that used to be there, that his schoolmate Adel had taken him to when they were in the ninth grade.

Most of the seats were broken, some were missing altogether. The owner had replaced the missing ones with stools or old chairs, or with cheap, fold-back benches wherever several seats in a row were missing. The place reeked of roasted meat, sour pickles, cabbage, and garlic. Beggars, laborers, and the unemployed sat and slept in the seats. Some would spend cold days there. The cinema owner had a kind heart. For the price of a ticket, he would let them stay until the last show, which ended around midnight, when they had to leave.

The film was a surreal montage. A cut from a Tarzan film ran for the first ten minutes, and while the King of the Jungle was still fighting a crocodile, the second cut began with a Flash Gordon journey. But it didn't last long either. Just as Flash struggled to save the beautiful Dal Arden, he was attacked by the evil tyrant Ming. The spaceship wobbled. Then a colorfully dressed Indian man started singing and dancing around a coy beauty. Suddenly a blond woman could be seen lying unconscious on a Caribbean beach with palm trees and white sand, a survivor from a shipwreck. In the distance a handsome musketeer from another film rode up on a white horse. But the audience never found out what happened to the woman, because two monsters were now fighting on the moon. They both looked like people dressed as lizards for a carnival. From the audience, someone called out, "Belly dancing's next," and sure enough an Egyptian woman started dancing across the screen. Before she'd even finished, a fighter plane with an Asian crew was shot down by the Americans.

The whole thing lasted ninety minutes and was made up of more than twenty different film clips. When the lights went up, Salman's head was buzzing. He tried to piece together the clips he could remember into some sort of absurd story, with correct credits at both ends. It was lots of fun, and a month later, Salman wanted to go back again. But when he asked Adel, he shook his head sadly.

The cinema had been torn down a week before, and a ten-story hotel was due to be built on the site.

When the taxi pulled up at the souk, Salman found a delicatessen where he could buy a good bottle of French champagne, which he packed into his new leather shoulder bag, before getting into another taxi. "The Thai embassy on Brazil Street, please," he said.

"As you like, sir," the driver replied with exaggerated obedience.

"Is the gentleman a diplomat?... I mean, because of the embassy."

"No," Salman replied, observing the driver. He was good looking, perhaps in his early thirties and well dressed, but a little too taken with his own charm.

"Is he planning a holiday in Thailand? I know somebody there..." His old-fashioned phrasing suggested that he had been to high school.

"No. I do business in Southeast Asia. And you? You weren't born a taxi driver, am I right?"

The taxi driver laughed. "No, but I got a woman pregnant when I was young and so I had to give up my studies. I actually wanted to study history. Meanwhile I've got six children."

"You do know that the contraceptive pill was discovered a good while ago."

The taxi driver nearly choked with laughter. "My wife has been on the pill since she was sixteen, but sometimes she forgets it and then I somehow find her particularly erotic. The pill is supposed to be responsible for the number of twins being born. But I think that it's my semen. In my family, all the boys only need to say hello to a woman and presto, she's pregnant. My uncle has thirteen wives, but I only have three—one I'm married to, and two lovers. I occasionally reach my limits and need a little help."

"What do you mean?"

"I beg your pardon, but at your age, I beg your pardon, you're bound to be using it. One Colossal tablet and the evening is saved. Afterward, your partner lies there like a happy corpse and you've saved face."

"And where can one obtain this Colossal?" Salman asked.

The taxi driver laughed, reached over into the glove compartment, and pulled out a red package. Salman saw there were easily ten more in there.

The taxi driver passed the package back. It held ten tablets. "How much is one package?" Salman asked.

"Twenty dollars at the chemist's. I sell them for ten, but for you let's say eight because I like the look of you." The taxi driver had suddenly started talking with him like a pal.

"Give me two, *akhi*, my brother," Salman replied, slipping into Damascene talk.

"You speak Damascene dialect, but with an accent, brother," he said, smiling at Salman. Living abroad, Salman thought, settles on your tongue.

"I've been in Dubai for twenty years, and they speak more English than Arabic there."

"And are you back for a visit? Family perhaps?"

"No, I've no family left here. My parents are long dead and my three brothers are in Canada. I'm here on business."

The taxi driver's questions felt like a trap. Many taxi drivers earned a bit on the side by working as informers for the secret service. Salman had read that the Syrian secret service employed some hundred and fifty thousand staff, and twice that number of informers.

~

At the embassy entrance, Salman got out and paid generously for both the fare and tablets. "For the six children," he said.

"Fine, thanks," the man called out, driving away quickly. Salman took several steps toward the embassy, but as soon as the taxi driver disappeared around the corner, he turned back and slowly strolled around the block. He stood for a moment in front of the Franciscan Church, then turned onto to Maysalun Street and from there back again onto Brazil Street, passing the Cosmetic Laser Clinic. Salman wondered how blemishes could be removed with laser surgery in a city where most people were forced to still live as they had in the eighteenth century.

A woman's revenge

The building where Rita lived was unusually magnificent, even by the standards of this well-to-do district. Salman rang the bell, which chimed a little tune. The front door opened. Salman went up the stairs to the third floor. Rita stood beaming at the door. "At last," she called. "I thought you weren't coming anymore."

"It took me a long time to find some good champagne," he said smiling.

Rita insisted that she had the most beautiful and expensive apartment in the whole building, as she proudly gave him a guided tour of her luxurious home. It seemed to Salman as if he was in a show apartment with the best of everything—paintings and furniture, crystal glass, and the latest in televisions. A fire crackled in the central fireplace in the living room. The effect was so perfect that it might have come straight out of a commercial. On closer inspection, Salman noticed that it was an electric fireplace with fake flickering flames and crackling wood.

Rita had redesigned the magnificent roof terrace as a garden, complete with a fountain and a marble floor. An elegant tent for intimate moments looked like something from an American film. No Arab would ever set up anything like it in the desert. "It's like paradise here in the summer. The tent has air-conditioning, so when it's a hundred thirteen degrees in the shade outside, it's always pleasantly cool in here," Rita explained.

She put the champagne in the refrigerator to cool and took out an expensive white wine. "We'll have the champagne later," she said, stroking her silk dress that subtly suggested her curves. Salman had always been against cosmetic surgery, but now he was close to changing his mind. Rita was more beautiful than ever.

She acted cool and direct, and didn't lose a moment getting down to essentials. She kissed Salman with passion. He could feel that she had no idea that he was being chased.

Soon they were lying on the big sheepskin in front of the fireplace. The situation felt as unreal to Salman as if he were in a film. He didn't think for a second about what he was doing there. Was it his pent-up longing for Stella? Or was he trying to forget his fear? Or could it still be that irresistible attraction that Rita had held for him since she was nineteen? He sank into a soft world perfumed with an exotic fragrance. Wherever he stretched his hand, his fingers met her smooth skin.

Only when he lay next to her, soft and perspiring, did he notice that he had not reciprocated any of the affectionate words she had whispered.

"Where do you get your strength? You're even wilder than you were forty years ago," she said admiringly. "Or are you taking potency tablets?"

"With your beauty and seductive powers, tranquilizers would be more like it," he lied.

The taxi driver had not made any false promises. A single tablet had been enough for several hours of virility. They drank the wine and ate delicacies Rita had prepared. She didn't seem the least interested in his life in Rome. He waited for her to ask him how long he would stay with her, but she didn't. After the meal, Salman and Rita lay back down on the sheepskin in front of the fireplace and talked and caressed each other until they fell asleep.

The next morning, Salman could no longer remember how he had put on his pajamas and gotten into bed. He heard Rita's voice. She was on the phone in the kitchen. He heard her laugh and say she was sorry, but she couldn't come because she had company. "An old friend, his name's Salman, but you don't know him," she explained.

Salman sat up, worried. When he went into the kitchen, Rita was just finishing her phone call with a happy "Bye-bye!"

"Who were you talking to on the phone?" he asked, his throat dry.

"My sister. She's blind and she lives in a nursing home where they care for her around the clock. She wanted me to visit her tomorrow. I excused myself by telling her about your visit. Actually, I'm bored when I'm with her, and on top of everything, she gets me depressed whenever I go and see her and she keeps talking about the alleged curse on our family."

Salman was relieved for a moment, but he decided to tell Rita about everything before she prattled away to the whole world about who was visiting her.

~

"I'm in trouble," he started, after breakfast. "Elias, my cousin, has tricked me. He took ten thousand dollars from my father to guarantee my family and myself that the secret service had nothing against me. Otherwise, I'd never have come despite the amnesty."

"Did your parents really pay the money? You've been away for forty years. Even a triple murder would come under the statute of limitations by now," she objected.

"There's a lot you don't know about Elias and me," he said, giving her a full report, while she silently served him a cappuccino and pastries she had ordered from the bakery while he was still asleep. Salman was careful to avoid any reference to his cousin Tarek, and he assured her that he needed only a couple of days until he fled to Lebanon and flew back to Rome via Beirut. Rita listened, pale and silent.

"It's not as easy as it used to be," she said. "The borders are under tight surveillance these days. I've often read that opponents of the government have been arrested at the Lebanese or Jordanian border. The secret services of the three countries have come to an agreement faster than their own peoples," she said.

"But you're welcome to stay here," she added. "Nobody can arrest you here." She sounded very sure of herself.

"Aren't you afraid for yourself, if this comes out?" Salman asked.

"No, my cousin is the president's first security adviser. He owes his advancement to me. I had an affair with his previous boss and persuaded him to take on this clever young man. We're still in touch, and I could ask Bassam if he can arrange for you to be protected here. But you won't be allowed to do anything political, and you'll have to put up with my being out of the house often—oh, and you'll have to go on a long walk whenever I have certain guests, you understand?"

Salman nodded. All he needed was to be safe for a few days, until he could contact Tarek and discuss the situation. It all seemed totally absurd to him, but the last few days had shown him that he no longer knew this society. Maybe in this state, different power centers had different protected territories. Just like in a science-fiction film, a new country had been born from forty years' dictatorship. The Syrians were ruled by several secret organizations, while ministers and important officials merely served as a front for those in power, who remained unseen. People still spoke Arabic in the street, but they didn't understand his language and he didn't understand theirs. Where else would a president proclaim an amnesty that the secret service later revoked?

Rita looked at the clock. It was shortly after ten. She took her smartphone, called Bassam, and asked if she could drop in to see him.

"A faithful boy," she said when she had finished the call. "He's in his office at the moment. It's not far away, only five minutes' walk. Make yourself comfortable. Hopefully I'll be back soon with good news," she said before leaving. With her bleached hair and her fur coat, she looked like a Swede.

Salman drank a second cappuccino and looked at the terrace through the big glass sliding door. From there he could see, on his right, the splendid Cham Palace Hotel, and on his left, in the distance, the large, famous Sepky Park, which he had known since childhood. Farther left, but close by, was the Franciscan Church.

What were people thinking about right now in all those houses? Salman wondered. What did they know about those who are persecuted, under arrest, expelled? Nothing? Or did they in fact know quite a lot and pretended they knew nothing? In this country, indifference grew in people's souls. The only good Syrian was an indifferent one. His mother had told him that a man had been shot by a passing driver in the middle of the street. Most people had walked on, a few had pulled out their phones and called the police or the ambulance, but no one had actually stopped. Dogs barked and tried to pursue the killer, but were dragged away by their owners. It wasn't much different in Italy, Salman thought, even without a dictatorship. There, it was the Mafia that had educated people to become indifferent.

~

It was nearly one o'clock when Rita came back. Her happiness had evaporated. When Salman helped her out of her coat, he noticed that her makeup had run. She looked glum and tired.

"What happened?" he asked anxiously.

"Yes, what? He can't help you. If you were a murderer, a smuggler, an arms dealer, he could have gotten you off the hook for my sake. He hates your cousin Elias. But he checked something on his computer and then said that the search for you has top priority. I asked him what that meant. He said it meant that the wanted person belongs to those who represent the greatest danger to the president. No one, not even the president himself, can stop the manhunt. Only the secret service can lower the level once they consider the danger has been averted."

"And that enables Elias to extort as much money as he wants," Salman said, while Rita fetched a bottle of red wine from the cupboard. They drank the wine in silence, and Rita smoked. Her liveliness and happiness had vanished.

"What's the matter with you, Rita? There's something else, isn't there?" Salman asked cautiously after a while. He didn't want to ask her directly whether she had just slept with the man, even though he was actually sure of it. He suspected that she had another unpleasant piece of news for him.

"Bassam has…" she finally started, before stopping again as if realizing that another explanation was needed. "You have to know," she added, pausing again, as if the words were stuck in her throat, "we, that is, Bassam and I, have a long-lasting relationship. He's married and not allowed to separate from his wife. She is the daughter of the minister of defense. But he does everything for me, and this is how I enjoy considerable protection."

Salman had to stop himself from laughing. These men used to be called pimps. Now they were generals, heads of the secret service, advisers to the president.

"You know," she went on, "I was very lonely after my husband died. All my attempts to get away went wrong, including before he died. No one wanted to flee with me. You didn't, either… At the time, I'd fallen hopelessly in love with you. Do you remember?"

Salman nodded and to his surprise felt ashamed.

"But no one would have me, although I was pretty and clever," she added.

"Maybe because you wanted too many," Salman said, providing a polite explanation of the situation at that time, when Rita, as the jokes went, changed men faster than the Damascene cinemas changed films.

"Possibly," Rita said drily, nearly angrily, "but I needed protection."

"How much more protection do you need? Bassam isn't enough?"

"Don't be cynical," she said. "After my husband died, I was completely on my own. No one wanted to help me. I've suffered a lot during all my affairs, especially when I was foolish enough to fall in love. Men feel that and they'll play with you. If at the beginning they feel a certain tender love that makes you their equal, later they elevate themselves to being patrons and you become the one who gets their charity."

"Did it happen that way with me, too?" Salman asked, although he knew the answer.

"Yes, with you, too. But that's all history now. I no longer bear you any grudges. Although..." Rita faltered.

"Although?"

"You must leave my apartment today. Bassam gave me twelve hours. Come midnight, he can't guarantee anything. You must go. You're far too dangerous for me and for my life. Bassam said it was only a matter of days before they catch you. I don't want to frighten you, but whatever Bassam says about the secret service, he's always right."

Salman saw a smirk peer fleetingly beneath her mask. Fear seized him.

"Okay," he replied. So that was her revenge. He decided to leave the apartment at once, not just to get some fresh air and organize his thoughts, but also to call someone who could take him in. He couldn't use her telephone because that might lead his pursuers right to him. "I need to get out of the house and walk a little. My head is spinning," he said, dressing warmly and setting off.

"Take the key, then you won't need to ring the bell," she called after him.

~

It was ice-cold outside. He trudged through the streets until he could make out a phone booth in the distance.

302

Shivering with cold and fear, he dialed the number for Adel, his best friend at school, who said he would be happy to see Salman. Salman asked if he should bring anything.

"No, I still have a few bottles of good wine in the cellar. Once we've drunk them, you can treat us to another one," Adel said.

"Do you know what I remembered today? I was in a taxi, and I recognized a building where that cheap cinema used to be. I thought about that montage we saw there. Do you remember?"

"Oh yes. At the time I was worried you might laugh at me. I was in love with you. You were like a hero to me. Come quickly, and we can really reminisce. We couldn't do that at your parents' house, so many relatives and chatterboxes! That's why I never came back. When will you be here?"

"In a half-hour. You live in Joule Jammal Street, across from the Central Bank, near Seven Fountain Square?"

"Yes. You'll recognize the white building. There's doctors' practices downstairs and a Syrian Airlines sign hanging on the first floor. Hurry up, I'm looking forward to seeing you," Adel said, ending the conversation. Salman breathed a sigh of relief. He felt some pride. All's not lost yet, he thought out loud.

~

When he opened the door to Rita's apartment, she was sitting near the fireplace. "I'm driving to Aleppo," he said.

"You're afraid of me, aren't you?" she replied, staring at the electric fire. "Maybe I shouldn't have told you so much. But I thought, if we want to be friends again, there's a few things you should know about me."

"You've just told me in no uncertain terms to leave your home. What am I supposed to do? Sit here and cry about my bad luck? I've asked my cousin in Aleppo to put me up."

"You're lying, you're not driving to Aleppo. You're afraid to stay here, that's why you're lying to me. Admit it."

"Sure, I'm afraid. It's all about one tiny detail, namely my life. You shouldn't have run off to Bassam to make a report. That way I could have stayed here."

"Don't be such a child. I'm not reporting to anyone. If I meant you any harm, I could have you arrested in five minutes," she said angrily, lighting a cigarette. Her hand was shaking and Salman knew that he had provoked her. "But I'm beholden to Bassam, otherwise I'll lose his protection in this wolf's lair. If I give shelter to a terrorist, that threatens his position. Everyone in the president's palace knows that I'm his lover."

"You really disappoint me," Salman retorted with a calm voice. "I'm not a terrorist. You talk like Elias and you want to tell me that you're independent. We'd better bring this to a close. I'm being picked up in fifteen minutes."

He picked up his bag of toiletries in the bathroom and his shoulder bag in the kitchen. Then he went once more into the living room and stood at a distance behind her. She refused to turn around, but went on staring at the fire.

"I hope for your sake that Bassam is wrong," she said, and her brittle voice made him realize that she was crying.

30

Snapshots from Jasmine Street

Damascus, 2005–2010

The inhabitants of Jasmine Street were worked up like never before. For the very first time, Karim heard these fearful people cursing the government, and the secret service as well. It was all about their neighbors Lutfi and Farida, who had been tortured for three days by the secret service and then sent back home. They were peaceful, helpful people, and everyone on Jasmine Street liked them. Lutfi and Farida were both nurses at the same hospital, and they would always give away medicines to people in need on their street. They were about forty and had a bright ten-year-old son. This pale young boy was always at the top of his class and his parents had great expectations of him. His name was Nagi—"the survivor." He was his parents' pride and joy, as he had come healthy into the world after his mother had several miscarriages.

What had happened? It wasn't just some pretext, like spying for Israel or for the CIA. No, the story going around was even more incredible.

Nagi's teacher had asked her pupils what they wanted to be when they grew up. One child wanted to be a doctor, another an architect, one boy hoped to kill all robbers and criminals when he was a policeman. But Nagi said, "I want to be president."

The teacher froze. The children didn't notice anything and continued to talk happily about what they wanted to be when they grew up.

305

With a heavy heart, the teacher reported what had happened to the principal because she was new and afraid that one of the children would spill the beans. And according to school regulations: "Withholding dangerous events, behavior, and statements is an offense."

"You did the right thing," the principal reassured her, and the teacher breathed a sigh of relief. He called Nagi to his office and, together with the teacher, tried to convince the little boy that he was definitely talking about becoming president of a football club or a chess club or the trade union, or even the police. But the boy insisted that, no, he wanted to be "President of the Republic."

With a heavy heart, the principal had to report the boy to the party and security authorities. The secret service turned up at the parents' house that very evening. Lutfi and Farida were arrested and interrogated separately, but the officer was unable to beat anything out of either of them. It wasn't until his mother cried out in desperation, "The boy's mentally ill" that the parents were released. They were not to breathe a word about their detention. But people have eyes.

Karim went to Lutfi and Farida's house. The visitors were spilling out onto the street. News of the couple's return had spread like wildfire. Karim was surprised by the neighbors' solidarity, but many avoided eye contact with him. They looked away as Karim pushed his way through the crowd so he could shake hands with Lutfi and Farida.

"Karim! I'm so ashamed," Lutfi said. "Please forgive our cowardice," he added quietly. Karim clapped the man on the shoulder and took his wife's hand in both of his. "You both have a wonderful, brave son," he said. Farida wept. Karim was moved too, and he was still lost in thought when he went home.

"And what happened to the boy?" Aida asked when Karim had finished his story.

"He's in the psychiatric ward, and when they let him out, he'll be sent to his grandparents in Dara'a, in the south. He'll go to school there and never talk about his future again," Karim replied.

~

Karim was an excellent cook. "Cooking is an art full of secrets," he told Aida, "a book with seven seals, only surpassed by the art of tasting. You tell me you don't like to cook, but I've never met a single person who has such a delicate sense of taste as you do, a blessing for any passionate cook." It was true—Aida liked eating and she ate a lot without ever putting on a single pound.

One autumn, Karim and Aida invited about twenty people from the Selfless to celebrate with them. Amal, Aida's friend, had told her that love was an infectious, but pleasant disease. Without lifting a finger, Aida and Karim's love over the past four years had infected another ten members. That called for a celebration, which in turn called for cooking and baking. Aida and Karim had shopped for all the ingredients, some of which were pickled, marinated, or soaked overnight.

Aida came very early. Although they had been together for four years, she still didn't spend the night at Karim's. The door was ajar, and Karim was at the round table on the terrace with two cups and a pot of coffee in front of him. He smiled at her. "I felt a bit restless and thought I'd make a start, but let's have a coffee first," he said. While they drank their coffee, they discussed all the cooking they had to do.

They laughed a lot and nibbled all morning, like two unruly children. Karim had set up several tables around the fountain. A colorful assortment of chairs, collected over several generations, stood around the tables. He had never hosted such a large gathering before. There was only a wobbly stool left for him to sit on, which he put next to the elegant chair with the high backrest, which he had chosen for Aida.

They didn't have any lunch because they were full from all the nibbling. They'd conjured up more than twenty dishes in only a few hours. By three in the afternoon, they were completely exhausted. They slept for an hour, had some more coffee, and at about five, they set out plates, cutlery, and dishes on the tables, which were now in the shade. On this hot day, the fountain provided some welcome coolness.

They showered together, laughing a lot. "I get the feeling you've set my clock back. I keep getting younger with you," Karim said, kissing Aida's eyes.

"You're not allowed to get any younger than eighteen, otherwise we'll have morality problems."

After they had dressed in light, summery colors, there was still an hour left, and they decided to spend it on the terrace. The garden had never looked so lush. Karim brought two small glasses of cold white wine. "Before the others come, I want to tell you how much I love you," he said. They clinked glasses and drank a sip before putting the glasses on the little table and hugging each other. After a kiss, when Karim opened his eyes, he saw something come flying over the garden wall and land in the rose bush with a thump. He couldn't quite make out what it was.

Aida heard the thump. "What was that?" she asked anxiously.

"I don't know," Karim said and he went down the steps into the garden, followed by Aida. A dead cat lay there, stretched out between two rose trees. They both froze at the sight of it. The cat was gray, with a gentle face, and seemed to be asleep.

After Karim got over his initial shock, he ran to the house door and out onto the street. There wasn't a soul in sight. In the distance, a man was cycling away down the street. Children were playing on Monastery Square. Karim went up to them and asked two boys if they'd seen anybody throw something over his wall. They both shook their heads innocently and returned to their game of marbles. Karim didn't believe them, and he found it strange that the street was suddenly completely empty. He went back into the garden with stooped shoulders. Aida was putting the dead cat into a plastic bag.

Carrying a shovel, Karim accompanied Aida to the monastery ruins. There they buried the cat close to the city wall, smoothed the earth over the grave, and Aida stuck a red rose on it.

~

One day, Karim played his piece on the oud really well, and Aida was so happy that she treated him to an ice cream at the famous ice-cream parlor Bakdash in souk al-Hamidiya. They went along Straight Street holding hands, and Karim noticed how some shopkeepers, who stood in their door-ways on this warm spring day, or sat on a stool outside, went back inside their shops to avoid having to say hello. Some young men whistled and made rude noises.

One of the men was still standing in the street because he'd noticed the couple too late. It was Ismail, the olive merchant. He smiled in embarrassment and Karim suddenly felt an inclination to scare him off as well. He went up to him with Aida. "Have you gotten the new olives?"

"Yes, but the delivery's not ready for sale yet."

"Can we try a few?"

Usually he would have invited his customers into the shop and offered them a variety of olives to taste. But he didn't show the slightest sign of wanting to do so.

"Yes, well," he said with a brittle voice, "perhaps not today. Maybe later." He looked around, unsure of himself.

"You don't have anything against us, do you?" Aida asked.

"No, why should I? You too are God's creatures, and I have nothing against Jews, blacks, or unbelievers," the man answered, trying to disappear back into his shop. But Karim held him by the sleeve. "Nothing against lepers either?"

"No," the man said, freeing himself from Karim's grip and fleeing into his shop.

"I'm relieved to hear it," Karim called out after him and decided never to buy a single olive from the coward again.

~

Karim dismounted slowly from his bike. His hip had given him problems since he was twenty. A young neighbor asked if he could help him carry his shopping in. Karim thanked him but declined. Whenever he worked hard in the garden, his hips would make themselves felt, but the pain was bearable.

"I'm amazed," the young man said, "at how lively you are. At your age, people should be happy to be still alive. In the old days, people died at forty, and here you are, pushing eighty and getting yourself a girlfriend!"

Karim was furious but he took a deep breath. "It's true," he said calmly. "I'm over seventy, but in my heart I feel thirty, so by your calculations, I've got another ten years to go. I'm not a creature from another planet. I'm a

Syrian, like you, just a bit older. I can look back on a rich life, something you can't necessarily say about yourself."

The man shook his head and walked away. "I wanted to help him and he insults me," he said out loud to another man who had been watching the conversation from a short distance away.

~

The widower Badri Safi was one of the few neighbors on Jasmine Street whose friendship with Karim had never faded. Badri, who was in his late seventies himself, walked slowly and with a slight stoop. People greeted him in a friendly fashion, but not without a certain amount of pity. He had been a famous singer in the seventies. Now he was bowed by poverty and illness. His white suit was the only reminder of his fame, although it hadn't been spared the ravages of time, as could clearly be seen from the collar and the sleeves. But there were traces of his good looks remaining, one only needed to look closely. "Ruins of a Roman temple," he would say whenever people flattered him by saying he looked good.

Catastrophe had struck at the beginning of the nineties. After a terrible car accident, Badri had spent almost six months in the hospital. His head and throat had to be operated on several times. His voice was ruined after that. Although he could still speak and make himself understood, he could no longer sing. As if that wasn't enough, his wife had left him after the accident. Karim supported Badri as much as he could, and often had him come over to eat. He was happy to do it because Badri was funny and self-deprecating, and because meals eaten in company simply tasted better.

After Aida and Karim became friends, Badri still came by to eat now and then. He was a gentleman, and

Aida liked his old-fashioned ways. He always kissed her hand when they met, without ever seeming overly familiar or obsequious.

"Death is awful for those who remain because they're alone with their memories. I'm unlucky because my voice died before I did, leaving me with the memories of the times we shared. My songs now rot in my heart for lack of fresh air."

On his doctors' advice, he had decided to cut down on smoking. After the accident, he had smoked two packs of cigarettes a day. Now he only treated himself to a cigarette every two hours—eight cigarettes if he was awake for sixteen hours.

"Congratulations—that's a big reduction!" Karim said to encourage his friend.

"Yes, but the stupid thing is, I can't wait for the two hours to be over so that I can finally light up again. How long have I been sitting here?" he asked.

"Half an hour," Aida said and smiled.

"Is that all?" Badri called out in dismay.

31

Expired Friendships or the Third Dead-End Street

Damascus, December 16–17, 2010

Dashed hopes

Salman's school friend Adel had become a successful dentist who lived alone as a bachelor in a large apartment. Salman's father had asked him why he still worked at sixty-five. Adel had replied, "In my practice I fight cavities, receding gums—and my boredom."

Adel didn't actually need to work since he'd already earned enough. He also owned the large building where his apartment was. Rents were extremely high in this central part of the city. There were two other doctors' practices on the ground floor next to Adel's, an optometrist and an internist. An airline leased premises on the first floor and a large insurance company occupied the second floor. On the flat roof above his third-floor apartment, Adel had created a summer residence, complete with an elegant privacy screen, swimming pool, trees in large tubs, lounge chairs, a bar, and two air-conditioned areas.

After Adel's visit, Salman's mother had told him that everyone knew that Adel didn't want any long-term neighbors because of his lifestyle. He had a weakness for strapping young men, preferably newcomers to Damascus. Strangely enough Salman had never had an inkling of Adel's preference for men when they were students, although they were together every day. Physical closeness was taken for granted among pupils. Adel had visited Salman twice since his return, and each time he'd invited Salman to his place. Each time they parted, he had offered his help, in no uncertain terms.

It was the ideal hiding place, Salman thought as he made his way to Adel's apartment, a modern building on a busy street with lots of clients and customers. It was likely to be safe because Adel had no political affiliations and he often had gentlemen visitors. In the old underground days, apartments like his were regarded as real "safe houses."

Salman put on his sunglasses, turned his coat collar up, and wrapped the scarf around his neck. It was less than a kilometer from Rita's apartment to Adel's. He went along Maysalun Street as far as al-Azmeh Square, and from there to 29 May Street, which led directly to Seven Fountains Square. He went around the square and turned into Joule Jammal Street. In the distance, he could already see the large sign for the airline. He kept his eyes on the modern building with the polished white stone facade and noticed the lively comings and goings at the entrance. He walked quickly toward it, went up the marble steps, and rang the bell at a front door of dark wood and colored glass.

Adel opened the door. He was wearing a bathrobe of wine-red silk over dark blue pajamas.

"Welcome," he shouted and stretched out his arms, laughing.

"Why are you still in your bathrobe? Your practice is open," Salman said in surprise.

"Today's Thursday. It's my day off, along with Sunday. A hardworking young colleague stands in for me. But come on in," he said and drew Salman into the light, spacious apartment. "I've got a visitor," he whispered to him. Salman was a bit startled, but at least he now knew that his school friend had no idea about the all-points bulletin out for him. He left his bag in the cloakroom, hung his coat on the stand, and followed Adel suspiciously, ready to turn back at any moment.

A young man was sitting in the living room, his bathrobe worn out and slightly too short for him. Adel introduced him as his friend Bashir. The young man had a handshake like a steel vice. "Would you like a coffee?" Adel asked.

"Yes, please," Salman answered. Adel gestured to Bashir with a slight nod of his head. He stood up immediately and went into the kitchen.

"Tell me about Italy," Adel said. "The men there are very handsome, aren't they?"

"Yes," Salman said, slightly embarrassed by the question.

"You know, when you were young, I always took you more for an Italian than a Syrian. And isn't it funny how in the end you actually became an Italian?"

"You're right. In Italy hardly anyone suspects I'm Syrian. I've even met an Italian actor who's the spitting image of me."

"Really?"

"Yes, his name's Francesco. Before the amnesty came out, I even toyed with the idea of coming over here on his passport. But the risk was too great for both of us." Adel was curious about how Italians lived, particularly about how homosexuals lived, and Salman explained to him that the Italians had become more tolerant, particularly in the big cities.

Bashir brought the excellent coffee, and for a while they chatted. Adel's companion rarely opened his mouth. When Salman asked him questions, he only answered with a yes or a no, stifling any further attempt at conversation. His reticence made Salman slightly nervous.

"Would you rather have dinner at a restaurant, or at my place?" Adel asked. "Bashir's a trained cook. He comes from a small village near Aleppo."

"In that case, I'd rather let myself be tempted by Aleppo's delicious cuisine," Salman replied, knowing that he would have to tell Adel as soon as possible about his situation.

"Fine, Bashir, you go and do the shopping—and please buy only top quality food. Our guest is a spoiled Italian." Both left the room. Salman heard them kiss, and then the apartment door closed. After a while, Adel returned, now dressed.

"Come, I'll show you my little secret paradise. A pity you didn't come in the summer."

~

Salman followed him. A small staircase led up to the roof terrace. Adel wasn't exaggerating. There was no trace of modesty, and several golden ceramic cherubs and cheetahs had found a place, as is often the case in wealthy Arab homes.

"This is where we celebrate once a week, like in Sodom and Gomorrah, from May to October. The best of the city comes, and you have to book well in advance. There's only space for twenty men and women. I'm booked out for the next five years."

Salman nodded and followed Adel absentmindedly. The sun shone and it had gotten warmer. Suddenly Adel looked straight into Salman's eyes. "What's the matter with you? You're troubled—or am I mistaken?"

"No, you're not mistaken. Your eyes are as sharp as ever," Salman said flatteringly. "I'm in trouble. Does the name Elias Baladi ring a bell?" Adel shook his head. "He's my cousin, a big shot in the secret service. He hates me, and a few days ago, he had an arrest warrant issued against me. I'm supposed to have murdered a woman, although I was still in Rome at the time of the crime. So, I'm a wanted man. I'd never have come back to Damascus if the president hadn't proclaimed a general amnesty. And on top of that, my parents paid this creep Elias ten thousand dollars for him to check whether there was still anything out against me anywhere. I only came over after he'd given the green light."

"So why is he persecuting you now?"

"No idea. Elias knows that I'm wealthy. Maybe he wants to blackmail me. They say he's up to his neck in debt. But I need to hide for a few days, until I find a way to reach Beirut safely. From there I'll fly back to Rome. I thought you could help me…" Adel remained silent.

"That's not possible, unfortunately," he finally said, poking a large plant tub with a small shovel. "I don't want any more trouble. I have enough as it is, you understand? The whole world's watching my ass. Do you understand? For years they registered all my visitors. It's only lately that they've finally left me in peace… and now here you come. So what's this all about? A test of my courage? My loyalty? Yes, I'm a coward. So what? I never had any friends. Where were you when I went through hell for six months because I loved a man? People who call themselves socialists had me raped every day in their prisons. The pain and the humiliation were supposed to reform me. I hate them all—government and opposition alike." Adel grew silent. He rammed the small shovel into the earth near the oleander. "It's not possible, unfortunately," he said again, barely audible. "You have to find yourself another friend. You can spend the night here, but tomorrow morning…"

They remained on the roof, in silence, for nearly an hour. Then they heard Bashir call. "Let's enjoy the hours we have left," Adel said, going down the stairs. Salman followed.

~

Downstairs, Adel was friendly and obliging. "You can rest here for a while. I'll call you when we're finished," he said, showing Salman a guest room with a bed, a desk, and a wardrobe. When Salman sat on the bed, he noticed a door to a private bathroom. He went in and looked at himself in the mirror. "What kind of a walking disaster are you?" he thought, gazing at his reflection. He pitied the sad-looking creature.

The dinner Bashir prepared was delicious, but Salman could not sleep that night. His thoughts were too loud, and the noises that came from the bedroom next door, even louder. Salman's thoughts went around in senseless circles. Should he call his cousin Tarek? He was afraid to jeopardize that last hope, too.

A gleam of light in the dark

The next morning, Salman woke up early. Bashir had left. Adel drank his coffee in the kitchen, already in his white coat. "You must be gone in half an hour because I can't leave you here on your own. But drink your coffee first," he said insistently.

"Don't worry. I'll leave soon. But I want you to know that I haven't committed any crime. I renounced violence forty years ago."

"You haven't committed any crime?" Adel shouted, almost outraged. "Just wait until they arrest you. Then you'll be happy to own up to a murder so that they don't beat a bigger crime out of you that will take you to your execution." He waved his hand dismissively. "I don't care if you're wanted as a terrorist. That's what counts, and I don't feel like losing everything I've built up just because of you. Our country is a perfect police state. But life's not so bad here, as long as you don't interfere and you don't support its enemies—and, well, you're officially an enemy of the state. By the way, last night before I fell asleep, I remembered that in those forty years you never even once sent me a postcard. Am I right?"

Salman nodded.

When Adel went to the toilet, Salman stood up and took his shoulder bag and his coat. He left without saying goodbye or touching his coffee.

Outside he breathed in the fresh air of the sunny morning. The streets and the cars gleamed. Where should he go? He hurried away from Joule Jammal Street and crossed Seven Fountains Square. On Bagdad Street, he discovered a little café. He sat down in the warm, small room. Only one other table was occupied, by two young women drinking tea. The waiter brought him a cappuccino, collected the payment, and retreated to the kitchen behind the counter.

Where should he run to? He didn't know anyone else he could trust. Absurd thoughts ran through his mind. He remembered an old story that he had heard when he was a teenager. A woman had been living for ages with two men. Her husband was the chief of police, her lover a criminal. He was wanted everywhere, except in the house of the police chief. So he lived there for years in a secret cellar where the husband never went. The woman had nerves of steel. She lived happily with the two men. Salman contemplated for a while going to Isabella, Elias' wife, and asking her to hide him in her cellar. But disgusted, he pushed the thought out of his mind.

The best thing would be to look up Hani. His old comrade-in-arms wouldn't abandon him. Fortunately, Hani had been the only one of his former comrades who hadn't been there that evening when Elias had visited his parents' apartment. Salman hadn't dared to go to any of the others because Elias had seen them there. And Tarek? Calling on him would be too dangerous for both of them.

His years in the underground had taught him never to underestimate an enemy, particularly when they were as cunning as Elias. He thought back to the moment that evening when Elias and his wife were saying goodbye. In passing, almost disinterestedly, Elias had asked, "Any idea what Hani's doing these days? Has he been by to see you?" Salman had been at a loss for an answer. To deflect Elias's curiosity, he'd shaken his head and said, "No, thank God. I heard he's gone crazy."

"Oh, right," Elias said, pretending more or less to be concerned. "The poor guy. I heard something like that too. I heard he was in a psychiatric ward."

After a while Salman left the café and went to the telephone booth that he'd spotted on the way. He hesitated briefly. Not far away from him, two older men were shouting at a young man to get in a car—something the young man did not want to do. The car's motor was running. The driver sat disinterestedly behind the wheel. The young man was white with fear. The smaller of the two who were pestering him flashed a badge, and the taller shook his gleaming bald head in indignation. He gave the young man a loud slap on the side of his head and shoved him into the car, climbing in next to him.

The other walked around the car and got in next to the driver. Then the car roared off. Passersby, residents from the surrounding houses, and customers in the café, all were rooted to the spot. Even the shadows along the wall seemed to disappear out of fear.

Without hesitating, Salman went into the telephone booth and dialed Hani's number. "I need your help urgently," he whispered into the mouthpiece.

"My help? Sure, come by now." Hani sounded concerned.

"Are you sure it's all right for you both? I'm not disturbing you so early in the morning?"

"Not at all, I'm on my own. It's been ten years since the secret service assholes bothered me, so no worries there."

"What do you mean 'on your own'? What about your wife?"

"She cleared out—to her parents in Aleppo for now. She doesn't want to live with me anymore."

"I'm sorry to hear that," Salman said, and he meant it. He was ashamed that he hadn't noticed that, among all his visitors, Hani had always come by himself, unaccompanied. Nobody had been aware of his broken marriage—not even Sophia. Salman had the impression that society had forgotten Hani completely.

"There's no need to be sorry. It just didn't work anymore, and we don't have any children, so the separation's not so dramatic. You know where I live, don't you?"

"Still at your parents' place?"

"Yes, from Bab Tuma Square go down Jura Street, and at the third street on the left, it's the corner house. Just come over. I've got a couple of good bottles of red wine—you like red wine, don't you?"

Salman said yes and hung up. He was sure that Hani didn't have the slightest idea just how bad his situation was. The sky seemed to have clouded over, but in the midst of all this gloom there was at least a gleam of light.

32

A Promise's Weight

Damascus, December 17, 2010

It was Friday morning and ice-cold outside. Karim had a doctor's appointment; his hip was hurting again. When he came home and opened the front door, first he heard Aida laughing and then Sophia's voice. Hers was a voice he could recognize among thousands. What was she doing here? He leaned his bicycle against the terrace railing, walked slowly up the few steps to the inner courtyard, and cautiously opened the door to the living room.

"There he is," Aida called out, jumping up. They were sitting at the big table in the living room, next to the sofa. The table had six chairs around it and also served as a dining table. The fire in the oven was blazing away. Sophia stood up, too. Her hair had turned snow white and her face was still beautiful. She had hardly changed, only she looked melancholy and sad. Karim seemed to have turned to stone in the doorway.

"What's the matter?" Aida cried, coming toward him with open arms. "Are you scared of two peaceful women?"

He smiled in embarrassment, gave Aida a quick hug, and held his hand out to Sophia.

"It's been a long time," he said softly, sitting down at the head of the table between the two women.

"What did the doctor say?" Aida asked. "Just tell me briefly, then Sophia can tell you why she's here, while I go and make us all some tea. I'm a terrible hostess. I was so enthralled by Sophia's story that I forgot all about hospitality."

"Well, the hip joint is infected again. He's prescribed me some painkillers and a new medication for the infection. I should go swimming when I can. That's good for the hip. And I shouldn't carry heavy weights."

"I've told you that ten times. But then again, I'm no doctor, just a hairdresser. Well, it's official now. No more heavy work in the garden, understood?" Aida said, acting severe.

"Yes, ma'am. I obey your every command."

Aida stood up to put the kettle on, kissing Karim on the head as she passed.

"A wonderful woman," Sophia said softly. "So genuine and attentive. After just an hour, I feel like we've known each other for years."

"Yes, she's remarkable."

"The reason I'm here," Sophia said after a moment, "is I need your help."

"My help?" Karim asked in surprise.

"Yes, it's about my son Salman. After the president proclaimed an amnesty for all exiles, he came back to Damascus to visit us for the first time in forty years. But now he's being hunted, and we don't know what to do. His life's in danger… they want to kill him…" Sophia began to cry.

Aida, who had just come back from the kitchen took Sophia in her arms and hugged her close. "It'll be all right, you'll see. Everything will be all right," she said. Sophia calmed down a little and Aida sat back down at the table.

"Sophia," Karim said, "a long time ago I promised you that I would always stand by you. And I keep my word. You can be sure I'll do everything I can to help you and your son. We'll find a way," he said and stroked her hands that were folded in front of her on the table as if in prayer. "Please tell me everything just the way it happened."

33
Hani's Scars

It had just started to drizzle when Salman left the phone booth. He quickly flagged a taxi that was speeding past. The driver braked with a screech.

"Are you free?"

"As a bird. Where to?" the driver asked while Salman climbed into the backseat. "Bab Tuma Gate."

"My pleasure," the young man said and turned up the radio. A young singer afflicted with a bland, generic voice went on about an unattainable blue-eyed, blond beloved—probably a tourist who didn't understand what he was saying. He was begging her to let their hearts speak. Just like in Italy, Salman thought. *Amore* rhymes with *cuore*, *calore*, *dolore*, *rumore*, and even with *suore*—nun.

At least the taxi driver left him in peace. Salman's thoughts went through him like jagged splinters, and he couldn't sort things into any kind of order. He was talking to himself, to Paolo, to Stella, and to God, reproaching himself for having come here. He had a life in Rome. What was he doing here? Stella, beloved Stella! You were right. I should have stayed in Rome. Paolo, light of my life, what will become of you if I die here before you've grown up?

Just what was he searching for here, Salman wondered. Proof that he had defied the dictatorship? Proof to whom? But then, what's so wrong with visiting your childhood haunts and giving joy to your parents? Even so, his father seemed just as cold as ever. Yusuf had never liked or understood him before. He was one of those fathers who should have remained a bachelor, one of those charming anarchists. What kind of society had the Assad clan turned out in this fear factory? Syrians—the loudest people in the Middle East—had been broken. They had become quiet cowards. They had been forced to creep and obey.

What should he tell Hani about the manhunt? How would he react? Where was Elias now?

Salman was jarred out of his maze of thoughts by a police car racing along Baghdad Street. "What's going on?" he asked the taxi driver. "Maybe somebody's bought their mother-in-law a ticket to the Creator. One-way, of course," he said, laughing. "And what if it's something serious?" Salman persisted.

"Well then, you wouldn't notice the police car. In that case, they'd sneak along without lights or sirens. So, where should I stop?" he asked as the Bab Tuma Gate appeared in front of them. "Near the Dar al-Yasmin Hotel, please." The taxi driver took his fare, said thank you, and drove off.

~

Hani's house was not far from the gate, and not even that far from Aunt Takla's. The rain had stopped. Salman hurried along. Two men were standing in front of the hotel, smoking and watching over the street. He only slowed down after turning onto Jura Street, which was quieter. He hadn't needed Hani's directions because he remembered that his friend's parents' house stood at the corner of Jura and Bakri Street. He rang the bell.

As if Hani had been waiting for him behind the door, it opened instantly and Hani smiled broadly at his friend. "Forgive me for visiting you in the morning already," Salman said. Hani smiled. "You're always welcome. Did you get bored with all those relatives? You've done well. I couldn't even have put up with it for five days," he said, hanging his friend's coat on the rack and leading the way into the living room. It smelled of heating oil. Provided you sat close enough, a modest stove gave out a little warmth in the damp ground-floor room. Hani had put a small bistro table and two chairs next to the stove. It all seemed shabby to Salman. Stella would have sarcastically called it a "bachelor pad."

"Tell me how things are with you," Salman started after taking his first sip of coffee.

"There's not much to tell," Hani replied almost reluctantly. "We'd planned and opened our café together. But then my wife suddenly became dissatisfied and wanted nothing to do with it. That was my downfall. I'd signed all the contracts, and every evening she'd tell me to give up the café. But the truth of it was, she wanted to leave me. I think she was disappointed in me. You don't get any better-looking at sixty. You get a little uglier with every failure. And my whole life is nothing but a streak of failures.

So I gave up the café for a loss. I'd inherited four pieces of good land from my parents, in the north of the city, and I was able to cover the debts by selling one of them. And how did my wife thank me? Three months later, after we'd had an argument, she ran off to her brothers in Aleppo. They're both well-to-do lawyers and now she does all the housework and looks after the children, so that her sisters-in-law don't have to lift a finger. But here, in my place, toward the end she wouldn't even empty her own ashtray. That's what happens when love dies. But the worst is, she won't speak to me anymore. Can you imagine? After twenty years of marriage? I can't. I wanted to talk and make up with her, and she just shouted at me that they'd been right to torture me in prison. Those were her last words, and they're still ringing in my ears."

"Why don't you go and see her in Aleppo?"

"I went there but her brothers wouldn't let me in the house. Supposedly, they were afraid for their sister's life. Afraid of me!" he shouted in outrage. After he'd calmed down, he finished his coffee. "How about you? Are you happy with your wife?" he asked Salman trying to change the subject.

"I'm happy with Stella, but we've had our troubles, and I also have a failed marriage behind me. That was more than thirty years ago, though," Salman replied, sipping at his second coffee. The only thing that could be heard was the flame sputtering in the metal stove. The silence was like a blanket; at the beginning it felt calming and soothing, but then it began to weigh on Salman's soul.

"They're looking for me," Salman finally said. "My cousin Elias is behind it all. You know him from our time in the underground," he added.

Hani looked at him keenly. "Do I know him! He had fun watching two of his men torture me in the camp."

"Well, he's tricked my parents and me. He took ten thousand dollars from my father to clear all my records, despite the fact that there was an amnesty and I had been in exile for forty years, so all offenses fell under the statute of limitations. But now he's framing me for a murder I didn't commit and he's blowing up the old story about the police station and the injured policeman. Do you know what became of him?"

"Yes, I found out because I was still hiding out in that area," Hani said. "Luckily, he recovered quickly and was running around after two or three weeks as if nothing had happened."

"Now they're looking for me for the murder of Fatima Haddad," Salman continued.

"Fatima Haddad?"

"She was killed by Islamists four weeks before I came back to Damascus, but now they've framed me. Don't you read the newspapers?"

"No, I haven't read that rubbish since my café went bust. Which newspaper was it in?"

"The official one—*Tishrin*, page one."

"My God, back then in the mountains, I never doubted that Elias was a revolutionary. Do you remember the two of us defending him against the leadership? Later, I always said that he was the one who betrayed us. Now I know that he had been infiltrated by the secret service right from the start. The secret service learned that from the Russians and the East Germans," Hani said bitterly, looking at Salman. "But why is he hunting you? Do you still have scores to settle? Is it about a woman?"

"No. Elias is pursuing me like an inquisitor. All these years, I've been really afraid of him, more than I wanted to admit in public. He never lost sight of me. I know that he found out a lot about me, my longing for Damascus, my conduct while I was on the run, my strengths and weaknesses. He wants money—a lot of money, at least a million dollars," Salman explained.

"Ah!" Hani shouted, as if getting the whole picture for the first time. "That's what's going on—he's not even your cousin, not even the son of a mother and a father. He's just one of the dictator's gnomes, a test-tube creature of an evil system. He should be killed."

"No, no, I don't want to kill anybody. I just want out. It was a mistake to come here…"

"Yes, you're running away, but what about the rest of

us twenty million? Where are we supposed to run to...?"

Salman had no answer to that.

Silence fell again.

When the church tower clock chimed eleven, Hani stood up.

"I'm hungry. Do you want something to eat?"

"Yes, please," Salman said.

"Okay, I'll get us a bite from the snack bar next door. I'll be right back. You can rest after the meal and then we'll see. You're safe here."

"Do you need money?"

"For God's sake, no. I have enough. Don't forget, you're in Damascus, as a guest. You're the noble prisoner of the host," he laughed, putting on his jacket and leaving. He turned back again at the front door. "Don't open this door for anyone! I'll lock it from outside so that it looks as if I'm home alone."

After Hani left, Salman took a look around the apartment. Two other rooms were crammed to the ceiling with cardboard boxes. A third room served as a bedroom. Salman was met by a stench of stale air, sweat, cold smoke, and old socks. But the kitchen was the worst. Fat maggots crawled and wriggled in the black mixture festering in a pan on the stove. There was a mountain of dirty dishes in the rusty sink and the tap dripped. Coffee powder had been spilled all over the table, which was covered with half-empty bottles, the contents of which could only be guessed at. Salman retraced his steps, fighting the urge to vomit. In the main room he opened the window. He closed his eyes and breathed in the fresh air. He was beginning to doubt if Hani's apartment was the right place for him. Finally, he sat down to rest on the sofa beneath the window and felt overcome by a paralyzing fatigue.

He was walking across a broad landscape and heard Paolo calling for him. But when he turned around, he noticed the ground opening up in front of him like an abyss. He woke up with a start. Hani was standing in front of him, smiling benevolently.

"You're tired, you poor devil," he said. He must have been back for quite a while because there was food laid out on the little bistro table by the stove, giving out a pleasant smell. There was hummus, falafel, cheese and olives, and crispy bread on a sheet of newspaper. Everything looked fresh and tasty.

To his own surprise, Salman was hungry and ate a lot. But after the meal, when he offered to help with the washing up and tidying the kitchen, Hani curtly refused his help. "You're my guest, not my wife," he said, almost as if he were insulted.

He carried the leftovers into the kitchen and came back with a bottle of red wine and two tall cocktail glasses. Without asking Salman, he filled both glasses to the brim. "Cheers," he said, and took a big gulp before lighting a cigarette. An overflowing ashtray lay on the floor next to the stove. Salman put it on the table. Hani took note of this impassively, tapped his cigarette ash on the edge of the ashtray, and took a second big gulp of wine.

The sojourn in hell

They sat there for a while saying nothing. Breaking the silence, Salman said, "Tell me about your time in prison."

"Each day was exactly like the one before," said Hani. "I can't tell the months and years apart. But I can remember the first few days very well, the torture and the uncertainty. Many of my comrades were executed. A secret service security expert decides that so-and-so is dangerous, and then the man is just dragged out and shot through the head from behind.

"As an explosives expert for a resistance group, I didn't think I stood much of a chance. They wanted to torture me before they executed me, and they stuck me in a cell with twenty Islamists. In their eyes I was an enemy in every way. I was from a Christian family, and an atheist. But even with all that, I was lucky. Except for one bearded idiot who kicked and slapped me every chance he got, even though he was ten years younger than me, the others left me alone. In the third year, the torture also lessened. I had plenty of time to think and decided I wanted nothing more to do with changes brought about by force. I read a biography of Gandhi that somebody had smuggled in.

"There were dark days when I would have preferred to end it all, if I'd had the strength. But then there were moments of joy. Sometimes, I laughed so much they must have thought I'd gone mad.

"One day I'll never forget was the worst of all." Hani paused for a moment and took a long swallow of wine.

"What happened?"

"One morning, the guard called out my name. I was panic-stricken. With the exception of the bearded idiot, all my fellow prisoners said goodbye to me.

"I asked the guard why he'd gotten me. He smiled and said, 'Captain Radi.' I can't describe my fear. The Devil could take lessons from Radi. He'd tormented all of us, sometimes in person. For almost a year, it seemed as if he'd forgotten about me. Now it was my turn again. Everyone knew 'wants you' meant rape.

"The guard shoved me into the captain's office and stayed outside. Radi was sitting at the table with a book open in front of him. Across from him sat a vicious policeman who everyone called *Aftas*, flat nose, because his nose had been broken in a fight.

"Radi said he had received a book containing new interrogation techniques he was unfamiliar with. He wanted to try out one of them on me. It was called 'meatball,' but he couldn't figure out how it was supposed to work. The translation of the book from Russian was confusing. I almost died of fear.

"The captain told Aftas to take the thin nylon rope and follow his instructions, and for me to sit on the floor and pull my legs in. Reading from the book, Radi told Aftas to take the rope around the neck and then from the right under the armpit down toward the left, then back across over the legs under the right armpit to... But Aftas couldn't get it. He crouched down next to me, and his foul breath was torture enough. They started again, but the book's translation is a disaster, start to finish. It said in some cases to use sunflower oil—what was that supposed to mean? It was like the fool typed in something out of a recipe, just to pad the text, like we were frying falafel!

Radi and Aftas went over the instructions like schoolboys. It was all gobbledygook. Finally I said, 'Maybe I can help? I know a bit about knots.'"

Salman nodded. He knew that Hani was not just an explosives expert but the best handyman he'd ever met. Give him a rope and few wooden planks and he could build you a solid chair or a bunk. And he could really do magic tricks with a piece of rope.

"The two looked at me like a pair of zombies. I said to just let me have a quick look in the book and I'd demonstrate the technique for them. So they untied me and Radi ordered Aftas to get undressed and squat down. Aftas tried to protest, but the captain shouted there were no buts about it, and Aftas took off all his clothes. In all my life, I'd never have thought that a sadist like Aftas could have such a smooth and hairless body. Even the captain noticed it.

"I looked at the book… it really was a terrible translation, but the illustrations and drawings were precise. In five minutes I'd wrapped the torturer up in a ball you could easily roll this way and that. Radi wrote down the steps. 'Fantastic, fantastic,' he said. 'Now fuck him.' That wasn't in the instructions! Aftas looked at me, pleading. I said I couldn't do it, it was dishonorable. Radi jumped up and punched me in the face, and I fell backward against the door. The guard opened it to see if everything was all right. The captain yelled at the guard, called Adnan, to show a eunuch like me how real men fuck. He told him to look at Aftas' hairless naked backside—not even his wife had such a smooth backside. And Adnan raped his colleague.

"Afterward, I showed the captain how to untie all the loops and knots, while Aftas wept. The guard led me back to the cell. I didn't want to tell anyone what had happened… I suppose my swollen eye said enough."

Elias and hell's deepest dungeon

Hani lit up a new cigarette and took another gulp of wine. "Elias arrived after I'd been there four years. By then he was a captain in the secret service. Murderers like him served a whole year in camps or prisons, and that was enough to destroy what was left of their humanity. At the camp, every commandant was a god. Laws meant nothing. The commandant was like a scientist studying insects. Elias had us crushed, killed, buried in the desert, without ever having to account for his actions. He had me tortured, and he laughed maliciously while they did it. I'd reached my lowest point—a former comrade was ordering people to torture me, and watching and laughing! Elias must have hated us. I asked him if I'd ever done anything to him, and the answer was no. I begged him to shoot me and put an end to the torture, but he just laughed. 'For God's sake, I want you to live long and suffer,' he said.

"And all the time he sat behind his desk, giving detailed instructions. I was going mad." Hani pulled a dirty handkerchief out of his pocket and wiped his eyes. He took another drag on his cigarette, as Salman waited. How Hani must have suffered... just listening to him was almost unbearable. Finally, Hani stubbed out his cigarette in the ashtray and lit up another one. "It was hell to be tortured by someone I'd risked my life for. Do you remember how we wanted to kidnap the head of the secret service?"

Salman shook his head. He hadn't been involved and knew little about this secret special operation.

"There were six of us—Elias, me, and another four comrades—two women and two men. We wanted to kidnap the head of the secret service, General Bukadir, and force them to free fifty of our people. Bukadir usually took leave using a false name in a village near Latakia. He passed himself off as a university teacher. But our informer got the date wrong and we attacked an empty villa. During our escape, Elias slipped and fell, and two policemen arrested him. We were able to escape. I kept thinking about Elias. The others didn't want to go, but I went back. I took the policemen by surprise and freed Elias. We left them handcuffed at the edge of an olive grove. We put on their uniforms and drove away in their Land Rover. Elias suddenly braked, reversed like a madman, until he was back where the handcuffed policemen were. He climbed out and shot them both. I was speechless, but he said they might have recognized him. He said he'd be grateful to me all his life, but I was to swear never to tell anyone about it.

"I reminded Elias about this operation and about his promise to show his gratitude some time. I begged him to spare me, but that made him even more angry.

Ten years later, when I was about to be released, he was also the one who, from his senior position, described exactly how that was to happen. The prison warden said almost apologetically that this was not really common, but the order had come from very high up—Elias.

Two men held me down. I was stripped to the waist, stretched out over a bunk in the open air and they tied my arms, while a third man lashed my back with a whip. He carved the map of Damascus into my skin to remind me that I was a Damascene, not a Russian communist. Later, once the scars healed, I asked a friend to take a picture of my back. I could identify all the streets and places that I knew. Straight Street, my school, my parents' house, the church, the citadel, and the souk al-Hamidiya."

"Really?" Salman said in disbelief.

Hani stood up, went into the bedroom, and came back with a large framed photograph—a close-up of his back. Salman managed to make out the outline of the city, and he followed Hani's description of places and streets with a mixture of pity and compassion.

"I suffered a lot in this school here," Hani said, pointing to a place near historical Straight Street. "And here, at Kishle bus stop, I was beaten up by an older boy when I wanted to take my pretty cousin to the cinema for the first time." He pointed to a dark spot. "And from that day on, she never wanted to go out with me again." His finger followed the map of his scars while he talked for more than an hour about the places where he'd suffered. Then he put aside the photograph and drained his wine glass. The first bottle had been finished long ago. Salman would have liked to warn him not to drink so much, but he felt like a fool.

"And then they gave me a dirty, shabby shirt that I had to pull over my bleeding back before I left the prison. A guard gave me one last slap, and I staggered outside into freedom. I hadn't the faintest idea that the prison was right in the middle of the city, because I'd spent three years in a tiny cell, seven floors below ground. When I'd been brought up for interrogation, they'd chained my hands and blindfolded me. There was an old lift which stopped with a rattle at every floor. It was only years after that I learned that the building had ten floors below ground and only three above.

I breathed in the fresh air and could hardly believe my eyes. People walked around laughing and happy, as if the prisons were located in a foreign country or on another planet. I felt like I was in a science-fiction movie, with a time machine sending people from one century to another. People on the street looked right through me.

It was then I realized that there were many Syrias. On the surface there's peace, and it's not just the tourists who think that the country is a paradise. The Syrians do too, as long as they know nothing about the other Syria. But an entire city of hell lies beneath Damascus, seven floors down, and spreads out... It's hundreds of kilometers wide and it mushrooms out of the ground in Adra, Saidnaya, and Palmyra. There are camps and prisons there for hundreds of thousands of innocent people. This hell is so well organized that the people who live above ground can't hear or feel it.

"Whoever has lived it and survived, needs to forget as quickly as possible if they don't want to go mad. You're pushed out of the gate, but it takes a long time before you've really left the prison behind you… It's as if it takes root inside you. All paths are paved with mistrust. Each curious question seems like an interrogation, and you keep trying to protect your head from unexpected blows."

Finally, Hani no longer wanted to burden his guest with his tormenting memories, and he searched in his memory for experiences they had shared. And there were many of these. They laughed and told each other stories from the past. One was about a comrade named Said who feared more for his penis than for himself when they were in combat. "What if it gets blown apart by a bullet and I survive? You can lose your home and win it back, you can even find a new home—but you can't replace that," he said. He made himself a tin codpiece that looked like a chastity belt and strapped it on before every mission.

When dusk fell, Hani stood up. "I'll get us something else to eat," he said, indicating the door.

Salman switched on the television. It was time for the news, but he only sat up and took notice when the speaker mentioned something about trouble in Tunisia.

By the time Hani returned with the food from the snack bar, he had found out more. Customers there said a rebellion had broken out against the Tunisian ruler Ben Ali. A policewoman had harassed a greengrocer, and as a result, he had doused himself with petrol and set fire to himself. That was the spark that set off a rebellion.

Hani and Salman ate the delicious warm dishes in silence.

The fate of revolutionaries

"Do you remember Isam?" Hani asked after a while. "He was my friend and comrade, my role model. I don't think I ever had a true friend, but at the time, I was happy when he called me friend. He was a born speaker, and we were all carried away by his charm. Later he would sing to an enthusiastic audience, and when his voice broke, he made millions with his artists' agency. In the eighties, I think he must have arranged for more female singers and pseudo-artists to land in Saudi beds than on the stage. At the time, the Saudis hadn't yet discovered London, Paris, Amsterdam, and Munich. Can you imagine? A communist pimping for the oil sheikhs.

"And have you heard from Safer? He was the one who grew a Che Guevara beard and wore a beret with a star. Now he's the mufti of Aleppo and the right hand of the head of the secret service there, who also happens to be his brother-in-law. The pyramids defeat time, and the clan always wins, even against political ideologies—Marxism, Leninism, nationalism. Safer bored us all with his atheism, and today he's advocating that atheists be publicly stoned. And how about George, remember, the son of Josef Assfar, the millionaire? He always walked barefoot and the peasants took a special shine to him because he was so modest?" Hani emptied his glass in one gulp and filled it up again. Of course Salman remembered George. He couldn't stand him at the time. The man never washed and gave such exaggerated sermons against materialism that he made you feel put off by the luxury of stale bread.

"George is the worst of them all. Nowadays he deals in Cuban cigars, Russian caviar, Hungarian salami, and other delicacies from the former socialist countries, and he's become a millionaire. I could have forgiven him everything, but when he started moaning, I spit in his face."

"You spit in…"

"Yes, you know why? The rich have taken everything—money, power, the nicest houses, gardens, beaches—and now they've even taken over moaning, which used to be a monopoly of the poor. Nothing's worse than a moaning millionaire. The son-of-a-bitch said that he no longer felt happy in this country and that he had to emigrate. They've even robbed us of our misery," Hani cried, laughing bitterly as if his woozy brain had heard a joke on another channel, then he coughed.

Fleeing from a dangerous dead-end street

Salman drank slowly. He wasn't enjoying the second and third bottles of wine. With every sip he felt the burning carve its way down to his stomach. But he said nothing. Hani knocked back the wine, but he remained sober.

"Fifteen secret services, fifteen civil services from hell are destroying our lives," Hani said to the silence. "Syrians rape Syrians, torture them, crucify them, so that the world up there can keep on turning peacefully. To save us all, we need to blow up the ones who run this system. Only then will Syrians be able to live together in peace."

Salman was overcome by fear. "Hani, I'm tired of fighting. I just want to live in peace. We should stop waging wars. What do we gain with violence…"

"Ah, our esteemed merchant wants peace for his business. But I want to end my failure of a life with something big. Not with something any shopkeeper can do. I want to leave my mark. How about murdering Elias? I'll call him and tell him that you believe he will save you and this is why you'll only surrender to him in person. But he should come alone, or with his bodyguards. And then I'll send him to hell. I've got three large cases of dynamite in the cellar."

"Dynamite? You're making this up?"

"Three cases, best quality. I got them for a song. A rebel group had broken up and needed the money. I tested one pack in the quarry. Excellent!" Hani's eyes gleamed. "Salman, you saved my life in the mountains, and out of gratitude, I'll kill this Elias son-of-a-bitch."

Hani had talked himself into a rage. He was drunk, but his words were crystal clear. His speech wasn't the least bit slurred.

"Not so loud!" Salman begged.

Hani got up and walked on his swaying legs to a little closet, opened the door on the left, and pulled a pistol from beneath a pile of shirts. He aimed toward the window and said, "Bang." Then he came back and put the pistol on the table. It was a macabre sight—the wine bottle, two glasses, a pistol on the table, and the two men in the dirty room. Salman's throat felt dry. He drank a sip of wine.

"You've been in Germany and Italy," Hani started again. "Sure, exile's not easy, but in the meantime I've been through hell. I don't believe that God, in His infinite goodness, is at all capable of creating hell. But those who govern hell on earth, they're monsters filled with malice.

Should I tell you about the prison in Saidnaya, or the prison camps at Palmyra or Adra? And what would be the point of telling you? To you it just sounds like the hallucinations of a sick man, and it kills me to talk about it. Not even my wife could take it any longer."

Salman looked at him sadly. "You don't have to tell me anything. I believe you."

Hani nodded, drank in silence, and then kept talking. Gradually his speech began to slur.

Just after midnight he stood up suddenly, muttering that he needed to go to the toilet. After a while, when he still hadn't returned, Salman decided to see if he was all right. He found him in the bedroom. Hani was lying fully clothed in bed, snoring. Salman covered him up and went back into the living room. He hid the pistol under the shirts and lay down to sleep on the old sofa by the window. He felt a cold draft, so he got up to stuff cloths he'd found in the cupboard into the gap in the window. Finally he made himself as comfortable as he could on the sofa, which smelled like dust and sweat. But it was a long time before he could fall asleep.

He was awakened by a noise. It was still dark. He sat up in bewilderment and it took a moment before he realized where he was. The cry had come from the bedroom. Hani was now whining and weeping softly. Salman didn't know whether to go to him or just leave him alone until he woke up. He decided to wait and lay back down again. But he felt too restless. He remembered what Hani said about explosives in the cellar. He put his shoes back on and crept out into the hall, where he'd seen a cellar door, and he found the light switch. Unlike the rest of the apartment, the cellar was scrupulously clean. The larger room was a sort of electrical workshop. When he pushed open the door to the smaller room, he froze. In the center stood three cartons, one on top of the other. The stencil on each one showed the contents—Semtex H, an internationally known plastic explosive.

All this was why his wife left him, Salman thought when he was back on the sofa. Nobody could tolerate it— explosives in the cellar, a loaded pistol, a sick broken soul. He decided to go to his cousin Tarek the next day and ask him again for help. But suddenly he was alarmed. Did he still have the key to the passage that led to the workshop? He checked his pocket. Relieved, he returned to the sofa and finally fell asleep.

When he woke up, it was eleven thirty. Hani was still asleep. The stove had gone out. The tank was empty.

Salman took a book off the little shelf and read. It wasn't until one o'clock that Hani came out of the bedroom and glanced at Salman suspiciously and with a certain amount of surprise, as if he'd forgotten that he'd spent the night there and then went into the bathroom without replying to Salman's greeting.

"Good morning," Salman said again as Hani came back into the room. Hani was mumbling incomprehensibly to himself.

"I'll get some fresh bread and we can have breakfast," Salman said.

"Don't bother," Hani reacted dismissively.

Salman lost his temper. "Then I'll go to a café and get some breakfast there."

"When will you be back?" Hani asked.

"Should I come back at all?" Salman asked earnestly.

"I don't care. If you need a hideout, you can come and live here. If I'm not here, look in the Abu Ali restaurant. It's close by, in the direction of Bakri Street."

"Right," Salman said and stood up.

"Good luck," Hani replied.

Salman buttoned up his coat, picked up his shoulder bag and left.

34

Tarek's Hand

Damascus, December 18, 2010

Guilt by association

Outside, Salman breathed a deep sigh of relief, but he also dreaded what awaited him—loneliness, fear, the threat of arrest. Four times he'd fled to what seemed like an oasis, only to find a mirage. Still, he had to move on, and the fresh air did him good.

He wandered through the Old City, went into a restaurant, and ordered grape leaves stuffed with vegetables, and stuffed squash, served proudly by the waiter with a side order of rice with toasted pine nuts. He finished the delicious meal with mocha with cardamom.

Then he walked along the tourist trail to the Orthodox Church of the Holy Virgin, from there to the Chapel of St. Paul, and from there to Zeitoun Street and the famous Catholic Church, to which the gates were open. Inside he became engrossed in the pictures and listened to the explanations of the tourist guides in the various languages. The city seemed more peaceful here. He knew that his cousin Tarek's two workers didn't go home until five o'clock. When the afternoon light began to fade, he directed his step toward Deir Street and slipped through the door into the underground passageway that led to his cousin's workshop.

It was a while before his eyes adjusted to the darkness. Finally, he found the telephone, dialed one, let it ring three times, and hung up. He repeated this three times.

The third time, the low door leading into the bathroom opened and Tarek beamed at him. "Come on in, you old nomad." Salman ducked his head, slipped through the door, and followed Tarek into the workshop, where his cousin then turned around and stretched out his arms laughing. Salman hugged him. More than a hug, it was like a drowning man holding on tightly to a great beam of wood in a churning sea.

"Now that's what I call telepathy," said Tarek when the two of them sat down in his office. "I've been thinking about you all day, and praying to the Virgin for you to hear my calls in your heart."

"What's happened?" Salman asked worriedly.

"Everything's fine. Yesterday I visited your mother and arranged with her to leave your suitcase at her house because the secret service may have fitted it with a transmitter so they can track it. Our apartment has been bugged as well. I've brought the money with me you left at home. Everything else you can buy brand new. Your mother has found an ideal hiding place for you at an old friend's. He's also agreed to help you get out of the country. She gave me the address. His name's Karim Asmar and he lives on Jasmine Street. Do you know where that is?"

"Is that the one between Abbara and Zeitoun Street, with the narrow entrance?"

"Right."

"Is Karim reliable?"

"More than reliable. Your mother once saved his life, and he promised her to repay the favor."

Salman laughed. He could hardly imagine his mother saving anybody's life. She'd never said anything about it to him. Tarek stood up, opened his safe, and took out a shopping bag and a thick envelope.

"Your presents for Stella and Paolo are in this bag. I opened and examined the wooden box carefully. It's clean. And they can't have concealed a bug in Stella's jewelry." Tarek handed over the bag and envelope to Salman. "Here are five thousand euros and five thousand dollars from your father." Salman started to object, but Tarek raised his hand. "That's your father's wish. He told me that he would be happy if the money could be of help to you."

Salman was close to tears. "I've underestimated him," he admitted.

"I used to think my father was a simple carpenter, until he traveled with me to Beirut for a week to buy wood. When I saw his skill in handling those merchants, I was ashamed of my arrogance. But there's something else..." Tarek said hesitantly.

"What? Has something happened?"

"It's turned out all right. It's just that Elias somehow found out that I hid you at Maria's. He had her arrested and pretty roughly interrogated. When my mother called his wife Isabella, she claimed he was still in Moscow or Prague. Maria held out and was tortured for two whole days until her father-in-law used his contacts and got in touch with General Shaukat, the president's brother-in-law. So the secret service immediately released Maria. She told me they'd said during the torture that I was next. Apparently General Shaukat gave Elias such a chewing-out that he thought better of it.

"How's Maria now?" Salman asked anxiously.

"She's regained her old spirit and visits Aunt Sophia every day," Tarek reassured him.

Salman felt ashamed. "My God, the trouble I've caused all of you!"

"I'll be grateful to you all my life for helping us when my daughter was ill. But now let's look ahead." Then Tarek slapped his forehead with his hand. "I was forgetting the most important thing. Sahar, whom I told you about, called Stella from Beirut and put her mind at ease. Stella says to tell you that she loves you very much. She and Paolo are sure that you're clever enough to outsmart all your enemies."

Salman couldn't hold back his tears. He felt so weak and so far away from Stella and Paolo.

Tarek left him alone for a while and came back with a clean towel. Salman took the hint, washed his face, and when he came back, Tarek was just putting a pot of mocha and two cups on the table. They drank the mocha in silence. In the meantime it had become pitch dark outside.

"There's a bike in the yard that belongs to Karim. You'll ride it back to him. His house is the last one on the street, on the left just before you get to the square with the monastery ruins…"

"Isn't that near the grave of those two lovers who were only united in death? When I was little, my mother used to go there with lots of other women one day during the summer. It was like a little procession… My father always laughed at her."

"My mother went, too. Unfortunately, I never accompanied her. Anyway, be there by eight. Karim will be waiting for you at the entrance to his house. Your mother totally trusts him. You'll be safe there because nobody knows you, and Karim lives alone."

"Okay. Maybe I should say goodbye to Hani," Salman said. He still had an hour before he needed to leave.

"No, I'll go to his place tomorrow and tell him that you've gone to Beirut with friends. He's a lunatic, who knows what he'll go around saying. We can't be making mistakes now." Tarek paused briefly. "By the way, the secret service has had all your neighbors and friends that

Elias met at your parents interrogated—including their families—and their homes searched. You were lucky that Hani wasn't on his list, at least not until yesterday."

"If they go to Hani, there'll be a hell of a firework display waiting for them," Salman said, "That's why I left."

"Forget Hani. I'll ride to the restaurant and get us a bite to eat. Then we'll have about an hour… My moped is just outside. I'll be right back. Don't open the door for anyone or answer the phone," Tarek added before going out. Salman heard the moped rattle away.

He used the time to look at the newspaper. To his relief, there was no more news about him. When Tarek came back with delicacies and fresh bread, they ate together and drank another mocha. Salman told Tarek about his adventures with Rita and Adel, and asked him to tell Maria that she was brave, and he was safe.

"No one should come and visit you at Karim's," Tarek insisted. "Only your mother and I know your hiding place. Neither my mother, my wife, or your father know. If one of them is tortured, God forbid, and betrays the place, you're lost and Karim is dead." Salman was utterly ashamed to have put these good people in mortal danger by visiting the country again.

It was already ten to eight. Tarek stood up and gave Salman a strong hug. "They won't get you, I swear on my life," he said, slapping Salman tenderly on the back of the head. Stretching out his hand to his cousin, Salman responded, "And you promise that if I get out of here alive, you'll come to us in Rome for Easter with my mother, Aunt Takla, Mona, and Maria. Give me your word?" Only then did he notice that Tarek was crying. He smiled in embarrassment and clapped Salman's hand as if making a deal. "I'd like to come to Rome someday," he said softly.

~

Salman slipped out of the house and rode away on the old bicycle. The light from the old bicycle lamp was very bright. He didn't take long. When he turned into Jasmine Street, it was five to eight. It was cold that evening and the street was empty, but when the lamp illuminated the square, in front of the last door, on the left-hand side, he saw a silhouette that seemed to be waiting for him.

He braked, said hello, dismounted, and followed the man through the door.

An exquisite inner yard opened out in front of him. Lanterns lit the garden path, the stairs, and the yard. Salman breathed a sigh of relief when the old man took the bicycle and shook his hand with surprising strength. "No one but the Good Lord will find you here."

Salman returned the man's handshake. Then he lifted the cardboard box with the presents and his shoulder bag from the luggage carrier.

After four dead-end streets—Maria, Rita, Adel. and Hani—Salman now had a feeling that he had reached a crossroads that offered several possibilities. He breathed in the cold air and followed the man up the stairs underneath an arch that led to a small courtyard.

Then the man opened the door to the house, and Salman was greeted by warmth. There was a fire burning in the oil stove with a rusty window, and a delicate, kind-looking woman was beaming at him.

IV

35

So Near and Far

Rome, December 15–17, 2010

One day a woman named Sahar Khoury called Stella from Beirut. She introduced herself saying she was a distant relative of Salman's. She told Stella that a warrant had been issued in Syria for Salman's arrest. He was wanted, but there was no need to worry. He was being protected, and people were doing their best to get him safely out of the country.

Sahar spoke good Italian, and sounded friendly, nearly motherly. "To assure you that I'm calling on Salman's behalf," she went on, "he suggested that whenever I give you some information, I also tell you something that only he could possibly know. Any news you may receive from someone else is fabricated and may be controlled by the secret service. Do you understand?"

Stella said she understood.

"With this call, I am to tell you that Salman is well and that he loves you as much as the first time you met in Heidelberg."

Stella didn't want to cry, but when the woman mentioned Heidelberg, she couldn't hold back her tears.

Sahar Khoury waited patiently. "I'm so sorry," she kept repeating, "but I've been instructed to keep in touch with you... I'm truly sorry..."

"No, I'm so grateful to you. I've been restless for days and now somehow I feel relieved... now I know that Salman has good friends, and you are one of them. I know he'll come home safe and sound, but…" and Stella began weeping again.

Sahar joined her. She cried over the misery being inflicted on this innocent woman in Rome, just because she had fallen in love with a Syrian man. But she also cried over her own misery at always meeting the wrong men. First Antonio, that hypocrite, for whose sake she had broken with her family, and who had vanished from Beirut one week before their wedding. And then Shadi—they were together for three years before death put an end to her short-lived happiness. He was twenty-nine.

"We'd better stop crying now," Stella said, ashamed of her tears and of infecting the woman on the other end of the line. She asked Sahar for her telephone number and said that she would call in two days and leave a message for Salman. The bus driver would take it to Damascus. However, Sahar would have to translate the letter into Arabic, because taking letters written in a foreign language across the border could get you killed.

~

Stella took two weeks' leave after confidentially telling her boss, the dean of her faculty, what had happened to Salman. He advised her to go to the Italian Foreign Ministry.

On Thursday, she planned to treat Paolo to a meal, so she reserved a quiet table at the New Station. Ricardo, the old waiter, asked whether Salman was already back. Stella replied that she would come with a much younger, and more handsome, man than Salman. Ricardo, who had known Stella for years, laughed. "In that case, you're coming with Paolo."

"That's right," Stella said, and a little breath of happiness fluttered in her heart.

At dinner, Stella tried to explain to her son that Salman had been delayed in Syria. She kept getting into a muddle. There was nothing left of what she had worked out to reassure Paolo, who listened in silence. After beating around the bush for a while, she finally managed to tell Paolo that his father was a wanted man in Damascus.

"Mama," he said. "Dad is a clever guy, and those assholes in Damascus won't get him. I promise you that. I know my dad," he said with all the confidence of an underground expert. He stroked her hand soothingly. Stella didn't know what to say. She took his head in her hands and, across the table, kissed his eyes and cheeks.

"I won't tell on you, otherwise my friend Salman will get jealous," she heard old Ricardo say.

~

That evening, Stella lay awake for a long time. She wrote Salman a letter and told him proudly how brave Paolo was, and how they both missed him. She must have rephrased it at least ten times before it sounded like a harmless love letter. The following day was a Friday and she dictated the letter to Sahar over the telephone. Realizing that it would be much easier if Stella sent the letter to Sahar either by e-mail or in a text message, they both laughed.

Stella put the phone down. For a moment, the sun shone through the window, directly through a break in the clouds above Rome. Before calling Sahar, Stella had thought about some friends—lawyers, journalists—who could help her. But now she knew that she didn't need anyone. She would get through all this on her own. She felt her love for Salman more deeply than ever before.

The cloud cover closed in again, as if the show had come to an end. Stella looked at the clock. It was time to go shopping. Paolo wanted to prepare an Arab dinner with her. She took from the shelf Salman's favorite cookbook of Damascene dishes, *La città che profuma di coriandolo—The City that Smells of Coriander*.

36

An Oasis: Aida and Karim

Damascus, December 18–24, 2010

Calm

"First get some sleep," Karim advised Salman at around midnight. He hadn't slept properly for days. The evening meal at Karim's, the red wine and stimulating conversation had soothed him. He ended up telling them his life story. Karim asked many questions because he really wanted to understand everything, especially why Elias was so hostile toward him. Karim and Aida thought that in addition to envy, he was motivated by the large ransom he hoped to get. Salman quickly felt at ease with them both.

When Aida left for home, she hugged Salman. "Don't worry. Karim and I will do everything we can to protect you." Karim accompanied Aida to the front door and quickly rejoined Salman. "I've prepared the room upstairs for you. The stove has been on since this morning because it was quite cold and damp. I haven't used the room for almost a month. You can keep the light on for as long as you like. The only window looks out onto the courtyard. No one will see anything from the street, and starting tomorrow, you'll be Habib, my cousin's son."

"Habib?"

"Yes, Habib Shahin, the son of my cousin Fatima. He lives in Canada and is about the same age as you. But we can talk more about that tomorrow. Get a good night's sleep first. Otherwise your mother will yell at me, and that's something I can't afford," he said laughing.

It was a large room with a tiny adjoining bathroom. There was a bed, a small, well-stocked bookshelf, a desk made out of dark wood, and a night table with a reading lamp. It was stiflingly hot. Salman opened the window and turned off the stove. It was December outside, and August inside. He heard someone playing the oud and he looked out the window. The courtyard was dark, but there was light in the semicircular window above the door. That meant Karim was still awake. Salman listened closely. The melody from the oud came from his room and the music was clearly by Beethoven—*Für Elise*. What a strange mixture. A Muslim living with a Christian, and playing Beethoven on the oud. Before long, Salman fell into a deep sleep.

Dreams

The next morning, he was surprised by what he had dreamed. In his dream he had been obliged to submit to a cruel inspection. Perhaps the dream was triggered by his conversation with Karim the previous day. Karim had recommended that he not leave the house until he had fully assimilated his new identity. Aida would give him a receding hairline, he would wear glasses instead of contact lenses, and he'd grow a mustache.

Salman didn't understand why he needed a receding hairline and a mustache. "Habib is a Muslim, should I also get circumcised?" Salman joked. "No, we're not in Lebanon," Karim said. Salman understood. During the Lebanese civil war, rival Christian and Muslim factions stopped trusting identity papers because everyone could get as many forged ones as they liked. Soldiers at checkpoints would order men to pull their trousers down. Whoever was circumcised was seen as a Muslim, whoever wasn't, a Christian. That could mean the difference between life and death.

Salman stayed in bed for a while. "Habib Shahin," he muttered to himself. "From now on you're a Muslim and your name is Habib Shahin."

His dream came back to him. He was queuing at a border post, surrounded by loud men. "They don't check your passport, but your foreskin," the man standing in front of him said. "They're Christian Phalangists. Anyone who is circumcised is shot," he added, shaking his head.

"How about you? Are you circumcised?"

"Yes, but I superglued a foreskin back on. You can't get more Christian than that," the man replied with a smile. But his smile vanished when a soldier looked at his penis and shouted, "It's an old trick, take him away!"

Salman felt safe because he wasn't circumcised. He pulled his trousers down and held them in his hands with his underpants because the floor was littered with cigarette butts and spit. "Have a look at that!" the soldier called out. He was a plump young man. He laughed, revealing a yellow and black mixture of teeth and gaps. The other soldier, a pale young man, was very surprised. "My God, there's nothing down there!"

Salman woke up with a start, switched on the lamp on the bedside table, took a quick look inside his pajama pants, and went back to sleep, reassured.

Camouflage

When he awoke, he washed, dressed, and went downstairs. Aida and Karim were just sipping the last of their mocha.

"Good morning, Habib," Karim greeted him.

"Good morning," Salman answered. He noticed an oud hanging on the wall.

"I'll get breakfast ready. Aida will have done your hair

by then," Karim said, taking the tray with the small cups and the mocha pot. "Come with me," Aida said, leading Salman across the inner courtyard to the bathroom near the stairs, which went up to the first floor. Aida set a chair in the middle of the bathroom and spread all her utensils on a small bistro table.

"If you please, sir," she said, and Salman sat down.

"I'll give you a receding hairline like Karim said. His plan is for you to look like his half-brother, a chocolate manufacturer in Lebanon."

"I thought I was supposed to be his nephew, Habib Shahin," Salman said, surprised.

"Yes, that's true, but only during the days you spend in Damascus. Karim will explain everything to you. When you leave the country, you'll need authentic, credible identification at the border. Karim will get it from his half-brother Hassan. Shortly after Christmas, Karim will visit him in Beirut. We're sure that Hassan will lend you his passport. Karim couldn't explain it to him over the phone, but we're close friends. The night before you leave, we'll dye your hair and your moustache white, so that you look even more like Karim's half-brother."

"Why don't we bleach my hair now?"

"Because we don't know how long it will take to get you out of the country. And anyway your black hair would grow back and we'd have to do it all over again. That's not healthy, and besides it would arouse suspicion."

Aida started cutting his hair and Salman watched his locks fall to the floor. "What lovely thick hair you have!" Aida said to her customer admiringly. "Let your beard grow. That will change your face and I'll shave you just before you leave—except for your mustache. I'll shave you so close you won't need to go to the barber's for a long time."

When she had finished cutting his hair, she put on blue disposable gloves and spread the cream on his head with a spatula. Just as she was leading Salman to the washbasin, Karim stuck his head through the door. "I'm off to get bread and I'll be back in five minutes," he called out. Aida washed Salman's hair, rubbed it dry, sprayed a lemon-blossom lotion on it, and covered his head with a dry towel. Only then did Salman take a look in the mirror. He almost cried out in horror. A completely different man with a huge bald patch was looking back at him wide-eyed. The gray stubble he had grown during his days on the run reinforced the strangeness of his new face.

"My God!" he exclaimed in a shaky voice.

"I must admit, when I saw the picture your mother brought, I had my doubts whether you could look like Hassan. But now you really look a lot like him! The only thing that's missing is glasses," she said, sweeping the floor. She opened the window and the door to the court-yard to air the bathroom, which was filled with the musty smell of the hair removal cream.

~

The table was laid and the tastiest delicacies of Damascene cuisine set out on small plates and in bowls. Pickled mini-eggplants stuffed with walnuts and peppers, several types of olives, various dishes, cheese, olive oil, Aleppo za'tar, honey, quince, and apricot marmalade. The room was filled with the smell of crispy bread, and a large teapot stood in the middle of the table.

Salman ate with a grateful, hearty appetite.

Once breakfast was over, Karim went out and locked the garden and front doors. "We don't need any visi-tors," he said, sitting down at the table between Aida and

Salman, only to get up again. He seemed to have forgotten something and went into the bedroom. He came back with a large framed color photograph in his hand. "That's us, Aida and I, with my half-brother Hassan, when we were in Beirut on holiday visiting him."

Salman froze. Then he stood up and got the little mirror from the bathroom that he'd seen on a shelf over the washbasin. He placed the mirror next to the photograph and looked at his reflection and then at the photograph. No doubt about it, he and the half-brother looked very much alike.

An army of half-brothers

"Tell him about all your half-brothers," Aida urged Karim, laughing and sipping her coffee.

"Well, my father was a rich timber merchant. He also owned land around Homs, where he grew sugar beets. He dealt in local, as well as imported timber, and traveled a lot. When he was at home in Homs, he played the pious one. Imagine, he even had my beloved sister Saliha killed because she married a Christian… That was when your mother saved my life.

My father was a hypocrite. It was only after his death that we found out that he'd had relations with more than ten women. All in all, he had twenty-two children in Beirut, Istanbul, Athens, Thessaloniki, Cairo, Aden, even Khartoum." Karim shook his head. "And all these years, he had been paying the women generous maintenance so that they left him in peace and all the children were well taken care of. Once he was dead, the women came to my mother in Homs one after the other, asking for their share of the inheritance. In addition to my mother, the court only recognized three women, as prescribed by the sharia. The other women went away empty-handed.

"I didn't get to know all of these women because my family had disowned and disinherited me. That's why I haven't been in touch with my clan for such a long time. But then a cousin came to visit and she told me that some of the half-brothers and half-sisters wanted to get to know each other, and a few also visited me as well. A deep friendship developed with some of them. The ones I got to know most closely were my half-sister Sarifa in Cairo, my half-brother Mehmet in Istanbul, and my other half-brother Hassan in Beirut. Sarifa's an architect and Mehmet's a spice merchant. The one I get along with best is Hassan, who has taken his mother's family name Mandur out of rage at our father. He founded a small chocolate factory. Today that factory is one of the best in the Arab world, Mandur."

Salman had never heard of it, but then he seldom had anything to do with chocolate. He only imported wine and arak from Lebanon. "But why must my name be Habib, first?" he asked, finding Karim's plans somewhat complicated. "I could be your half-brother from the start."

"It's not that easy, unfortunately. Hassan's very well-known here. He visits me several times a year. He's very generous and each visit brings enough chocolate for the whole neighborhood. And then, of course, he's always invited—for coffee, for a glass of wine—and often to dinner because the Damascenes are always trying to prove to the Lebanese that they are the better cooks. People might notice small differences between you and him. He's fatter than you and his hair is snow-white. And he speaks Lebanese dialect. The few phrases you'll need later for a passport or street control you can learn by heart, but you won't be able to convince anyone on this damned street that you're Lebanese. So you need another identity. Your mother tells me your French is perfect so, like my nephew Habib, you'll live in Canada, in Quebec. People here don't have the slightest interest in Canada. I've got three good books about the country, and if you read them you'll know more about Canada than everyone in Damascus put together." He smiled.

"For as long as you live here, you're my nephew, Habib. Nobody here knows Habib. He's been in Syria for a month now, but he won't be visiting me. He's very rich and wants to open a chain of supermarkets. As you know, the secret service has spineless informers on every street who work independently of each other and report on anything and everything that changes on a street. What matters to secret service headquarters are the names of agitators or foreigners who suddenly turn up here. So, as soon as they hear that Habib Shahin from Canada is visiting his uncle Karim Asmar on Jasmine Street, they'll check the data: Is the name Habib Shahin on any of the lists of state enemies? Answer: no. Did he come from Canada? Answer: yes. Is he Karim Asmar's nephew? Answer: yes. Is Karim actively working against the government? Answer: no. Habib Shahin is clean.

If the name is totally unknown, they'll have the person photographed and get ahold of his fingerprints and other details until headquarters is convinced he's really harmless. But to make the country attractive to tourists and investors, they avoid arrests as much as possible. If, at any stage, a name is suspicious, the secret service will require more comprehensive reports. That's why informers are so important. They don't get any money, but they get a point for each catch. If they supply wrong information, they get a point deducted that they then have to make up the next time they denounce somebody. If they rack up three minus points, they're tortured and sent back to work. That way, headquarters keeps a balance between senseless, hysterical overzealousness on the part of their informers and dangerous laxity. It's a cheap and effective system. In addition to the hundred and fifty thousand regularly employed secret servicemen, there are over three hundred thousand assholes who freelance for the secret service. The leadership of the secret service consists of highly educated Alawites. They even have an academy for the training of senior secret service officers these days. That's why the first meeting between you and our invisible informers must be one hundred percent watertight and not just ninety-nine percent."

"But what if your nephew Habib turns up after all?" Salman asked anxiously.

"He won't come here because he despises me. And even if he did, he wouldn't have any contact with the neighbors. He hardly knows anyone in Damascus. The last time he was here was ten years ago and we had a bad disagreement. Unlike his mother, my cousin Fatima, he admires my father and, like him, he's a sanctimonious hypocrite."

"Should I look out for anything when I'm talking to your acquaintances and neighbors?"

"Talk as much or as little as you want. Just relax, but please, not a word about Italy or Germany. All the informers, even the stupid ones, get a search template. The key items around your identity are: Rome, merchant, import, Christian, Italy, Germany, married to an Italian and things like that… and you mustn't have *any* contact with your parents or go anywhere near their apartment. The surveillance and monitoring for them and the apartment is currently higher than for a government minister. Elias knows all about your great love for your mother. You know what has to happen to save a drowning man?" Salman didn't understand what Karim was driving at and shook his head. "If the drowning man doesn't follow his rescuer's instructions, they both drown. And my beloved and I both have a few things left to do in this life. So, are we agreed?"

Salman nodded thoughtfully. "Yes, I'll do everything you say. I don't know these Damascene waters anymore and swimming was never my strength." He had never imagined that a poor country like Syria could possess the kind of perfect control system found in wealthier countries. In his homeland, where the postal system, the electricity and water supplies, and the schools and universities didn't work, the dictatorship had succeeded in surpassing even the worst visions of dystopian novels. Salman admired all the more the care with which Karim had planned and prepared everything.

And as if Karim had read his thoughts, he continued, "You know, you should always assume that the enemy is smarter than you first thought. One mistake and we're both dead. I'd be embarrassed in front of Aida if I were to bring our wonderful love story to a close too soon. And I'd stand before your mother with my head bowed in deepest shame because I wasn't able to save her beloved son. So, just stay in the house for a few days and practice your new identity with us and our visitors. And then, when you feel safe, go out on the street and to cafés and cinemas. Avoid nightclubs, they're crawling with secret service types and shady characters. Going for walks through the city will give you confidence and help you to appear relaxed and natural. And remember, there isn't a secret service on earth that can check everything."

"You're doing all this for me? Why are you risking your life for somebody you never even met before yesterday?" Salman asked.

"It's a long story," Karim answered, and told him of

his love for Sophia—the beginning of all tales, as he called her. Salman interrupted him with questions. When Karim came to the murder of his sister, he had to weep, and Aida kissed him. Salman stroked his hand. "Saliha was so beautiful, so peaceful, and she hadn't done anything to anyone," Karim said, his voice cracking. When he calmed down, he told how Sophia had saved his life and about his second love, Amira. He also talked about Maha, his daughter, whom he had loved and who had declared war on him since he and Aida were together.

Salman listened attentively.

"Are you sure that I'm not your son?" Salman ventured, mischievously.

"You are Sophia and Yusuf's son. I saw your mother again in 1950 after more than seven years. You were already five years old. She never brought you with her to Aunt Munira's where I was in hiding, although I asked her to. She said you might betray me with your childish innocence."

The next morning Karim went with Salman to an optician's in Bab Tuma. Even without his contact lenses, Salman felt safe walking alongside the older man. He was surprised at how modern the shop was and how wide the selection of fashionable glasses. He decided on a frame with round lenses in a warm orange-red.

~

As they had agreed, he grew a mustache. He was surprised to see that his beard, which he shaved every day in Rome, was now quite white, without needing any bleach.

Aida and Karim practiced his new name with him. For the first two or three days, he didn't always react when he heard it, but he gradually became used to his new identity.

The two of them would often leave him in peace and

busy themselves in the garden or go off to visit friends. Salman envied their tenderness toward each other. They were open and relaxed, even when he was there, so free and light-hearted, as if they forgot both the world and themselves when they kissed. In Rome only young lovers behaved like that.

Sometimes Karim would walk via back ways through the city to meet with Tarek. Three days before Christmas, Tarek reported that Stella was worried. She was even starting to doubt that Salman was still alive because there were reports of armed clashes in the country on the Italian news. Sahar Khoury, her contact in Beirut, was unable to put her mind at rest. She was asking for a new sign that he was alive.

Salman was heartbroken to think he was the cause of Stella's suffering, she who had given him all her love and caring in Rome. And now, what was he giving her in return? "I am so sorry," he said. "I'll think of something."

"But there's something else," Karim said and hesitated. "Your father has agreed to pay fifty thousand dollars to get you out of the country, on one condition. He'll only pay once you've reached safety and phoned him. An air-force general and close friend of the defense minister took a look at the case and refused. He'd be happy to act for anyone on the run because of murder, smuggling, drugs, or money laundering, but your case is way out of his league. He thinks whoever is involved is angling for millions, so it's not just Elias who is involved, but someone very high up." Karim took a sip of water. "And that bodes ill for us, because Elias now has even more power and backing from outside his secret service department. Whenever a secret service officer wants to be sure of results, he involves one of these big criminals. It's no wonder that the president's brother earns about three hundred million dollars a year, thanks to his involvement in three hundred juicy cases like yours. All he needs to do is give his blessing for it to happen."

There was absolute quiet in the living room.

~

The following night, Salman again heard the oud being played. He didn't recognize the piece, but he could tell that Karim wasn't satisfied. He kept stopping and starting, repeating a phrase again and again.

The following day Salman wrote to Stella a few words on a slip of paper and gave it to Karim. "Please let her know that today I thought of the Sardelada Festival in Grado and about how we both used to leave the polenta untouched."

"Polenta? It's a chicken dish?"

"No, polenta is a sticky mixture of corn semolina."

"Italians eat that?" Karim asked in surprise.

"Yes, especially in the north. It's been a mystery to me, too," Salman replied and laughed.

Days that feel like years

Karim and Aida's days had become full since Salman had moved in with them. But they still managed to find time for each other.

Salman would go off into town after lunch. One day, Aida had an irrepressible desire for Karim, who was sitting on the sofa reading a little book. He laughed repeatedly at her playful teasing but kept going back to his book. He seemed unaware of all her attempts to attract his attention while they were doing the dishes. Even Salman, who was drying the dishes, laughed at Karim who was ignoring "the hot little bee" at his side. "I'm off. The two of you should have some privacy in your own home," he said laughing and slipped out of the house.

Aida looked at Karim. How handsome he was in his dark blue pullover, white shirt and blue trousers. He had pulled up his sleeves and the little silver-blond hairs on his forearms looked very tempting. And whenever he embraced her, she was aware of the smell of him, which reminded her of green leaves, bamboo, and cardamom.

"Are you going to read for long?" she asked, hoping for a "no."

"Why?" he asked to her dismay.

"Because I want to have a nap with you, and I can't get to sleep if you're not there," she said.

He finally closed his book and lay down next to her.

When he kissed her, she was seized by a stream that was both cool and hot, strong and soft. She closed her eyes and saw little colored dots against a dark sky. She laughed and perspired and floated above the world. He caressed her skin.

She lay next to him, feeling soft and content.

"I'm getting so ancient that sometimes my will and my desire don't reach down to the tired old man between my legs. He's hanging there like a limp rag, even though I feel so much desire," Karim said sadly.

"Why aren't you satisfied? It was really beautiful," Aida said, laying her head on his chest.

"It's always beautiful. Just accompanying you when you soar away is beautiful. I wanted to go with you."

"But lovemaking doesn't always have to mean that," Aida said, nudging him gently.

It's funny, until now I've never wished that life could go backwards—be born as an old man and get younger each new year."

"I'm noticing that the older I get, the greater the losses

become. I've already lost so many friends and relatives. Things which were once important to me are losing their value. My capacities are stealing away."

"But getting old isn't a one-way street," Aida protested, sitting up. "There are pluses. Even forgetting is nature's wisdom. Many people go to all pains to delay it. But forgetting also means letting go. I sometimes forget a person's name, where, when, and why I met them, but I never forget whether I liked them or not."

"Feelings seem to have a better memory," said Karim.

Christmas memories

The day before Christmas, Salman longed to be with Stella and Paolo. Ever since he and Stella had lived together, they'd always celebrated Christmas in style. Neither of them had been religious, but they enjoyed the Christmas season in Rome, particularly since Paolo's birth. Salman took a childlike pleasure in it. In Damascus, Christmas was never a special celebration, Easter being the greater festival. But in Rome everyone celebrated the birth of Christ. Like all Italians, Stella decorated a Christmas tree in the large living room on the eighth of December, the feast of the Immaculate Conception. A small crèche decorated with beautiful, delicate papier-mâché figures stood in one corner. From when Paolo could first walk, on Christmas Eve, he had solemnly taken the baby Jesus out of the box, carried him to the crèche, and laid him carefully in the manger. He would get excited days in advance and ask whether Jesus was born yet. Even when he started secondary school, he would still insist on laying the Divine Child, made out of paper and wallpaper paste, in the manger himself.

For years, Salman had refused to travel on business

during the Christmas season. From early December, he limited himself to office work and inventory. He loved the atmosphere of Rome's brightly lit streets, the decorated Christmas trees in all the big squares, and the Christmas markets. Near the Piazza Navona market, Paolo and he were fascinated by the exhibition showing Christmas Nativity scenes from all over the world. The previous year, Paolo had counted more than a hundred and fifty crèches. As usual, the most impressive one was in St. Peter's Square and was unveiled on Christmas Eve. Salman and his family also went several times to the Auditorium Parco della Musica during the Christmas season. The musical performances and choral recitals did Salman's soul good.

On Christmas Eve, he would go to St. Peter's Square with Paolo and Stella. And Stella, who seldom went into a church on her own, would even go to Midnight Mass in St. Peter's with him.

In return, every year on Christmas day in the afternoon, Paolo and Salman would accompany Stella to the ice rink in front of the Castel Sant'Angelo and admire her as she elegantly skated, although she did so only on Christmas. "I practiced a lot when I was a young girl, and your body never forgets. It's just like riding a bike. I'm a little uncertain for the first five minutes, but after that it's okay," she said, laughing. Paolo never wanted to skate. As a small child, he would cling to Salman whenever Stella tried to take him with her. "Paolo's lower half is Arab. It always freezes when it sees ice," Salman said, defending his son.

All these memories came welling up in Salman, and he told Karim about them. At the same time he felt a deep hatred for Elias. Karim smiled benevolently. "Careful, my friend. Hate is poisonous. You could poison the whole

Mediterranean with the hate you feel for Elias. You should rise above the baseness of his spirit and look at the whole picture from above, with the serenity of a good soul."

In the meantime, Aida had become curious and she wanted to know everything about the way Italians celebrate Christmas, so Salman told her everything in great detail.

Deadly traps

On the evening news, they heard that the farmers in a village near the Lebanese border had surrounded a suspicious bus and taken all its passengers prisoner. According to the newscaster, they were twenty wanted Muslim Brothers who had broken out of prison two months previously.

"All lies," Karim said. "Those were no farmers. They were secret service informers. No government can completely control all its borders. Syria has almost twenty-three hundred kilometers of border. People have escaped to Turkey, Iraq, Lebanon, and Jordan, and in the old days also to Palestine and across the sea to Cyprus. At first, all the secret services of the Arab countries agreed to deport their opponents. But since the Syrian regime was sometimes on bad terms with all its neighbors, it came up with an ingenious and treacherous system, back during the early days of Hafiz al-Assad."

"The secret service enlisted the aid of drug smugglers all along its borders with Iraq, Jordan, and Turkey," he continued. "They usually came from border villages and knew the borders in these remote areas better than anyone else, and they would hand over any fugitives they caught. In return, they were allowed to smuggle drugs with impunity. If anyone slipped through their fingers, they were held responsible. So the clans kept a tight watch on the borders.

Sometimes they would even pocket escape money from the fugitives and then hand them over to the secret service.

"The Syrian secret service ruled in Lebanon from day one of the civil war in 1975 until 2005. During those thirty years, not one Syrian dared try to escape via Lebanon. The secret service then used a trick that had been thought up by security in the former Czechoslovakia. Imagine a false border with barbed wire and watchtowers. The smugglers, working with the secret service, would pocket huge sums from the fugitives and then bring them to this location which is supposedly only lightly guarded. They then say that they're only responsible for getting them over the border, and after that the fugitives are on their own. So the smugglers accompany them as far as the barbed wire. From there, they can make out a tarmac road and, in the distance, the lights of a gas station. The Lebanese flag is flying everywhere. So they wait until the soldier in the watchtower goes away or falls asleep, they pay the smugglers, jump over the low fence and walk happily toward the gas station to travel on to Beirut. But in reality, the Syrian secret service is waiting for them, because the whole thing takes place on Syrian territory—the Lebanese flags, the barbed wire, the watchtower, and the gas station are just a decoy. There have been cases where the secret service has encouraged famous people, sometimes sons of rich families, who were not even part of the opposition, to flee so that a senior officer could then pocket millions in ransom.

"These methods are far more effective, and they spread more fear in the population than just arresting anyone looking for someone to help them escape. That's how the secret service developed into a kind of insurmountable wall. But it isn't. We'll overcome it. It won't be long now.

My half-brother Hassan will be back from the Ivory Coast, where he buys his cocoa, two days after Christmas. Then I'll drive over to see him and ask him for help. If you want to write something to Stella, I'll take it with me to Sahar Khoury in Beirut."

Salman nodded, almost in a daze. Never before, not even when he was in the armed resistance, had he felt such fear as on that evening when Karim described the Syrian fugitive scenario to him.

"Tomorrow we'll celebrate at my place," Aida said and asked him what he would like to eat for Christmas. Salman was close to tears.

37

Christmas and Memories of Flowers

Damascus, December 25, 2010–January 1, 2011

Christmas

Christmas at Aida's was lovingly prepared. On the previous evening, Salman had heard from Karim that his message had reached Stella in time and that she was very touched that his friends had reacted so quickly. She wanted Salman to know that she and Paolo would go to the places where the three of them had always celebrated the holidays, and that she would skate in his honor. Salman could picture Stella on the ice, waving and laughing at him, then vanishing in the mist.

Aida noticed that Salman was very quiet. She stood up and stroked his head. "It'll be all right," she said. "Come, let's celebrate." And Salman decided he would not hate Elias, or anyone else, but enjoy the celebration. He went into the bathroom, freshened up, and came back smiling. "Merry Christmas," he said.

Aida had prepared everything days before. She had gotten hold of recipes for a Roman Christmas meal and even remembered the mandatory panettone.

"Where did you get all this?" Salman asked her, slightly embarrassed by all the trouble she had gone to.

"I went to the Italian deli and asked the assistant what to cook for an Italian guest."

After midnight, Salman felt tired. He wanted to leave, but Aida wouldn't let him go out into the driving rain and stormy winds. "The weather's terrible, and anyway it's not healthy to go out into the cold after so much wine. You can stay the night."

"So do I have to go home alone?" asked Karim, who was never allowed to stay the night at Aida's."

"No, we'll make an exception this time for Salman's sake," Aida said, laughing.

"Great. I say, Salman should never go back to Rome," Karim replied, gleefully happy.

The guest room was small and pretty. A splendid, age-old cast iron woodstove made the room pleasantly warm. Aida had obviously anticipated the bad weather, and the stove had been well stocked with wood that afternoon. There was a fragrance of burnt resin.

It reminded Salman of a childhood Christmas when his father had wanted to celebrate Christmas properly, in the snow. He had seen photos in magazines and was fed up with the rainy weather in Damascus. So he rented a small apartment for the family in al-Zabadani, a popular holiday resort about twelve hundred meters up in the mountains. Salman was ten or eleven years old at the time, and this was his first contact with snow. He played outside all day and couldn't get enough of it. And no matter how often he experienced snow later, in Germany, the memory of the snow of al-Zabadani remained the most magical.

While he was lying in bed, he heard Aida and Karim talking, before sliding calmly off to sleep.

~

On the second day of Christmas, Salman went walking through the streets of the Old City, armed with an umbrella against the rain.

He felt safer in his new identity, complete with bald patch, mustache, and glasses. It made him think of the

English television series, *The Avengers*, which had been so popular in the seventies, and he grinned to himself.

It was here, in the Old City, that Damascus had changed the least. But Salman noticed a religious revival, among both Christians and Muslims. The Christians hung up pictures of saints everywhere, even in a small bar. Nearly every street had a niche with a statue of the Virgin Mary, often with flowers in front of it, even on a winter's day like today. There hadn't been anything like that before. Salman had already noticed that many Christian women wore golden crosses and icons, and never before had he seen so many Muslim women in headscarves and long coats. Damascus seemed to him more bigoted than in the sixties. Why was that? In Karim's opinion, people embraced religion and revered saints because the state didn't offer them any security, be it social, political, or economic. And when people felt the need to cling to saints, superstition was not far behind.

Salman remembered a conversation with Stella, who was grumbling about the Italian state for leaving people in the lurch. Countries where good health insurance was available needed less incense, she said, and she was right. How else could you explain that, for the Italians, a controversial figure like Friar Padre Pio rated even higher than the Virgin Mary when it came to begging for miracles?

When Salman returned, Karim and Aida agreed with him that a new kind of religiosity was spreading, one that separated people instead of bringing them together. It was a belief system based not on love, but on separation. "I've been in despair ever since Maha started behaving in such an inflexible religious way," Karim said. "She used to be so lively, and now she's forcing a piety on herself that stifles any joy in life. That can't be God's will."

Rejecting temptation

With each passing day, Salman felt safer in his new identity, and so he occasionally accompanied Karim and Aida to gatherings of the Selfless. They both seemed to enjoy going there, even though Aida would make ironic remarks about the group. Salman felt protected by the politeness and reserve of people there. But at one of the gatherings, temptation reared its head.

Malika, a young woman who was there with her husband, flirted with Salman. She was not at all discreet about it, and he was embarrassed. Her husband pretended not to notice. Salman wondered to himself whether Stella might have learned about his erotic escapades in Rome and simply pretended not to notice as well.

But then his attention was drawn to the speaker, Professor Fardani, an elderly philosopher who was giving a short talk on love. He spoke clearly and with subtlety, peculiarly craning his head every now and again like a chicken drinking.

"Love is an earthly religion of this world, which contradicts the religions of the next world. Every human being who loves is a follower of this religion," he said. There were quiet murmurs of protests, but the professor was unfazed. "The religion of love feeds on positive feelings, freedom, security, and trust in a beloved human being, not on fear of punishment like the religions of the next world. They have invented a hell to convince their followers and turn them into obedient sheep, to deprive simple people of the right to dignity and freedom. They all approve of murder and war. Not so the earthly religion of love, which has always sustained human life, while other religions promise life in the next world. I personally don't believe in life after death. But I'm convinced that there is a fulfilled life before death..."

An outcry of voices objected. "Stop!" "That's going too far." "This isn't choir practice for atheists."

When calm was restored, Aida spoke up. "I'm convinced that this religion of love will remain human until the time when it comes to power. But then…" Aida paused.

"She learned that from music," Karim whispered to Salman who was standing next to him. Everyone was staring at her.

"…but then, it will wage war against the loveless in the name of love, against those who cannot or do not love, or do not wish to be loved."

Several clapped, many laughed.

The professor raised his hand. "Is there a single human being who cannot love, who resists love?" he asked almost indignantly.

"But that's just the problem with religions," Karim chimed in. "They bring disaster on everyone who doesn't want to believe in their unique, kind and merciful God—in this case it would be love. Love is precious, that's why we should keep it away from the state and politics."

Salman felt a hand on his back. He turned around, and Malika was standing behind him, smiling.

~

The following day, Malika showed up at Karim and Aida's house. Karim had left for Beirut early that morning to visit his half-brother Hassan. He intended to be back the same day, and Salman was waiting anxiously to hear if Hassan would offer his passport.

Salman was preoccupied with his own problems and not in the mood for small talk with Malika—still less, to flirt. He wanted to be alone. He apologized, saying that he wanted to visit a friend, and left Malika with Aida. When he came back in the early afternoon, he found out that Malika had left the house shortly afterward.

"It wasn't me she wanted to meet, it was you," Aida joked.

Emboldened by her comment, Salman confessed to Aida about his previous life and his infidelities, which he now regretted. Aida advised him that Stella was probably well aware of them, but that she had carefully weighed his infidelity against his kindness, and he could be sure that she loved him. But if the scales should tip toward his infidelity, Stella would leave him—in an instant—without so much as a goodbye.

Salman was shaken. Aida's tone was not preaching or moralizing, but cool and sober. She reflected for a moment.

"Will you really tell her everything?"

"I'm not sure yet," Salman replied, candidly. "I think so. But it won't be easy."

~

Karim came back in the evening, and he looked happy. He closed the front door behind him and went into the living room. "Hassan is coming to Damascus the first week of January. By then he'll have an Italian visa in his passport. As usual, he'll spend the night at Cham Palace Hotel, where I'll pick up the passport. Then I can book you a flight to Rome."

"But won't he need his passport to get back to Beirut?" Salman asked, surprised.

"No, the Lebanese don't need a passport. When they cross the border, they get a control slip, which they have to hand back when they leave the country. But this time he'll give it to you as well. He won't need it when he drives back to Beirut. He'll just need to have enough Mandur chocolate for the border officials. They know him by now and look forward to his gifts. With the control slip, your disguise as a Lebanese citizen will be complete. He's also given me a suitcase for you, filled with chocolate, ballpoint pens, and a funny wristwatch for Colonel Maher Makhlouf, the head of the secret service at the airport.

~

The next morning, Karim wanted to visit an old friend who was ill at home. The day was warm and sunny, a treat after so much cold and rain. The former teacher lived with his wife in a small cabin in the Tabbaleh district. In the seventies, the whole area had been one illegal slum constructed out of metal and clay. "Today it's been legalized, but poverty couldn't care less," Karim said.

Karim wanted to walk to his friend's home. "It's about half an hour's walk at most," he said, and Salman went with him. He was looking forward to having a quiet talk with Karim about the Selfless, since their meetings had left him puzzled.

"Why are you following a master even though you aren't a believer? Isn't that like worshipping a saint?" Salman asked, intrigued by this contradiction.

"To me he isn't a saint and he never was. He was a wise man. He started out as a communist in the armed struggle, then he renounced all forms of violence, became a social activist, and built a large following who called themselves the Selfless, after his example. He didn't preach revolution, but a dynamic development of society based on relinquishing. Love, not hate, is the way to victory. Not as an ideology, as Professor Fardani misunderstood it, but in the sense of relinquishing selfishness. There's a deep idealism behind these ideas, and it will take a long time before they become reality. The master was a thorn in the government's side. He was arrested and only released from prison after three years. He was murdered soon after, because he refused to shut up. But just as he taught us, his person is transient—not his ideas."

"How can the Selfless meet undisturbed?" Salman asked.

"Because we're peaceful and we've never been political. The regime allows a castrated society to worship as many saints as they wish, provided they're politically silent. Every now and then they check whether our balls have grown back."

Salman laughed painfully at the idea.

"But it's true. Once when a member of our circle joked that the dictator should be healed from his lust for power by the power of love, the man disappeared overnight. And he had just said 'heal', not 'topple'."

"There must be an informer," Salman insisted. "Don't you check out new members before you accept them?"

"What an idea!" Karim laughed. "We're not allowed to check anyone. Everyone is supposed to be welcome, otherwise we'd be banned the next day. It's a desperate attempt and a balancing act to preserve what's left of our dignity."

They were still deep in conversation when they noticed two military vehicles close to the Eastern Gate. Soldiers in battle gear stood around, smoking and laughing. Karim explained that there had been a series of arrests and hinted that something must be up. The rebellion in Tunisia had also shaken the Syrian government. "The government pretends to be at ease, but they're nervous. You can tell from how often people are checked entering and leaving the city."

When they reached the house of Karim's friend, Salman saw an old woman who could barely walk tending a small pot of basil in the neighboring apartment. She was removing the wilted leaves with a shaking hand, and watering the plant with an old scratched watering can, smiling blissfully the entire time.

Memories welled up, of an event from Salman's time in the armed struggle that was etched deeply in him. Together with some twenty fighters, they had occupied a sentry post at a major crossroads. They went to the nearest village to buy cigarettes and food. The village was dirt poor. The farmers had to travel five kilometers for well water. People were friendly toward the guerrillas, who looked just as ragged and poor as they did. They offered them bread, water and dried fruit. Salman was the group leader, and he only accepted when they agreed to take money for it. While they ate and chatted with the farmers, Salman saw an old farmer's wife who obviously hadn't taken the slightest notice of the freedom fighters. She was watering a tiny flowerbed in front of her hut, barely a square meter in size, planted with marigolds, basil, and carnations. She was stroking the flowers and smiling. More than tending a small garden, she embodied hope and love of beauty in a most perfect form.

~

On the way back, they went through a narrow alley, flanked by dense rows of small houses with grimy façades. Chickens were clucking in backyards, an old skinny dog crossed the alley slowly as if he was afraid that his ribs would tear through his mangy fur.

A whole pack of children ran after them, competing loudly with each other to offer them sewing kits, dusty old sweets, stationery, and other cheap Chinese goods from their trays. Salman declined politely and walked on quickly with Karim. He saw pale girls in cheap thin dresses standing at the doors of their huts. There wasn't a glimmer of joy on their careworn faces. The children, who had seemed

friendly a moment ago, now shouted abuse at them in disappointment, and a stone just missed Salman. Karim turned
around in anger and suddenly the children disappeared,
leaving only the echo of their shrieks in the alley.

Salman thought to himself how quickly children aged
in poor families. At the age of seven or eight, they were
more cynical than their parents, and their faces more sor-
rowful than their grandparents'. The girls matured early,
many looked like adults as early as twelve, but they were
worn out and often already pregnant. "By the time they're
twenty, they sometimes have as many as six or seven children," Karim said, looking at a young mother standing at
the door of a hut with two children clinging to her skirt,
and a third at her breast.

~

That evening there was another power outage. Salman
cursed. It must have been the tenth one since he'd arrived in
Damascus. The Damascenes had gotten used to it long ago.
Aida and Karim would find their way safely in the dark,
light candles, and place them in different spots in the room.

"Stop moaning, put something warm on and come
with me," Karim said to Salman, while putting on his thick
jacket and a woolen cap. "I'll show you something beautiful." They went upstairs, past Salman's room and out onto
the large terrace on the first floor.

"Look how beautiful Damascus is," Karim said. A
panorama of dimly lit houses stretched out in front of them.
Candles and kerosene lights stood on every street corner
and entrance door. Salman's soul was gently soothed and
his anger calmed as fast as his face…

"And now some hot tea," Karim said.

They went back down the stairs again, and a pleasant
warmth greeted them. Salman ran to the oven and warmed

his hands. When the power came back, they played two hands of cards before Salman went to bed.

~

For a long time, he lay awake and reflected for a long time on old Karim's vitality. He hadn't gone slowly up the stairs, but leapt up two steps at a time. How strong had he been when he was a young man? Karim often passed over his age. Just now, as they were having tea, when he couldn't remember an accident that had happened forty years earlier, Aida had helped him remember. "Every now and again I lose the key to the kingdom of the past, and you help me find it," he'd said, kissing her in gratitude.

"But forgetting can sometimes be a mercy," Aida had said. "Had my parents been graced with it, they would probably have lived longer. But their memories killed them—they all revolved around my brother's death."

"You're right. If I thought day and night about my late sister, Amira, who was killed, or my ungrateful daughter Maha, I would have to cry all the time and might die soon. But I forget them and prefer to think of you," Karim had said cheerfully.

Karim and Aida's love is a rebellion against death, Salman thought, lying there in the dark. What about Stella and me? he asked himself. But he fell asleep searching for an answer.

A musical New Year's Eve

The next morning over coffee, Aida told Karim and Salman that Amal had called and said the friends had decided to celebrate New Year's Eve at Karim and Aida's in honor of "Habib," Karim's nephew. Karim smiled mischievously, and Salman got the impression that it wasn't Amal but his two hosts who had set up this charming plot. Full of anticipation, Karim, Salman, and Aida went shopping together, made all the preparations, and cooked. Some twenty guests were to be entertained. Given the number of dishes, though, it seemed to Salman that Karim and Aida were expecting a hundred.

In fact, the twenty friends who had been invited turned up—with another forty friends and relatives in tow. The guest list included two professors, a Jesuit, a young sheikh, and several famous judges, a singer and three actors. To keep his behavior under control, Salman decided not to drink.

"I understand you," Karim said. "You can hold your drink, so at least sip on the red wine, otherwise people will think you're feeling nervous or insecure. But please lock your room because people will be milling around. And if someone asks you innocently how long you're thinking of staying in Syria, just say three or four weeks. You still have business deals to finish up. And you can't talk about them because your business partners wouldn't like that."

Salman had already noticed that Karim and Aida weren't particularly fond of their neighbors. But the fact that they hadn't invited a single one of them to the party was striking. It meant that neither of them was afraid of a confrontation with them. "The secret service will see that as a sign that we're not hiding anything," Aida said.

~

After such a long time, Salman was glad to socialize with so many people again. The atmosphere was warm and informal. When he opened the door to the bathroom, he surprised a couple in a close embrace. "Sorry," he said and quickly shut the door. He told Karim, who laughed. "Yes, that's Khalil and Nura. They make the most of every party because they live in two rooms with their six kids, their in-laws and two aunts. That means control, day in, day out—nights too."

A genial old man—a carpenter by trade—sang song requests from the guests. Salman found out from Karim that the carpenter had been imprisoned for twenty years. "How could you endure it?" Salman asked the man during a break. "Because I loved life and I believed in the good in people," he answered, to Salman's awe and bewilderment.

Salman had fun all evening, and he felt more confident that he could play his part as Habib well. He joked with guests and enjoyed Aida and Karim when they played the oud.

Aida gave an excellent rendition of *Asturia*, a piece by Isaac Albéniz, which reminded Salman of a scandal in the Arab countries about this brilliant piece of music. Farid al-Atrash, an excellent oud player, but less recognized composer, had included it in his song *Awal Hamsa*, the first whisper, without crediting Albéniz, and the fraud was discovered. When Salman compared the two pieces, it seemed clear that al-Atrash had copied Albéniz.

After Aida performed, the guests began chatting about music, and Aida started arguing with a professor who claimed that music was the "best education." Aida disagreed, saying that academics try to put everything at the service of education. Music was a simple joy, just to be enjoyed. "Music moves the soul, lets it dance and frees it from worries," she said. "Everything moves with music, especially when we speak. Written speech is nothing but an ink dot dancing on the melody of the words." Listening to her, Karim was filled with pride and happiness.

"God is a musician, too," an old man called out, and everyone laughed.

"So why don't you believe in God, then?" a religious woman asked.

"I don't believe in Picasso, but I love his paintings. Don't tell me you believe in Mozart or Fairouz?"

The woman waved him aside. Salman wondered whether Karim would play Beethoven's *Für Elise*, which he often practiced at night. He asked him about it, and Karim smiled conspiratorially.

"That's meant as a gift for Aida at the next party. I'm not there yet."

~

Isolated, hesitant fireworks went bang. Salman glanced at his watch. The impatience of youth, he thought. It was three minutes before midnight. All stood there with happy faces, holding their topped off champagne and wine glasses. Then the whole sky was lit by one and then a thousand colorful flashes. The guests kissed and hugged each other.

"Stella," Salman thought, closing his eyes. A hand touched his face. When he opened his eyes again, Aida was beaming at him.

"A blessed year to you and your family," she said, kissing his cheeks.

~

It was nearly three in the morning when the last guests finally departed. Salman was so calm and cheerful that he almost felt ashamed. Before going to sleep, he wrote in his notebook that if he was allowed to leave this country alive, he would dedicate 2011 to purifying his soul. He would hand over most of the responsibility for his business to Chiara, his faithful and experienced employee, and use his time to meditate and spoil the two people he loved most.

Their joy would be his happiness.

38

A Glimmer in the Labyrinth

Rome, December 18, 2010—January 6, 2011

Stella had been able to use her connections, through a cousin and his sister-in-law, to contact a senior civil servant at the Italian Ministry of Foreign Affairs. She visited him and asked him for help because, although Salman held a German passport, he had married an Italian. The sixty-year-old gentleman was an experienced diplomat who had spent half his life abroad. He was obliging, listened carefully to Stella's request, and had his secretary bring her an espresso. "We could and would get him back from any country in the world—except from his native country."

The man spoke at length about the Geneva Convention and Syrian law. He explained to her that developing countries strongly resisted European interference, and described in detail various cases where Syrians and Iraqis had been arrested in their native countries, even though they had been living in Germany, France, or Italy for many years and had become citizens of those countries. Some held senior positions in business or politics. In one instance, a personal adviser to the foreign minister was dragged away from his delegation as soon as he arrived at the airport in Damascus. The delegation immediately flew back home and vehemently protested against the adviser's arrest, but this changed nothing. Then the diplomat told her, "Signora, these dictators know very well that the Europeans will sulk for a few days, but then they'll come crawling back so as not to jeopardize business deals worth millions with the country in question. And wherever oil is bubbling, the Chinese are lying in wait like highway robbers. They are always ready to step into a deal, without demanding that anyone be released from prison. It's never mentioned officially, but that's the way it is."

There was nothing that could be done.

Even a cousin of Stella's mother, whose best friend in the Vatican was the right-hand man of a supposedly influential cardinal, refused to help. The case was too complicated and had more to do with Syria's domestic policy.

"All we need now is for the Vatican to accept the Syrian secret service's accusations against Salman," Stella said in despair. During all her years of research, how had she overlooked the ways that her own country, and the world, was changing?

~

Paolo noticed how much his mother was suffering. She hardly went out of the house, and was often on the phone with a woman in Beirut and with her old friend Luca, the counselor, and she was losing weight. Paolo worried about her. But he trusted that his father would come home. He knew things about his father that Stella didn't, and he was sure that his father was capable of tricking even the CIA.

Although Paolo didn't know about his father's time in the underground, he admired his skillfulness at their computer games. Without ever playing, his father knew which tricks and fighting methods to use to free the encircled virtual heroes. In carnival games, he would score a bullseye nine times out of ten, always winning his amazed son the toy he wanted. Stella wouldn't have anything to do with those games. When he described them to her, she only gave a tired smile.

Paolo would have liked to take his mother out of the apartment, and her sorrow, but he couldn't think of a way. Time dragged by and going to school every day became more and more difficult. He felt angry at the Syrian regime for persecuting his father. He vented his frustration by playing violent computer games, and started arguing more with his school friends about politics. His friends said that those days in December 2010 changed Paolo. He was no longer the charming, laid-back computer geek. Now to some he had become a rabble-rouser, to others a more self-assured but aggressive young man. But everyone who knew him was astonished that, at this particular time, Paolo should fall in love.

~

He was seen with a certain girl in the city nearly every day. Her name was Nora and she was fifteen, the daughter of the Calabrese family who lived on the fourth floor. When he was a child, Paolo had been very much afraid of Nora's father, a tall man with dark skin and an impressive scar on his face. That was why, for a long time, his contacts with Nora had been limited to a quick greeting on the landing, or at the front door. No matter how often Salman and Stella assured him that Nora's father Stefano—despite being very conservative—had a tender soul and loved children, it was all in vain. Stefano only needed to utter a lion's roar or make faces on a child's birthday, and little Paolo would hide behind his father in fear. Sometimes Stefano also pretended to be King Kong or Dracula. The explanation he gave was, "I'm preparing the kids for life. Compared to real monsters, mine are sweet and cuddly."

Nora seemed to be shy, until the day when word spread in the building about Paolo's father being persecuted in Syria. The neighbors expressed their concern to Stella.

Then Nora worked up her courage, rang Paolo's door, and told him that she was sorry about his father, whom she'd always thought was really nice.

Paolo was speechless. He felt awkward about inviting her into the apartment, but she saved him by asking, "Do you feel like going to the cinema with me tonight?" It sounded as if she'd prepared the question well in advance. "There's a good film playing by Tim Burton with Johnny Depp."

Paolo liked Johnny Depp. He smiled. "Fine. When and where shall we meet?"

"Downstairs at the entrance," she said. "At six."

"And...your parents?" Paolo asked.

"Mama agrees and Papa's in Palermo. Grandma's sick. He's got to stay with her until Christmas."

"Fine, see you downstairs at the entrance at six o'clock," Paolo said, watching Nora depart before softly closing the door. The pale young girl had grown into a young woman.

It was some time into the film before their hands found each other and wouldn't part. Later they would forget who had first looked for the other's hand. But it was definitely Paolo who kissed Nora at the end of the film, before the lights came on again. "Thank you—that was a good idea. And the film was great," he said.

"If you kiss me like that, I'll want to go to the cinema with you every day," said Nora.

~

Perhaps it was his being in love that gave Paolo an idea for how they could celebrate Christmas that year. "I'd like," he told Stella the next morning, sitting at the edge of her bed, "to go with you to places where I've been with Dad but without you, and then you invite me to places where you've been with Dad, but without me."

Stella looked at him, wide-eyed with surprise. "Great idea. But what time is it now?" she asked, yawning sleepily. She had been reading until three that morning.

"It's ten o'clock. I'm just going into the city with Nora, but I'll be back in a half hour. You can be ready by then, can't you?"

"Have you already had breakfast?"

"Yes, there's a brioche waiting for you in the kitchen," Paolo said and left the apartment.

~

During the following days, Stella and Paolo went out together a lot, and they often took Nora with them. They went to markets, to grocers, and even to Mille Articoli, a shop selling cheap goods, which was only a few steps away from their building, behind a tiny IP gas station, and where Stella had never gone before. Stella took Paolo into bars where she had been with Salman and along the banks of the River Tiber. But Paolo found them a little boring, and also they were too cold.

A few days before Christmas, Paolo wanted to visit the Christmas market on Piazza Navona with Stella, because he had often been there with his father. As a child, he had wanted a toy there every time... and had usually gotten one. Stella didn't like the hustle and bustle, but she went along. Paolo and Nora ran ahead of her, holding hands, over the Garibaldi Bridge and from there through the city, all the way to Piazza Navona and its famous Bernini fountains.

Nora and Paolo would often invite Stella to go to the cinema. Both of the teenagers were surprisingly well informed. They knew many actors, and even their family backgrounds, their incomes, and scandals they were involved in. Stella hadn't been to the cinema for a long time and she dove enthusiastically into the atmosphere. She resolved to go regularly with Salman as soon as he came back safe and sound, and munch on popcorn with as much gusto as Paolo and Nora.

Paolo showed his mother places in Rome that she had never known about. He surprised her with restaurants that Salman had taken him to, now and again. When he and Nora sat opposite each other, billing and cooing, Stella thought about Salman and the first time they met. Paolo was very much like his father. Nora, however, was nothing like her. She was a dark-skinned beauty. She was also a lot braver than Stella had been in her youth. Stella had met her first love at the age of seventeen and lost him soon thereafter. That had been six months before her final high-school final exams and the trip around Europe, during which she had fallen in love with Salman the Syrian in Heidelberg.

Nora was funny and sometimes bold with Paolo, who let her get away with murder. Amazing, Stella thought, how love changes us. This sensitive boy who used to flare up at every wrong word, just like his father when he was younger, is as gentle as a lamb with Nora. He now took so much care in his appearance that it seemed almost overdone.

And all this was supposed to be caused by hormones like oxytocin, dopamine, and serotonin? Years ago, one of her former colleagues had been part of a team researching such questions at the University of Pavia. At the time, they had been striving to unravel the secret of falling in love from medical, psychological, and biochemical angles. They had found that the newly smitten had high levels of neurotrophin, but that the concentration declined over time, returning to normal levels in about a year. Stella shook her head, driving away all thoughts of research, medicine, and lectures. The gaiety that Nora always brought with her made her very happy.

When Stella had to choose another place where she had often been with Salman, she decided on the beach at Santa Severa and drove there with the two of them. After only an hour's drive from the city, you entered another world.

Nora wasn't familiar with the beach and was completely taken by surprise. Paolo was able to show off a bit with his knowledge, because he'd been there so often with his parents. He loved the castle that dated from the ninth century. Stella enjoyed the long walk along the beach with its semi-circular inlets that had been cut off from the sea by the rocks dumped there to form breakwaters. The view of the open water calmed her. Here she felt again the peace that had eluded her in Rome. Salman had always compared Santa Severa to Beirut.

~

Whenever Stella's worries became too acute, she would telephone Sahar. There wasn't fresh news about Salman every time, but Sahar had a wonderful voice that comforted Stella. She promised her that she would be honest with her if news about Salman was bad. "We women are hardy by nature," she said. When she read out Salman's most recent short love letter over the telephone, about the two of them not liking polenta, Stella had to laugh and knew that Salman was well, since he was able to send her something to laugh about.

Another time he told her that he yearned for a fish dinner with her in Nemi. That brought tears of joy; it could only have come from Salman. When the summer in Rome grew too hot for them and they didn't want to drive to the coast, they used to drive to Castelli Romani where the air was noticeably cooler. As Paolo grew older, he stopped wanting to come with them. They would be like two lovers and stop for a break in Marino or Castel Gandolfo on the shores of Lake Albano. They would eat something and then continue their drive through the cool, shady chestnut woods, until they reached their favorite village of Nemi, not even forty kilometers from their front door.

Deep down, Stella felt a gleam of hope stir. Memories of outings together strengthened her confidence in Salman's safe return. But then they would fade, and Stella—almost ashamed of her own insecurity—would have to call up Sahar again.

V

39

Leave-taking

Damascus, January 1–5, 2011

Salman slept almost until noon. When he woke up, the house was so clean and tidy that no one would have believed that sixty people had been partying there until the early hours. Karim and Aida were still sitting in their bathrobes. "Did you spend the night here?" Salman asked. Aida smiled. "Your visit has been a turning point," she replied. "I can't leave this guy alone for a second now."

"And when did you clean up the whole house?"

"We haven't lifted a finger," Karim replied. "This morning, we were woken up by a cleaning squad led by Amal. Ten people did everything. We weren't allowed to touch a thing, just give instructions... and make lots of coffee. They were finished by eleven."

After breakfast, Salman read the newspaper. The previous night, two madmen had climbed up the gate of the psychiatric hospital, loosened one side of the sign saying *assfurije*—aviary—and turned it to face the street so that the gate now served as the entrance to a crazy town.

He read aloud the short article to Aida. "Why do we call the psychiatric hospital an aviary, anyway?" she asked. Salman didn't know. "Because people want to forget that people are kept and mistreated there. So they call helpless prisoners colorful birds in a cage," Karim answered.

~

The next morning, a cold, sunny Sunday, Salman went for a walk by himself in the Old Quarter after breakfast. He watched children playing, and in his mind, he suddenly became one of them. He felt a bittersweetness that he could almost taste on his tongue, and he had to accept that the world of his childhood was gone forever. The children took their smartphones out of their pockets and started showing off to each other, comparing who had the newest model with the latest apps.

Half an hour later, he reached beautiful Sufaniye park. He sat on a bench and watched the well-to-do mothers with their small children. The children were dressed up like dolls and bundled so heavily that they could hardly move their limbs.

Nearby, a couple was locked in an intimate embrace beneath an oak tree. The woman suddenly pushed the man back. She laughed out aloud. "You'll eat me up!" Salman heard her call out. "You're supposed to kiss me, not to eat me."

Looking at the lovers made him feel wistful. "Stella, beloved Stella," he thought. He recalled the time before he left, when they had so often disagreed, and he felt remorseful. How could she have understood him? He'd had to accept that there was no point sharing with Stella dreams and longings for the places of his childhood, places for which she felt nothing. She didn't know Damascus. She couldn't understand the allure of the alleys of this city. She had always lived on wide streets where children were not allowed to play. She had never experienced dictatorship or expulsion from a homeland, or the realities of opposing a powerful regime.

Stella always insisted that longing for places of one's childhood was a silly invention of poets and nationalists, a mirage that disoriented your senses, leaving you feeling hopeless. She despised nationalists and didn't trust those who read complex diseases into bellyaches or fatigue. Talking with friends, or a few days' rest often brought relief faster. "And that applies to homesickness too," she had said venomously.

They had nearly quarreled just before his departure, when Salman read her a poet's longing for his native land. "He's a hypocrite," Stella had said. "None of these places people long for will ever hold up to expectations when people go back there. The past is gone. All that remains is a frightening, colorless monotony."

In Damascus, he now was forced to think back on those words. Here, in my own homeland, I am defamed and hunted down by my own cousin. Everything we live by is being destroyed—Arab family, Damascene hospitality, the peaceful ways Syrians have always dealt with each other… "It's all become smoke and mirrors," he murmured aloud.

~

Salman wanted to get up at dawn the next morning, but a leaden fatigue pulled him back to sleep. As he slept, he saw his house in Rome burning. The house was not on the Viale di Trastevere but stood alone on a wide plain. Someone was playing the accordion and Salman was dancing the tango with Stella. The neighbors all had fled from their apartments and a large crowd had gathered around the burning house. But neither he nor Stella were worried by the fire. They were dancing, undressed. He soon became dizzy from all the turning, and they laid down in a soft hollow covered with thick grass. He felt no fear. Paolo had whispered to him that he was a judo black belt and would protect him and Stella. Paolo was standing not far away from the hollow, with his back to them. He was wearing his white judo uniform and was barefoot. And he was brusquely sending away curious onlookers. Salman heard Paolo's voice, "Move along, this is a family matter! Move along, nothing to see here. Please move along!"

And then he heard Elias call out, "Salman! Where have you been hiding? I'll find you!" Salman felt the earth shake.

He awoke with a start on the floor. It was still early, but it was now light.

Salman opened the window, went back to bed, and wrapped the heavy woolen blanket around himself. He enjoyed the fresh air and felt warm. "I'll never come here again," he said out loud and thought of the crying boy that he had seen on his first visit to Rome.

Stella had taken him with her to see all the sights, which had to include the well-known Trevi Fountain. Fellini's *La Dolce Vita* starring Anita Ekberg and Marcello Mastroianni had helped the fountain to win its worldwide fame. Salman saw the many coins in the basin and the tourists standing with backs to the fountain, throwing coins into the fountain with the left hand over the right shoulder. He noticed that many people would throw more than one coin and he asked Stella why. "The locals say one coin brings you safely back to Rome, two coins means you'll fall in love with a Roman, and three coins means you'll marry them."

Salman stood with his back to the fountain, shoved his hand into his right trouser pocket and then stretched it out to Stella. There were three German coins in it. Stella laughed and kissed him on the cheek. Salman put the coins on the palm of his left hand, closed both hand and eyes, and threw the coins over his right shoulder into the fountain.

The noise of the water splashing and the chatting, laughing tourists around them was deafening, but it couldn't drown out the loud crying of a little boy standing nearby. His mother did her best to calm him affectionately, while the helpless father looked after their small daughter who was also close to tears and kept pointing to her brother. Salman couldn't understand what she was saying, but when he heard the woman speaking German to the boy, he asked her why he was so sad. "Seven days ago, Jonathan threw a coin into the fountain, but now he's tired and doesn't like Rome anymore. He never wants to come back to Rome and so he'd like his coin back."

"Jonathan," Salman called out to the boy. "Don't you know how to break the spell?" The boy looked at Salman and shook his head. "My grandmother hated Rome and she showed me a trick to make sure that you never come back. All you have to do is stand with your face to the fountain," he said. The boy had stopped crying and was only sniffling now. "Look up at Oceanus, that poser with the beard up there, and shout, 'Oceanus, I hate you.' And then take a coin in your right hand and throw it over your left shoulder into the city. Oceanus will make sure that you never come back to Rome again."

"Is that true?" the boy asked, full of hope.

"Sure, my grandmother never came back to Rome. Even when she wanted to, it wasn't possible. That's why you have to think about it carefully. Do you really never want to come back to Rome?" The boy beamed at Salman. "Never," he said fiercely, and asked his mother for a coin. Then he glared at Oceanus. "I hate you, I hate you, you hear? I hate you," he said and threw the coin with his right hand over his left shoulder. The coin flew in a high arc down the steps and rolled into the narrow passage between the fountain and the shops on the Piazza di Trevi.

Waking nightmare

Around ten, Salman got dressed and went downstairs. Karim and Aida were out, and they had left a note saying that they would be back around noon. He had breakfast alone and looked out the window. It was sunny, so he decided to go for a walk. He put on his black trousers, red turtleneck pullover and black leather jacket, stuffed plenty of money into his wallet, both lira and euros, and left the house.

He avoided the official buildings and some streets that Karim had warned him about because they were equipped with video cameras. Every member of the opposition knew about them. It was enough for a senior officer of the secret service to live there and the whole street was under surveillance. Salman reached Straight Street around eleven. He walked westward. He wanted to see the spice market once more, and then go to the Omayyad Mosque, where he had sometimes gone to rest when he was a student. He thought mosques were much more inviting than churches. Their floors were covered with beautiful carpets and if it didn't happen to be prayer time, anyone could go in, regardless of their religion, to sit down and read or simply meditate.

Then Salman planned to go back through the maze of streets that ran nearly parallel to Straight Street. He knew them well and they had hardly changed, as he had discovered during several walks. But he never got that far.

When he reached the spice market, he recognized many of the old shops he had known as a child. The only difference was that now the sons—sometimes the grandsons—stood there, selling spices like their fathers and grandfathers. Ever since he was a child, Salman had loved the bright colors and the opulent range of spices from all over the world. When he arrived at the market, he slowed down, reading the signs of the goods for sale. But he soon noticed that there was hardly anything new to be discovered. Aleppo was a more interesting city for his spice business in Italy. There, trade relations with India and other spice exporting countries were stable and reliable, and the quality, too, was much better. Whoever saves on spices regrets it when the meal is served, that was his motto. He chatted a while with the merchants. Afterward, he wanted a strong mocha.

He went into one of the traditional cafés. It was quite plain inside, and relatively dark, so he took off his sunglasses. He sat down at a small table near the large window looking out on the street. And in that moment he discovered his pursuer. He was a heavyset man in his forties, stuffed into an undersized suit that only just contained his large body. He stood on the pavement opposite the café, acting disinterested and talking on the telephone. But one sharp, searching glance thrown at the café betrayed him. An alarm went off in Salman's head. He stood up, nearly knocking down the waiter who was just about to bring him his mocha. "Is there a back way out of the café?"

"No, why?" the waiter asked.

Salman glanced once more at the man in the ill-fitting suit, who was just walking toward the café, then he jumped out of the door and started to run. The man was not built for sprinting, so Salman was able to quickly put distance between them. The street was busy, with cyclists, tourists, shoppers, and stinking taxis everywhere. Salman thought that he had shaken his pursuer when he saw another one, more athletic, running toward him. This one kept his cell phone close to his ear.

Salman spun around and ran back toward the large man, who stopped abruptly, opened his arms, and shouted, "Stop, Aref Safadi! I'll shoot!" His face was deeply flushed. Salman shoved the man aside with all his strength and ducked into a back alley. The man stumbled to the ground, his cell phone flying from his hand.

"Aref Safadi!" his pursuer's shout echoed after him.

There were hardly any people in the alley, which curved eastward. He slowed down so as not to attract more attention and moved unobtrusively in the narrow shade of the houses. But he had lost his bearings. Soon he imagined he could hear voices, then everything became deathly quiet again. Whenever he reached a junction, he took the narrower, darker alley. Eventually he stopped at a crossing where two alleys met, to catch his breath and calm down. He thought he had gotten rid of them, but suddenly he saw his pursuers, who had spotted him. They were still a ways off.

Salman started to run again. In the distance he heard the two men shouting after him. A narrow alley suddenly opened to the side, so he slipped in. It wasn't two meters wide. He passed an old woman sitting on a stool in front of her house, and it was then that he noticed that he was in a dead end. He cursed the alley and his bad luck.

The old woman, a widow by the look of her black clothes, heard him cursing and sat up.

"What's the matter, my boy?" she asked, stretching out her hands as if to touch him. Salman realized that she was blind. "I can't go a step more," he answered, breathing heavily. The woman pushed open the door which was ajar and whispered to him, "In you go!" Then she sat back on her stool.

Salman leaped into the house and quickly pushed the door closed from the inside. He was standing in a small courtyard. A young woman, also dressed in black, sat at a table, peeling potatoes. When she noticed Salman, she stopped. Salman put his finger to his lips. A pretty little girl came running and hid behind her mother, but kept peeping out anxiously.

Then Salman heard hurried steps. "This is a dead end," someone called out, gasping for air. "Have you seen a man with a bald head? Sixtyish?" the other pursuer asked. "Yes," the woman called out. Salman nearly broke with fear behind the door. "Where is he, Grandmother?" the man asked again, blowing his nose in a handkerchief. "Here he is, hidden between my legs," the woman answered, laughing loud.

"She's blind, just look at her," the other man called out. "And she acts like this was all just a game," the large man said angrily as they both walked away.

Weak with relief, Salman took a few stumbling steps forward and leaned against the wall. A long moment passed, and then the old woman slid the door open and came into the house, shutting the door behind her.

~

"Are you hungry, my boy?" she asked, feeling her way into the courtyard.

"No, thank you, but I'd love a glass of water." Salman followed the blind woman on shaky legs. "Farida, bring our guest fresh water and please make us a coffee," she called out to the young mother. "Just go into the living room and take Leila. I'll be right with you," she added, but Leila was shy and she eyed Salman suspiciously.

"Who's Grandmother's beloved?" the old woman called out. "Leila," the child answered. "And who's going to help your Grandmother find her way to the living room?" Leila came running, took the blind woman by the hand, eyed Salman almost angrily, and pulled her grandmother toward the sitting room. It was warm and there was a pleasant scent of cinnamon.

"What did the criminals want from you?" the old woman asked. Her granddaughter stood next to her, holding on to her hand. "They've confused me with a man called Aref Safadi or something like that. But my name's Habib Shahin and I haven't committed any crime."

"Just like my youngest son Said. He came from Saudi Arabia where he'd been working with my other son. He was longing for his wife and his little daughter. That was two years ago. Leila was four. They mistook him for a dangerous terrorist. He died while he was still at the airport. Afterward they said he'd slipped and hit his head… may God punish them."

Salman drank the coffee.

He told the old woman and her daughter-in-law that he lived in Canada, that he was just here for a visit, and that he was staying in a beautiful hotel in the Christian Quarter. The young woman was curious and asked about Canada. Salman answered her calmly, from his newly acquired knowledge about Canada. He told them a few stories from his first years out of Syria and changed Heidelberg to Quebec. The two women insisted that he should stay until sunset and only then return to his hotel. Late in the afternoon, they prepared a snack of roasted potatoes, onions, and scrambled eggs.

During the meal, Salman laughed all of a sudden. "I hope you won't think I'm crazy. I was thinking about films from the fifties and sixties, usually shot in Egypt. There were always chases and when it got really thrilling, the director would interrupt the story and make the fugitives land either in a nightclub or a wedding party where a belly-dancer had just made her appearance, wasting ten minutes of the film."

"If you'd told me that you wanted to see that, I'd have rolled my hips for your pursuers," the old woman said as she began to laugh, too.

At dusk, Salman stood up. "Please wait," the young widow said, bringing him a dark coat which seemed brand new.

"It's cold outside and no one will recognize you this way. Said only wore it once," she explained. Salman was deeply moved. He took out his wallet and emptied the contents on the small table. There were over a thousand euros and several thousand Syrian lira. "Please accept this as a gift. Leila should get everything that she needs, and as much chocolate as she likes. Tell her later that it's from Uncle Habib, who was saved by Grandmother."

"Chocolate…" Leila said in wonder, and smiled. Salman handed the money over to the young woman, hugged the blind old woman, and left.

Words of disguise

It rained that night, but when Salman opened his eyes the next morning, the sun was shining over the city. The clay rooftops steamed like huge flatbreads fresh from the oven.

Salman had breakfast with Karim. Aida had been invited to her friend Amal's, and Karim never went with her. When Karim asked him about his plans for the day, Salman said that he wanted to relax and read. Karim smiled as if he didn't believe him, so Salman confessed he was afraid to leave the house after his close encounter the day before.

"No, my friend, you have to go out. Disguise yourself well and go without fear. You didn't make any mistake yesterday, you defeated them. It's like driving a car. Just because you're in an accident, you don't give up driving."

"Okay, I'll go into the city," Salman agreed reluctantly. "Perhaps I'll find something for Paolo and Stella," and Karim encouraged him to do so. He had to work on a couple of long overdue repairs, and couldn't go with him.

Salman actually wanted to look for a present for Aida and Karim, to express his gratitude. It was warm outside in the sun, so he could go out without a coat. He wandered along Straight Street toward the souk al-Hamidiya, which had a wide selection to choose from.

He sometimes paused to listen to the sounds of the market and noticed, now even more than when he had first arrived, how afraid people seemed. They spoke a lot, and loudly, but what they said only served to disguise what they couldn't say. People were not allowed to say what they thought. He wondered why he was noticing it especially today.

Ridiculing of slavery

As he walked past shops, Salman observed how the glorification of dictators sometimes produced comedy. Regardless of what products they sold, made, or repaired, all the shopkeepers displayed photos of the Assad trinity— Father Assad between his two sons. A fishmonger advertised *We only sell fresh fish*, with the three photos hanging underneath, and just below shelves with the crates of fish. The cobbler stuck the photos underneath a board with the sentence *We repair all kinds of shoes* scribbled in large letters.

Libraries, clubs, a dam, an airport, and whole districts bore the name of the president. Salman was astonished that, although he himself never wanted to become politically active again, this family dictatorship made him want to rebel against this enslavement in which twenty million

Syrians were forced to remain silent. They lived and breathed beneath an oppressively heavy, stultifying blanket. But they joked about it, for the dictatorship allowed this outlet. They laughed about the silliest talk shows, the cheapest films, and were moved to tears by the ridiculous soap operas on television. Every country has its Mafia, but here the Mafia ran the entire country.

And Salman was amazed at the countless clubs and centers for bodybuilding and yoga, which boasted exclusive certificates from Europe or America. The market was flooded with cheap imported goods, replacing traditional Syrian handicrafts. On the walls of buildings between them were posters—or remnants thereof—calling on people to fight America and Israel.

Salman decided to look for a piece of silver jewelry, since Aida never wore gold. One shop displayed beautiful work that caught his eye, and when Salman asked the owner if he had made the jewelry himself, the stout man laughed. "It's not worth it anymore," he said. The Yemenis make it for half the price. Look at this beauty." He pointed to a silver belt made of the finest silver wire, with Arab ornaments in filigree work. It came with a brooch and a bangle. Salman had it packed up in a jewelry box.

The shopkeeper looked at him in surprise. "You speak Damascene dialect and you don't bargain!" he said, and only then did Salman notice that he had put the requested price on the table without haggling, something unthinkable for a Damascene. "I've been living in Canada for years. People don't usually bargain there," he said in embarrassment.

The shopkeeper insisted that Salman drink a coffee with him and sent the errand boy to bring two cups of mocha from the nearby café. They sat down underneath a photo of the president. The shopkeeper was funny, smart, and experienced, but conversation with him went round in polite circles. After forty years of dictatorship and after the whole world had acquiesced to it, all resistance had collapsed. The Syrians had swallowed their defeat and learned the art of meandering.

The regime was a high wall, taller than the pyramids. Whoever wanted to survive accepted it and went around the wall by detours. Limits were quickly internalized, from the very first slap at school if not sooner. Before a thought was fully formed, the invisible obstacle had already been avoided.

Salman had noticed that although Karim repaired everything at home, he only owned cheap tools of poor quality. After a long search, Salman found a large case with a complete set of tools, fit for a craftsman.

Foolhardiness

The following day, Salman woke up at six. He had been troubled during the night, had hardly slept, and spent most of the night reading. Would he get the passport today? Or would Karim's half-brother back out at the last moment and the whole plan fall through? Then Salman would have to start again from scratch.

He went to the large window and enjoyed the view of the courtyard, which was still quiet. He looked up at the blue sky and wished that Stella could be at his side. Karim came out of the kitchen. He was carrying a tray with a mocha pot and two small cups. As if sensing Salman's gaze, he looked up and smiled at him. "Come down," he called out to him, returning quickly to the kitchen to get a third little cup.

Aida and Karim were already dressed.

"Couldn't you sleep well either?"

411

"Well," Salman said, "today's a special day." They drank the coffee in silence, as if no one wished to intrude on the other's worries.

"I'm supposed to be at the hotel reception desk at eight," Karim said after a while, breaking the silence. "Hassan called just now. He arrived at seven. He must have gotten up at five in Beirut. He wants to freshen up because he has his first appointment at nine. So I think I'd rather leave as early as possible. Aida will come too— Hassan likes her. That way we'll greet him together."

Salman hugged them both and went back to his room.

When he was alone in the house, he made himself some tea. "Stella," he thought silently, "can you hear me? We're almost there now. All this torment will be over." But what if everything went wrong? For the first time in his life he contemplated suicide. But he quickly resolved to deny Elias that triumph—and not let Stella down.

He drank his tea slowly and listened to the news. An explosion in front of the French embassy in Mali, a dioxin scandal in Europe that was spreading, a bomb threat against a Turkish airliner. The inquiry into why the Church of the Apostles Saints Mark and Peter in Egyptian Alexandria had blown up grabbed his attention. More than twenty dead and eighty injured... Salman switched the radio off.

He was too nervous to read or listen to music. He paced up and down in the courtyard like a caged animal. When the telephone rang, he didn't know how long the feeling of faintness lasted. He picked up the receiver and, as arranged, said nothing. "My brother says hello," Karim shouted into the receiver and hung up immediately. Salman understood. He could have screamed for joy.

412

Aida and Karim came back shortly before ten. They had taken a taxi and had brought freshly baked bread for a celebration breakfast together.

"Here's the passport with the visa for Italy and the check slip to exit Syria. Look at the photograph," Karim said, holding out the Lebanese passport to him.

"It's just the hair that needs to be a bit whiter. The mustache is already perfect. Hassan also has a gray mustache," said Aida.

~

Salman wasn't sure where the crazy idea came from. Perhaps it was his enthusiasm about the passport, maybe he wanted to make one final check. Or was it a longing to say goodbye to his mother? Karim and Aida wanted to visit a girlfriend and, on the way there, to buy the air ticket to Rome at a travel agency in Salihiya. "Not an Arab airline, if possible, please," Salman said, giving them the money. They arranged to meet at five and go out to dinner.

Salman got dressed. Light gray suit, dark gray turtleneck pullover, white scarf, and dark gray coat, the present from the woman who had rescued him. He looked really elegant. He bought a daily paper at a kiosk and crossed Bab Tuma in the direction of al-Akhtal Street, north of the Christian Quarter. He headed for George Khoury Park and took the route through the quieter streets and lanes. It took less time than he'd thought. He'd reckoned on an hour's walk but was there after only thirty minutes, despite having stopped for another coffee at the Glass Palace.

It was a cold, dry day and the sun caressed both houses and people with its warm hand. Many inhabitants, happy to have escaped the dark and damp, were sitting in front of their houses and shops. Salman reached the park at a quarter to three and sat down next to a couple on a bench. Shortly afterward the couple left the park. Salman read the newspaper, or pretended to.

His mother came at just after three. She was pushing his father in his wheelchair. Aunt Takla walked alongside her. Both women looked well. They were already dressed for summer, and the only reminder that it was still winter was the blanket over his father's legs.

They both walked past without recognizing him, deep in conversation about the misery in Syrian hospitals. Salman coughed quietly. He was counting on the fact that his parents would be shadowed, and indeed he saw two men following the group at a distance. At that moment, the two sisters swapped places and Aunt Takla took over pushing the wheelchair. Salman's mother seemed to steal a glance in his direction, but she could have been turning toward something else.

They stopped at the old oak, as they always did, and the two sisters sat down on the bench there. But Salman's mother immediately stood up again to push the blanket over his father's legs to one side, so that they could be bathed in the warm sunshine. His father waited until she had sat down again and then pulled the blanket back across his legs. Salman smiled. Two headstrong children, he thought. None of them noticed him. Sophia closed her eyes, pretending to sleep. After about fifteen minutes, Salman left the park.

Now he was sure his disguise was perfect.

40

A Mother's Soliloquy

Damascus, January 5, 2011

Sophia just wanted to take Yusuf out for a quick breath of fresh air. He loved to be wheeled through the park after his nap and coffee. Takla came every day for coffee and would stay with them until early evening before going back home. But that day she didn't, and she couldn't be reached by phone, either. Yusuf grew restless. He relished the fresh air and sunshine. Just in case Takla showed up after they left, Sophia told Naime, their neighbor across the street, that they were leaving.

Ajami, the grocer down the street, greeted them and asked how she was doing. Sophia looked up to the sky in exhaustion, and he nodded understandingly. How was a mother supposed to feel when her innocent only son was being hunted like a criminal? Ajami was in his early seventies and had three sons. Two were professors in America and didn't want to come back, while his third and youngest was an alcoholic and couldn't take over the shop.

Suddenly, Yusuf asked, "Where's Takla? It's three o'clock already."

"God knows where she is," Sophia replied, hoping that nothing had happened to her sister. Takla was Sophia's greatest support. She couldn't bear life without her, her nephew Tarek, and her niece Maria.

It was only five minutes to George Khoury Park, and as they turned into Ibn Bitar Street, they saw Takla coming toward them. Yusuf beamed at her. "I thought you weren't coming today."

"What do you mean, not coming?" Takla answered, cheerful as ever, giving first Yusuf and then Sophia a kiss. "I've got to come and visit my brother-in-law and his beautiful wife every day, otherwise I'd be out of sorts."

Takla explained that Mona, her daughter-in-law, had had severe pains during the night, and that Tarek and she had taken her to hospital after lunch. It was something to do with her appendix. Tarek had stayed with her.

"Which hospital is she in?" Yusuf asked, concerned.

"Here, in the French one," said Takla.

"That's good," Yusuf said. "They still treat you like a human being there. The other hospitals have turned into slaughterhouses. They sell organs to rich Saudis who've ruined their livers drinking."

Two men had followed Takla at a distance, and she indicated this to Sophia silently, with a wave of her hand. Yusuf and Sophia already had been followed from their front door by two others. Even old Ajami had noticed them and tipped off the couple with a nod of his head. The men pretended they were out for a walk, and meanwhile Sophia, Yusuf, Takla, and the grocer chatted as if nothing unusual was going on.

Tarek once warned them that the secret service could hear every word of a conversation using directional microphones. But as soon as they noticed that they'd been discovered, they would switch to more crafty tactics. The best thing for Yusuf and Sophia to do was to act as if they were senile, half blind, and hard of hearing.

Yusuf had anticipated yesterday that security would send two groups, on purpose. One would behave really obviously, trying to attract attention, so that the second group could shadow them undisturbed.

The secret service kept surveilling and entering their apartment while they were out, just as Tarek had predicted. Their neighbor Naime had seen them, but she hadn't dared ask what they're looking for. Whenever they were out, she would keep watch on their apartment through her peephole and afterward tell her if someone had been there.

Funnily enough, Sophia never noticed even the slightest change anywhere in the apartment. She set traps for them, set up things to fall down if they opened a drawer. She even stuck hairs on door frames, just like she'd seen in spy films. But no, everything seemed untouched.

Only now and then, if one of them had a particularly strong body odor, would Yusuf notice right away. He had an incredibly good sense of smell. When that happened, Yusuf would look at Sophia and hold his nose, and Sophia knew that the secret service had been there. He once wrote to her on a slip of paper, "The stinker has been here again." But perhaps the secret service was aware that the couple knew, and just acted as if they didn't? Sophia shook her head to rid her mind of such brooding thoughts, and in that moment spotted Salman.

~

For a second, she thought she was hallucinating. Her heart raced. Salman, that's Salman, she thought. But he looked different. And what was he doing there? Why was he looking at her with such a poker face? Was it a trap? Had they sent a lookalike to fool her? Takla didn't notice anything at all, but Sophia was sure. That was definitely Salman. Only Salman had eyes like that. She thought she was going to die.

Yusuf couldn't see him because he was nearsighted. He only wore his glasses for reading. But it was Salman.

He was sitting there on a sunny bench, like many others were that day, and he was reading a newspaper. But he kept glancing at her. He had a bald patch and a moustache, and wore glasses. It was a really clever disguise, but it didn't fool Sophia. Salman was an elegant and handsome man... Yes, she knew that even female apes thought their sons more handsome than gazelles. But women were crazy about him, it had always been that way.

Takla noticed that something was the matter with her sister. She was born observant. Sophia still remembered, as if it was only yesterday, how Takla looked her in the eye searchingly when she was just three weeks old, as if she wanted to ask, "Who are you and what do you want from me?" Sophia was five at the time, and she took an instant liking to her. Takla was her doll. She said to her, "I'm Sophia, your sister." Takla seemed to nod in agreement. They loved her—everyone loved her. Takla laughed a lot and would chatter on endlessly when she was only a year old. But Sophia never forgot this clever look of hers.

"Sophia, what's going on?" Takla asked, but Sophia didn't dare answer her. She spotted a man in a parked VW bus looking at them and pointing something at them that she couldn't make out. "Nothing, nothing," she said. One word, one false move, and Salman would be arrested or killed on the spot. She knew full well that Elias and his secret service people were incredibly angry that they hadn't caught him yet. And Tarek had let them know by roundabout ways that Salman was just about to make his escape. Karim had organized everything to perfection. You could rely on Karim. He promised that she'd be the first to know, as soon as Salman was safe.

When they passed Salman, he coughed slightly. They walked on to Yusuf's favorite spot near the old oak tree.

Despite herself, Sophia turned around one more time. She would curse herself for being so foolish, but it was as if an invisible hand had turned her head. She quickly looked away again. In her heart, she was talking to Salman. No one had noticed anything.

"Salman, my beloved Salman, you look so different, but your mother recognizes you. Salman, my heart, can you hear me praying to the Virgin Mary to protect you? When you were a young rebel, you once told me to stop pestering the lady who couldn't even help her own son. You had a temperature at the time, and I thought you were already asleep, otherwise I wouldn't have prayed out loud to the Virgin Mary. Do you remember how we laughed? Your father came out from the other room and said, 'Salman, I thought you had a temperature? And now you've given it to your mother as well.' He said it so seriously that we had to laugh even more. The next morning, you were right as rain and we argued about whether it hadn't been the Virgin Mary after all who had laughed along with us and cured you as a reward. But you insisted that it had been the effect of the penicillin.

"Salman, may the Virgin Mary protect you. May my lips remain sealed and not utter a word that might betray you. I'm closing my eyes. That doesn't mean I don't wish to see you. I've seen you in my heart every second since your birth. But this may be the only sign I can give you without putting you in danger."

Fifteen minutes later, Salman hurried out of the park, and Sophia breathed a sigh of relief. Only Salman walked like that. The secret service was not as clever as it claimed.

~

Sophia wheeled Yusuf back to their building. In the lift he whispered to her, "What on earth was he doing in the

419

park? Holy Virgin, protect him!" Sophia bowed down to Yusuf, kissed his eyes, and put her index finger to her lips.

Takla let out a shout of joy when Sophia wrote on a slip of paper in the kitchen, "Salman was in the park." She clapped her hand over her mouth to hold back a torrent of words.

41

The Peculiar Sensitivity of Doves

Damascus, January 6, 2011

A fugitive's worst enemy

"For the next three days, until you leave, I'd better lock you up in the storeroom," Karim said as they were having their morning coffee. "Just so you don't go off on some dangerous adventure, now that we're only a gate away from freedom." He was half-joking, but Salman sensed that he was afraid and restless.

Aida was more relaxed. "Everything's gone well. Let's look forward and hope that everything works out." The evening before, at the restaurant, Karim had been irritated with Salman when he'd told them about the incident in the park. Karim had frequently warned him not to go near his parents. Salman promised not to take any risks without asking him—and look what happened!

Karim, whose attitude toward most rules resembled a young anarchist, respected the age-old law of hospitality—the guest is sacred. So he swallowed his anger. But it stayed on his mind and wouldn't let him sleep. He acknowledged to Aida that he was afraid—for Salman, for Aida, and for himself. Salman had not kept his word and had disappointed him. Without even consulting him, he had done something foolish and dangerous. He was like his mother Sophia; once he was set on doing something, there was no changing his mind. What if his mother had recognized him and been unable to resist approaching him?

Aida stroked his head and kissed him on the eyes. She couldn't see how deadly dangerous this was, Karim thought, but he was wrong. Aida clearly perceived the danger, but she had tried all her life to overcome her fears. So she tried to seduce Karim, hoping that their lovemaking might make her forget her own fear. But he didn't respond.

Karim arranged for a meeting with Salman's cousin Tarek to go over the final steps. The two got along well. But when Karim returned in the early afternoon, he seemed unusually serious.

He hugged Salman and kissed him on the forehead. "My heartfelt condolences," he said. Salman froze. "Your father died of his cancer, early this morning, at the hospital."

Aida cried out in despair and clapped both hands to her lips as if to stifle herself. Salman sank down on a chair in the kitchen and wept bitterly. Karim took both of Salman's hands. "The cancer had metastasized all over his body since May, and he didn't want any chemo or any other therapy, only painkillers. He had asked Sophia not to say anything so that you could enjoy your time here without worrying about him. As much as I disapprove of your high-handedness, you actually gave him a parting gift. Your courage must have made him proud. Perhaps he called out to you and you heard him in your heart."

But Salman couldn't be consoled. What a lonely life his father must have had, with a wife who hadn't married him for love and a son who didn't understand him. Salman wished he could apologize for his many silly assumptions about his father. But it was too late now.

Later, when Salman wanted to go for a walk, Karim insisted on accompanying him. He was afraid that Salman in his grief might do something foolish. But Salman wanted to be alone and he shouted at Karim that he wasn't a child and knew how to look after himself. But Karim wouldn't relent. "You'll have to get past me if you want to go out alone. I won't let you out of here," he replied, blocking the door of the living room. Salman glared at him.

"The last thing I want," he said after a while, in a calmer voice, "is to push aside the man who's offered me his hospitality and saved my life. But please let me go."

Still, Karim refused to budge. He wouldn't let Salman approach the door. Aida seemed frozen. She knew that no matter who she sided with, the situation would escalate.

"Your worst enemy isn't Elias and his organization, or the Syrian army of informers. Your worst enemy is inside you. It knows you better than any other enemy and more than all of them put together, and it can ruin your plans," Karim insisted. "Now do as I say!"

Salman sank down on a chair and remained silent for a long time. Finally, he agreed that Karim could accompany him.

So the two of them took a walk through the city. They trekked silently along Straight Street, all the way to its western end, and then onto Revolution Avenue, before turning left at a mosque, past the Suez Canal Hotel to the city center and Marjeh Square. Karim followed Salman. They soon reached Yusuf al-Azmeh Street and the square, where the statue of the martyr Yusuf al-Azmeh stood. He had been an officer in the Ottoman army and Syria's first minister of defense after the country was liberated.

But this liberation, under the leadership of Prince Faisal and Lawrence of Arabia, turned out to be a beautiful sham. Although thousands of young men gave their lives on the battlefield, the Arab countries had long ago been invisibly divided up in a secret agreement between the French and the British. Syria and Lebanon would be the spoils of the French. The Syrian army had eliminated the king beforehand, so that the French could occupy the country without meeting any resistance. But Yusuf al-Azmeh, the proud Kurd, would not be subjugated and he called upon the people to resist the French. Some three thousand men followed him, singing and dancing. Many didn't carry guns, but daggers and hookahs. The Damascenes hadn't waged war in centuries. They were an Ottoman province. Even those members of the four-hundred-strong cavalry with war experience had no idea of what was in store for them. They were armed with swords and muzzle loaders.

In Maysalun, some twenty-five kilometers from Damascus, they found themselves facing the modern French army, with a full military arsenal and led by General Henri Gouraud. Within hours, the French with their tanks, planes, and modern weapons killed over five hundred men, among them, thirty-six-year-old Yusuf al-Azmeh. The year was 1920. In the entire history of the Arabs, he was the only minister of defense to have died on a battlefield.

Salman gazed at the statue, which stood amid the chaos of traffic and the stink of diesel fumes.

42

A Lover's Distraction

Stella wanted to start work again on Monday. Still in bed, she phoned her secretary and told her to collect all the mail that had arrived for her while she was out, and she would come by and pick it up some time during the day. Then she'd have the whole weekend to read through it and be ready for Monday. The secretary offered to drop it off, but Stella refused. "No, thanks a lot, but I'm going to have to get used to driving in to the university again."

Stella kept her work strictly separate from her private life. Only seldom had she invited her boss or colleagues and coworkers to her home. Salman had to learn to get used to that. From his experiences in Syria and Germany, he was accustomed to having friends and colleagues over to his home. Whenever Stella invited colleagues, they mostly went to a restaurant.

But Paolo had other plans for his mother. "You can pick up your mail later. You have to come shopping with me." He informed her that Nora's father had invited him and Stella for dinner to get to know his daughter's boyfriend better. Paolo wanted to bring gifts for Nora's parents and her little brother, Giacomo, who was six years old.

Right now he was off with Nora to the Piazza Venezia, but then he'd be back to go shopping with her for the presents for the Calabrese family.

"Ciao, see you!" he shouted and hurried out.

Stella was amazed at how much life changed all the time. She didn't get up immediately but treated herself to another half hour in bed. Here was Stefano, the strict Sicilian, inviting his daughter's fifteen-year-old boyfriend—with his mother—to dinner, and Paolo wanted to go! From thinking about ways her son had changed, she returned to her own life.

Stella's mother was her total opposite, a typical Italian *mama*, on the plump side, good-natured and slavishly devoted to her family. There was never a meal with fewer than three courses, no laundry that didn't smell like fresh detergent, no underwear that wasn't ironed, and her father never had to wear a white shirt twice.

Her mother would have preferred to have three children. She would have pampered and coddled them, and raised them to become *bamboccioni*, those big babies who still live at home at thirty-five and start or end each sentence with "*Mama*." Stella, on the other hand, wanted to leave home at sixteen. In this, her father encouraged her. He had always dreamt of a son and had raised her as if she were one. When as a little girl she cried, he would even sometimes say, "But, Stella, brave little boys don't cry."

But her mother, like her grandmother and great-grandmother, concentrated all of Stella's education on the fact that girls should please men: "Men like that." "Men don't like things like that." "What would they think of you?" "You'll never find a good husband that way!" Her remarks got on Stella's nerves. Stella had no idea what she was going to be in the future, but she was certain she would never be a woman who conformed. Above all, she would never be a housewife. The world was full of wonders and she wanted to understand a few of them. Her mother had probably caught on to this wish of hers, and so she repeated even more often what men expected from an Italian woman. One day, it was too much for Stella. She screamed at her mother in fury, "I don't want a husband, Mama. I don't want a family." Whereupon her mother wept for an entire afternoon and told her father that Stella was ill. He calmed her down, saying it was just the hormones playing up at her age.

But now, strangely enough, according to everything Stella read in the newspapers, this phenomenon was on the way back. The number of young Italian women, and particularly young Italian men, staying at home with Mama, was on the rise again. Stella had been convinced from very early on that there were other paths for women to follow. That was why she had filled her bookshelves with works about famous women: Camille Claudel, Joan Baez, Marie Curie, Hypatia, Clara Schumann, Catarina Cornaro, Natalia Ginzburg, and many others. And her greatest supporter was Salman. They shared the housework and the child-rearing. Once they started to earn more, he employed a housekeeper, but one who never had to look after Paolo. "That's reserved for the boss," he said.

Stella was still lying in bed when Paolo came back. She jumped up and dressed quickly, laughing in embarrassment. Then she drank the espresso that Paolo had made for her and ate the *brioche con marmellata* that he'd brought her back from the baker's. They then spent many pleasant hours together, first in town and then at the Calabrese's.

The dinner was excellent and the delicious Sicilian wine crept up on you. Paolo and Stella didn't leave their neighbors' apartment until about ten. A slightly tipsy Stefano hugged and kissed Paolo at the door. "My son-in-law," he called out, "from today you are under my protection. If any suicidal dog should happen to insult you, just let me know and I'll finish him off," he announced and kissed Paolo again. Nora and Stella rolled their eyes at the same time. Nora turned away in embarrassment.

Stella was pleasantly tipsy and soon went to bed. Just before she fell asleep, however, it occurred to her that she had forgotten to drive to the institute and pick up her mail.

~

The following morning, to take her mind off worrying about Salman, Stella decided to finally look through her mail. She drove to the university, but on Viale delle Scienze she noticed the little university chapel, and a sudden desire to go in overcame her. She found a parking space just next to the entrance to the campus and walked over to the chapel. There were only a few people around. Sitting in front of the round chapel was a young woman who recognized Stella and nodded to her.

Stella had seen the chapel countless times over the past fifteen years, but this was the first time she'd felt drawn to it. She had heard that famous choirs sometimes performed there, even Christmas programs, but she had never been interested.

She entered the church and her glance was drawn to the statue of Our Lady of Mercy on the left wall. In her mind she compared the statue's simplicity to the perfection of Michelangelo—this modest figure in white stone radiated sadness, despair, but also fortitude. "Holy Mother, protect Salman," Stella whispered. She murmured a short prayer that came out falteringly. Then she looked up to the cupola and read the quote along its bottom edge: *In principio erat verbum et verbum erat apud deum et deus erat verbum et verbum caro factum est et habitavit in nobis. In the beginning was the Word, and the Word was with God, and the Word was God. And the Word was made flesh and dwelt among us.* For years she had thought that these were the first words in the Bible. But Salman had corrected her, explaining that these were the opening words to the Gospel of St. John. Salman, dear Salman, where are you now?

The statue of Mary was unlike the picture of Ignatius Loyola to the left of the altar, in which Loyola seemed like an officer, waging war for the faith. She knelt down and spoke from her heart.

"Holy Mother of God, I don't know how the prayer goes, but I'd like to speak to you, in all humility. I know I haven't prayed to you in years, but I always felt you close by me. Please protect Salman. I love him, buy we lost sight of... we both got so lost in... work... ourselves. How stupid we were. Now I miss him so much. Please help, Holy Mother. Please help me... help us..." She began to cry.

A Jesuit priest was standing between the altar and the statue of Our Lady of Mercy. He approached Stella as she wiped away her tears and was getting up to leave. "Do you need any help?" he asked. "No. Thank you, Father. But please pray with me that my husband comes home safe and sound," she asked, feeling small and helpless.

The priest was the church chaplain. Stella confided to him about Salman. He listened to her and as she was leaving, he pressed her hand firmly. "I will pray for Salman every evening, Signora," he said. She felt relieved.

She climbed into the car and drove home.

It wasn't until she had parked that it occurred to her she had forgotten her mail again, and she began to laugh. She had no idea of how long she had been sitting behind the steering wheel laughing when a young policeman knocked at her window. "Good day, Signora. Can I help you? Are you all right?"

"Oh, I'm fine," she replied, climbing out. "I just won

a prize," she said still laughing.

"Congratulations, Signora. What sort of prize is it?"

"I discovered a drug that makes people forget. And it just won me the prize for the worst discovery of the year."

"How's that?" the policeman asked, wanting to detain this beautiful woman a little longer. "Because people are forgetful all by themselves, even without any drug," she said, and ran off into the building.

She was lying in bed that evening when she heard Paolo whistling their signature tune. Salman, Stella, and Paolo often split up at the entrance to big supermarkets when they went shopping. They would disappear in different directions and bring back what they'd found to the shopping cart every now and then. Whoever was at the shopping cart would whistle the tune and the others would whistle it back. Sometimes other shoppers would laugh when they were heard whistling to themselves, but nobody grumbled because it was a pretty tune.

Salman had declared, time and again, that he'd whistle this tune in Heaven until Stella and Paolo found him. "Heaven would be a wasteland without the two of you," he said.

That night, when she heard the tune, she got up and went to Paolo's room. He was lying in bed and looked at her in embarrassment. He didn't look like a teenager. He looked like a seven-year-old boy. "I'm sorry," he said. "I was whistling so that Dad would find us."

43

On a Tightrope

On the day before his father's funeral, Salman asked Karim if he'd deliver an envelope to Tarek. Salman had written a farewell letter to his father, for his cousin to slip unnoticed into the coffin.

"I'd be glad to," Karim replied.

Salman drank his coffee but skipped breakfast and lunch. He filled a small notebook, stuck it in a large envelope, and gave it to Karim. Afterward he felt relieved.

Karim and Aida were engrossed in the news. Widespread rioting had broken out among the poor in Tunisia and Algeria. Tunisian president Ben Ali said the trouble was being instigated from abroad. Karim just shook his head.

In Egypt riots were continuing after Islamists carried out a terrorist attack against a church in Alexandria. "More than twenty-three innocent people died," Karim fumed, cursing the fanatics with a well-chosen swear. Aida agreed.

Early in the morning, Karim rode off on his bicycle and was away for many hours. Aida's heart began to sink. Salman, too, kept glancing out toward the house door.

When Karim came back shortly after seven, it was already dark. "What happened?" Salman and Aida admonished him before Karim even had a chance to lean his bike against the wall.

"Nothing happened, it just wasn't easy to meet Tarek without being noticed. He stayed at your mother's for a long time. I only managed to speak to him when he went to the florist's. We were lucky, the big shop was full and we could talk unobserved. I gave him the letter. He plans to slip it into the coffin this evening. Your father will be laid out overnight at your parents' apartment for the neighbors to say their last goodbyes."

"Your mother's well," Karim continued, smiling. "If you'd kindly treat me to a mocha instead of leaving me here to freeze, I could tell you something nice."

"Of course," Salman shouted, running into the kitchen. Aida hugged Karim and kissed him.

"You can be proud of your mother," Karim began after warming up at the oil stove and taking his first sip of coffee. "Your parents' apartment is packed with friends and neighbors offering their condolences. Even the goldsmiths have come. Your mother's very touched. She had no idea how loved your father was. Now she's hearing for the first time just how many people he discreetly helped over the years, or even saved from ruin. So, today your mother was sitting in her living room like a queen, with Tarek, Takla, Mona, and Maria all there. Around twelve, Elias and his wife Isabella arrived. Tarek said that the mourners—about seventy people—all froze. Just as Elias was about to offer his condolences, your mother jumped out of her chair as if she'd been stung by a tarantula and shouted at him, 'Get out, you traitor! Clear out! You swindled us and now you're persecuting our only son. No one despised you more than my Yusuf. Get out of here, you and your whore!' Elias at first tried to dismiss the accusation in a friendly way, before insisting that Sophia had to be confused or crazy. That's when your mother retorted, 'I may be crazy, but I've kept my dignity, you despicable traitor. Go ahead, denounce me. I'm sure you'll think of something, perhaps I killed someone

432

before I was even born. Get out of here! Out!' She was screaming so loudly that two of the neighbors summoned up all their courage—which usually disappears into thin air whenever Elias is around—and escorted him politely but firmly to the door. That's our Sophia!" Karim said proudly.

Salman nodded. He was smiling, but his eyes were filled with tears.

~

"It's time to discuss the situation at the airport," Karim said the next morning after breakfast. "Can you remember everything I wrote down for you about my half-brother and his family?"

"I've learned the whole two pages by heart," Salman answered.

"Aida will bleach your hair in a minute, and then you should stay in the house until seven tomorrow morning. At dawn we'll sneak through the streets, catch a taxi on Straight Street, and drive to the airport. Your flight doesn't leave until nine, but you still have to check in and go through passport control."

"Wouldn't it be better to stay over at my place? Then the taxi could come right up to the door," Aida chimed in.

"Yes, but if we go to your place with a large suitcase, the carrier bag with the presents, and the shoulder bag, it will attract attention and we'll have informers on the scene. But early in the morning, most informers are still in bed, and if my nephew Habib takes a taxi to the airport, that's normal and credible because he's flying back to Canada. Informers couldn't care less because they know that the checks at the airport are strict enough to catch any suspects."

Salman drowsed as Aida bleached his receding hair-line with hydrogen peroxide. She finished by shaving his three-day growth of beard.

The clean shave brought out the moustache, and Salman looked very much like the passport holder. His face was a bit thinner than the portly chocolate manufacturer's, but Karim had drummed it into Salman that if anyone asked him about it, he should describe in detail a successful diet he was on, one that sounded so tough that officials would lose interest.

~

Aida wanted to prepare a three-course meal for dinner. For starters, she would she would make tabouleh salad, Karim wanted stuffed grape leaves as the main course, and Salman wanted crème caramel for dessert. Karim and Salman went into the guest room on the first floor so that Salman could rehearse the airport checks and practice answering the trick questions calmly. Time and again, Karim reminded his friend not to be nervous, because the inspectors actually knew nothing about him.

"What if the trap that Elias talked about is waiting for me there?" Salman said despondently.

"I think he's assuming that you'll try to escape via Lebanon or Jordan, so that's where he's set his traps, at the border crossing points. He definitely doesn't expect you to have the guts to escape via the airport, with all its controls. That's what I'm counting on."

"And what would you have done if I didn't look like your half-brother?" Salman asked. "We have our friends, even at the passport office," Karim answered. "It would have been more complicated and would have cost a few thousand dollars, but I would have brought you a genuine Syrian passport with the name of someone they'd never look for."

"You're boasting! Is there anyone in this country that they'd never look for?" Salman interjected ironically.

"Yes, he died fifteen years ago. The forgery only consists of raising him up from the dead for a short time, just on the computer, before we let him die quietly again, as soon as the fugitive is over the border with the passport. That's how my friends have managed to get three wanted philosophers and poets out of the country."

"Oh," Salman said, ashamed.

Karim clapped him on the shoulder. "Back to our rehearsal. What about the gifts? Which Mandur chocolate has hazelnuts?" Salman looked at the chocolate bars and chose three. "Good," Karim said. "Which ones contain alcohol?" Salman knew those as well. As a chocolate manufacturer, he couldn't allow himself to make the mistake of offering chocolates with alcohol to a conservative Muslim.

Thanks to his half-brother, Karim knew the names of the officers who worked at the airport. None of them were strict Muslims—unlike the ordinary soldiers and policemen on duty there, some of whom were very conservative.

They rehearsed for a long time and were having fun like two schoolboys when Aida called them down for dinner. Karim grabbed Salman's hands. "Listen carefully, dear friend," he said seriously. "It's been a pleasure to stand by you. Like a gift to someone beloved, it is a great joy to the giver. At the beginning of this story, I gave my word to Sophia. She's the beginning of our story, isn't she?" Salman nodded and smiled. "But Aida and I have grown fond of you these past days. Remember that tomorrow. When you go through the airport, it will be like dancing on a tightrope—no tricks, no safety net. You're all prepared, so act like a circus artist, light and playful, as if it was the most natural thing in the world."

"I'll do that because my guardian angels will be there," Salman replied, hugging Karim tight. "Go on down, I'll be with you in a minute."

When he opened the door with his elbow and entered the living room, Aida and Karim were kissing.

"Stop that! Not in front of the children!" Salman scolded, putting the presents on a small table.

"What have you got there?" Aida asked.

"Here, this is for you," Salman said, giving her the beautiful box with the silver jewelry. "And for you, Karim, this box is so you can do better repairs." They were both really astonished. They got up and kissed Salman on the cheeks from both sides.

Salman calmly handed them an envelope. "Easter is late this year, and Rome is really enjoyable the week before and after. This is a small gift for you. My wish is that both of you, my mother, Aunt Takla, my cousin Tarek and his wife Mona, and my cousin Maria and also your half-brother from Beirut and this nice woman, Sahar, who's been reassuring Stella all this time—will come visit us in Rome. I especially wish the two of you would organize this, because whatever you touch is bound to succeed. I'll show you all the Eternal City. I think Stella and Paolo will be very happy to spoil my saviors and…" He couldn't continue because of his tears of helplessness and gratitude toward these two people who were risking their lives for him, without even mentioning it. He handed Karim the envelope.

"The money is enough for return air tickets. You are my guests in Rome. I'll rent a big apartment for you all, near where we live. That'll be better than a hotel because then we can cook and have fun together. Will you grant me my wish?"

"Isn't that too much for you?" Karim asked.

"It is too little thanks for you," Salman replied.

"To your health," Karim said, raising his wine glass. "We'll miss you a lot. This is a good idea of yours, and we'll see you again soon in Rome," he added.

The telephone rang. Karim got up, blew his nose loudly in his handkerchief, and picked up the phone.

"Who's calling?" he asked, puzzled. He listened for a while. "No, I can't tonight. I've got to go to bed early because to be up at five tomorrow and drive to Aleppo." Karim frowned while he listened. "Yes, Aleppo, what's so surprising about that?" He listened again. "No, I'm only there for two days. You can call again on Wednesday. First I've got to check with Aida…" "Well, call her what you like, but I won't do anything without Aida's okay… so forget it… Yes, I know you're my daughter, but there was also a time when you forgot that I am your father… Call me on Wednesday and then I'll tell you if you can visit us, or if the two of us can meet somewhere else. Yes, bye," he said in a firm but friendly voice, and hung up.

"Maha?" Aida confirmed.

"Some people refuse to change in spite of their intelligence. She wanted to visit me because she's not feeling well. Her husband is mistreating her, and although she's the one who needs help, she wanted to set conditions."

~

Aida waited until she saw the light come on in the guest room and knew that Salman couldn't hear her before hugging Karim. "Soon Salman will have made it out, and for the rest of my life I'll be proud to have been part of it."

"Wouldn't you rather travel to Beirut tomorrow morning and watch things from a safe distance? If everything goes well, I'll be with you in the evening."

"And what if things go wrong?" Aida asked.

"If they do, my guess is they'll need three hours to figure out that it's us. By then I'll be long gone."

"No, you're lying because you love me. If they arrest Salman, they'll have you too, before you can even leave the airport, and you'll be dead on the spot."

Karim said nothing. He knew she was right. The secret service continually checked their many surveillance video recordings at the airport. That way, they could quickly and accurately identify anyone accompanying an arrested person.

"No, then I'd like to die with you," Aida said determinedly.

44

The Leap over the Abyss

Salman awoke at dawn, refreshed after a night's sleep. He was surprised at how at ease he felt before this last critical step of getting to the airport and taking off for Rome. After all the turbulence of the past weeks, he now felt strangely calm. When Salman mentioned this to Karim, he responded that this was good, since only calm water could understand and reflect the sky. It wasn't indifference but certainty that the final act of this play would end with deliverance or catastrophe.

At half-past five, Salman said goodbye to the rooftops of his city. He freshened up in the bathroom, went back into the bedroom, opened the window, and took in a deep breath of fresh cold air. The clear sky seemed to promise a sunny day.

Time had passed so slowly in Damascus. It seemed to him like an eternity. But when he added up the days between his arrival in December and today, he was even more surprised. Just five weeks had gone by.

His packed suitcase stood near the door, along with the large plastic bag filled with presents for the control officials at the airport. He knew the contents by heart and could give a lecture on all the different chocolates manufactured by Mandur.

Downstairs, Karim came out of the bedroom, already dressed, and walked to the kitchen through the courtyard. "Good morning," Salman called out to him.

Karim smiled at him. "I bet you'll sleep for three days

once you're back in Rome. Come down and let's have a quick coffee."

~

At that hour, there was almost no one out on Jasmine Street. Salman carried his suitcase and led the way with quick, quiet steps, followed by Karim carrying his shoulder bag and Aida the plastic bag with the presents. When they reached Straight Street, the green grocer greeted them from a distance. "Karim, if you're emigrating, take me with you," he called out.

"I'm not emigrating. Where else could I find another sly fox like you?" The green grocer laughed. Just then a taxi coming from Bab Tuma turned into Straight Street. The driver hesitated for a moment before he spotted the trio, drove straight toward them, stopped, and got out.

"To the airport, please," said Karim. "With the meter," he added once he was seated in the back next to Aida. Salman sat in the front.

"All right, all right. A blessed morning to you all. You're my first customers." The driver had put the suitcase and the plastic bag in the trunk. Salman kept his shoulder bag and all his papers with him. The drive took half an hour. The taxi driver had many questions on the tip of his tongue, but Salman, Aida, and Karim let them fade away the moment they came out. They didn't seem to hear anything and kept staring ahead, so that the driver soon stopped talking. "What kind of a rude mob do you think you are?" he would have said, had he been honest, but he couldn't if he wanted to keep his job.

Once at the airport, Salman went straight to the Alitalia counter to check in and get his boarding card. He still had an hour left, but he wanted to get it over and done with.

"I'll say goodbye now. Listen, I'll never forget your

kindness and your hospitality, no matter how things turn out. I used to think this sort of thing happened only in stories."

"But our life is an adventure story, too, and thanks to you it's been much more exciting," Karim said, hugging Salman. He kissed him. His eyes were moist.

"We are also in a love story," Aida said. "And we love you very much. May the Holy Virgin protect you!" Aida kissed him, and she too was fighting back tears. We cry when we part, Salman thought, because when we say goodbye, we die a little. But he was not crying this time. He was already concentrating on his own tightrope walk ahead.

Salman went to passport control. He was fourth in the queue. At this early hour, there were only a few travelers. Karim and Aida stood at a distance, holding hands.

"Good morning," Karim whispered in a Lebanese accent to Aida, inconspicuously reporting the passport official's lines. Salman pushed underneath the glass panel the passport and the slip, duly completed, that the Lebanese had to present when they left the country.

The official put the passport on the scanner, examined it, compared it with the slip, leafed through it, and then looked at Salman.

"Are you Mandur? The chocolate manufacturer?" Karim whispered to Aida, now with a Southern Syrian accent.

"Yes, sir, it's also written in the passport," Karim said, switching over to Salman's role as the Lebanese Hassan Mandur.

"I don't know your chocolate," Karim said, smiling. "Do you happen to have a sample for my children?"

"Of course I do, and for you, too," Karim said just as Salman put his hand into his bag and took out two bars of chocolate and two ballpoint pens. "These are good ballpoint pens."

"Oh, thank you so much, sir," Karim went on, trying to mimic the exact tone of an experienced, corrupt customs official.

The official turned around in his booth and called for his officer. Salman took a box of chocolates out of the bag and handed it to the officer.

"Enjoy with care. They're filled with liqueur," Karim said. Aida had to laugh. "How can you know what he says? Do you have a directional microphone too?"

"No, but we've been rehearsing this *ad nauseam*," whispered Karim.

Two men were queuing behind Salman. They looked bored.

"Is Colonel Maher Makhlouf on duty today?" asked Karim, who had also prepared Salman with this question.

"And who is Maher Makhlouf again?" Aida asked.

"The head of airport security. My brother always brings him a watch. Maher Makhlouf is a cousin of the president, and he's in charge of important deals. He has a passion for collecting watches."

The officer shook his head, but Salman gave him a box that contained a watch.

"The colonel will receive it today at noon. Corruption is the only reliable instrument of our State," Karim said as the official handed Salman back his passport with a theatrical salute. Salman now pushed the bag with the remaining five chocolate bars and the ten ballpoint pens through the opening.

"Please distribute what's in it with my best wishes," Karim wrapped up, mumbling Salman's final line. Salman put his shoulder bag on the conveyor belt and another official frisked him. Finally, he went to the door leading to the departure lounge.

He waved one last time without turning around.

43

The Inner Song of Your Beloved

Damascus, January 9, 2011

The day had started off sunny, but since midday grey clouds had begun to blanket the city. "Why do I love stubborn women?" Karim asked. "Well," said Aida, "because you love smart women, and they just happen to have their own opinions. The moment a woman has her own opinion, men say she's being stubborn."

"I can't sit behind you like this while you pedal."

"You'll manage," Aida said laughing. "Just hold on to me tight."

"People will laugh at us," Karim objected but realized right away he was talking nonsense.

"Since when do you care what those losers think about us? I want to proudly enjoy driving my teacher around," she said. "But out of the goodness of my heart, I'll make a deal. I drive you there, you drive me back." She outstretched her hand back to him over her shoulder. Karim shook it softly and kissed her fingertips.

So Aida cycled him around, and Karim sat behind her with his oud slung over his back in a brown cloth bag. Passersby stopped and turned. Some shook their heads in disbelief, others were inspired by the sight. Forty well-behaved schoolgirls, standing beside their suitcases waiting for a bus—apparently on a school trip—clapped and applauded when Aida cycled past them, calling out "Bravo!" after her. Emboldened by their applause, Aida waved back to them.

"Both hands on the handlebars," Karim reminded her, quietly proud of Aida. He embraced her and pressed the side of his head against her back, taking in her pleasant warmth on this icy afternoon. She reminded him of a song and he tried to remember which one, but it wouldn't come to him. "What's that song you're singing?" he finally asked.

"I'm not. My tongue would freeze in this wind," she said. "Maybe it's my soul singing your love." My brain's the director, she thought. My heart's the drummer, my lungs are the organ, my stomach has taken over the oud, my guts are the trumpets, my kidneys are playing the flute and my skeleton's playing the xylophone. Laughing, she waved to an old man who bowed to them in admiration, calling out as they passed.

"Impressed, aren't you?" she asked, swelling with pride.

"Yes," Karim smiled. Aida didn't know that he planned to play his oud for her at tonight's meeting of the Selfless. He had been practicing secretly for two months for the highest reward from her, the heavenly smile of his beloved.